The Time Tsar

Book Two in the
Tales from Apple Island series

Hilary A.B. Lambert

The Time Tsar is the second book in this series.
The first, *Ten Thousand Secrets National Park*,
was published in February 2020.

Both are available by order online, in print and Kindle formats:
https://www.amazon.com/stores/author/B07P1N17QQ

ISBN: 979-8-218-90693-1
hlambert0@gmail.com Facebook: Hilary A.B. Lambert

Linda Healey, editor: www.linkedin.com/in/healio
Frank Muller, cover design and photos: veganphoto@gmail.com

Dedicated to
James F. Quinlan, Ph.D.

Table of Contents

Prologue

What happened next?

A friend has urged me to tell the story of what happened next, but I had not planned for a "next." I thought it would end right there when I blew the place up.

I did not anticipate that – in spite of my best efforts – both of my grown children would get involved in my lone wolf action.

When I first planned that action, I was on my own. My comrades and colleagues from the western park were dead or in hiding. I had edged away from my son and daughter, made a break, gone into hiding. I wanted them far away, innocent of my planned violent action against property on behalf of nature, which some call ecoterrorism.

But then my daughter came looking for me, and I helped rescue my son from strange circumstances, bringing him into my living quarters – just before the timer began ticking on the bomb.

This is the story of what happened next. I became determined to live, and to remain free through the aftermath of my actions, to make sure my children were safe.

Also, above I refer to “a friend.” In the aftermath, I have made friends. This is bizarre, that someone would know who I am, and what I did, and still be friendly! In my isolation I had grown unaccustomed to friendly interactions – this is something I am re-learning.

The story of what happened next is not all mine. It is mostly about Tom King. He thought he was a really bad guy, and was proud of it, until he came across pure evil. He the predator became prey. I wonder if he understood that. He was arrogant, and ignored the danger. Others warned him.

So, I stayed free. I accepted my loving responsibility for others. And now I have met good people who can work together to protect nature, sometimes using unconventional methods. Tom King was not so fortunate.

— Janet Harper

Part I
The sign you have been waiting for

Chapter 1

Upon departing 1600 Pennsylvania Avenue, Washington, D.C.

In the spring of 2017, the newly appointed federal Time Tsar met with the USA's newly elected President.

As the car pulled away from the White House, Dr. Tom "Cat" King leaned back against the leather seat and looked at his chief of staff, Mary Anne Washington.

"I'm going to say it," he said. "The big guy might be crazy. And not in a good way."

"Oh now sir," she replied. "He was just thinking outside the box. Just – you know – brainstorming. Trying to be helpful – creative." She said this while nodding her head in agreement with King's words. Mary Anne assumed that someone was always listening in, and spoke accordingly.

"But Mary Anne," he said. "He has taken the implications of my report to a whole new level that even I cannot support." King rubbed his face with his hands and stared out at the May drizzle, the bright colors of flowers and blossoming trees magnified by moisture.

He watched a squirrel run across the street on a power line and went on, "You heard him, he said we could go back to 1910 when the coal was still in the ground, mine it, and bring it to the present to 'make a fortune.'"

"It's an idea," she replied, unhelpfully.

"And when I told him that would prevent people from using it back then, so we would not now be where we are today – you heard what he said!"

"Yes," Mary Anne said, "he told you, 'Who cares about the past, I want that coal now.'" She gazed out the car window, wondering if she should quit immediately or wait a bit longer. It was time for a change in her life.

"Could he really force us to do that?" King asked, continuing, "And how about his other 'time travel ideas for making America great again' – inviting Ronald Reagan to visit him at his Florida estate. That is weird enough, but what about his suggestion that we send someone back to kill Winston Churchill by bombing 10 Downing Street in 1940. What the *heck* did he have in mind with that one, do you have any idea?"

King stared wild-eyed at Mary Anne, at his wits' end for the first time in a very long time. Her response was not reassuring.

"All I can come up with is that with Churchill dead, England would have surrendered to the Germans."

King stared at her in silent horror, and sat up straight. "Look," he said rapidly, "those were just fun ideas of his, right? He was not directing us to do those things, was he?"

The car was drawing up to the curb at their office complex. As they left the car and crossed the sidewalk to the big glass doors, Mary Anne replied, "Not sure, sir. I'd wait to see if there is any follow-up from his aides. If you ask me – and you did – I think he meant it, and I think he has more ideas coming."

Several big buildings, grassy lawns, and busy streets away from King's office.

Around the same time.

Ravi Sen-Ellis's phone was overheating in his hand, so he turned it off and set it on his desk to cool. He closed his eyes to rest from the glowing screens in his cubicle, in the adjoining cubicles, and on the walls around the big room. His report was due at noon tomorrow to Senator Liz Maximus, but all he had to give her was private conjecture and unreliable press releases.

Ravi got up and stretched; it was 3 p.m. on a warm, rainy Tuesday, that day in the work week when we wonder how we will make it to Friday afternoon. His brain was freezing in the refrigerated offices, so he walked past his colleagues, down two flights of stairs, and out the building's side door. The rain muted the hum of Washington, D.C. traffic, and the wet air carried the scent of spring flowers. Ravi leaned against a tree and stared up at the unfurling new leaves. He closed his eyes and took a meditation break, the city fading away as he focused on the tree in the rain.

When he re-emerged, Ravi thought, 'A cup of coffee sure would hit the spot.' He remembered a name from the previous year, someone who might fill him in on the time travel program. That park science guy, Steve Roberts. That is, if he hadn't been fired in the mess last fall. Re-energized, Ravi went to get coffee and grab his phone.

Central Ohio, in a prosperous western suburb of Columbus.

The afternoon of that same day.

That morning, Steve had been only a couple of buildings distant from Ravi, but was now disembarking from his flight in mid-Ohio, undecided about whether he should go to the office or just head home. He was worried about what his supervisor Dr. Tom King had told him and the Time Agency staff about the new President's ideas for the federal time travel program. He needed to think it through.

Steve made the right choice and was soon sitting in the family living room, staring without seeing at the birdfeeders outside the big window. The garden was emerging from the deep freeze of an extreme winter, the ground still cold in early May.

King had filled them in about what he called the President's "laughable" ideas. But they sounded like direct orders to Steve, a longtime bureaucrat. It was bad enough working for King, who was gutting the time travel safety procedures developed by his predecessor Ed Zanetti. To Steve, the President's suggestions felt like action items. So he sat unmoving, brooding about everything at once. His beloved wife arrived with the kids at 5:30 p.m., and he woke guiltily to cook supper.

A nondescript warehouse area in Horseheads, NY.

On an indeterminate date.

The days were getting longer. When Brian Owen emerged from the windowless building where he had spent his weekly check-in, it was a beautiful evening. The clouds were high and the sunshine was bright in the cold spring air. Brian smelled garlic cooking, drifting his way from a restaurant down along the highway. But he was not hungry.

Since late the previous fall, Brian's life had belonged to the Department of Homeland Security. Thanks to something his mom had done – no one had told him exactly what – Brian had been incarcerated for four months, and questioned mercilessly with tools of dubious legality and vicious intent. But someone in New York State had rescued him. He had recently been released, in return for wearing an electronic tracker and checking in weekly at the nondescript little building in the industrial park next to I-86 in Horseheads.

Brian had not been fired from his software management job at the museum in Corning. They trusted and supported him.

So he drove back and forth between his apartment, work, and the grocery store. He checked out movies at the store to watch at home, and read books. He was not allowed personal email or social media communications, and his work was surveilled.

Like the late-arriving cold springtime, Brian was just beginning to emerge from this traumatic period. He avoided friends and familiar places so as to not get them involved. His special pals Harris and Rita had come to talk to him at his front door, but he would not let them in. They must not endure what he had been subjected to.

On his way home from the check-in, Brian drove past Mushroomy Fields Forever and, as usual, saw Rita's car in the lot. He kept going, heading home to a solitary vegan stir-fry. That night, after watching *Moana*, Brian fell asleep easily for the first time since his release, moonlight shining in through the open window.

He woke gently at around 2 a.m. into deep stillness, to hear two barred owls calling, "Woo-hoo hoo-hoo… who cooks for you?" They were in the big maple tree in the backyard of his apartment building. One flew to his windowsill. Man and owl contemplated one another for a long time. The big grey bird cocked its head at him.

"I've been wondering," said Brian, "if the tracker could follow me there, to Apple Island." The owl stared out into the darkness and then turned its soft brown eyes back to Brian, who took this as an invitation to give it a try.

"Okay, I'll see you there," he said. The owl and its companion flew off, and he fell back to sleep. Birdsong woke him at dawn.

The New York-Pennsylvania borderlands in the hills south of Corning, NY.

In the hidden Hollymount community.

May Day, the first of May, had long been a festive day for the animals, fairies, and their human allies in the woods around Hollymount. This immigrant Irish fairy community was hidden deep in the hills of the New York-Pennsylvania borderlands, and its residents looked to the fairy Maeve for leadership and indulgence.

It was customary on May Day for everyone to wake early and stay up late so as to not miss a moment of the parade and feast. Maeve always led the dancing forest creatures on a winding path through the woods and fields, visiting every burrow and nest. Food was plentiful, welcome after the deprivations of winter.

Along the paths were set small fragrant bonfires, and even the tiniest beasts leapt the coals for luck. Not one was ever harmed. In the woods near where the paths crossed, a venerable serviceberry shrub and its descendants bloomed reliably around this date through the centuries. Its white-blossomed branches were decorated with bells and baubles otherwise stored by Maeve in her cellars.

Thus she had adapted the ancient customs of Beltane to this colder climate for the enjoyment of her mortal animal friends. In the early years, long ago in the count of animal generations – though only a brief time to Maeve – she had attempted to rouse them for Imbolc, in early February, but nothing doing. They needed their cold weather deep sleep. In the past few winters however, the weather had become unpredictable and downright weird, and some were waking earlier. This just-past winter had been particularly capricious, waking even the bats with warmth in March, followed by a killer deep freeze into April.

The warming days had finally arrived, and it was May the first. But there was no celebration, because this year Maeve lay silent, wrapped thickly in spiderwebs, curled up in long grass around the roots of a big patch of briars. She was slowly healing from the punishment unleashed on her the previous Halloween, when she had failed to pay her taxes in full to the demon who had accompanied her long ago from Ireland, and who had taken up residence deep underground.

Without Maeve, it had been difficult for her community to find warmth and shelter. Not all of them had survived the deadly cold. But May Day was the date for renewal, and Maeve needed to wake up. Surely she must be ready. So they unearthed her. The Innkeeper pulled her out from her thorny shelter into the daylight, where the mice and squirrels carefully unwrapped her from the soft silver webbing.

Maeve reluctantly opened her eyes to see worried friends clustered around her. Her voice creaky, she said, "Hello, my dears. Is it May, then?" and they sighed a giant sigh of relief. She sat up, twining her hair around her neck, and got carefully to her feet.

"Come back to the Inn, Lady, it's warmer there," said the Innkeeper, leading her gently up the slope, followed by the mice, squirrels, possums, and chipmunks who revered her. This procession would have to suffice for the annual Beltane celebration. The Hollymount community's Board of Directors – the fox and her husband the black cat, the crow, and the old woman in the pink tracksuit – all walked slowly with the two fairies to the big white Inn between the towering holly trees.

A few days later, Maeve was sitting in a chair at the foot of the Inn's broad front steps. She had come out seeking sunlight, was wrapped in blankets and held hot tea in a big cup in her hands, but she was shivering.

"Surely this is February, not May, and you fooled me into waking early," she snapped at her long-suffering Innkeeper, who stood nearby, scanning the fields and pathways for signs of spring to show her. The beautiful landscape was grey, worn down by months of unrelenting cold and snow. Not much greenery yet. Even the skunk cabbage, food for dragons, had yet to emerge.

"Rough winter, very slow to warm," he replied patiently.

"The sun says it is May, I know that," she replied, chastened. "But I have never felt this bitter cold so late. Maybe it is time to return to Ireland, and see the family," she said, taking a sip of tea.

"It was deadly cold there too, Maeve," he said. "We need you here – those men have been asking for you all winter. They kept coming to the Inn. They brought a mechanical thing here, a ve-hicle they called it, through the deep snow. I was afraid it would tear a hole in our world, with its noise and smells."

A cabin in Green County, Kentucky.

Springtime warming after a cold winter.

The residents of this green county, 20 miles east of the federal park, know how to keep a secret. Unbeknownst to Lena and Janet, information about their presence was widely shared and carefully guarded. Everyone knew who they were. Who else could they be, two women showing up at that cabin about a week after the big blast over there at Ten Thousand Secrets National Park? And they were so – secretive!

In these parts, the long tradition of rural church-centered life keeps people skeptical of what they hear and see on television and the Internet. Casinos are anathema in church country, so someone blowing a hole in the one at the Park, well, that wasn't necessarily a bad thing.

Janet and Lena were down at the small river near their cabin, fishing. What a beautiful morning, the sky blue, the temperature almost warm enough under the springtime sun. It was the first of May. The trees were greening up, the redbuds on the far slopes were magenta, the dogwoods blossoming white.

"Here, take this," said Lena, handing her mother their fishing pole. The Amish farmer across the river had shown them the basics. They had gotten pretty good at it, and the bass were biting. They sat on the riverbank, trying to keep the fishing line from tangling with trees that had toppled into the water.

Fifty feet above in a sloping field stood their cabin, facing sunny uplands. The cabin belonged to a friend of Janet's who did not come here very often. It had been a good place to hide after fleeing the blown-up casino at the Park.

But the winter had been cold. They used the cabin's woodstove, hoping that no one would come to investigate the smoke. Their neighbors knew who they were, and kept their mouths shut. No one could drive down their gravel road unobserved, and they were left alone.

Janet and Lena were aware of the packs of drones and big black helicopters that swarmed overhead during the winter, searching for them. They did not know that the surveillance terrified and enraged the hamlets and households in the green valleys and sinkhole pastures around the Green, Green River.

Sympathy for the fugitives grew as children on their bikes quailed below the buzzing, snooping eyes in the sky. Kids asked their parents if they were going to be bombed. People lost sleep – and left gifts of food and firewood at the top of the rise near the cabin.

January and February were frigid across Kentucky, and the uninsulated cabin was not spared. Janet and Lena lived cold, wrapped in the sparse blankets and bedding left by the cabin's summertime resident. They hiked through snow up the wooded gorges and across icy pastures to the Amish store for beans, cheese, and other essentials. Low on cash, they bartered with bags of black walnuts, a local foraging currency.

They had been feeling warm only in the past few days, as the sun started to make headway, heating the cold fields and valleys. Janet lifted her head to listen to the pickup truck driving past their cabin on the gravel lane. It was headed down to a hunting cabin where the riverbank flattened out, ready for a rowdy weekend of male camaraderie.

"When do you think we should leave here, Lena?" she asked, watching her line drift downstream, tugging it away from a pesky snag.

"This weekend," Lena replied, her head turned to hear the truck's engine. "This place will get pretty busy from May through October. And we need to get to work on what Steve asked us to do."

"We also need to hear from Brian," said Janet.

She was worried about her son, Lena's brother. She had learned that he was being punished for her actions.

Their visitor had arrived in late April, on the last frosty night, well after midnight. The loud knock on the door was shocking. They rolled out of their blankets and into their boots, ready to climb out the window and head for the river.

"It's me!" came the voice of Steve Roberts, the Park's science chief, whom they had left behind last November in the collapsing ruin of the Casino at Ten Thousand Secrets National Park & Entertainment District. "I left my truck at the top of the road and walked down here. Let me in!"

Janet unlocked the door. Steve stepped inside, glanced around the one-room cabin, dropped his backpack, shut the door behind him, and stomped his icy boots on the mat. The two women stared at him by the low light of the woodstove, which Lena began refilling. No one knew how to start talking, so Janet gestured to him to sit in the rocking chair near the stove.

She said, "Don't take off your coat or hat, it's cold in here." Steve held out his hand for a friendly shake, but Janet was too anxious, and shook her head. They both sat down, she on her camp cot.

"I'll warm up some food," said Lena, turning toward the cooking area. Her bold outlaw identity had vanished instantly on seeing her recent work supervisor, whom she had abandoned when she ran off with her mom the ecoterrorist. She set the pot holding last night's leftovers on the woodstove, and gathered bowls, cutlery, and a pan of water to heat for coffee.

Janet was trying out sentences in her head, unsure of what to say.

"I'll start," said Steve, not displeased at their discomfort.

"Wait. How did you find us? Have you come to arrest us?" Janet was finally fully awake. She stood up, listening for footfalls, weaponry, vehicles outside in the pasture around the cabin. Lena abandoned her hospitality efforts and climbed the ladder into the loft to peer out the window into the darkness.

"Calm down, I'm alone," Steve said. "One of our maintenance staff lives up the road here and knows all about you. Took him until last week to get up the nerve to tell me – he thought I would turn you in. I've been throwing out hints to people for months, and he finally decided it was safe to tell me about you."

"People leave us food, and honk when they drive by," said Lena, scrambling down the ladder. "I thought it was just rural hospitality."

"I think everyone around here knows who you are," said Steve. "You are a well-kept local secret. I figured it out when I heard people in the Munfordville grocery talking about 'our own Thelma and Louise.'"

Lena and Janet put on their coats and moved in closer to the stove and to Steve. "Has there been any news about a young man named Brian Owen?" asked Janet.

"Your other non-child?" Steve asked. "He was taken into custody in New York State last November. Not a word since." Janet put her head down and tried to breathe.

Steve went on, using words that would sting. "They assumed that because he was a guy, he must be the ringleader ecoterrorist, but then they realized you used to work for the Nevada federal park that had its historic red light district blown up."

While Steve was upset with Janet for her destructive actions, revenge was not his reason for coming here. He sat back, shook his shoulders loose, and stared around at the dark, comfortable cabin space.

"I thought I could keep them both uninvolved," said Janet quietly.

"Life doesn't work like that," said Steve.

Lena handed them each a mug of instant coffee, and to Steve a bowl of stew, spoon stuck upright. But her voice was unfriendly.

"What do you want?" she asked.

"I came here to tell you that I am upsct and hurt about what you did. It was all your work, right?" He looked at Janet, who nodded briefly.

"So now you can go," said Lena. Janet sat up straight, her daughter's voice a tonic.

"But, I also came to tell you – " Steve tried to slow down, breathing in and out slowly, "that you are safe with me. And you are heroes to local folks who hate the government, and gambling. But you need to get out of here soon. That Turner guy is hot on your trail. He takes this real seriously. Also, the bigshots are moving right along with their plans to revise U.S. history. Your explosion did not touch them."

He thought this must be bitter news to them, but could see little expression beyond their gleaming eyes in the flickering light.

"And I have a big favor to ask, that I fully expect you to fulfill. What are your plans?" The coffee was better than he expected, and the mystery leftovers warmed him up, along with the stove's heat on his boots and face. Extremists like Janet irritated Steve. He had worked very hard to get where he was, quietly putting up with the harms and insults of being Black while working. But he was more on their side than not.

"You expect us to tell you what our plans are?" asked Lena in a tone of deep disdain (they did not have any plans).

"Might fit in with what I'm asking you to do," he said, venturing a smile.

"What's that?" asked Janet, who was thinking she needed to head to New York State and track down Brian.

"I bet you're thinking you need to rescue your son. Don't do that," said Steve. "Lost cause, right now. They would grab you. And he has friends there. Remember Ravi Sen-Ellis?" They stared at him, the name seemingly out of a distant past. "The Senator he works for has teamed up with her New York colleagues and their Governor, calling for Brian's release. Let that sit for a while."

Steve remembered he had brought supplies, and leaned back to grab his heavy backpack. He opened it and pulled out food and socks and gloves and toilet paper, coffee and chocolate.

"I need your help," Steve said, "because some of us think that Hugh Hynes might be alive."

The Park's scientist had been presumed dead when Tom King turned off the Pleistocene Era time switch, returning underground passages to their stone-choked present-day state.

"But – !" gasped Lena. "The passage behind me turned solid with rock and debris. He was trapped in there." She began to cry at the shocking memory.

Janet felt a tiny jolt of joy. "Why do you think this?"

"His family demanded that we go look for his remains. Tom King is in deep legal trouble over his death, so the federal park service is calling for a big investigation. Last week a team of cavers went into that big cave room from the Pleistocene side. They found a campfire, and outside nearby they found some human poop."

The dawn light outside was strengthening. Steve sped up his pitch. "I have to get out of here before daylight. I'm driving back to Ohio, not over to the Park. I learned a trick from you desperadoes, and purloined a hider gizmo powerful enough to conceal a truck. Got it from the new military warehouse at the Park."

He stood up, pulling a bundle of papers out of his coat pocket. "We're keeping the discovery about Hynes secret, to protect him from King. But we want him found and rescued – right? I have some instructions to leave with you for getting into the Pleistocene via the back door – at a secure place down near Oakland."

He handed the papers to Janet. "The sooner you get there the better. There's a team in place that needs your help. And I'll be in touch." Janet held the papers, silenced by his transformation from bureaucratic boss to ally.

Steve said, "I gotta go," and was out the door. They did not hear his truck depart.

And now, sitting on the riverbank in the chilly May Day sunshine, they knew they too had to go.

Chapter 2

As Administrator of the recently established federal Time Travel Agency, Dr. Tom King is the USA's Time Tsar.

In his office on Pennsylvania Avenue NW, Washington, D.C.

"You know who's surprised me," said Tom King to Mary Anne Washington. They were talking a few days after their meeting with the new U.S. President. She tilted her head in a questioning way.

King continued, "It's Steve Roberts, the federal parks science guy in Kentucky. Since they let him out of custody, he's been a very good employee. I mean better than that, he's been loyal to me, and he's insightful about the time trips program."

"You trust him?" asked Mary Anne, who was helping King review the details in their new Time Travel USA reservations system. It was intensely detailed work, so she was grateful for a break.

He replied, "No, I don't trust him. I warned him that he would be out of government service permanently if I saw any further hint of misbehavior. That caught his attention. And he's doing good work."

After the explosion at Ten Thousand Secrets National Park, Steve Roberts had been detained for questioning by Homeland Security and the FBI. As work supervisor for the presumed perpetrators, he was first in line as a suspect.

After all, the authorities argued, he was with Janet Harper and her daughter Lena Owen when the two made their escape. They eventually let him get back to work, but he was now beholden to Tom King for his job.

"From what I heard," said Mary Anne, "he says he had no clue what they were up to. Hard to believe." She excused herself to check the morning's email at her laptop in the front office.

The Time Travel USA reservations website was a few days away from its launch, to be held at Ten Thousand Secrets National Park in Kentucky. The public would soon be able to take economy-priced family day trips to Venice, Italy (1959); Oxford, England (tentatively 1910); and Bar Harbor, Maine, USA (1920, when it was still named Eden).

King was aggressively micromanaging his staff, needing to be sure every detail dovetailed. Mary Anne had already accumulated three pages of his "suggestions" for the web team. Steve Roberts was managing the workload at the Park.

Waiting for Mary Anne to return, King thought about how much easier it was to get things done without tree-hugger fanatics like Hugh Hynes around. Sure, King was in trouble over the manner of Hynes's disappearance – presumed dead, locked into the rock, when King adjusted time settings at Ten Thousand Secrets National Park – but people would forget about it eventually.

Scientists are such sticklers for rules and regulations, King thought. With Hynes out of the way, and the procedures-obsessed Ed Zanetti forcibly retired outside the D.C. Beltway, change had been swift. Under King's command, the Kentucky federal park was becoming a high-tech top secret research center for time travel.

(Who could blame him for the small human adjustments he had made last year? Thus he justified killing human beings for "the greater good.")

Mary Anne returned, a worried look on her face. She had printed out a lengthy memo, with "Office of the President, the White House" at the top. "Sir, not the best news," she said, handing it to him.

"Just tell me what's in it," he said, tired at the end of a long day. He hated difficulties late in the afternoon. King put his hands behind his head and leaned back, feet on his desk, and closed his eyes.

"'The President is very excited about the potential for time travel development,'" she read. "'He gives full approval to begin work on the projects you and he recently discussed, in addition to several new initiatives that will benefit our nation and business community. These are detailed below.'"

King's eyes opened and he sighed deeply. "This will put us behind schedule if we have to consider his pet projects."

Mary Anne rushed on, to get it over with.

"'We are opening an official White House Office of Time Travel Development, to be overseen personally by the President and his closest business associates, with his son.'" Mary Anne stared wide-eyed at Tom King, who stared wordlessly back. They had heard about the sons. She continued. "'…his son as project liaison. He will personally meet weekly with you. Bids are being taken from a number of top international companies for this work, which will be privately funded.'"

"This is a nightmare," said Tom King. "A disaster. Give me that list of projects," he said, grabbing the pages from her.

Mary Anne backed away.

"Sir," she said, "I have to let you know that – "

"Oh no you don't," he said. "You're not quitting on me now. You and I and the staff have to figure out how to manage this mess so that it doesn't destroy our programs. Let's see what he has here."

Papers in hand, he glanced at Mary Anne, saying, "Bonus pay. Juicy incentives. So just don't even go there."

She sighed and looked sorrowful; she had already read the letter. King's eyes scanned the two pages.

White House Office of Time Travel Development
Top Priorities

- Track down Nazi art robberies and bring the best stuff to my Florida estate for safekeeping.
- Invite Joe Stalin to the White House for a big party. We'll give him a Medal of Honor.
- Give Rommel a hand, I like that guy's style. (Suggestion: Make time hole big enough for jet fighters to fly through, so we can help him out.)
- Help Russia in Crimea (bombers for this one).
- Move Abe Lincoln's fatal encounter with John Wilkes Booth to 1860.
- What we already agreed on about mining coal and gold. Also oil in Venezuela. These are just off the top of my head as good places to start. Looking forward to a long and profitable partnership!

The President's giant signature was scrawled across the bottom of the last page.

King said, "Mary Anne, will you get drunk with me?"

She shook her head, grabbed her bag, and departed.

He sat back and wondered how to handle this situation: Clearly the new President did not know how government operated! King and his national security, military, and academic allies had worked with powerful Congressional partners for over ten years to get the Time Travel Agency established. They were moving forward with top secret plans to carry out pinpoint changes in history, to enhance the USA's present and future global dominance and security.

The President would wreck the whole thing if they did what he wanted, looting the past like it was a candy store.

Maybe someone – not himself – could make a presentation for the President about the dynamics and rules of time travel?

King sent an email to Mary Anne asking that she reply in his name to the White House, stating that, with all due ceremony and respect, these were interesting ideas, and should be discussed further. Then he forgot about it and went back to work.

Nearby on Capitol Hill, Washington, D.C.

The Hart Senate Office Building.

Ravi Sen-Ellis and Senator Liz Maximus were in her office. He was reporting about the President's plans for time travel. The prominent California Democrat was giving him her full attention. Her time was valuable, so he had to make every word count.

"Please, separate conjecture from fact for me," she said, looking at him over her half-glasses. It had been a long day, and this was the final item on their shared schedule. And it could not be postponed or ignored.

They had moved from the Senator's official desk to the comfort of the sofa and easy chair below the big window. A low table sat between them. Soft evening sunshine illuminated their empty cups – his coffee, hers tea – consumed in a desperate 6 p.m. attempt to muster energy for this last, important task.

"It is fact that the President has met with Tom King," said Ravi, "and, to quote the Prez from a White House press release, 'Time travel technology is the best thing since sliced bread. I am working closely with Tom King to develop this very important tool to help make America great again.'"

Ravi looked up from his screen at the Senator, and continued. "Under 'conjecture,' we have gossip that the President has notified a group of top investors that he wants them for a 'time travel development task force.' I could not verify that."

Senator Maximus shrugged. "Not much to go on, Ravi dear. But do continue."

Appalled by the new White House administration, Senator Max was an increasingly vocal opponent of the President's dark and chaotic approach to governance. She listened to Ravi.

"Yesterday I got solid information from Steve Roberts, the federal park service scientist who got caught up in that bomb mess last fall. He's working for Tom King in the time travel program at Ten Thousand Secrets National Park, and he learned disturbing stuff in a staff meeting."

"Roberts – that's the man who was with the ecoterrorists when the park blew up, right?" asked the Senator. She added, in a sharper tone, "You went on that time travel field trip to Venice with the alleged ecoterrorist herself, *and* you helped rescue her son. The very same young man we recently helped to extricate from indefinite secret incarceration."

She smiled at Ravi, but not sweetly. "How fortunate that we have been able to keep you out of all that. I don't think you should be in contact with Steve Roberts."

Ravi did not like to be chastised or sidetracked. He replied, "Roberts was totally open with me," gesturing with air quotes. "He said that Tom King held a staff meeting to announce that the President was putting 'time travel development on the front burner,' that 'big investors were interested,' and that the President has a lot of 'interesting ideas' for 'making America great again' via time travel investment."

Ravi saw that this had her full attention. In fact, she was glaring at him. He piled it on. "According to King, a couple of the President's ideas included inviting a historically famous dictator to the White House to receive a Medal of Honor, and capturing the Nazis' World War II stolen art and bringing it to his Florida home. That's just the start."

"I hear you, young man," said Senator Max. "We have to defuse this. If we let that incompetent crook loose in the past, horrible things will happen."

"Horrible things *have* happened," said Ravi. "Maybe he had a hand in them."

"Don't confuse me with time travel hocus-pocus. We stop him before he starts, OK?"

She stared into the distance for a moment, then continued, "Is my respected Senatorial colleague back on track after the explosion at his personal national park? Maybe we need to find out what he's up to. He has his claws pretty deep into Tom King." The Senator was referring to her political opposite, conservative Republican power-wielder Harlan Styce, senior U.S. Senator from Kentucky.

Having skipped lunch to pull together his report, Ravi was getting hungry at 7:30 p.m. Instead of replying, he pulled a packet of peanut butter crackers from his pocket and with an apology to the Senator began to eat.

Liz Max got up and prowled her office, adjusting books on the shelves and staring out the window at the red tail-lights of homeward-bound commuters. "I have an idea," she said finally, as his stomach growled loudly. "Just take this suggestion home with you. We have a long fight ahead of us, on this and other precious things that we have to protect from the crook in the White House. So let's start small."

The Senator walked over to the coatrack, took down Ravi's jacket, and handed it to him. She gestured toward the door.

"I also want to keep you away from your fascination with time travel. That could lead you into deep trouble. But first, find that naive man who ran the federal time travel program until last year when he was dismissed. I assume by King."

"Ed Zanetti," said Ravi.

"Oh my gosh, yes," said Senator Max, her hand on the door security panel. "That *wimp*. Find out what he knows, enlist him to help us, if you can. Protecting the past – that will appeal to him. And – I may regret suggesting this to you – find out what the personal aide to Senator Styce has been up to."

"Ard Sprinkle!" said Ravi, with a grin. The Senator felt uneasy when she saw that grin, his law school attack dog grin.

But she said only, "These are the people that King will be leaning on for help with the President. Start there."

She opened the door and watched him walk down the empty hallway, calling after him in a hushed voice, "But only one hour on each. The big push right now is for my fundraisers next week. And we need to make sure the CDC has funding for their pandemic emergency response program – that's on the President's chopping block."

Ravi waved as he rounded a distant corner of the long marble hallway, and she went back into her office to make phone calls.

The New York-Pennsylvania borderland hills south of Corning, NY.

Apple Island itself.

Brian knew he was approaching his destination when protest signs showed up along the south side of the highway: "Illegal road to nowhere" – "Destroying nature & history to save 5 minutes drive time!?" The name of Harris's group was at the bottom of each sign: SoTierNatureFirst!

For the final mile, a chain-link fence blocked his view of the project area. The Canisteo River lay low on his left. Beyond the river, hazy blue hills flanked green valleys. At the Highway Spur Project Site the tall metal gate hung open. Brian turned into the highway construction site he had last seen the previous October 31st when his quiet life had been derailed.

The project had been halted over the deadly cold of the winter months. The parking area next to the trailer was empty, there were no big machines, and there was no sign of recent activity. Sunshine warmed Brian's shoulders under his green cloak as he locked his car and gazed at the graveled roadbed that would one day be a highway, curving past the white church spire toward the hills.

He was not interested in encountering Maeve, so he crunched across the fields and walked around the church clockwise, remaining in our mortal world. The roadbed ended in a flurry of survey flags, and he continued forward on the hiking trail toward the hill ahead.

Brian had walked this route in his mind many times during his months of incarceration and interrogation. He still wondered if they mapped his brain activity, because they had asked him about it.

"Tell me again how you planned to kidnap Tom King and hold him hostage in that Inn."

He was back in that room with the questioner. "How many times do I have to tell you that I knew nothing about that guy?" This was his weary response, yet again.

And her counter-accusation came, for the nth time.

"We know for a fact that you, your mother, and your radical group planned to grab him and kill him. He says you threatened him."

"That's ridiculous. I was helping a community group get funding for a road improvement project. I never heard of King, except when I met him once on the trail. And I'd been out of touch with my mom for over a year."

Brian closed his eyes to rest them from the bright lights in the small, airless room.

"Open your eyes when you're talking to me. How come we can't find any records of this so-called 'community group'?" The questioner leaned forward. The guy behind her stared at the ceiling, craving a smoke.

In a voice rendered toneless by repetition, Brian said, "You can talk to the highway company. Talk to her Congressman. They all know the group's leader. I only knew her first name, Maeve."

Brian shuddered at the memory of Maeve's voice, screaming at him as he ran away from the blazing Halloween inferno, down the path to Apple Island. He wondered what had happened there since? What had his mom *done*, anyway? No one would tell him. They had simply grabbed him from his apartment and started shouting at him, months ago now. And how did his sister Lena figure in? They kept mentioning her as if she were part of this mysterious plot.

His questioner shifted her weight to rest her back, and went on, "The highway company Walden 2 is missing a consultant, and we think you know what happened to him. Congressman Speed's office knows nothing about this group, or anyone named Maeve. We can't find any Inn or any community, it's all woods up there. And where did the grant money go? The grants office thinks you pocketed the money."

Synthetic sympathy oozed from her tired voice: "You are in such big trouble in every direction, so just tell us the truth. We can work out something for you."

But Brian was not about to tell them about a scary, sexy fairy queen, the gates of Hell opening, maybe even some elves, and time travel.

That would land him in heavy drugs limbo for life. The unreality of this solitary confinement was eating away at his ability to think straight about the strange events of the previous year. So he held tight to a memory of Apple Island and the sense of homecoming he felt there, and answered the same questions the same way, over and over.

Late one night, some weeks later, they let him go. He had been trying to rest in his tiny cell. The lights shone down from the ceiling, hot and bright on his closed eyelids. The awful 1960s music had been turned down, though he could still hear it whispering. His blanket was thin and he was cold.

Two big men entered soundlessly, pulled him upright, yanked his arms back, and propelled him down the hallway through a set of doors into a room he had not seen before. There was a two-way mirror in one wall, a table and chairs, and a door on the far side of the room with a glowing red EXIT sign above it.

One man pushed Brian into a chair and bent down to fasten a tracking device around his left ankle. The other man handed him a plastic bag with his long-lost coat, wristwatch, phone, keys, and wallet, while talking.

"Some bigshots are forcing us to let you go, but we'll see you once a week at the address in here. You screw up in any way, you're back inside for a long time." He tossed over a packet of instructions and talked on, fast and angry.

"You can't contact your family and you can't use the Internet. Just be a very good boy and we'll see you next week." The man walked over to the other door, pressed buttons, and it popped open, swinging outward. Stinging cold and blessed darkness streamed in.

"Now go – git!" snapped the guy, pushing Brian outside, the door slamming heavily shut behind him. Brian pulled on his coat, found his gloves in the pockets and put them on. He was standing in an empty parking lot next to a metal building in a quiet commercial and residential neighborhood. A security light burned brightly above the locked door, which had no handle.

Cars hissed past in the cold. His watch read 2 a.m. They had to let him go, but they weren't making it easy.

Down the road to his right gleamed an all-night golden arches. Brian headed there, to get food (his wallet revealed a $5 bill) and to figure out where he was. He eventually arrived back at his apartment a little after dawn, having savored every cold minute of his six mile walk under the stars and streetlights, belly filled with hot food and coffee.

Brian's car was in its garage space. He turned on the lights in his apartment, bracing for disaster, but it wasn't bad. They had made a mess, for sure, but not to the extent of ripping up cushions and pillows. His green cloak hung untouched in the closet; his houseplants were stone dead. Bills and junk mail were piled up inside the door. From the bottom of the pile, Brian picked up a newsweekly dated the previous November and began to get caught up on what his mother had done.

Now headed toward Apple Island, Brian knew that he should be in his apartment living his new quiet life until this storm blew over. He should not have come here, but he was sick of doing nothing. Time to take assertive next steps.

Brian followed the trail from the parking lot up the slope, past the tumbled stones that, in Maeve's world, held the entrance to her personal Hell where the demon resided. The vegetation was matted, brown and crushed by the long winter. Here and there green spears of springtime growth poked upward. Tree limbs lay where they had been blown down by wintry winds.

He crossed the creek on the small footbridge and turned right along the base of the cliffs. He moved quickly past the green dell where, in Maeve's world, he had fought for his life and had tried to rescue that highway consultant, Gregg, from Maeve's clutches.

Last fall, the survey flags for the proposed highway spur had been lined up in two rows, marching up the slope and into the woods ahead. Today, on this chilly May morning, the small neon flags had been pulled up and were piled in a colorful heap, surrounded by winter-worn, hand-painted signs.

These read "End of Road Work!" and "Protect Us from Ourselves!" More of the SoTier group's work.

Brian walked up the hill, hearing birdsong, and wondered what the birds were talking about. At the place where the paths crossed, he turned left on the Apple Island Trace and was soon walking down the steep slope toward Apple Island. He smelled woodsmoke.

At the bottom of the slope, across the log bridge over the stream, Acton stood waiting, and Greenwood waved from beside the fire. Brian crossed the bridge. His watch face went blank, and the electronic device around his ankle fell off. He bent down to pick it up, put it in his pocket, and rose to hug his friends.

Farewell to the cabin.

Paddling the Green, Green River.

With a sigh of thanks for all it had provided, Janet locked the cabin's door, pulled on her backpack, and followed Lena into the long grass. Under hazy stars they clambered down the steep wooded bluffs to the river. They were borrowing (perhaps permanently) a small purple canoe that they had found stored at the cabin. Janet pulled it downslope toward the water, Lena carrying the two paddles.

Soon the little river was carrying them steadily downstream, northward toward its confluence with the Green, Green River. The trip ahead was not long, less than 60 miles, but filled with places they could be spotted, especially when they paddled below the interstate highway bridge.

Eventually they would have to hide the canoe and hike along the eastern edge of Ten Thousand Secrets National Park to reach the small town of Oakland. According to the papers Steve had left for them, people there would help them enter the Pleistocene to look for Hugh Hynes.

"How long will I have to live like this," thought Lena, paddling at the stern, both women warily watching the dark banks and water ahead.

The little river emerged from a tunnel of budding trees into open land, stars overhead. A single light shone on the left bank outside a small cabin. They smelled a cookout, and marijuana smoke. Hugging the right bank, the canoe crept quietly along in the shadows, but had to pass through a sliver of light from across the water.

Their movement was seen, and a voice called out, quiet but clear, "Hi, ladies – are you on the move again?" They picked up speed but could still hear the man's voice behind them. "Folks are watching out for you. We honor you for what you did. Don't be afraid to ask for help."

When the light had faded behind them, Lena whispered, "What do you make of that?"

Janet's paddle bit deep into the water as she replied, "Nothing we can do about it – so let's make the most of it."

Springtime rains had raised the little river's water level, and they made better time heading downstream in a well-made canoe than they had the previous November, during those grueling four days when they'd paddled upstream to the cabin in an inflatable raft.

Then, they had slept in thorny woodlands, been chased back onto the water by farm dogs, and held their breaths beneath a steep limestone bluff as a searching helicopter rumbled overhead, blasting the steep-sided river valley with its violent churning.

The fugitives had felt invisibly supported by the communities they paddled through. On the second night, when the inflatable raft edged toward shore, a voice from the darkness hissed,

"Not here! Too dangerous! Look for the black boathouse!" They escaped upstream just before spotlights poured down the slope behind them. The black boathouse had provided quiet cover through the next day, as they listened to the drones buzzing around overhead.

Now, rested and toughened by the long cold winter, they came to that boathouse again. It was just upstream of the confluence with the Green, Green River, where they would turn west toward the park and their destination in the flatlands to the south.

It would be dawn soon, time to get under cover. They paddled into the boathouse under the wooden roof, and felt for the dock in the darkness. Janet held the canoe steady as Lena prowled the building's small interior and checked the path outside.

"All clear, I hope," Lena whispered on her return, taking the bow rope from Janet's hand and tying it around a metal upright at the end of the dock. "Here's an old cooler – that wasn't here last fall."

Janet climbed up next to her and felt the cooler's smooth plastic surface, with a button at one end to open the sliding cover. "We can check it in daylight," she said. "Let's eat, and you sleep first."

They ate bread with dried fruit from Steve's supplies, and then Lena climbed into the gently rocking canoe to sleep. Her mom sat watch above her, drowsing on the narrow dock, listening to the flowing water and the rising hum of birds and insects as morning arrived.

Daylight was growing when they woke soon after dawn. Sunlight entered through cracks in the wooden walls and shimmered on the flowing water below, as they bathed their faces and limbs. Wasps floated over their heads.

Lena climbed up to Janet on the dock, saying, "Your turn to sleep."

"Thank you, I'd like that – but first let's look inside," Janet replied, pulling over the red-and-white cooler.

"It's probably full of old dead fish or bait," warned Lena, edging away.

"Maybe, maybe not," said Janet, sliding the lid open. She peered cautiously inside. A piece of paper lay on top, with a handwritten note dated four days earlier. Janet moved the paper into a shaft of sunlight and they read it together:

I check this once a week.
There's food here for secret travelers — they hungrily glanced into

the cooler to see wrapped packages — and some advice, which I update when I can. You are a quarter mile upstream of where our little river joins the Green, Green River. I strongly advise that you go upstream. There's good people in Greensburg. Look under the dock at the town landing for information. They can help you to safety.

However I think you are going to go downstream, back toward the Park. Dumb idea! I suppose you want to paddle all the way to the Ohio River and escape that way. That's a lot of river miles. This past winter we paddled the Green, Green River all the way through the Park, and could not detect any surveillance or security checks (retired military, we know what to look for).

A warning – there is a guy with land and guns on the east side of the Park. We are hoping you stay on the water, and slip right past him. So be cautious if you have to travel overland. He is watching for you. His name is Gene, and he is part of the local militia group and has a lot of influence. Not a good guy.

Thanks again for all you have done to protect our land and values.

Your friend,
Rose

They dug into the food packages and found summer sausages, peanut butter sandwiches, chips, water, cookies, and more – enough for a feast, and supplies for another day. After their meal they both fell deeply asleep in the warm little boathouse, the water rippling and flowing below.

At dusk they set out again, and soon came to the confluence where the brisk clear water of their little river merged with the wide green flow of the larger waterway. Turning downstream and west onto its shallow waters, they hugged the southern bank. In the dark they kept running into snags and sandbars, so they moved to the center, paddling to pick up the pace.

They hoped to reach the eastern edge of the Park in two to three days via the sinuous loops of the Green, Green River.

From there they would hike south to Oakland. Mind you, the

entire trip would take an hour and a half by car, if they had one, and could travel without being observed. This longer river route would have to do, for fugitive ecoterrorists.

Restless in the Pennsylvania-New York State borderlands.

Maeve becomes herself once more.

Warmth seeped into the cold folds of the hills, and bright sunshine called forth tree buds and green grass. Redwing blackbirds returned, flowing into the old pasturelands, singing. Soon after dawn on a bright morning in mid-May, Maeve felt good enough to take a walk, and set out along the path from the Inn. She passed the small houses of her friends and neighbors, who waved encouragingly.

Shana, the woman in the pink tracksuit, waved at the slow-moving fairy from her front porch, where she was visiting with a squirrel couple. Shana had moved to Maeve's community from a nearby human village some years back.

"It's great to see her back on her feet," she said to the squirrels. These three animals did not have a common language, nor did they share familiar physical gestures. Fast moves by Shana would cause the squirrels to leap off the porch and watch her from the base of a tree in the middle of the front yard. So she interacted in slow motion, and relied on tone to communicate.

In response to her conversation, the squirrels tilted their heads and stared at her fixedly from the other side of the small table. They sat on the table, she on a white plastic chair. Her pot-bellied pig rested at her feet. He understood everybody.

Shana was lonely, so she took the squirrels' nervous gaze as a social cue and said, "I hope that Maeve can bring in some food for hungry folks. Care for more nuts?" She was striving to emulate Maeve, who spoke sweetly and intimately with all the animals.

Shana held a bag of baseball peanuts, around which this social breakfast visit was intensely focused.

She counted out four nuts, placed them in the middle of the table, and the squirrels crept back for their portions. The pig snuffled a reminder from below, and she dropped three nuts for him.

Everyone in the Hollymount community was hungry following the cheerless winter. Shana was putting off the long trek into town. She and the little lady who lived near the entrance hiked to a bus stop where they got a ride to the Walmart in Painted Post. She needed to warm up more before attempting all that, but being almost out of coffee was a great motivator. Shana had found the bag of nuts in the dark corner of a cupboard along with an ancient jar of crusted instant coffee, nasty but better than brewing tea from the emerging dandelion greens.

Maeve sensed her neighbors' gaze as she made her way through the small Hollymount settlement, up the slope, and into the woods. She felt stronger and more aware with every step, and decided to pay a visit to the overlook above Apple Island. Turning into the woods, Maeve passed through the trees, gliding silently above the ground until she stood at the edge of the Apple Island gorge. Below on the island, apple blossoms gleamed in sunshine. The vivid pinks and whites stood out against winter-grey woodlands that stretched into the distance on the far side of the creek, curving out of sight around a bend.

Maeve gazed and listened, hearing animal friends breathing and sleeping miles distant. She knew where each returning bird was nesting, and her mind accounted for three humans on the island below.

At the far edge of the woods, she could feel the heat of the Others Entrance, as she named the tunnel, and turned aside in remembered pain. The old orchard below her had been scoured of apples by her community during the cold winter. Where was there food?

Maeve was lonely for her kind: the overwrought, crowded fairy community she had left behind in Ireland so very long ago. They were family, after all, though spiteful and mean. Once spring returned to the Pennsylvania border hills, her mood would improve.

But these disheveled grey woods and waters of early spring sapped her spirit.

The door to return home was on Apple Island, and all she wanted was a quick visit to Ireland's green bower. Maybe she could bring a few blithe spirits back with her, to make life among the animals more amusing, and to wreak a little mayhem among the clueless human beings.

Every year for four hundred years she had felt this springtime craving. Until the families of Acton and Greenwood had arrived, she had been able to take her jaunts to Ireland, and would bring back flowers, plants, new fairy settlers (who regretted the move and flew away), and the latest songs from the fairy court. But now the portal to her Ireland was blocked.

Below on Apple Island, the three men were waking after a night of talk and beer. Brian had been promised answers and explanations in the morning light. He was expecting big revelations of magic power, and romantic tests of his ability to handle them. He craved transformation, new beginnings, wisdom and purpose.

They were sitting in sunshine on the slope above the orchard finishing off the food he had carried in when Greenwood stared at the hillside and jumped to his feet.

"She's up there," he hissed, stepping protectively in front of Brian. The three scrambled down the slope into the dark cover of the hemlock grove.

"Every spring," Acton whispered to Brian, "she becomes homesick and longs for her people and comes to ask us for permission to go through. After the weather warms up she gets over it and forgets. This has been going on since I was small, and that's a long time now. Our parents and uncles stayed here before us, to keep her away. It's why we're here."

"What's 'a long time'?" asked Brian, thrilled at getting some real information about this opaque situation. He could not feel or sense Maeve's presence, and was vaguely disappointed for not having yet acquired the necessary sixth or seventh sense that these supernatural entities surely took for granted.

He wondered what was meant by "go through," but had an inkling because of the portal he had been pushed into on his previous visit.

Greenwood and Acton exchanged glances. The three were huddled together beneath a big hemlock tree. Brian noted that Acton's brown jacket was a familiar name brand, not a handmade elven garment. His face was youthful, yet mature. He did not glow with a mysterious inner force or fire suggesting a mystical origin. Who and what were these guys?

"She's about to go into her cry for permission," whispered Greenwood. "No time now for big revelations."

"Oh c'mon, guys, give me a break," said Brian. "I'm in violation of my parole by being here, and may be thrown in jail as soon as I get back to the highway. You invited me big time."

Greenwood craned his neck to stare through the branches toward Maeve, and finally gave Brian what he sought. "Those were the owls who called you here," he said, "but we're glad you came."

"Wait – you're *not* the owls?" Brian asked, astonished. Greenwood rolled his eyes, glanced at Acton, and jumped back on his feet to gaze up at the forlorn fairy.

"I'm 175 years old," Acton replied, "and Greenie here is around 180. We don't count it like you do, we're on a different scale, but that's about right. And we've been coming here off and on since we were what, fifteen of your years. Give or take."

"But you're *human?*" Brian asked. He felt a tingle of fear.

"Sure – of course, what did you think? But humans pick up other things – abilities and skills – when they live a longer life," Acton said, as he and Brian rose to their feet.

Brian's mind and body roiled with confusion. Not magical – just extremely old human beings? He wanted to get away and figure out how he felt. But this was no time to bolt for the bridge and run. He held himself still. Above them Maeve was calling.

"I want to go home," Maeve shouted. "Let me pass through."

"It's springtime, Maeve," Greenwood called to her. "The buds are swelling on the branches. Your winged friends are returning from far away. Your community here needs your help."

"Congratulations on your narrow escape, and recovery," Acton added diplomatically.

"Let me pass, you terrible young men," she replied. "It is unjust that you block my passage home." She rose off the bluff and slowly descended toward them. Acton tossed a handful of dirt onto the smoldering campfire, and a sheet of glittering fog rose above them, obscuring even the fairy's view. The two older men moved around the base of the central hemlock tree, a giant, to stand guard on the portal she sought.

Greenwood picked up a smoldering branch from the fire and spoke warily. "We can't allow you to do that, Maeve," he said. "My great-great-grandparents let you go back and forth, and you brought deadly powers and sickness back with you."

Floating downward, Maeve emerged through the sparkling smoke. "You got in my way," she cried. "I drove off the people who were here before me, and then you moved in and began to plow and plant and kill my animal friends. It was too much to bear." She was hovering closer, now just overhead.

"You want to go to Ireland, take a plane," said Acton.

Brian moved to guard the other side of the big tree, keeping what he hoped was a safe distance from the portal, and Maeve saw him. Still weak from her winter ordeal, she had been concentrating to stay afloat. But now her strength failed and she plummeted to the ground. The three men scrambled to surround the doorway to Ireland, with its dim green glow, barely discernable near the base of the giant hemlock.

Maeve sat up and shook twigs from her black hair. She was near enough that Brian could see her pallor and lines of pain from the hard winter. Maeve stared at him, and saw that he was no longer a fool or plaything. Their mutual attraction of the previous year had been extinguished by the punishment each had received.

"Brian, watch yourself," whispered Acton.

"Come here, Brian," said Maeve, in the thrilling voice he remembered. She had pulled him here, compelled, back when he was willing to move mountains for her. But the cord had been cut.

Brian's incarceration and torture – he named it – and the long winter cold had burned away his sweetness and trust. He stood next to the old tree and glanced at Greenwood, and at Acton. Then he looked at Maeve.

"There is nothing for you here, Maeve," he said quietly. And not a word more. He felt the other two exhale, reassured by his response. They stepped forward toward Maeve, leaving him to guard the glimmering opening.

"We fed your woodland friends all winter, Maeve," said Greenwood, "with apples from the orchards. Go take care of your chosen community." He pointed with the smoldering branch to the tree-trunk bridge across the stream. Acton took a step forward.

Exhausted, her energy spent, Maeve turned away and walked toward the bridge, crossing slowly, but with dignity and grace. They watched as she climbed the steep path and vanished into the hemlock woods. At the crosspaths she would turn left and head back to the Inn, past her neighbors, and receive their sympathy.

The two men continued to watch the hill and sky, vigilant. But Brian knew she was gone. He stepped away from the trees and walked around the campfire to get a clear look at Greenwood and Acton.

"She's gone, back to the Inn, so relax," he said. "I've got to get back to town and check in with my handlers," he continued, surprising himself by what he was saying. "So if you can answer a few questions, I'll let you get back to work."

"We need your help here, Brian," said Acton, "to guard the portals on Apple Island." The two men re-seated themselves.

Brian stood on the far side of the fire. He asked, "Who and what are you?"

"Our community is through a portal down there near the water," said Greenwood, gesturing toward the orchard and creek beyond. "We settled here around 1800. Families came over from England. We planted the orchard. But Maeve made it bad for us, so our forefathers moved everyone through the portal. It led our families to rich woodlands and farmland, near the Kentucky-Tennessee border."

Acton spoke. "We grew up there, and we are here on a two-year community service mission to protect our homeplace from her. Everyone has to do this. And we need you to help."

"But how can you be so old?" asked Brian. "You both look like you're in your forties."

"It's the effect of passing back and forth through the portal," said Acton. "If you do it often, it extends human life. Most everyone in our community is at least 150 years old, except for our grandchildren. And great-grandchildren. Mine are in high school."

"What year is it at the other end?" asked Brian.

"Same as here," said Greenwood. "Your time. We voted in the election last fall, like everybody else."

Brian turned to look up the path, and said quietly, "I voted, and the next day they arrested me. I doubt I'll ever be allowed to vote again."

"Well, we're real happy about the new President," said Greenwood. "He is going to fix things. He'll restore what this country has lost." Greenwood and Acton toasted one another with their cups of tea.

Illusions were spilling off Brian in a shower of sparks and jolts. These guys were not the dreamy wood elves of his imagination. He had a bad feeling they were not liberals.

Controlling his urge to run, Brian asked, "Your farmland through the portal – where exactly is it located?"

Acton looked away. "Sorry, we can't tell you that right now. Not until we're sure you're on our side. Things have changed since last fall, since the election. Please just say yes to helping us."

Upset by their lack of trust, Brian said, "Look, I have to get back and check in. I'll be in touch with you again, once I talk to my friend Harris." He edged toward the log bridge, worried that he was being abrupt and rude. "Thanks again for this cloak!" he said, weakly.

"We had nothing to do with that. Those owls stole the cloak from Maeve," said Acton. "But Harris and the dark girl can't come back here. The President says we have to stay away from people who aren't Americans."

"But – " stuttered Brian, shocked. "He's from Ithaca – she's from Utica! They're – New Yorkers!"

"That's not good enough, Brian. We've been arguing about this back home, and the elders said we can make an exception for you only."

Greenwood held out a friendly hand to Brian, a sad expression on his face. Brian did not take the offered hand, but walked quickly across the bridge and up the slope, turning right at the crosspaths toward his car.

Chapter 3

A warm day in Washington, D.C.

Ard Sprinkle reveals his true loyalty.

It was 10 a.m., and hot sultry weather blanketed Washington, D.C. In a deeply chilled conference room, Steve Roberts was meeting with Tom King, and Ard Sprinkle was taking notes. Their faces reflected the glow of Steve's slide presentation.

Sprinkle was feeling good. As Senator Styce's point man for time travel research, he enjoyed advising King's agency about the tourism time travel project. And nowadays he took everything he learned straight to the President, because he felt that guy understood a thing or two about respect for the past. He would make this federal parks program shine! As soon as this meeting ended, Sprinkle was headed to the White House to report.

"We've completed the launch areas and entryway," Steve said, using his cursor to delineate the Time Travel Vistas project being built along the Green, Green River near the casino and hotels area of Kentucky's Ten Thousand Secrets National Park. These had been shut down after the terrorist blast the previous fall.

Steve pointed to a sinuous line winding around the edge of the colorful graphics.

"The TimeLink Tramline should be running in ten days. So people will go directly from the parking lots to their Time Travel Vista check-in. We'll be offering limited day trips by Thanksgiving this year. Can't offer overnight stays in the Park until the hotels reopen."

The next slide displayed the Green, Green River's south bank, with yellow circles delineating four sites. Steve continued: "Each of the four launch areas is completely self-contained, with full facilities including a destination-themed gift shop and local foods café."

Images of frosted tea cakes, corn on the cob, pasta platters, grits and gravy biscuits, and people wearing lobster bibs flashed past.

"This launch area is Venice, Italy, 1959; this one is Oxford, England, around 1910 – we need to finalize the date. The third one will open by December – Bar Harbor, Maine, 1920 – that's the premium site. And this fourth one" – the green laser dot circled a mist-swaddled paddlewheel river ship under a moonlit sky – "is the proposed Tennessee Rivers Ghostlands Cruise. That's a three-night cruise on a hovercraft paddlewheel-extended dance ship, with 95 percent invisibility features. Anyone back then – the 1850s – seeing the ship for a moment or two would credit it to the supernatural."

Steve glanced at his small audience. "The trip visits riverfront plantation mansions, and guests will enjoy authentic period mega-feasts. We'll import the food from Tennessee farms in our era. It's ambitious, and it's the brainchild of an esteemed Southern Senator. We got his vote to approve the program as a whole by promising him a home state featured trip. It's at least a couple years away from opening, and I personally doubt it is feasible. We are looking for a solid date."

He paused, then added, "May also be in violation of the Civil Rights Act and other modern laws, if our park personnel have to act the part of enslaved persons, but that's tough to assess. You know, do we go with what's legal then, or now? In any case," and his voice rose as he finished his presentation, "we are pre-building the docking area for it."

He turned off the presentation and sat back, looking at the two men. "These are all river or canal rides with water arrivals," he went on. "Venice and Oxford include a narrated cruise and a twenty-minute walk. Eventually we'll add a refreshment stop with authentic local foods. Bar Harbor costs a hundred more per person, and includes a lobster dinner."

King gestured to speak, and Steve paused.

"Venice and Oxford are twenty-five dollars a head, right?" King asked.

"Correct," said Steve. "Ninety-five dollars for a family of four. With a choice of cap, T-shirt, themed plush doll or plastic animal toy."

"I heard the exploration team lost a boat in Oxford?" asked King with a slight smile.

"They did not understand inebriated river etiquette and their punt was rammed and sunk, yes," said Steve. "We are looking for a quieter time and date. Plus sunshine for two full hours. It rains there so much! All our research teams come back soaking wet."

He shrugged and continued, "On the other hand, Oxford is an easy place to travel to, because loud Americans and modern women were already a norm by 1910, so we won't stand out. People of color were there from across the British Empire. Once we've tried this for a while and worked out any rough spots, we'll add in a pub lunch or high tea. Not allowed to bring in any modern food or drink. The consultant we're working with says their input-output studies show almost no effect on food supplies of that era. I guess England was doing pretty well."

King grinned and said, "When I visited Oxford twenty years back, we estimated that every third person we passed on the street was a time traveler. It's a popular destination."

But Ard Sprinkle was not amused. He said to Steve Roberts, "You didn't mention the President's project."

"Ah, yes," said King, "his Classic Casinos Culture Tour." He gave Ard an amused glance, but received a cold stare in return.

Ard went on, "What's wrong with a casino trip? It would keep the President happy, and that's good for the program."

"The federal parks service already has a gambling park, Ard, out in Nevada. It's up and running again."

"But that's a sleazy Old West cowboy fantasy," said Ard. "The President wants a classy tour, highly luxurious – to famous gambling joints. You know – Havana in the 1950s, or maybe Monte Carlo. He says those would be easy. Did you see his list? His big favorites are Ancient Roman Games of Chance, and Gambling for High Stakes with Catherine the Great."

Tom King sat up straight and crossed his arms, anxious.

"We've been over this before, Ard. I told you and Senator Styce, and I sent a report to him and the President, that none of those are viable. The health impacts alone are overwhelming. Our visitors and ancient Romans would be trading diseases, lice, bedbugs, you name it. These things do change history, big time."

"But Tom," said Ard, deeply earnest, "he said he can get the Russians to help, and he has close friends who knew Meyer Lansky, so the Havana Riviera or Nacional is a shoo-in. These trips are ready-made for success." (The President had said, "I could work with Meyer Lansky, he's my kind of guy, but Lucky Luciano, he's not so nice.")

King replied, "Our rules and regulations state that we can't do trips to unstable places. And we can't work with the Russians on time travel — that might clue them in about matters of national security." This was a touchy subject for Ard, who knew the President was sharing with his pals in Moscow every detail that Ard brought him.

Steve chimed in, "Ard, those places and times violate all the rules of the federal time travel program. Homeland Security and the Federal Parks System fully agree that – "

Ard whipped around to face Steve, his finger pointing into Steve's face. "I'd be very careful of what you say, Steve, if you want to keep your job." His usually pallid, bland face was red, and the pointing finger trembled.

"I'm just telling you the rules and laws that are on the books, Ard." Steve leaned away, replied calmly, felt uneasy.

Ard snarled, "The President is aware that you are on this team, Steve. He thinks that's a bad idea. Says you have an agenda. He says you're planning to take over the past for Black radicals. You're taking guns back to them." Aghast, Steve sank back in his chair, glancing at Tom King, who shook his head slightly.

"That's right, Steve, you shut your mouth," foamed Ard. "Be a good *boy*. Do what the master says." Steve started to rise, but King held out his hand to stop him and spoke.

"Ard, you can't speak to Steve like that. Do you and Senator Styce meet with the President often?"

Ard replied carefully, still staring at Steve, "I talked personally with Senator Styce on the way over here. He's expecting a report from me. Also, the President is gonna be plenty mad when he learns that you two are setting up roadblocks."

A silence fell. Ard caught his breath and mopped his face and neck with a big handkerchief. King was deep in thought, wondering what Ard was up to. Steve was fuming at Ard's racist aggression, but felt constrained by his job to stay quiet.

King said, "Maybe you need to fill me in, Ard. Why do you persist in thinking that the President has any say in what we do here? As far as I'm concerned, he can make suggestions, and we can consider them, and let him know the rules. And really that is where it ends. Especially with the dangerous ideas he's been suggesting."

Ard stood up, collecting his papers and bag. Dropped his phone, picked it up. He walked toward the door and spoke from the doorway. "You need to understand that the President is shaking things up, changing how we do stuff. He wants to open up the past for development and investment. To make America great. He is a visionary, and I love him. Your trips and research are just a waste of taxpayer money. You guys are on the way out."

Sprinkle's voice rang across the big room outside King's office, where the young Time Team staff sat in cubicles under security domes, working on every aspect of the time travel tourism program. They all heard his angry finale.

Some stood up to look over their cubicle walls to see who was speaking.

And sank down when their boss appeared in the doorway.

King, mindful of this listening audience, called to Sprinkle as he stormed out through the glass doors, “We’ll do what we can, but the rules are the rules.” He went quickly back into the conference room and shut the door.

Steve’s head was up and his eyes were gleaming, the only visible signs of his emotions as he stood waiting. King regarded him for a moment, seeing the self-discipline in how Steve stood in his green federal parks uniform, holding his wide-brimmed hat under his arm.

King said, “I apologize, Steve, for Ard Sprinkle’s words and behavior.”

Steve shut his eyes, and replied tightly, “Apology accepted, sir. But I think that a problem is emerging with the new Administration.”

“Be careful where you say that, Steve,” said King in a low voice. “But also, hold onto that thought.” Then he spoke for listening ears. “I need you to focus on the good work you’re doing to launch our upcoming tours. Can we talk about the staff training? Have you got everyone you need?”

Steve replied, “That security staff you recommended for the Time Ranger Team turns out to have a lot of potential.” He was grateful for the change of subject. “I particularly like the Park’s local guy, Lee Turner. He sets the bar high for everyone else.”

“He strictly enforces the rules and regulations,” said King, sitting back down at the table. He wondered where Ard was headed with all the information Steve had provided. Ard’s behavior felt stealthy. Was he on his way to the White House? King shook off this thought and focused on Steve, who had also settled back into a chair.

“Last fall at Ten Thousand Secrets Park, Officer Turner disobeyed me in order to enforce the Park rules, and I have come to appreciate that. We need a belt-and-suspenders guy to keep us on track. Especially with Ard Sprinkle on the loose.”

Without realizing it, King was shifting from being a rule-breaking iconoclast to protector of his status quo (this happens often in human affairs). He looked over at Steve.

"I took matters into my own hands, to get this program started," said King. "And maybe I'll get away with it. Maybe not. But this guy – " he nodded silently at the official photo of the new President, on the wall over his desk. "He has created a new appreciation in me for the rules, and why we have them. So we need someone like Lee Turner. And you."

"Thank you, sir," said Steve, shocked at the compliment.

They looked at their watches simultaneously, and realized they were both late for their next meetings. Rising to their feet, they mapped out future meeting times and dates, and departed via elevator and stairwell.

Lunchtime in Washington, D.C.

Ravi and Steve compare notes over trending food.

Top on the new President's agenda was raising the Capitol Hill free-will reduction levels to include middle and upper-level federal agency staff. An Executive Order that he signed during his first day in office ratcheted up the electronic behavioral-cognitive control system to 50 percent.

Loyal employees were rewarded with a higher level of free will and a special lapel button. Only senior agency administrators still received full free-will reduction waivers, and some of them – the ones the President was rapidly removing from their jobs – felt kind of punky and low energy most days.

Steve slipped down the broad marble staircase and out a side door of the behemoth building housing the Department of Time Travel. He decided to walk the half-mile to where he was meeting Ravi for lunch, so he could think through what he wanted to say.

Once he emerged from Capitol Hill's security force field, Steve felt a rising surge of emotions about the words Ard Sprinkle had said to him. He pulled out his phone to call Ravi as he jogged toward the sports bar. Remembering he was in uniform, Steve slowed to a dignified fast walking speed.

Already seated at their table, Ravi had just ordered an iced tea when his phone rang. He had been expecting a terse, formal exchange with Steve. Instead, an upset man unloaded on him.

"He said that to you?" Ravi asked, horrified. "Can you do something about it?" Steve entered the sports bar and spotted Ravi on the balcony talking to him on his phone. He climbed the steps to their table and continued talking as Ravi ended the call and slid a menu across the table to him.

"I mean, where the heck did he get off talking like that?" Steve said, sitting down. "It's like everything that I am, and that I have achieved, was erased. I had to keep my mouth shut with both hands, you know?"

Ravi was there to get information, but first he had to help this person in distress. He asked, "What did Tom King say, when Sprinkle said that racist shit to you?"

Steve took a deep breath, looked at Ravi and around the wood-paneled, quiet space. He forced himself to focus on the neon-green-edged menu. The freshly shaved in-house vat-grown lettuce block salad, with sautéed local cave-harvested truffle slices and hand-formed tofu gnocchi, would help him calm down. He wondered about the vat-grown food items. His wife, Becky, needed to know about this menu.

Turning down the waiter's beverage suggestions, Steve drank a long cold glass of water. Ravi was working his way through his enormous iced tea (no sugar). He watched Steve regain his equilibrium and spoke again, gently.

"Ard Sprinkle is a big problem. I sure hope that your boss reports him for what he said."

"It's a weird thing, but I think King was almost friendly to me today," Steve replied thoughtfully, turning the empty glass in his hands. A waiter hurried over to refill it, and Steve nodded his thanks.

"How do you mean, 'weird'?" Ravi asked encouragingly.

Steve lifted his eyes to meet Ravi's, and went on. "I think he's paying attention to me, not just telling me what to do next for the time travel program. I think *his* new boss has really scared him."

"How do you mean that?" asked Ravi, as the food arrived. Steve stared in wonderment at the plate of handmade, vat-grown luscious blocks of green and brown taste sensations, surrounded by garlicky knots of gnocchi. He decided it would be undignified to take a photo for Becky.

"You think this food is our future?" asked Ravi, tucking into his own similar platter, with Terra-Form Taters on the side. He slid the plate toward Steve to share. Steve took a Tater, then pulled out his camera and snapped photos after all.

"My wife is a future foods researcher at the Ohio State University, so, yes I do," said Steve. "First time I've seen these outside their lab kitchen. But back to our topic. The new President is putting heavy pressure on Tom King to do some really bad things with our accessible history resources." He took another delighted bite of the salad block.

Ravi commented, "That's the official time travel jargon now, huh, 'accessible history resources'? Can you give me examples of the really bad things the President wants to do?"

Feeling uneasy about mixing friendliness with work, he added, "You need to know I'm preparing a report for *my* boss, Senator Max. We're trying to figure out what's going on. We think the President is up to no good."

Steve shrugged, replying, "That's for sure. I can fill you in, as long as my name doesn't go beyond the Senator. I already told you some things, but here's the specifics – the President's kids and in-laws and five of his cronies have a start-up, IITP. Stands for Invest In The Past. They even have a mission statement, 'Invest in the past for a wealthier tomorrow.' And there's a bunch of investors who've already put a lot of money into it."

Steve listed big names and dollar amounts. He paused for a final bite, then completed his summary. "So there's a lot of pressure on Tom King to carry out targeted assassinations and other deranged and illegal things the White House has dreamed up."

Ravi lost his appetite at these words, but continued to eat mechanically. A wave of fear rippled along his spine. He said, "Tell me more, please."

Steve considered the possibilities, and replied, "Well, as examples, a coal company magnate in the IITP proposes to take modern mining machinery back to 1900 and bring out coal from when it was cheap and plentiful. The President is focused on getting to the gold in California and Alaska before the first prospectors found it, and bringing out the best quality ore. And he wants King to use his 'assassination talent' to take out liberal leaders and union organizers, so they can't cause any trouble."

Steve drained his glass of water and gazed at Ravi, who was having difficulty understanding what he was hearing. He asked, "But they can't really do that, right? If they kill famous past people and change things, wouldn't we already know?"

Steve caught the eye of the waiter to order coffee, replying, "Who's to say, at this point, that what we're experiencing today is not the result of their actions? Also I think they have something on Tom King, to control him. You need to talk to my ex-supervisor, Ed Zanetti. He knows something really dark about King, from back before the Park bombing last fall."

"Like what?" asked Ravi. They held mugs of coffee and drew closer together, heads down, voices lowered.

"I think that the country is where we are now, with this dangerous President, because of something that King did," said Steve. "Last year King altered something – it was violent – and I think it kicked our country sideways. And Ed Zanetti can fill you in."

Steve saw Ravi shiver.

"So, the past *can* be changed, you're saying?" asked Ravi. "There is no big self-correcting device that adjusts things back to where they were headed?"

Steve nodded. "Yes – there is no self-correcting mechanism to make things come out all right. If there are parallel universes, we're not in one."

He drained his coffee, and continued, "Further, when you tweak a thing in the past, you have no clue how that will ripple forward to affect us today. That's what has me so worried about this IITP group. They map out an action to take in the past, and draw a straight line to the big bucks, the enormous profits, for everyone involved."

Steve looked at his watch and stood up, needing to catch a train to the plane. "But it doesn't work that way. What happens next is wide open. Can't predict the effects. I asked some friends at a couple universities to start researching the physics, but that takes time."

They shook hands, and Steve departed. Ravi had another cup of coffee and sat and wondered how Senator Max would react to what Steve had told him. Would she believe a single word? Then he dialed Ed Zanetti's phone number.

Traveling across Hart County, KY toward Ten Thousand Secrets National Park.

Lena and Janet are trapped by cave country politics.

Roped lightly to a snag, Janet and Lena's canoe floated next to the river island until the sky was fully dark. They ate the last of the peanut butter sandwiches and cookies, watching as tired paddlers on the river's south shore loaded coolers and kayaks into the back of a pickup truck.

Lena said she recognized these ecologists and water quality scientists. They were from the university in nearby Bowling Green, probably staying at their field house. She did not mention that she deeply missed this work and these people. They had been part of her job at Ten Thousand Secrets National Park until she escaped the casino bombing with her mom, the eco-perpetrator.

Now she was a criminal on the run.

The research group stood around and talked quietly, relaxing with cold beverages. Soon they climbed into the truck. It rumbled away up the steep dirt road, tail-lights vanishing into the woods, engine hum fading. Trees sighed in the darkness, and insects clamored.

"I bet they're going to eat pizza," whispered Lena. Three days of sneaking past life's amenities was getting to her. As they paddled the Green, Green River she glimpsed the glowing signs of fast food chains, and intense food cravings inhabited her mind.

During the river trip they had passed springs pouring out of green hillsides, crept close along the riverbank below a two-lane highway, and narrowly avoided being seen by fishermen camped at a boat launch. Their final push had taken them past the city park in Munfordville and underneath the Interstate 65 highway bridge, trucks roaring and billboards shining through the trees above. The land was beautiful, but they were both ready to get off the Green, Green River.

Janet bent to untie the canoe rope from the snag. "Did you see the bumper sticker on that truck? 'No to the Casino Rebuild.' Maybe we have some allies around here." Lena shrugged tiredly as they paddled over to the landing area. She jumped into the water to help push the canoe onto the bank. They removed their gear, turned the vessel over, and slid it into a tangle of grapevine and jewelweed, paddles underneath.

It would stay hidden until the plants died back in the fall. Both gave quiet thanks to the beautiful little purple boat, hoping that it would find its way back to the cabin via the owner's name and registration number.

They shouldered their packs and set off uphill on the dirt road that the pickup had taken. They planned to hike south along the eastern boundary of the Park during the night, sleep during daylight on a high point of the wooded escarpment, and then hustle southwest across the open fields of the sinkhole plain to the server farm situated between the airport and the small town of Oakland. This was the power source for the computers at the Park.

Their instructions petered out at this point, so they had to trust that someone would meet them.

As they walked uphill, they saw a light across open fields to the east. "That's the university research station," whispered Lena. "I swear I can smell the pizza. Their showers are to die for. And the bunkbeds."

Her tone was wistful as she walked with her mom, their boots softly brushing through the spring grass under the blooming trees. They heard the lonely hum of a car, its lights illuminating a road ahead. At the top of the slope they found a tangle of small roads and quiet houses, with dogs who barked in a friendly fashion. They crossed into woods and fields.

Their southward path was less than a mile from the eastern edge of Ten Thousand Secrets National Park. That boundary loomed large in their minds. Janet had seen no surveillance cameras here when she worked in the online crowd management system, but her domain had not gone beyond the now-ruined casino's parking lots. And security might have risen since the unfortunate events of the previous autumn.

Perhaps they were too focused on walking at a safe distance from that boundary, and not sensing far enough ahead. In the dark cedar woods Lena felt something grab hold of her ankle, and she stopped moving. But it was too late. Janet hissed a warning – as a net dropped over her head and pulled tight around her neck. A super-bright light stunned their dark-adapted eyes.

"Right on schedule, ladies," said the person holding the spotlight. "Dumb as a couple of does. Caught trespassing, red-handed!" The tall male figure approached Lena, who had kneeled to remove the plastic loop that was tightening around her ankle. The man reeked of bug spray.

Janet pulled out her knife and sawed away at the plastic loop around her neck. It broke easily. She slipped her head out of the net and stepped away from the light, circling behind the smelly guy who had grabbed Lena's arm. He turned with the bright light and caught her again.

Janet shut her eyes tight against the glare and said, "Just let us pass on by, please. Show us to the edge of your property."

"Come off it, Miss Janet," he replied. "And Miss Lena here," he said, holding her arm while bending down to snap the loop off her leg. He continued with a bizarrely polite introduction. "I'm Gene. My people have been tracking you since you left the cabin, and reporting in to me."

Janet remembered way too late the note in the cooler: "There is a guy with land and guns on the east side of the Park. We are hoping you stay on the water, and slip right past him…" Oops.

Lena was beginning to strongly resent the big hand wrapped around her bicep. But Gene sensed her next move and kicked her legs out from under, while dragging her forward. He was big, moving fast on ground he knew, and the spotlight was blinding her eyes. Janet ran behind them.

"Sorry for the poor treatment, gals, but I did not want to miss you. I got snares and pits all over the place here and – " Gene teetered on the edge of an unseen hole, stepping back just in time. "Let's us get back to my truck safely with no adventures. I got a big friendly welcome set up for you at my house."

In the dark they came up hard against a pickup truck. The driver side door swung open, and Gene shoved Lena up and across the front seat. Climbing in next to her he said, "C'mon Janet, jump in the back seat, I got your daughter safe and sound up here," and started the engine.

Janet scrambled into the open truck bed and Gene said, "Wow, smarty pants! Now I can't trap you in the locked cab!" He jerked the truck forward and Janet almost fell out.

The massive vehicle rumbled through the woods with the headlights off. Janet and Lena were able to keep track of their basic direction – southward, deeper into the woods just east of the Park. They went down into and up out of a gully, and a gate with a massive gleaming metal "Don't Tread on Me" flag slid open as they approached, and locked shut behind them.

"Electric fence, gals, to keep us safe from undesirables," sang out Gene.

A building came into ghostly green focus on the dashboard display. They rolled up to a garage door which opened to embrace the truck and close behind it as the engine stopped.

Gene had kept a hand on Lena's arm, and now he dragged her out his door and let her fall to the garage floor. Her backpack landed next to her.

Janet jumped from the truck bed onto Gene's back and pulled his head back sharply. He twisted her off onto the floor, picked up Lena and her bag and threw them through an open door into the adjoining building.

"C'mon, Janet," he roared, "it's nicer inside." He slammed the door shut and locked it behind him, leaving her alone in the garage next to the cooling truck. Janet pulled a jack stand off a shelf and began whanging on the door, smashing into the lock, and screaming a lot of swearwords. Another door opened to her right, and Gene leaned through.

"Please put that down," he said, "and come in ladylike and nice. I got good food and clean beds for you both, and no hanky-panky. This is serious political business, and we need to seal the deal before you move another step."

He turned to shove Lena back from the doorway as Janet rushed in, entering a handsome living room with cathedral ceilings and big soft couches and chairs, all in calming pastel colors.

"My wife is away at her sister's," said Gene in an apologetic tone, "but she got some nice food for you ahead of time." He gestured toward a gleaming bathroom. "Who goes first?" Lena grabbed her bag and stalked off toward the balm of a hot shower.

Gene shouted after her, "It's all locked up, you can't sneak out." He swiveled to look at Janet, who was standing hands on hips scanning the nearby kitchen area for potential weapons.

"Everything's put away, Miss Janet. And all my guns are locked tight in the gun safe so the grandkids don't mess with them. How about some iced tea?" He reached into the refrigerator and handed her a bottle of sweet tea. "It's all pre-packaged, don't want you to think I'd try to poison you."

Steely ecoterrorist Janet was feeling overwhelmed, after eight months essentially outdoors. She took the tea, sinking into one of the big soft chairs, and snapped the bottle open. She chugged the bland, sweet brown stuff, and let the air-conditioning wash over her.

"Thank you," she said, for the moment skipping over Gene's assault and kidnapping.

"Just as I thought," he said, sitting on the big soft couch with a tea in his hand. They could hear the shower down the hall. "You gals need a break, a little bit of nice treatment." He handed her a folded flyer from the coffee table.

"You are big heroes to a lot of people, you know. We want to join forces with you." Gene was a wily old sociopath, and knew when to hurt and when to back off. He watched Janet closely as she examined the front of the flyer, and listened for Lena, who soon returned refreshed from the shower, reeking of fancifully scented shampoo and conditioner. She sat down next to her mom, who wordlessly handed her the flyer and walked toward the bathroom.

When Janet returned, scoured by the powerful shower, Gene was sliding a frozen pizza into the big oven. Lena was pushing buttons on the microwave, an empty lasagna box on the counter. Gene turned to Janet.

"Got a feast nearly ready, Miss Janet," he said. "All pre-packaged, like I said. OK?" Janet shrugged and pointed to the flyer on the coffee table.

"Can you give us some background on that, please?" Lena started to speak, but Janet held up one hand, pointing to Gene with the other.

"Well, we had to take some liberties with your persons for that photo, but liberty's what we're after, you know," Gene said smoothly. He did not give a rat's ass if they liked it. They just had to face the facts.

The flyer's title read, "Take Back the Commonwealth of Kentucky!" Below was a faked photo of Janet and Lena standing in the dark entrance of a cave. Janet held a cartoon bomb in her hand, its fuse burning. Lena brandished a submachine gun. "These two heroines did what no one else dared to do!" roared the caption.

The following lines expanded the theme:

Will you join them?

They will lead our army into the

Stygian Darkness of the Caves
to confront the Blue Berets!
The time has come to eradicate the Evil U.N.
and its plans for Global Government!
Yes, this is the sign you have been waiting for!

Neither woman wanted to read any further.

Gene beamed at them, blue eyes watchful. "You girls are a real shot in the arm. Nobody had the nerve to act, all these years, just talk, talk, talk. And then out of nowhere you come along and blow the place up!"

"Can I speak?" Lena asked, looking at her mother, who nodded. The microwave dinged, and Gene went over to rotate the lasagna. "Dinner's almost ready!" he chirped.

"What's this about the U.N.?" Lena asked. "You mean the United Nations? What do they have to do with Ten Thousand Secrets National Park?"

Gene was delighted. The girl was asking questions. She could be educated! Her mom, though – not so much. She was a nasty b-word. He put plates and cutlery and more bottled tea on the dining table, and gestured for them to sit down. Good to get them fed – turns enemies into allies.

"Dig in, ladies, while I answer your excellent question, Lena." He smiled benevolently, gesturing at the food. They dug in, famished and excited by the bright colors and odors of the supermarket food – pepperoni – melted cheese – hamburger – tomatoes – fat, salt. Intoxicating.

Gene ducked his head for a moment of silent prayer and picked up his fork. "Back in the late 20th century, a guy we thought was a friend of ours, the first President Bush, signed an agreement with the United Nations that handed our country over to the globalists. We were stripped of our sovereign rights!"

Lena reached for her third slice of pizza, her eyes slightly glazed. She said, "I never knew that!"

Janet's mind surfaced out of her gluttony to consider how they would get out of here. She could not bear this stupid man's nonsense.

Gene polished off a slab of lasagna and pushed the still-ample dish toward Janet, whose plate was momentarily empty. She hesitated, then spooned out another helping as he continued, "Our group was formed to protect the Commonwealth of Kentucky from this threat. The U.N.'s soldiers are holed up in the caves, waiting for the signal to emerge and take over."

Lena stole a glance at her mother, who rolled her eyes behind Gene's back. He whipped around, but missed it.

"Take over where?" Janet asked.

"They will impose global government nationwide," he replied.

"You really believe that?" Lena asked. Satiation was beginning to hit, but she continued to eat, luxuriating in the flavor and salt. She leaned back and looked at Gene, who frowned for a tiny moment, disappointed at the doubt in her voice.

He said, "They are invading our federal parks. You can tell by the ones that say they are Biosphere Reserves. That's the U.N. program that uses global funds from the financial overlords to steal our land and guns and strengthen globalization." Gene was getting louder with enthusiasm, hoping to carry them over the finish line with his argument.

"So you think I'm some sort of criminal mastermind?" asked Janet. "You want me as an ally, me and my innocent child?" She pushed away her empty plate, wondering if she could pick up the table and throw it, to distract him.

"I beg your pardon!" cried the outraged child. Janet held up her hand again, and Lena quieted, glaring.

"Well yeah, kinda-sorta," said Gene, waving his hands. "We want to take your approach nationwide. It's an incredible model. Two brave women, blowing up symbols of oppression and wickedness." He beamed encouragingly and went on. "We need you to visit some other parks, get people trained. All expenses, 24/7 protection for you."

Gene excitedly jumped to his feet. “The new President is sending secret signals that he likes our style. It’s time!”

“What exactly do you have in mind for us to do?” Janet said, quietly.

“I thought you’d never ask!” said Gene. He popped open a laptop and clicked around to find a document. “Here’s our draft plan,” he said. They bent forward to read, as Gene intoned the solemn words.

The Plan to Take Back Kentucky
Blueprint for Action!

Last November, the pillar of flame shooting into the night
sky from our stolen land was the call to action —
the signal fire to move forward!
We will always remember where we were
when that call came.
All of us witnessed the destruction of
the face of Evil in our midst.
Since that glorious night when the Casino was consumed
by cleansing flames and heavenly torrents, we have
been preparing to take our positions of power.
Everyone knows the roles they must play.
Sadly, violent acts may be necessary.

A small sound at the front door distracted them. Was Gene’s wife returning early? She did not like his “foolish antics.”

A God-fearing, law-abiding woman, Chrystal did payroll at the Park, and her job paid the bills. These thoughts flashed through Gene’s mind as the door lock rotated, and the door began to open. But Chrystal always called his name when she came back, and entered through the garage door, not the front. He dived for a kitchen drawer and pulled out a handgun.

“Gene, put that away,” said a woman. Not Chrystal.

A man walked in and nodded to Lena and Janet. He was followed by the small dark-haired woman who had just spoken.

Gene said, "Aww, shit," set his gun down on the table, and collapsed into his chair. The man stepped forward, picked up the gun, walked back to the front door, and tossed the gun out onto the lawn. Janet paid close attention to where the gun would have landed.

"No gun, no problem," the man said, closing the door. Gene swore at him. The woman spoke to Janet and Lena.

"Glad we finally caught up with you. We were tracking your progress on the river, but good ol' boy Gene got to you first."

"How about some respect, Gabby?" Gene said to her, heading for the refrigerator. He pulled out more iced teas and set them on the table. "I am not no damn *boy.* We are a prominent leadership group of men and women, bringing heartland America back to its senses. Can we talk?"

Gabby and her companion sat on either side of Lena at the table. He gave her a wink. She recognized him and Gabby Greene from the Park's caver team. His wink stopped her from saying his name, Dave Davis, known as Dave Caver.

"What just happened?" asked Janet, slumped tiredly in her chair, overwhelmed by the rich, heavy food. It had been a long day. She was unaccustomed to people, and felt claustrophobic as the room filled up with strangers.

Gabby smiled. "We came to an agreement with Gene a couple years back, that he does not interfere with our business. You are our business."

"And I know how to get into Gene's so-called fortress," added Dave. "That electric gate is child's play." He picked up the plastic tray and began eating the remaining lasagna with his fingers. This did not look as bad as it sounds.

Looking at Janet, Gabby spoke carefully. "You had a visitor in April, right?" She put her finger to her lips to indicate they must not say Steve Roberts's name. Lena and Janet nodded.

"Well, we are your escort for the next step. You took your damn time getting here."

Lena said, "I know who you are, and him, too."

Gabby shrugged. "Yes, you sure do. We trained you for the cave science work. Big thanks we got for that! I don't like what you did to the Park and my cave. So now you can help us out." She opened a tea, took a sip, and picked up a slice of pizza.

"Make yourself at home, huh?" said Gene.

Gabby smiled at him and took a bite.

"Gene, what were you planning to do with our guests here?" asked Dave, opening his tea and drinking deep.

"Take them over to the firing range, meet with the group and plan for implementation," said Gene, snapping the laptop shut on his beautiful plan.

"We'll just skip that step for now, Gene," said Dave, "and thanks for the grub." He placed the empty tea bottle on the table and rose to his feet, gesturing for Lena and Janet to follow him out the front door. They grabbed their backpacks and went, with Gabby hard on their heels, eating her pizza slice. Behind them, Gene stood up as the door closed.

Outside in the humid evening air, Dave ran to the driver's side of a passenger van, bat logo on the door. "Fast, fast," he hissed, opening the front and rear doors. "He might start shooting from upstairs." Dave climbed into the driver's seat and started the engine as Gabby got in next to him.

Lena scrambled in the rear door with her pack and slid across the seat to make room. Janet, fully revived from her food torpor, scooped the handgun off the lawn and into her pack before climbing in. Dave backed the van down the driveway.

Gene's voice shouted after them, "Take this, you f*ckers," as shotgun blasts hit the asphalt just short of their tires. They tore through the open electric gate, which was sparking and popping.

"We're cutting a couple of days off your incredibly slow trek to your destination," said Gabby from the darkness of the front seat. Lena leaned forward to listen.

"I guess our big secret trip wasn't so secret after all," said Janet, arms wrapped around her pack, pushing the gun deeper inside.

Gabby grinned. "Not very secret. Many people knew where you holed up, and have been reporting your every move."

"Whose side are you on, exactly?" asked Lena. "Mom, I don't like this situation."

Dave interrupted. "Gab, do you think he'll come after us? Let's change cars." He turned left off the small road onto a bumpy unpaved lane that wound through thick woods. They emerged suddenly into open pasture, where the springtime insects were singing loudly. The lights of the interstate highway twinkled in the distance; stars gleamed overhead.

"Get ready to jump," said Gabby. A small sedan was parked along the lane. They jumped out, climbed in, and were off again.

"OK, gals," said Gabby. "Can you get down on the floor? It's less than a half hour to your destination and we don't want to screw up. Nighttime is the right time, but let's play it safe. We need your help, but don't want you around any longer than necessary. Maybe that tells you whose side we're on, maybe not."

They soon arrived at a highway intersection on the eastern edge of Ten Thousand Secrets National Park. Janet felt uneasy, being so close to her old job and less than a mile from the destruction she had caused. Dave turned to drive along the Park's southern edge. Soon they were descending from the sandstone plateau, heading through the woods and onto the sinkhole plain. They turned south at the old road toward Oakland.

Janet gazed out the window at the darkened farmland, dotted with groves of trees and quiet homes. Although it was less than a year since she had ridden here with Brian to the bus station in Bowling Green, it felt like another lifetime. A wave of guilt and fear for him suddenly engulfed her. She must have made a sound, because Lena reached out and took her hand.

Dave steered the car around a couple of right-angle turns and they slowed, approaching the village of Oakland.

"We are arriving at the deceptively normal household where worlds collide," Dave said portentously, in a voice of doom. "There you will rest for the night. Tomorrow we'll take you into echoing corridors that connect strange places and ancient times."

"I really need to put my head down for a few hours," said Janet, "but maybe you can explain what the heck you mean by that?"

They passed a fenced-off area containing warehouses, sheds, and electric pylons. It was bright and noisy in the quiet night.

Gabby tilted her head toward it. "When the feds installed this massive server farm to bring the Pleistocene into the Park, there were some unanticipated consequences," she said. "We cavers have been exploring and mapping the openings that appeared. We call them time tubes. When Hugh Hynes got killed, we went into them, looking for his remains."

They drove along Oakland's main village road, lined with trees. Driveways led to well-tended small cottages and Victorian-era homes. Dave put on his left turn signal and they entered a driveway edged with stone, rolled past a lawn and flowerbeds, and pulled up next to a house where a light shone through a curtained window.

"And you found signs that he's alive, right?" asked Lena.

"That's what Steve told us," added Janet.

Gabby nodded, smiling tightly. Dave opened his car door, got out and stretched. The others followed, and they all entered the quiet old house.

New York State's Southern Tier.

A glad reunion, coupled with disillusionment and confusion.

Brian shrugged unhelpfully at the officer he was reporting to this week. "It just – fell off," he said, the ankle monitor on the table between them.

"They don't just fall off, Brian," she replied. He had dealt with this nameless officer several times, and she was a bully. Now she moved into his face, and he resisted leaning away.

"To open it, you need the code we have right here in this office. Tell me again, how did you remove it?" They had been going back and forth like this for twenty minutes, and Brian wasn't feeling cooperative. The windowless little room was deeply air-conditioned, and he pulled the green cloak over his shoulders.

"Feels like a meat locker in here," he said.

"I beg your pardon!" she said, vaguely outraged. "The other thing we need to resolve are many missing hours in your record. We lost track of you for five hours and fifty-eight minutes. You parked your car in that construction site, walked along that trail, and – poof, gone. And now here you are with a bogus story."

"I hiked in the woods, and came straight here when I realized the monitor wasn't working, ma'am," said Brian tiredly. The metal chair was digging into his back. "Doing the best I can," he said, and stopped being helpful. He did not care if they believed him. Brian was feeling low and sad. The two guys he had looked up to, Greenwood and Acton, were just creepy old bigots. His vision of going to live with them in the woods and be a magic wood elf was in ruins.

The officer ducked outside the door, spoke to someone in the hall, and came back in. "We'll overlook this one, because you have been fully compliant until now," she said. "But next time, you go back to prison. Here's your papers to sign. There's an invoice for the cost of the monitor – you'll be billed for it. We'll take it out of your paycheck at the museum." An officer came in with a new monitor, which he affixed to Brian's ankle.

"You're gonna make me *pay* for this f*cking thing?" Brian asked, his exhaustion boiling over into unguarded language.

His assigned officer smiled, delighted at having hit him where it hurt. "You broke it, you bought it," she said cheerfully. "Complain to your fancy Ithaca friends, damn dirty hippies. You *f*cking*" – she rolled out the pungent word – "trust fund babies, liberal snowflakes! Our new President is gonna make you *pay*, all right."

They threw him out the door, reminding him to show up on time next week. As he drove away, Brian cast around desperately for what to do. He decided that he would *not* return next week. Things had to change, now. It was his life!

Suddenly intent on seeing his friends, he drove straight to Mushroomy Fields Forever. Rita's car was in the lot, as it was every week when he went past after his appointment. Brian parked and got out (inside, their heads lifted as they saw him!). He walked toward the door, counting two more things that he knew for sure. One, Maeve was real. Two, those portals went places, and connected with people. Maybe he could find his mom again, like last time. (And what about those owls?)

Inside, the familiar scent of pizza and beer rushed to meet him, along with his friend Harris, who dodged around people at their tables and hugged him tight, almost crying. "Every week, man, we've been waiting here for you," he wailed. Brian sat down at their table, and Rita slid over a paper plate with a pizza slice so big that it overlapped the plate at both ends.

"We've watched you drive by, week after week," she said.

"You knew where I was, what I do, each week?" Brian asked.

"Everyone knows, man!" said Harris. "We all want to help, and you just ignored us. But today you finally stopped and came in! What's different this week? But eat some pizza before you answer!" Brian closed his eyes and inhaled the scene. He felt as if color and sound were returning. He did not know they had been gone. He picked up the 'za and savored a big bite.

"How do you mean, 'everyone knows'?" Brian asked, as the impact of the first bite flowed through him.

"The Internet, man," said Harris. You are *so* famous. You are a *cause*." He waved his phone at Brian, who said, "I'm not allowed any of that, keep it away."

Ignoring this, Rita pushed her phone toward him. "Here's our Brian Owen Safety Watch page. Seventy thousand followers." She scrolled through photos of him entering and leaving that small building, him in his truck, him at the grocery store.

"They don't dare touch you," she said. "They know we're watching." Brian had a small sip of beer, his first in many months.

"What is the world coming to?" he asked, mildly. "This is really weird. I feel kind of creeped out by those photos."

"Nobody knows what the world is coming to, Brian!" Harris replied. "The world has gone in a very strange direction recently. At least we got you back! Maybe normalcy will return. But this election – this new President – "

"We're all frightened, Brian," said Rita.

"Heck, I'm not scared," said Harris, piling pizza slices in front of Brian.

"Scared of what?" asked Brian. "I've been out of it. Not allowed to read much news. What did I miss?"

Rita looked at him thoughtfully. "Where should we start?" she asked.

"Well, what did I do?" he asked, starting in on another slice. "And is it really true about the new President?"

"Let's start there," said Harris, who looked wide-eyed at Rita for support. "But – you don't know what you did? What does that even mean?"

"The President part is easy," said Rita. "A mediocre television celebrity is the President of the United States, as of Election Day last fall."

"That's what I thought," said Brian. "But I'm not allowed any newspapers or TV or Internet, so I have just been trying to grab what I can from thin air, and what I hear people talking about. What is the truth? I just have no clue. I don't get how that guy got elected President. What's going on? I just eat my meals and watch old movies."

Rita got out of her chair and leaned over to envelop Brian in a hug. Harris was trying and failing to not cry. Tears were squeezing out of his eyes, and he had a hard time catching his breath.

"And you don't know what you did," he whispered. "You didn't do anything, Brian. Why didn't you come find us sooner? Why didn't you open your door? You knew it was me."

"See this?" Brian asked, lifting his ankle to show the monitor. "They already know that I'm breaking their rules, by stopping here. And now I've dragged you two into it. That's why I've been staying away."

Harris wiped his eyes on his sleeve. He pulled out his phone, took a photo of Brian's ankle with monitor, and began typing. He looked up to say, "OK, seventy thousand people have been informed where we are and what the threat is. You should be safe for a while, so come home with us."

"Can I finish the pizza?" Brian asked plaintively, picking up the next to last slice, and draining the beer in the pebbled plastic glass. The other two settled back down. Rita refilled Brian's glass.

Two helmeted young people on bicycles appeared out front, locked their bikes, came inside and signaled to Harris, who responded with a nod.

"See?" he said to Brian. "You're safe."

"I see two high school age persons," replied Brian, in a skeptical tone. "You're saying they came because of what you just posted on Facebook?" Rita and Harris nodded vigorously.

"There'll be five hundred if we need them," said Harris. "We're in a strange new world."

They followed Brian in their car to his apartment building, accompanied by the two-bicycle security escort. He filled a suitcase, gathered up his laptop and new houseplant, and drove to their place. Rita hid his car in the small tumbledown garage next to the small white wood-frame house with a green, flower-filled front and back yard. The bike escort departed with a wave.

"Since when do you guys live in a house? And together?" asked Brian, sitting on the couch while Rita made up a bed for him in the spare room off the kitchen.

Harris plopped into an old armchair and replied, "We're roommates, comrades, whatever you want to call it." He was arranging a pot of hot tea, cups, spoons, and honey on the low table between them. Brian's houseplant (a fern) had already found a new home on the windowsill. Rita joined Brian on the couch.

She said, "Brian, a war has started. People need to gather and organize. You are joining us here."

Harris nodded, drew in a deep breath, and said, "Something that worries me right now is that you haven't laughed or even smiled since you came in the pizza place. You notice that, Rita? Where is our laughing funny friend Brian?"

"What's there to laugh about?" asked Brian, leaning forward to accept the cup of herbal tea. He stirred in some honey, and looked up at the other two.

Drawing breath, he said, "All right, I'll tell you. And you already know some of this. Since last fall, a wacko fairy queen tried to sacrifice me to the underworld, and I think my co-worker Gregg didn't escape. I ran away and hid on Apple Island. The next morning I was pushed through a hole into the past by a guy named Ricky. I got sick and almost died, got rescued by Ravi" – he glanced at Harris, who rolled his eyes in delight at that name – "AND by my actual *mom*, who put me on a bus back home to here."

Brian sipped his tea and went on, "A few nights after I got back, I was fast asleep in my bed when the door was kicked in and these shouting guys in space-enforcer costumes and big guns dragged me off to a secret hell-space and beat the shit out of me."

Harris said, "That explains a few things. Rita and I got to Apple Island a little too late. We talked to Ricky, but you were gone. What did he do, exactly? What do you mean, pushed into the past?"

"Into some kind of portal, man, I fell in, and came out in Venice. In the past." Brian looked defiantly at them, wondering if they would believe him, but Rita said, "We are in a weird new world."

Harris said, "Wait, and your *mom* and Ravi showed up in Venice?"

Brian shrugged. "She and some other people were testing a time travel tour for the federal parks service. I have no clue why Ravi was there."

"But the past is a mighty big place," said Rita, holding her teacup close. "Why did you end up where they were?"

Brian shrugged again. They all fell silent.

Then Brian told them some more. "The security hell-people used drugs and waterboarding and other stuff I'm not going to mention. I don't know for how long. Weeks or months. They were mad at me about my mom and sister – wanted to know my 'role' in something really bad they'd done. But I didn't know what that was! I told them my mom paid for my bus ticket home and gave me cash for new boots. That was all I knew." He wiggled his beautiful boots.

"What did they say about that portal?"

“They thought I was making it up, so they hurt me every time I mentioned it.” The three friends sipped their tea, Harris shaking his head in silent anger.

Brian whispered, “I haven’t talked to anyone about this before. You pretty sure we’re safe here tonight?” He stared worriedly at the old wooden front door and the open windows.

“We’ll close it up before we go to bed, which should be soon,” said Rita. “It’s safer than it looks. We’ve been working on it.” She lifted a handheld-size plastic box with shining red and blue buttons. “We’ll explain about this tomorrow.”

Brian rushed to get his story out. “Late one night they gave me back my cloak and wallet and boots, opened the door, and threw me out into the cold. I walked home, where I read an old news magazine and finally found out what my mom did.”

He leaned back against the couch cushions and closed his eyes. “Since then, I report to them every week, being a good boy. But this week I paid a visit to Apple Island, and that means trouble for me.”

Harris said heatedly, “Seventy thousand people and three U.S. Senators got you out, man. You aren’t going back in there. Trust us.” He got up to shut the windows and lock the doors, and entered data into the small device. Rita waved goodnight and headed upstairs to her room.

Brian walked to the doorway of his bedroom and slumped against the doorframe, needing to talk a bit more. “It was so great to see my mom,” he said to Harris. “I hope she and Lena are somewhere safe. I want to find them, so I’ll start with the portals on that island. It’s as good a place as any to start looking.”

Harris was starting an enormous yawn but cut it short and said, “You saw those two nature guys on Apple Island?”

“I did. And they can go to hell,” Brian replied, crawling gratefully into his bed. “There’s lots more to tell you,” he said as sleepiness overtook him.

Chapter 4

To the Hollymount community above the Canisteo River.

King is captivated, and Mary Anne finds her path.

A black luxury pickup truck with darkened windows charged onto I-86 westbound, heading from the Elmira, NY airport to the Highway Spur Project Area. Dr. Tom "Cat" King was driving, drinking coffee and staring out at the wide flat valley as they passed a small veterinary office and a regional health center. His trusted executive office manager, Mary Anne Washington, sat next to him taking notes on a laptop, her coffee in the door cupholder.

"What do you mean, 'non-detect device?'" he asked, continuing the conversation they had started on the private jet that had flown them to Elmira from Dulles Airport. He had commented then that he hoped this trip could be kept private, and Mary Anne suggested he use a non-detect device.

"Surely, sir," Mary Anne replied tartly, "you have encountered those little tech-y doodads that mask your presence. You leave no trace on security cameras, and no digital trail. It's a sonar reflective device, developed by bat researchers."

"Bats, huh," replied King absently.

He was fighting off a panic attack and felt as if the truck were about to accelerate and fly off the road. He sucked in deep breaths, got into the right-hand lane, and slowed the truck to a stop on the shoulder. Cars whizzed by.

Mary Anne dug around in the small cooler tucked between them and pulled out a prescription pill bottle and a breakfast sandwich from the airport coffee shop. She shook out two pills and placed the sandwich where he could see it. Mary Anne was an excellent employee.

King downed the pills with coffee and rested his head on the steering wheel. “What is wrong with me?” he asked, out loud for the first time ever. “My nerves are shot. I can’t concentrate to do my work.”

He unwrapped and took a big bite of the eggy sandwich. “Thank you for this. But I can barely remember why I wanted to go see the project,” he said, looking at Mary Anne, who stared out the windshield at the grey morning.

“If you are asking me for my opinion, sir, I think you are trying to do too many things at once, and also the President is getting on your nerves.”

“It’s not that,” King replied, looking briefly in the rearview mirror before pulling back abruptly onto the highway, forcing cars to scatter out of the way of the hulking truck. He talked between bites of his sandwich.

“Last year everything was going well, I was taking over the program from those federal parks people, and dumping the idiots and dreamers. Then something happened. I mean, maybe I went too far. And ever since, things have been a mess.”

“I have never known you to miscalculate, sir,” Mary Anne said. “What do you mean?”

“Back in grad school, I did research that proves without a doubt that you can change history without bad outcomes in the present. You know about that?”

“I read about it, yes. The Grandfather Paradox.” (See Appendices, page 298). Mary Anne stared out the window as they drove past the Corning exits, keeping her voice light and steady. She had become frightened of her boss after reading about “harvesting” his grandfather in pursuit of academic glory. Maybe it was time to get out of the D.C. rat race.

"Exactly. I built my whole career on that work, you know."

King was feeling better, driving fast in the left-hand lane. He smiled over at Mary Anne and added, "You owe your job to that work."

She gazed fixedly at the cars they were passing, thinking, 'I need someplace better suited to my country self.' Mary Anne had grown up in a Baltimore suburb, but her heart belonged to her grandparents' small farm in western Maryland.

King went on, "So last fall I carried out another targeted cull, or harvest, if you prefer that weasel word. I was in danger of losing the entire time travel impetus to the bureaucrats and liberals. Had to do it."

He enjoyed the sound of his voice and regarded Mary Anne as a grateful receptacle of his wisdom. "And it worked. The entire time travel initiative fell into my lap – and here we are, riding high."

"But…?" Mary Anne prompted.

"But there are things – unanticipated outcomes – that are starting to worry me. I might have gone too far, tipped something off balance."

"Here's our exit, sir," said Mary Anne. She did not want to hear any more, and she needed to get out of the truck into the open air as soon as possible. What he'd done was disgusting, shocking.

As he slowed the truck and swerved into the exit lane, King added, "Don't worry, Mary Anne, I will spare you the details." 'She is a total professional,' he thought admiringly.

"But that's why I want to keep this trip private, even from Ard, OK? He knows what's going on down here better than anyone, checking it out since last fall. I need to see for myself. And figure out what the options are for fixing what I did."

Mary Anne sipped her coffee, and replied, "Whatever you say, sir."

"But it's probably not fixable," he said, turning south onto Route 15 toward the Highway Spur Project Area.

An hour later they had traversed the roundabout and walked

the trail and stood at the crosspaths in the woods. Mary Anne had switched to her phone and was reading from Ard Sprinkle's most recent report, which she had downloaded earlier.

TOP SECRET
Naturally Occurring Time Openings
Highway Spur Site, Steuben County, NY

Mary Anne read aloud, "The highest density of openings is found at the foot of the slope, on Apple Island. Approximately 50 acres in extent, the island is 75 percent covered by a large, well-maintained apple orchard. A remarkably stable microclimate appears to ensure a year-round springtime bloom of apple blossoms. Little is understood about this phenomenon, and it requires further study."

"Let's check it out," said Dr. King.

They walked down the steep trail to the bottom of the slope and crossed the small creek to Apple Island via a well-worn tree trunk. The weather brightened and warmed around them, and blue sky appeared overhead. The sun shone through the evergreen trees on the slope they had just descended.

"I thought I smelled woodsmoke," King said, walking toward a cluster of tall old hemlock trees and a smoldering campfire at their foot. No flames: It had recently been doused with water, and fragrant smoke rose up through the trees. They stopped to listen, but heard no one. King shrugged and sat down on a log seat, gesturing for Mary Anne to sit nearby. She gazed around apprehensively.

"We won't fall into one of those time holes, will we?"

"That's why I sat down," he replied. "Safer that way until we check out the map." He pulled out his cell phone, but to his dismay found a blank screen. "My phone is dead!" he growled.

"No reception here," remarked Mary Anne, who glanced at her phone, then slipped it back in her pocket. She looked around carefully and stared through the shady hemlock grove to the apple trees beyond, blooming white in bright spring sunshine.

'It's beautiful here,' she thought, 'so quiet and calm.'

"Look – Mary Anne – shh," King whispered, and she turned to follow his pointing finger toward the base of the tallest hemlock tree. They saw a shimmering of green-gold particles around an opening between the tree's old twisted roots. Mary Anne froze; the hair on the back of her neck rose, and a prickle ran down her back. They held their breaths.

Mary Anne stood up slowly and backed away, toward the bridge and trail up to the crossroads. King rose and looked at the sparkling circular opening for some time before deciding that he needed more information.

"Let's go talk to the local residents," he said in a low voice.

They walked across the bridge and up the trail to the crosspaths, where they turned left toward the Hollymount Inn. Across small fields they saw its white walls gleaming in the sun, punctuated by deep green shutters around multi-paned windows.

"When I stayed there last fall," said King, gesturing toward the Inn, "the community leader I told you about, Maeve, said they were ready to work closely with us. She didn't seem to know about the time access holes, so I talked about the highway project and the benefits it would bring to these rural poor folks. She wanted money." The two of them walked past small homes as he spoke, unaware of several observers and listeners. All of whom were surprised to hear themselves described as "rural poor."

Mary Anne scrolled through Ard Sprinkle's report as she walked, keeping an eye on the crow circling overhead. She bent to pat a beautiful big golden-eyed black cat who sat in the path at one of the houses. It meowed in a loud and friendly fashion but stayed where it was, watching them approach the Inn's broad entrance stairs.

The place looked shut down. It had been a hard winter, when the polar vortex came to visit from the Canadian Arctic, and stayed for many weeks.

"They found seven time holes on that island," Mary Anne said to King, "and maybe there's more. I have never been so scared in my life. Who knows where we might have ended up?"

King said, "I have to find out what happened to that highway consultant, Gregg somebody, who disappeared here last October. He signed out at work saying that he was attending a community meeting and seasonal party over here, and he never came back. He was part of the survey team."

"I thought that terrorist, Brian Owen, killed him?" asked Mary Anne.

"Nah, that loser has nothing to do with it. I read his interrogation reports. Owen was camping out on the island after the party and was pushed through one of the time holes by a low-life guy on the highway team. We can't find that guy, either." King climbed the big steps of the Inn and stared at the lifeless building.

"You think this place is abandoned?" he asked, and banged the holly leaf-shaped door knocker several times. The heavy sounds echoed from the thicket of holly trees on the hillside above the Inn. The door creaked open two inches, and a pallid dark-haired man – the Innkeeper – looked out at them.

"My lady Maeve is indisposed," he said, opening the door wider. "She asks what business do you have with her this day." Mary Anne gasped aloud. She was not expecting a beautiful Irishman, seemingly straight out of her favorite screen shows about otherworldly Celts and time-traveling Highlanders.

King glanced at her and said to the Innkeeper, "Is your dining room open? We'd love some coffee. And scones," he added, recalling Mary Anne's love of all things related to clans and glens.

The door swung wider, and the Innkeeper said, "That we can do. Welcome back. It has been a long winter here, and my lady has been ill." The Innkeeper and Mary Anne exchanged deeply interested glances as he showed them into the dining room, seating them at a gleaming round wood table near the fireplace. He placed logs on the glowing embers of an earlier fire.

"Two coffees and scones, on the way," he said, and went through the kitchen door.

Mary Anne stared around, her face shining and animated.

"Sir, I never knew about this! I'll see if I can come back and stay for a few nights – maybe they have musical events." She looked around in vain for tourism brochures.

"Ard's report leaves out a lot of interesting detail," King said, smiling. "What exactly do *you* think is going on here? The lady, Maeve – don't have her last name, another detail to check – told our highway consultant that she emigrated here from Ireland, with that guy you like and a couple others, over 400 years ago. Totally ridiculous."

He leaned forward and whispered, "I think she's a hippie. Kind of cute, if you like the type. We need to find out who owns all this, buy it, and move these folks out. This is that priority site for the Departments of Homeland and Defense you've been taking notes about."

Mary Anne stared at him, shocked. "Sir! I cannot believe what I am hearing. *This* is the place you plan to bulldoze and install a state-of-the-art lab for time travel research?" She rose from her chair and looked out the window, back the way they had come.

"How would people get here to do the work?" She turned to him, her face stern. "Surely you don't plan to allow that highway project – "

King had to nip this in the bud. She was useless to him if she took this attitude. At that moment, the Innkeeper emerged carrying a tray with a jug of coffee, cups, sugar and cream, and a platter of currant scones, with lashings of butter and jam.

"Ma'am and sir, here you are. Please relax and enjoy. My lady Maeve will join you briefly, after you have completed your repast."

The Innkeeper winked at Mary Anne and vanished through the doorway, leaving her with the feeling that he knew who they were. She threw herself into buttering and jam-slathering and pouring coffee just the way Tom King liked it. Perhaps for the last time, she realized, gazing around at the beautiful, welcoming room.

"Sorry, sir, I forgot myself," she remarked, retreating into her work role. She saw him relax at her calming words, and knew she had to be very careful. What might happen to her if she objected to his plans?

"That's really OK, I understand. This is a cute, charming old

old place, isn't it? Just be glad you got to experience it before we hmm … update the infrastructure, shall we say?" He smiled at her through a mouthful of scone, and she had to hide a sudden revulsion – against him, and against herself. All those times he had convinced her not to quit. She felt ashamed. And now she was stuck. Or was she?

They ate and drank quietly in the old room as the heat from the crackling fire saturated the air around them and sounds of birds came through an open window. Warm sunlight shone in the many-paned windows, illuminating floating dust motes. Wholesome spiders spun webs in the uppermost corners. Mary Anne felt at home here. Was this what she was looking for, in our one and only precious life? She compared the Inn and community to her city life of convenience, ease, and stress.

Absorbed in their own thoughts and plots, she and Tom King missed Maeve's arrival until she was sitting across from them at the table, the air shimmering around her. The Innkeeper brought her a cup of tea and stood behind her chair.

Maeve said, "Good day, Tom King, we meet again after a harsh winter. I gather you, too, have had good and bad times since we last met. How is your power holding? Is your wealth intact?"

King, startled at her sudden appearance, was silent for a moment. Maeve shifted her gaze to Mary Anne, and liked what she saw. She distrusted human women, regarding them as rivals for power over human men. She knew that Mary Anne understood Maeve, and would support her. 'And she fancies my Innkeeper,' thought Maeve with amusement.

"Hello, I am Mary Anne Washington, Dr. King's office staff," said Mary Anne. "I love it here," she said firmly.

"I know that," Maeve replied. "Perhaps you have finally found the right place." Mary Anne's eyes filled with tears at this remark, and she bent her head away so that King would not see, but Maeve and the Innkeeper saw. They smiled at her, as King found his voice and his sales pitch.

"So good to see you again, Maeve," he said heartily. My end is solid, but you're right, it was a rough winter. And how are you? I just dropped by to see if it was time to do business." Mary Anne was astonished at how tone-deaf he was to this situation and resolved to let him reveal himself. This time, she was not going to help him out.

"When you visited last autumn, we had a pleasant conversation, but I cannot quite recall what it is you wanted from me," said Maeve. "Could you remind me?" King realized he was distracted by her blue eyes and her black hair shining in the sunlight. He shook himself out of this reverie and became businesslike.

"Frankly, I'm thinking of the future, Maeve – the future of this community. Times are changing. We're going to build a new little town for everyone a few miles away. All the modern amenities, ecologically conscious – heat pumps, community solar, cell service, composting toilets maybe. While we update this property." His smile was, he thought, empathic and kind.

King's listeners reacted in different ways to this strange assemblage of words. The Innkeeper stared at the floor, too ashamed for the man to even look at him. Maeve's head tilted and her eyebrows rose. She understood very little of what King had said, beyond seeing straight through his lying self. A flickering, sickly aura surrounded him.

Mary Anne had long ago trained herself to keep her face blank around her boss. She watched Maeve and the Innkeeper, and wondered how she could possibly return to D.C. in King's company after this humiliating experience. What would he say next?

Oblivious, King continued, hoping to seal the deal, the one that only he could see. "I'm just here on a brief courtesy visit, Maeve, but my team will follow up with you this coming week. Gives you time to tell your neighbors about the big money coming, and a better life for everyone." He wondered why Mary Anne was not helping with this stuff the way she always did. He saw deep disapproval on her face and figured she was as impatient as he was to get this project moving.

"Mary Anne, I think you're delighted by the old-fashioned charm of this place. Can you fire up the laptop and get some details here? Full names, dates, banks, accounts, family contacts. You know the drill." His voice was warm, his gaze cold.

Mary Anne said, "You'll have to excuse me for a moment," and turned to the Innkeeper. "Where might I find the bathroom?"

He smiled and said, "We had one built just outside for you – for humans – for visitors." He gestured toward the door.

Maeve said, "Please go with her, dear." Outdoors, Mary Anne spoke quickly. He stood a bit closer to her than he might have.

"I want to help. I want to be here and help. That man is very dangerous and will destroy this place." The Innkeeper reached out and touched her cheek (his style with women not being of the modern era).

He said, "You should not fear for us or this place. There are powers here that Tom King has no knowledge of. But we need your help, and we'd love" – he paused on this word – "love to have you here. Can you go back with him, and find out his plans? We must prepare for this fight. Then gather your things and come back. We have room for you." He gestured toward the Inn.

"And I can help, be of use to you?" Mary Anne asked, moving just a tiny bit closer. But she stepped back as the door opened and King emerged, Maeve next to him in the doorway.

Indoors, King seized the moment alone with Maeve to flirt, a tactic that he mistakenly believed brought women into line.

"You look like you could use some warming up, Maeve," he said silkily. Maeve was not accustomed to her prey being quite this stupid, so she waited for him to settle into her trap. Some would call it a spell.

"Come visit me in D.C.," Tom King continued. "I have a hotel suite where I can put you up, and show you the sights of our nation's capital. My team can arrange the details." He cocked his head on one side, only in his mind looking vulnerable and attractive.

There. She had him.

Maeve replied, "All in good time, Doctor-Mister Thomas King. Your people visited here over the winter while I was ill and deeply upset my community."

King sat upright and began to apologize, but she held up her hand to stop his words – and his voice froze in his throat.

She stood up, which pulled him to his feet. A torrent of gold sparkles surrounded her as he followed her to the door. It swung open, revealing Mary Anne moving away from the Innkeeper.

Maeve turned to King and gestured for him to leave. The warming May day shone down on them, and he saw that she was beautiful. But he could not speak.

Maeve said, "I hear you have a new warlord in the D.C. palace. I do not like such tyrants. I came here to escape their scheming, their lying courtiers and slaves. You may send your people to talk, but none of your wheeled wagons with their filthy, smelly engines and loud noises. We will not have that here. Now go."

Tom King stumbled down the big steps, sapped of volition. Mary Anne stepped forward to steady him, and they turned toward the pathway to the distant parking lot through the woods. The Inn door closed quietly behind Maeve and the Innkeeper.

A Maryland suburb –

Flowers blooming everywhere.

Perched on a stool in the Zanettis' kitchen, Ravi Sen-Ellis gazed through the open French doors across a stone terrace to the lawn and newly planted garden. The morning breeze was fresh, but the heat of the day was building. Ed Zanetti refilled Ravi's coffee cup, his own, and that of Steve Roberts.

"I'm putting in raised beds and loading them up with this incredible compost I got from a working farmshare," Ed said, sliding the remaining waffles in Ravi's direction.

Ravi picked one up and nibbled it, keeping his cool as Ed continued to talk about converting his large suburban lawn into a vegetable and fruit garden. Ravi dreaded being shown neatly labeled rows with seedlings coming up. Suburban gardening by the upper middle class was, to him, empty elite posing.

"I thought I'd jump right back into the agency rat race after Tom King kicked me out of my old job," said Ed, "but then I started helping my kids with schoolwork and doing a better job of sharing housework with my wife, and eight months later – here I am."

He gestured around at the handsome home and two children, who were bent over small screens in the next room. Ed had given his kids a half-hour of screen time so that he could chat uninterrupted with his old work colleague Steve. He was slightly leery of Ravi, who was top staffer for the notoriously wonky Senator Liz Maximus. Why was he here?

Steve wiped his plate clean of syrup with a final bite of waffle. "I'm glad you're taking a long rest, Ed. You really needed it after updating the agency's time travel Best Management Practices. That was grueling work, coordinating all the reports and triple-checking the data."

Ed replied, "But King has thrown it all out. All my work. Under him, the agency is going ahead with dangerous new time travel tours. I'm keeping track of the Time Tours publicity, which is offensive and stupid. They – and I mean *you*, Steve – don't seem to care about the high likelihood of time change impacts."

Steve smiled and shook his head, not responding. He could see that Ed was jittery and did not want to scare him away from talking about what had happened the previous year. "Actually," he said, "we're using your Best Management Practices in every aspect of our trip development."

"*Except,*" said Ed with rising heat, "BMP #1, which if followed to the letter as required by law, would mean you would not develop *any* of these tours. So unsafe! Irresponsible. I mean it's a potential catastrophe, letting the general public – children! – take time tours! The potential for damaging, cascading time impacts is incalculable."

His children raised their heads at hearing their tribe mentioned, then went right back to their games. They were hoping Dad would forget about the half-hour cutoff.

"Ed, there will be time travel tours. King wants them," Steve replied, looking directly at Ed, who glared back.

"But we've done a lot of research with your time impacts BMPs as guidance, to minimize risk. We select for times and places where a few more tourists won't be harmful. The calculations all work out."

Ignoring Steve's attempts to pacify him, Ed drained his coffee cup and continued, "Heaven knows what damage has already been done. Sometimes I wonder if last fall's election results are the outcome of that disruptive time event last year." He looked at Steve. "Remember? You were there."

Ravi sat up, because this is what they had come to talk about. He and Steve exchanged glances, and Ed caught it.

"Wait a minute – " Ed said uneasily. "I'm not interested in getting involved, you know." He stood up and started clearing away dishes. "Let's go out in the backyard," he said, now aware of why they had come to visit.

Outdoors the warm air was filled with the fragrance of cut grass. Mowers could be heard from two neighboring backyards. The men skirted the ambitious vegetable garden and walked to a rear corner of the lawn, where the mowing noise was loudest. They stood casually with coffee mugs, apparently three suburban dad guys.

Ed said, "You first."

"Last year," Steve began, and Ravi nodded encouragingly. "After lunch at the office, Ed and I went through the portal to our little bench overlooking that French meadow, Loire Valley, 1860s."

Ed replied, "Yes, like we often did. We could talk there."

"And we encountered an anomaly. A person who was supposed to be there – he was there every time we visited at the same time on the same date – was not there. That triggered BMP #2, 'Abort trip.'"

Steve raised his eyebrows at Ed and continued, "We came back to our time through the time portal in the office hallway, and things had changed, right?"

Ed kept his head down, hiding his reply from observers, "You're quite right, Steve." The riding mowers, one operated by a mom and the other a dad, roared their closest approaches just beyond the fence, turned their corners, and the sound diminished. Families were preparing for backyard birthday parties, to which a close mow adds a note of property perfection, serenity in a troubled world.

Steve, also gazing down, spoke to Ravi. "In violation of every workplace practice, a security guy in a uniform I'd never seen before grabbed Ed in the hallway and said that an order had just come down that Ed was a security risk and potential traitor. He took Ed to the nearest capsule Exit – "

"And that was the last that Steve or anybody saw of me," said Ed. "I was tossed out on the street that afternoon, after twenty years in my job."

A jet overhead had its noisy interval.

Ed went on, "Why are you still working there, Steve? Those guys are dangerous." Steve nodded, did not speak.

"These are Tom King's thugs?" asked Ravi.

"No," the other two replied together.

Steve said, "They didn't exist before we encountered that anomaly. Someone went back and killed that person – a landscape painter. We found his obituary in old French newspapers, murdered with a knife as he painted, by persons unknown. And that murder has changed things into the present. I think that the crazy stuff we're all dealing with now, including the election of this President, started right then."

He looked at Ed and asked, "What do you think, Ed?"

"Wow," said Ed. "You found his obituary? I didn't know about that." They started walking back to the house, the meeting nearing its end.

"And I agree, Steve," said Ed just before they stepped back indoors, "it all started then."

"Who do you think ki – " Ravi began, but the other two shook their heads sharply, so he stopped speaking and set his coffee mug down on the table. Ed ducked into the adjoining room.

"OK, kids, time's up," he called, and returned to the kitchen, ignoring indignant wails of "No fair!" and "It's not a half-hour yet!" He walked his guests to the door.

"It was great to see you again, Steve. And good to meet you Ravi. Give my best to Senator Maximus – we got along pretty well, and she found us a lot of funding."

"She has a soft spot for good science," Ravi replied, shaking

Ed's hand. "Can we stay in touch, have coffee soon at her office?"

Ed said, "I need to think about it. What they did still hurts pretty bad, you know. I put up a good front about the changes in my life, but – "

"Let's leave it there for now, Ed," said Steve. "You need more time. But we may need your wisdom if the situation gets worse." Ed bowed his head and closed the front door.

Beneath and beyond the village of Oakland, KY.

"Glowing tubes, man."

Too close to the aggressive Kentucky city of Bowling Green for its own peace of mind, the 200-household community of Oakland is a haven of small old homes, quiet families, and tall shade trees, surrounded by farms. A beloved mayor once said that his main task was to keep the cows off the streets. Though it is hemmed in by unwanted development, independence and autonomy abide in little Oakland.

Rumors of caves below their houses have always thrilled the residents, and one family dug by hand deep into a sinkhole, but was never able to break through into the vast space they were certain lay below.

Until, that is, the day that the new server farm north of town was activated. Powered by western Kentucky coal-fired power plants, this enormous computing capacity was enough to shift several hundred acres of land in nearby Ten Thousand Secrets National Park from the Late Pleistocene Epoch into the present day. Night and day, the computers hummed and the coal combusted, keeping the Pleistocene accessible to secretive federal government agencies.

The government was unaware that the surge of energy had opened up other places into our normal daily existence. Wondering about a stiff breeze blowing from their cellar, the family in Oakland found a new deep opening, a hole three feet across, in the cellar floor. They called that guy everyone knows, Dave Caver, who threw a rope down the hole and found a cave passage. It was big enough for a carriage and four horses, just like the old local stories promised.

Dave returned from his first exploration trip unable to describe what he had found beyond "glowing tubes, man." He called in Dr. Gabriella Greene, the only cave scientist he trusted, swearing her and any others involved to secrecy "on pain of death, no joke." They recruited a small group of resourceful caver scientists to investigate what Dave had found. Only they and the local family knew about it, and pain of death was guaranteed to anyone who talked. Cavers can be like this.

Janet woke to the smell of coffee, and for a long minute luxuriated in the feeling of clean cotton sheets and a firm mattress. Lena snored lightly, curled up at the other side of the bed. The coffee pulled Janet out of bed, into the brick-walled bathroom with a giant claw-foot tub, past fantastic paintings and Americana collectibles, and around a column into the kitchen, where she found fresh-baked coffee cake and life-giving coffee.

It was unlikely they would meet their hosts, who preferred to stay in the background. The night before they had welcomed her and Lena and shown them their room, then faded into the background. Gabby and Dave had stayed a bit longer, whispering to the two women about "time tubes under the house," before heading out.

Janet carried full cups and plates back to Lena, who woke slowly. "I could get used to this," she said, sitting up to accept the coffee and cake. "You know, like life used to be."

"Maybe after we find Hugh," said Janet, "wc can look for somewhere quiet." But she knew that back in the normal world things would be different between the two of them.

Lena's life plans and career prospects had been ruined by embracing loyalty to her mother and going on the run together after

Janet blew up the Park casino complex. This fact lay between them. Their mother-daughter idyll was ending, at least emotionally. Lena's feelings might be shifting into resentment. Janet was storing up a treasure chest of memories from their winter together, anticipating the deep loneliness that would return when Lena inevitably departed.

"I had a weird dream," said Lena, still a bit sleepy.

"How do you mean?" asked her mother.

"One of those time tubes, that they talked about last night, that are under this house. It led me to a place to live, and to be myself again." She got out of bed, grabbed her clothes, and disappeared into the bathroom.

Janet sipped her coffee, rueful that Lena had not included her in that dream. Shook her head free of melancholy – what's done is done – and climbed into her clothes, staying focused on the task of going in search of Hugh Hynes, the head scientist at Ten Thousand Secrets National Park. He had been lost in a caving disaster last fall, and she felt in part responsible.

What's worse, she had learned from Dave and Gabby the previous night that with Hugh gone, Ten Thousand Secrets National Park had been quickly taken over by Tom King and his federal defense agency partners. Almost as though Tom King had pushed that button on purpose, to get rid of Hugh. But Janet had no interest in what she dismissed as "politics." She had her own goals to achieve – protection of nature, cost what it may. And, of course, to find Brian.

The night before, Dave and Gabby had said that Hugh might be found and rescued at the other end of "a glowing time tube." It would be a miracle to find him alive, Janet thought. As she looked out the window at the placid gardens and neighboring homes, Janet felt energized about the time tubes, "piled up like spaghetti," Dave had said, underground beneath their feet.

According to Gabby, they had probably been there for millions of years. The tubes were pulled into the present day, along with the Pleistocene, when the server farm powered up.

"Dave is here," said Lena, leaning around the doorway. They picked up their packs and left the warm bedroom, aware that their accommodations might not be so nice going forward. Dave was sitting at the big round table in the front room, maps scattered on its surface.

"Feeling refreshed?" he asked, as they refilled their coffee cups and sat on either side of him. "We're fortunate that the family who lives here is willing to host our exploration work. They dug down into the top of this strange phenomenon years ago, but didn't quite connect. So they're happy to help, but want to keep it quiet."

"Is this work sponsored by Ten Thousand Secrets National Park?" asked Janet. "I never heard about it when I was there, but maybe it's another of the ten thousand secrets?"

"Sheesh no," laughed Dave, who was setting up a small projector on the table. "The Park knows nothing about this little caving project. Even that scientist guy Steve Roberts. He asked to be kept out of it – unless there's an emergency. When we found signs of Hugh Hynes being alive, we figured that was an emergency. So Steve was our emissary to you in that hideaway that everyone knew about! This here is also secret – our caver secret."

"Wouldn't the Park administration want to find him alive?" Lena asked. "He was their chief scientist!"

"The man now in charge of the entire time travel program – including its military applications – for the U.S. government is Dr. Thomas King. You know about him?" Dave's eyebrows were way up.

"Sure!" said Lena tartly. "We had all winter in that cabin to think about him. He pushed that button to turn off the Pleistocene when he knew mom and I and Hugh were in the cave. His action killed Hugh, and endangered mom and me. We know about him."

"Well," said Dave slowly, "he's in a lot of trouble over that. Everyone knows that Tom King did not like Hugh Hynes. And he took over Hugh's position at the Park as soon as he was gone. People are asking, 'Was Hynes's death really an accident?' There's going to be a Congressional investigation. Our President wants King gone and is looking for a reason to fire him."

"I understand why you need to find Hugh," said Lena, "but – why me and my mom? Why don't *you* go get him?" Her question hung unanswered in the air as Dave pressed a tiny red button on the little projector. A glowing image took form above the table. He tapped an arrow on the projector, and the floating image grew into a pile of spaghetti of different lengths and sizes. Dave tapped the device to enlarge the image further.

They peered at it as Dave concluded his previous topic.

"King wants Hugh dead. Easier for him. Us rescuing Hugh is secret, for everyone's safety. And you owe us for the damage you did with that blast."

He raised his head to stare at them. Not in a friendly way.

"Also, we really mean it about secrecy. We don't want the President to hear about these time tubes. I mean, I voted for him and I love the man" – startled stares from both listeners – "but he is not a scientist. He might screw up if we give him too much information. So if you talk about this, you will die. And no joke."

It dawned on Janet and Lena that they were expendable. If they vanished, no one would ever know. They traded quick glances but did not speak.

The glowing image was now large enough to see the individual tubes. Dave tapped the arrow, and some of the tubes took on unique colors. He picked up a pencil and pointed to one end of a bright-pink tube.

"These are the piled-up cave passages that connect with other places and times. We color-coded them in this 3-D map to simplify wayfinding. I'll lead you to this particular tube entrance. We installed a glowing pink light just outside."

Janet squinted and leaned forward, trying to see into the tube.

"Mom, this is just a map," said Lena with embarrassment.

"Right," agreed Dave. "This image is a gross simplification. When we climb down in there" – he pointed to a larger sloping tube off to the side of the glowing pile – "you'll be in a regular cave passage. You walk around a corner and go into a domed room. This heap of craziness is in the center. It looks like a pile of rocks, a typical cave breakdown pile, except for all the sparkling holes."

He enlarged the view a bit more and concluded, "That's where the time tubes are."

Placing the pencil adjacent to a neon green tube, he continued. "This passageway is directly above the pink-coded one. You have to crawl around boulders to get into it. We set a glowing green light at the entrance. But – don't go into it," he said craftily, making sure they saw where it was.

"So each one has a glowing light at the entrance?" asked Janet, who was feeling frightened and did not dare look at Lena, not wanting to spook her. But Lena thought it was cool, and reached out to point at several of the other labeled tubes – orange, yellow, red.

"Have you explored all of them? Where do they go?" she asked.

Dave sat back and looked at them both. Gabby had told him that it was Janet and Lena's obligation to find Hugh, that they owed the cave a lot after the damage they had done. And she had told Dave not to rescue them if they got in trouble. He now needed to set the bait, to trap them into doing this. For the moment he simply answered Lena's question.

"We've explored all the ones that are color-coded, yeah. Twelve so far, in eighteen months. We estimate a total of maybe thirty." They could see the uncolored tubes, grey in the image.

"And we know where each of the color-coded ones comes out," he added. Janet began to ask where they all came out, but Dave got there first. "You don't need to know where they all come out," he said. "At many different places and times, is all you need to know. It's our secret research, OK? I'm just going to tell you about the pink one and the green one. So let's get going," he added, standing up.

He unlocked a door and led them into a windowless room filled with ropes, backpacks, helmets, headlamps, pre-packed food and water containers, gloves and knee pads. Soon outfitted, the two women watched silently as Dave pulled up a trapdoor in the floor, revealing the top of a round metal culvert, about two feet across. He swung himself onto the ladder inside and descended out of sight, and they followed.

"Leave it open, would ya please?" he called, waiting for them below. Dave wanted to keep this short. He had other things to do, including a movie date in Bowling Green. Gabby said to not mention some things, like the effect tube-time had on aging. Beards, body hair, and nails did not grow on these trips. No one knew what this might mean, but cavers minimized the amount of time spent inside these passages. Why worry these disposables with details?

He was a good distance along the sloping cave passage by the time the others were down the ladder to the cave passage. They hustled to catch up as he disappeared downhill around the bend. The passage stayed wide and high, descending toward a dim glow that strengthened as they entered a bigger room.

Across an open space lay a hill of rocks and massive limestone slabs, apparently fallen long ago from the stone dome that arched overhead. Sparkling nodes of pulsing white light shone out from all over the stony hill, marking the entrances into this tangled pile of time tubes, or portals.

Janet saw a pink square down on the right, and pointed.

"Look uphill from there – see the green?" whispered Lena. Dave liked that they had spotted their target areas. Now it was time for basic instructions – keep it real simple. Soon they would be out of his hair.

They followed him over to the pink glowing square, set just outside a cave tube near the base of the stony hill. The interior of the round passageway shimmered. Above them on the slope was the green sign on a stick, next to a rounded cave entrance somewhat obscured by fallen rocks. Their eyes soon acclimated to other colored squares and shimmering small entrances on the hill above them.

"So," said Dave briskly, "we figure this trip will be short, but you have supplies, water, and food packets for three days, with basic medical supplies. Just walk in there and proceed, and after maybe, oh, twenty minutes, you come out the other end of the tube into the Pleistocene. Here's a map."

"Wait – this passageway comes out on the north side of the Green, Green River?" Janet asked with some incredulity, taking the folded map. She gestured in the direction of the forty-five-minute distance they had traversed in his car from the Park.

"Why don't you just take a Park boat across the river and enter the Pleistocene through the front door like we did last fall? Why not rescue Hugh with a team of experts, like those security guards?"

She wound up with, "Why do we have to sneak in via this creepy hole in the ground and risk being arrested? Maybe you *want* us to be arrested?"

Dave tried to slow her down. "This passageway comes out right near the place where we found modern human poop and a campfire," he replied. Janet and Lena stared, waiting for more.

"Has nobody explained anything?" he asked, irritated. Yet again, he grumbled to himself, he was left to do the hard work. He went on in a whiny tone. "Wow, well I don't have a lot of time to spare right now, but let me fill you in a little bit. Your mission is to find Hugh and bring him out. Like we've been telling you, we have to keep his situation a secret until he's safe."

The two women nodded, and he sighed.

"Now I gotta explain why, I guess, since nobody else has. We can't use the front entrance to the Pleistocene any longer. After you blew up the casino, King shut down tourism access to the Pleistocene. That entry point is now exclusively for secret military training uses. They widened that portal and are taking tanks and drones and troops over there."

"Into the past?" Lena asked, staring. Janet picked up her equipment, trying to cope with the shock of this news by focusing on the task of rescuing Hugh.

"Yes, into the damn past, your precious untouched past," said Dave, angered out of his muted dislike of these women. "They're playing war games over there, killing animals and polluting and – " he paused and drew a deep breath. "Until last week, they kept the time setting to a single day, so that it was wiped clean daily for them to start all over. But now they want a permanent base. They're ramping up their occupation, switching the time setting to a week or a month, or longer. We also found out that they're deciding on a target date for their next Time Fort."

Dave's voice rose to a shout. "And we want to keep this place here out of their hands. Secret. OK?" He fell silent, angry at himself for venting and maybe telling them too much. Good thing Gabby wasn't here.

Janet and Lena walked over to the pink-labeled cave passage. "Tell us again what we do once we are in the Pleistocene," said Janet quietly. Dave was relieved that they were focused on their task. He continued in a calmer tone.

"At the other end of this tube, we built a cairn and wrote a note that we left under it, for Hugh. We put some food nearby. We're just hoping he found it before the war games assholes showed up. So this is urgent. This is an emergency. And secret. You two have taken far too long to get here."

"Are we walking the entire distance from here, under Oakland, all the way to the north side of the Green, Green River?" Lena frowned, trying to understand how long the trip would take.

"Are you what, exactly?" Dave didn't get the question.

"Is this time tube fifteen miles long?"

"Oh – heck no. Some of these tube trips are a little bit longer than others, like the green one is maybe ten minutes longer than this pink one. But they're all about the same. Twenty minutes. Even if they go somewhere long ago. Someday maybe the scientists will figure out how it all works."

Dave remembered just in time that this was all top secret on pain of death. He had been about to tell them where another tube went. He abruptly pulled a small heavy device from his top pocket.

"Just use your smarts. He can't be far away at the other end of the tube. This compass" – he handed it over, reluctantly, because it was expensive and he did not expect to get it back – "also works as a tracker to get you back to the time passage and back here. OK? And don't let anybody see you, right? Except Hugh." He paused, making sure he had their attention. Now it was time to drop the bait, the poison bait.

"And the green tunnel up the hill?" He pointed up to the green sign. Do NOT go in there. Come right back out when you find

Hugh. We saw a man come out of the green tube a few days back. He walked around for a while and then went back in. He just had a flashlight. We think he is named Brian Owen, from New York State."

Both women began speaking at the same time, but he overrode their frantic questions.

Dave held up his hand and said, "I know, I understand your feelings! Gabby really wanted me to tell you about this. We know that he's part of your family, and she cares!"

When Brian had headed back into the green-labeled tube, Dave and Gabby followed him far enough to see that it was collapsing – a potential death trap. But Lena and Janet didn't know that, and would go after Brian. Maybe they could get through, but for sure they couldn't come back. This was payback for the harm they had done to Ten Thousand Secrets Cave.

Dave turned away and began walking fast across the wide dark space toward the passageway to the surface. He called back to them, "Just get Hugh and bring him upstairs here, and then we'll help you find out what Brian Owen is up to. And we'll come looking for you, if you don't climb back up that ladder by tomorrow."

He put on a burst of speed and was soon out of sight.

How Brian found the green time tube.

"Magic, is that what you call magic?"

Saturday bright and early, Brian and Harris stepped off the log crossing onto Apple Island and walked under the sunny blue spring sky to where Acton and Greenwood sat, tending their watch fire under the hemlocks. No one was feeling friendly. The two guardians had told Brian that Harris was not welcome, because he was "not American." But Brian had brought him anyway.

During the drive to the highway spur turnoff, Brian and Harris had translated the phrase to mean "Jewish," and snickered at the stupidity. But facing one another in person was unpleasant for all of them.

Acton moved first, pouring and handing them each a small cup of tea from the pot simmering next to the fire. In return, Harris shared out chocolate chip muffins, fresh from the grocery store bakery. They stood there eating and drinking, gradually coming around to smiling and joking. Surely people can just get along.

"If you think we're bad," said Greenwood, "wait until you meet our replacements." He snorted and eyed Acton, who nodded as he reached into the bag for another muffin, then took over the tale.

"Our tour of duty here has another few months to run before we hand it off to the next team. They think we're way too lax and friendly to outsiders. They won't be letting any of you New York crazies across that little bridge." Acton was smiling, but the words stung.

"How do they plan to stop us?" Harris asked, upset.

"We're still figuring that out, and we sure won't be telling you," said Acton. The feeling of shared fellowship began to fade. Brian decided they had better push their plan forward.

"While we're here, can we explore a bit? You know, go through some of the holes? I know the one over there goes to Venice, and that one" – he pointed to the shimmering base of the hemlock tree – "goes to Maeve's Ireland, right? So where's the one that takes you two home?"

Greenwood gestured toward the spring sunlight and apple orchard. "It's on the point of land out there near the lake. We might show it to you, but only because we don't want you near it. I can show you a couple of other time holes, sure, but in return you have to help us."

"All right," said Harris. "Doing what?" And the four of them felt a little bit better, sitting down to drink more tea.

"What we really need help with," said Greenwood, "are some of the visitors. We thought that quiet times would return after that trouble last Halloween" – he glanced at Brian – "but there have been some people coming here that we don't understand at all. They seem dangerous. Maybe you know how to talk to them."

Brian had a sinking feeling that he was not going to get away from his problems by coming to Apple Island. "Like who?" he asked.

"Three different groups of people," said Acton. "First is a man named Ard Sprinkle. He says he works for the most powerful man in Washington, D.C., who wants to pay us cash for the time holes. Of course we kept our mouths shut. That Sprinkle is a bad man."

Acton turned to Greenwood and said thoughtfully, "Once Maeve gets to feeling stronger, maybe we can help her catch and feed him to that devil of hers down there."

He turned to the round-eyed, rapt Brian and Harris, and said mildly, "I think that Mr. Sprinkle is coming here again soon. I can find out from Maeve, because he wants to meet with her, too. Can you be there for that?"

"Tell them about the others," said Greenwood.

"Oh, yes. The second group is the men with powerful machinery. They did a lot of damage along the creek last fall, and now they want to come onto Apple Island and up the hill to where the paths cross. And around the Hollymount Inn up there where Maeve lives with her Innkeeper. They say they want to improve our lives, but that we'll all have to move away."

"You mean the company building the highway spur is bothering you?" Harris asked. "I thought that was just in our – what do you call it – dimension? Multiverse? Not yours."

"I never know what you people mean when you start talking that way," said Greenwood. "I think these men want to control the time holes. They came here as soon as the snow melted, before Maeve was awake. We held them off, saying they had to wait for her to heal. So they'll be back soon. They brought the machinery right up to the edge of the woods, that time."

"And the third group of visitors," said Acton, seeing the shock on Brian and Harris's faces, "was the man from D.C. who has been here before. He was here again a few days ago – Tom King, with his underling – a woman named Mary Anne. We think he sent the machinery last winter."

"We are just sick of these intrusions, you know?" Greenwood took up the tale again. "So we hid when we heard those two coming to the crosspaths and down the hill to our little campfire. We listened to them talk about time holes, but they took fright and went to the Inn to see Maeve. King told her that everyone has to leave and go live in new houses. She told him no, and spelled him to her control. And Mary Anne told the Innkeeper she will help." Greenwood was finished. He and Acton gazed expectantly at the others.

Harris said to Brian, "I guess we asked for it!"

He turned to the two men.

"All right, we'll commit to helping you rid your land of these intruders. But you gotta be nice, and don't be forbidding us to come here. We're on the same team."

"Until our replacements arrive, we can work like that," said Greenwood. "Now come look into the time hole that takes you to Kentucky. That's the one Brian wants, right?" He smiled at their surprised reaction.

"Magic, is that what you call magic?" Greenwood asked. They placed their teacups on a stump, and headed up into the sunlight.

Chapter 5

Meetings are held at Ten Thousand Secrets National Park.

Welcome to Deep Space!

The auditorium in the Park Visitors Center was packed and overheated. Consultants from Washington, D.C. along with Park staff spilled out into the hallway, where they leaned against the wall listening to King and others speak from the lectern inside.

A voice boomed, "Those terrorists did us a favor, blowing up the Casino. Don't get me wrong, too bad about the mess, but now it's full speed ahead with making America great again. Time travel is gonna make all of us stinking rich – the most patriotic news since I won the election."

These were the glowing tones of the nation's President, weighing in via phone from his Florida estate. He finished with, "Catch you later, Doctor-Professor Tom Cat King." The world's media captured his fade-out comment, "That pompous guy is a load of sh…."

"Glad you approve, Mr. President," said Tom King, to dead air. He looked out at the darkened room. "We've made great strides.

Thanks to the Park's own Steve Roberts and our agency's Time Tours staff, we're opening affordable time travel trips to the public starting this fall."

King was distracted for a moment by a fleeting vision of Maeve at the Inn. He drew in a deep breath and drank from the water bottle in his hand. Sitting nearby, Mary Anne had a good idea of what was bothering him but was not inclined to help. King grabbed the lectern hard with both hands to remind himself where he was and spoke into the microphone. The world's screens shared his words.

"We invite the American public to register for the first trips in our new Time Travel Vistas program. These will commence just in time for the holidays. And thanks to the federal parks service, the price is right for a family to take a premium time trip at an affordable price."

At King's side, Steve Roberts smoothly took up the story, flicking through the pretty pictures of plans and designs. "The public will be able to visit the beautiful uncrowded past in Venice, Italy; Oxford, England; and Eden/Bar Harbor, Maine, starting in late November of this year. You can enjoy a water cruise in small vessels, a short walk on land for those who wish it and, coming soon, refreshments. We hope to have overnight accommodations arranged for Eden/Bar Harbor by early in the new year."

Screen images from Time Team research visits showed picnic baskets in punts, blue skies, pigeons in the piazza, waves crashing on rocky shorelines, lighthouses.

Steve continued: "These places were selected for their long-established tourism presence. Our visitors will fit right in and will have zero impacts as we pass through. The science is good."

Replying to a planted question, Steve said, "Yes, the Tennessee Rivers Ghostlands Cruise is in the works. We hope to have it up and running soon, for the spooky autumn months." He paused, then went on to insert small-print details. "Of course, there are age, health, and U.S. citizenship guidelines, and other rules governing these trips. These places will be as accessible as we can make it at our end, but we cannot – *must* not – alter conditions at the other end. That's also good science."

An unknown voice in the dark room called out, "When do the casino tours start? The President said they would be a top priority!"

King emerged from his spellbound misery at these words and softly whispered, "Shit," which was picked up by his mike and emanated through the media as a long drawn-out sigh, noted by those who wanted him fired. Not loyal!

Covering for his boss, who had been under the weather for weeks, Steve spoke assertively. "The casino time travel tours are in the early planning stages. We are working closely with the President to determine their feasibility. Our tours need to be stable and without impact on the past. That's our duty to science, and Mr. President knows we're working on it!"

Steve touched the lights, ending his presentation on a positive note. "Learn more about it at our media sites. We are looking forward to greeting the first members of the public to travel through time!"

The crowd stirred and broke up, heading toward lunch. Steve soon escaped from the cameras to drink coffee in his office, desk cleared for his plate of buffet food. He wondered what was wrong with King, who recently had been arguing against his own programs and losing track of what he was trying to say. 'He needs a break,' thought Steve, 'but we don't have time for that right now. There's tours to launch!'

Not hungry, King skipped the lavish buffet. He was driven around the rebuilding of the Park Casino and hotels, making positive noises as it was all pointed out for him. They pulled the car up to an unobtrusive back door to the Casino and led the way under construction scaffolding into a narrow hallway and a gleaming elevator door.

"Sub-basement coming up, sir!" said the excited Park staffer. King closed his eyes and leaned back as the elevator descended. He knew that Mary Anne was next to him and he had heard Ard Sprinkle's voice as they stepped into the little box. Everything was hazy to him, except for distant Hollymount Inn and the land around it, which stood out sharply in his thoughts. Why was this happening? Ever since that visit with Maeve, he'd felt confused and restless, unable to sleep. Sometimes it seemed that she was actually in his mind talking to him, but that couldn't be true.

He thought vaguely, 'Maybe it's a sinus infection or something. I'm years behind on doctor checkups, don't want to hear what they'll tell me. Maybe – ' King yanked himself into the moment as the elevator stopped and the group stepped into the lobby of the gleaming new underground research and development space. Here they would securely and secretly plan the military aspects of the "past improvement initiative."

No expense had been spared in throwing Department of Defense money at this subterranean expanse, code-named Deep Space. All the latest conference facilities had been installed. There were four calling booths or huddle spaces, equipped with small couch, table, and chair – each in a distant corner of the giant room, walls in each one shimmering with a mild electronic buzz to prevent intrusion. A series of larger team rooms ranged between the huddle spaces, walled off and comfy, with space for eight to ten people to meet for secure confabs.

Three conference rooms with breakout space capacity stretched across the vast center area. Today's attendees were shepherded by the security team toward the glass doors of the middle room. A bar and informal dining area lay beyond, next to a wall of waterfalls with its soothing white noise. In an unobtrusive back-wall spot the red EXIT sign gleamed, containing the emergency capsule to the surface for anyone who thought too hard about how far underground they were.

While King and the glittering Joint Security Agencies Meeting settled in – it was their first meeting in this new facility, with two presentations on tap – the larger, hidden space that surrounded the Deep Space conference complex was buzzing with activity. Here were the security forces, teams on alert to protect and defend the visiting big shots, along with the emergency response and hospital services. The aesthetics were bare walls and wires, and the edge was cutting.

Beyond them lay secret labs, still being built, where research would soon be underway to connect the Park's engineered Pleistocene entry point to future time points, eventually linking to the present day. These carefully researched intervening time points were termed "inflection points," where small military, political, or social system actions would gradually tip the balance of history in the USA's favor.

In fact, this area of the program was in a state of chaos, a hard fact that Ard Sprinkle and the top military talent hoped to conceal from Dr. King at today's meeting. The expert hired for this extremely delicate research, Dr. Hrudlu Vatson, had been recommended by the President. There was nothing they could do to stop his installation at the top, even though he did not have a well-established science background, and his citizenship and security background pointed murkily toward Moscow. Overall, the research process was in disarray.

King sat down at the head of the gleaming table and surveyed his brief notes for the meeting. This would be consequential, so he had to stay alert and on top. But the humming in his head wouldn't go – was getting worse. Mary Anne slid him a cup of coffee.

It had been negotiated in advance by all parties (the interagency scientists, Homeland-Interior, spy agencies, and profoundly interested military entities) that this high-level, top secret group would be collegial and informal, because the task at hand needed a creative and elastic approach.

Speaking words of welcome, King explained that the two ten-minute reports would be followed by a break. Then they would open up a one-hour brainstorming session, no holds barred. Committee and task assignments, deadlines, and meeting dates would follow.

The lights were dimmed, and Ard Sprinkle stood to speak. Mary Anne placed another cup of coffee in front of Tom King. But he did not notice, quickly caught up in Ard's report about plans that would transform the "quaint Hollymount community" into a "national research center for temporal transfer real-world applications." Following these opening remarks, Ard checked his notes and looked up to smile at the group.

"We've established full communications with the elected and appointed leaders in this charming community. They are members of our advisory task force. By year's end, the transfer of all residents to an attractive, modern, off-site new village will be complete."

A series of screen images paraded past – the apple orchard in bloom, small homes along the path to the Hollymount Inn – neatly segueing into the spread of low white glassy research structures, with a protective dome over Apple Island. At a distance, happy residents could be seen in new small homes with gardens, the sun setting through the palings of white picket fences.

Ard continued his talk. "You have all seen my preliminary report, so you know that the quaintly named Apple Island is at the heart of this project. We will continue to study the seven-plus naturally occurring temporal openings here while we build a permanent protective envelope around this priceless military asset. It is key to making America great again." King had specifically asked him to not use that phrase, but with a glance of defiance at the boss, Ard spoke the words of a loyalist to the new President.

Sitting behind King, Mary Anne was flashing cold and hot with panic and horror. She was overwhelmed by the helplessness she had felt since returning from their field trip to Hollymount Valley. How could this be happening? What could she do to stop it?

And King was distracted by a voice in his ears – or in his head? – he could not figure it out. He leaned back to Mary Anne and whispered, "Is Maeve here?" Mary Anne shook her head tightly.

"But I hear her clearly," King whispered. "Can't you?" The room was focused on Ard, so the two conversed quietly.

Mary Anne whispered, "What is she saying?"

"She says that woman leaning against the wall – see her?" The woman was outlined by diffuse light. "Maeve says that she's telling secrets to someone far away. Look, could you just – check?"

Mary Anne slipped out of her chair and moved around the edge of the room. She walked among the standing attendees, who were focused on the brief questions Ard allowed from the group. Coming up behind the stranger, Mary Anne watched her whisper into her phone. As Mary Anne turned to look for security, a hand touched her arm.

"Is there a problem, ma'am?" asked Lee Turner, head of the project's security team, who had been following her movements. He saw the problem. Stepping behind the woman, he whisked the phone out of her hand, steered her away from the wall and quickly out the conference room door. Mary Anne watched security staff surround the two. They headed to an unobtrusive door in the outer wall that opened to admit them and closed seamlessly behind them.

Ard was winding up his ten minutes as Mary Anne settled back behind Tom King, who still struggled to focus on the meeting.

"Mary Anne," he said, as the lights came up in the room, "Maeve just told me that she will destroy this project. She said we're living in an illusion of power." Mary Anne felt a fierce burst of joy, but did not speak. She was still trying to make up her mind if she should quit this job, or at least pay a visit to Hollymount on her own time. She could try it out on vacation – but then King would find out.

King turned to the attentive audience and said, "Thanks Ard, you're moving this project forward quickly. Now let's hear from the man who will connect the dots through time, and give us the big picture, right here in Kentucky, Dr. Hrudlu Vatson."

King had been practicing the name, so it came out pretty smoothly, but the urbane black-haired man with the high forehead chuckled as he stepped forward. "Thank you, Professor King," he said. "Believe it or not, great-grandparents Americanized name at Ellis Island."

This comment got a laugh, but startled the officer in the room who was in charge of documenting Vatson's elusive personal history. 'That's strange,' she thought, 'he told us he emigrated here in 1995 with his parents.'

"OKAY!" said Vatson. "My question is, how do we get from

Pleistocene, across pretty little green river, through time, to new, improved, glorious global American future?" He rubbed his hands, readying a little joke.

"I ask good people of faith to trust me with this timeline, which goes back long way before Scripture allows!" More chuckles, and silent consternation from a few of the attendees. Vatson continued talking beneath the hot room lights.

"For past ten years, I have been working with world's top military historians to determine exact time points where desired military outcomes became failures. We have classification scheme, soon to include miniscule inflection moments where calculated action improves outcome. History is littered with military events to fix. Disastrous Gallipoli campaign in 1916, for example, and 1941 attack on Pearl Harbor." He shook his head and looked around the room.

"But those are classified 'too big to fix.' Too much slop, too many factors, too many players, too long time span. We want small, easy-to-manipulate inflection moments."

King noticed that Lee Turner had returned to the room and was speaking quietly into the ear of Ard Sprinkle, seated along the table to King's right.

Mary Anne walked slowly past, straining to hear. "Ard is in hot water," she reported to King, and settled back in her seat.

"Professor King," said Vatson, the teacher catching out an inattentive student, "please toss out famous lost battle or maneuver as example. It is instructive to play with these ideas." He looked happily around the room.

But King was not in a playful mood. "Dr. Vatson, let's keep the spotlight on your important work. Can you tell us when you will begin your micro-tests for improvement? Where in the time span of history between the Late Pleistocene and present do the most promising inflection, or change, moments lie? That's where you need to focus today."

This was rude – not collegial. Hrudlu opened his mouth to snap back, then thought better of it. Through the distracting buzz in his head, King knew he had been rude. He filled the awkward pause with a softer remark. "As a time traveler myself, and considering the difficult choice I had to make, you must know I appreciate your work."

He was referring to his pioneering experiment, when he had traveled to 1902 to "harvest" his grandfather, proving that this could be done without altering the present day. The implications of this study for targeted alterations of the past had revolutionized military appreciation of time travel, and had earned King his Ph.D. in Applied Time Travel Mechanics.

The risk he had taken – that he might prevent himself from being born – was greatly admired by many. Others found his work horrifying. Several people nodded their appreciation of King's diplomatic tone, and of the point he was making. This was King's theory – why wasn't Vatson further along in developing its application?

Hrudlu Vatson bowed his head in respect and said, "I eagerly await brainstorm session. With software provided by friends at War College, models will soon be running in lab. Happy to relinquish" – glancing at his watch – "one minute to group." He sat down.

King said, "Thank you. Let's take a break."

The attendees stood up and flowed out the glass doors toward the sound of falling water and scent of coffee. King looked around for Turner, but Ard arrived first.

"That damn zealot Turner has insulted my guest!" Ard glared angrily at King and leaned in close, aggressively. King stared back, wondering yet again what Ard Sprinkle was up to. Officer Turner approached and stood quietly behind Sprinkle.

King spoke to Ard in a low voice. "There are no guests allowed in this meeting. It's for specific people with top secret clearance. For this project only. So I authorized Turner to remove her."

Ard struggled to control his outrage. "But – sir – she is the President's official envoy!"

King's eyes widened. He said, "Envoy from where, Ard?"

"The lady in question says she is from the Russian Embassy in Washington, D.C., sir," said Turner, stepping forward. "Her name is Martina Putina. She does not have any identification with her, but we checked and she appears to be telling the truth."

Ard pointed a bony finger at Turner. "This ignorant fool and his thugs are holding Ms. Putina hostage," he said to King. "The President is gonna have your head for this." Seeing King's expression, he realized he had gone too far.

King smoldered, but stayed cool. "The Executive Office is not included in this briefing meeting, Ard. You knew that. Did you let this Russian diplomat in here?" Ard did not reply.

King spoke to Turner. "We'll have to review our security procedures, Officer Turner. For now, get her out of here. Put her in a meeting room at the Science offices, with every courtesy of course. I'll talk to her later."

Ard was gone, shouldering his way through the crowd, headed out the door. The attendees were returning, eager for the brainstorming session, balancing brownies on their cups of coffee. King did not want them hearing this discord. Lee Turner stood waiting for final instructions from Tom King.

"Don't let Mr. Sprinkle remove this person from the premises before I have a chance to talk to her. I should be back up there" – King looked at the wall clock – "by 4:30 p.m."

Turner nodded and moved toward the door, speaking into the radio clipped to his vest. The noise in King's head was gone – Maeve had departed. King shook his head to clear it, feeling relieved but apprehensive. What exactly did she think she could do to stop the project?

"Still time for a five-minute break, sir – there's a private door right behind you." Mary Anne set down two napkin-wrapped brownies and fresh coffee as she spoke. King felt an unexpected jolt of gratitude for the loyalty of good people like Lee Turner and Mary Anne Washington.

He patted her arm and said, "Don't know what I'd do without you, Mary Anne." And she thought, as many others in similar situations have thought, 'You may soon have the chance to find out.'

Senator Elizabeth Maximus's offices, Capitol Hill.

Notes are compared.

Ed Zanetti sat with the others in comfortable chairs at the low table in Senator Elizabeth Maximus's spacious office suite. While they waited for the Senator, he looked around at the handsome high-ceilinged room and at his companions, Ravi Sen-Ellis and Steve Roberts.

Ed felt anxious, being back on Capitol Hill eight months after an unknown security force had thrown him out, with no warning and no word since. Would he be punished for this visit? If so – by whom? And why?

Today he had been escorted here from his home by Ravi, the Senator's top aide, so there had been no objections to his entry. Also, he hated the nasty feeling of loss of control imposed by the free-will reduction barrier – maybe that was the worst part. Ed didn't have the upper-level employee exemption, so it had hit him hard. Maybe he did not belong here any longer.

The three men rose as Senator Maximus breezed in. The door to the outer offices closed behind her, and Ed felt the hush of being in a closed-off, soundproof, monitored space. Did not feel good! He glanced out the window at green trees and wanted to go home to his garden and family. Ed took a deep breath and masked his claustrophobia with polite words and a handshake with the Senator, who sat down on the couch across the table from them. Coffee and tea were brought in on a tray and served by a young staff member.

"Thank you, Ravi, for setting this up," said the Senator, her spoon tinkling against the porcelain cup as she stirred in milk and sugar. They all took quick sips and she continued, addressing Steve and Ed.

"We've been following the actions of Professor Thomas King for several years. I am concerned that he has taken advantage of changes at the White House to remove the safety measures that protect the past from our meddling. Ravi says that you both are well placed to comment and inform me about this."

She nodded at Steve, who responded. "Last fall, the twenty-year working agreement between Homeland Security and Department of Interior was dissolved, giving the Department of Defense a bigger say in time travel management and use."

Ed followed up. "I was the Homeland-Interior liaison for the time travel program. For twenty years – since the beginning. My specialty was the safety rules, the Best Management Practices that keep the past safe from us crazy modern people. But they kicked me out with no warning. I was left in the dark until Ravi and Steve came looking for me last week."

Senator Max was about to ask a question, but leaned back as Steve explained. "Ed vanished last fall, right when Tom King took over – now with the official title of Time Tsar. King put me in charge of time travel tours for the American public, all that's left of the original science research program. And King is also secretly moving forward with military access to the past. They're using the Pleistocene entryway at my park, Ten Thousand Secrets."

"They kept you around even though you were a known associate of those ecoterrorists who blew up the Park's casino complex?" The Senator needed clarity on that point.

"Ma'am," said Steve heatedly, "I had nothing to do with that. I was cleared for work again quickly. That behavior goes against everything the federal parks service stands for." Ed felt compelled to speak. This program was his carefully reared baby they were talking about, morphing into a monster before his eyes. He broke in.

"As I told Steve last week – mind you, he's a good friend – he and his team are moving forward with those Time Travel Tours in an irresponsible and dangerous fashion. Did you hear about them – Oxford, England; Venice, Italy; and Eden/Bar Harbor, Maine?"

The others nodded – they had seen the media coverage; Steve had made the main presentation at the park, and witnessed what had happened with the Russian envoy afterwards. He was not sure he should mention that. But maybe these were the right people to share it with.

Ed went on, looking at his good friend. "You say you're following the BMPs, but how about the whole fifty-page subset that deals with time travel beyond our national borders? There's a section of management practices for dealing with historic and diplomatic relations, treaties, sovereignty, international agreements, even insurance coverage. It was still kind of theoretical, like space travel planning, but you guys are ignoring it!"

He had bumped up against the restraint on his free speech, and fell silent. Ravi put out a calming hand. Senator Max remembered that she had found Ed Zanetti pedantic and fussy, and began to understand why he was like that.

Steve snapped back, "Ed, Tom King is my boss. And it is pioneering work, that we are developing responsibly, for the enjoyment and edification of the American public. We *are* using those BMPs – our first meeting with a British time representative is scheduled for next week. They want us to provide an insurance policy. Italy doesn't understand what we're talking about. They say they already live in the past and don't need this American nonsense. So we're still in discussion there. The State of Maine's tourism people have already OK'd it – they love it."

Ed was set to deliver a sarcastic and profound rejoinder, but Senator Max stepped in. "Ravi," she said, "I think you have something to tell us about the bigger picture. This might be a good time to for us all to hear about the other developments."

"Right," said Ravi, as Ed and Steve subsided, "Senator Max sent me out to find more." He asked Steve and Ed, "What do you gentlemen know about natural time openings?"

It seemed that a bird was at the window – a red flash – then gone. The early summer sunshine streamed in.

The Senator murmured, "We should not be wasting a day like this indoors. We have only two or three of them each year." They drained their coffees and set cups back on saucers.

Ed said, "Never heard of natural time openings. I thought that the engineered portal at the Park was the only way in. Natural time openings sounds kind of like science fiction."

"Or a fairy tale!" said the Senator with a wink to Ravi. Ravi smiled, noting that Steve Roberts had sat up straight and set his mouth in a line, as though to hold in his words.

"Yes," Ravi said, "it seems that there are places in nature where time travel passageways are found. Clustered – several in one place."

"Holy smokes," said Ed, "are they being protected? Can you tell us where?" He was excited, but disbelieving – like a person who learns that space aliens have finally contacted us. Steve said nothing.

"Do you have anything to add, Steve?" Ravi asked gently.

Steve said merely, "Sounds crazy." Ravi resolved to tackle him separately, later.

"How did you find these passageways?" Ed pressed on, excited. "What do you mean by 'clustered'?"

Ravi replied, "I was checking up on Tom King and Ard Sprinkle – you know, Senator Styce's trusted assistant – and found out they were spending a lot of time in a rural corner of New York State. I've now visited there several times, and understand part of what's going on there. But I don't know what those guys plan to do with it." It appeared to Ravi that Steve relaxed on hearing that the location was in New York State. What in heck was he sitting on?

Ed was dazed. He did not understand, he was thrilled, and he was apprehensive. So the questions spilled out of him. "How do these openings work? It takes a lot of electrical energy and constant monitoring and adjustment to keep the Pleistocene site open. Where – to when – do they go? Are they protected? How did King and Sprinkle get there first?" And finally, plaintively, "Can I go there with you?"

Senator Max smiled at him, delighted to get a glimpse of the original young scientist, buried under decades of deadening bureaucracy and infighting. She said, "Ravi, can you give them a brief overview? They can learn details later."

Max leaned forward. "What we need from this meeting is an agreement to continue talking. And we need to decide how to get this amazing place in New York State into safer hands."

Ed realized that beneath her steely, crisply tailored exterior,

Senator Max was a tree hugger. He said, "And then we need to get out into the sunshine," to which she nodded.

Steve finally spoke. He had decided that the best way to avoid thinking or talking about the passageways under Oakland, Kentucky, which had to remain secret, was to give the Senator and the others something else of significance. "I need to tell you about a worrisome thing that happened at the Park last week, after the time trips media event."

"Worrisome?" asked Ravi.

"Really worrisome – based on what you're saying about this place in New York State. That afternoon, I was aware that a top secret meeting was going on, something to do with the Pleistocene. Tom King went to the meeting after lunch, and a whole bunch of big shots arrived and attended."

"Where, in the Pleistocene?" asked the Senator.

"Not likely," snorted Steve. "Those guys like their comforts. A big new secret military conference and command center has been built underneath the Park's Visitors Center. I'm not supposed to know about it, but something that big can't be kept totally secret." (In fact, every single person over the age of five in all the towns and counties across central Kentucky knew about it.)

"During that meeting I was working in my office, and suddenly there was noise downstairs – a guy yelling, and a woman shouting in a foreign language, and lots of footsteps coming upstairs. I stepped out of my office to see Ard Sprinkle hitting the helmets of the Park security guards who were escorting an elegantly dressed woman into the conference room across the hall from me. She was shouting at the guards, 'Give me back my phone, you thugs!' and then she would veer into another language – I learned later it was Russian."

Senator Max leaned back and closed her eyes, saying, "I was so afraid you were going to say that."

"Yes, ma'am," said Steve. He paused to make sure they were all paying close attention and went on. "Officer Lee Turner and two of the guards hustled her into the conference room and closed and locked the door. Ard was yelling in the hallway. He was banging on the glass walls and saying, 'We'll save you, Madame Envoy! The President will rescue you!'"

"What the heck," said Ed.

"Then he sees me and barges into my office and starts flinging insults and commands. Like 'Get someone competent in here who can rescue this woman!' 'Go find your supervisor, you damn – ' not going to repeat what he said then."

"I'm sorry, Steve," said the Senator. "Did you find out what this was all about?"

"OK, let me cut to the chase. The Park Superintendent showed up. He and other staffers managed to get Sprinkle to quiet down. They all came into my office and shut the door, and Sprinkle spewed more insults at me. He was just out of control."

"Revealed his true self," offered Ravi.

Steve nodded and went on. "Let me sum up. This woman, a Russian envoy from their Embassy in D.C., was in that top secret military meeting. Ard let her in. King had her removed. He came upstairs later and went in and talked to the envoy – her name is Martina Putina. Then she was escorted out of the building by the guards, with Ard on their heels. He and she got into his car and drove away." Steve leaned back in his chair and regarded the group.

The Senator shook her head and said, "What can you find, Ravi?" He opened his laptop and got to work as she asked, "Is that the same envoy we've had on our radar?" Her voice put quotation marks around the word envoy.

"Yeah, but the lady ain't no envoy," he replied, a bit distracted as he read and scrolled. He turned the laptop around so they could see a photo of a pale white woman in her early thirties with long reddish hair. She sat quietly, hands folded.

Ravi said, reading, "She's a graduate student at American University, but a more accurate way to describe her is as an activist in Russian and American gun rights groups. Says here she's 'working with our President's staff and family members to strengthen links between the two countries.'"

"There's something really wrong with this," said Ed. He felt shocked that his science program was becoming involved with an international scandal.

"Whatever she learned at that top secret meeting about our military use of time travel is in other hands by now," said Senator Max. She shook her head, thinking of colleagues to contact. This story would be public soon, and she shuddered to think how the White House would react. The President liked Russians.

Senator Max pushed the meeting toward a close. "I guess we all understand that the security of time travel is under threat – and it appears that the President is sharing top secret information with our global adversary. Ravi," she asked with a smile, "do we have a world-ending supervillain apocalyptic plot on our hands?"

"Not if I can help it," he replied. "Look, ma'am, I know you have some phone calls to make, so I'll take these two into the other room to give them the full story about the New York State site." The three men stood up.

"Before you go, the homework for our next meeting is to focus on rescuing the Hollymount community in New York State from all these bad guys," said the Senator, as Ravi escorted Ed and Steve out of her office.

"Also, just a friendly reminder," said Ed to Senator Max. "We kind of agreed that we need to go outdoors after this meeting." Senator Elizabeth Maximus smiled, watched them depart, gazed wistfully out the window, and picked up her phone.

The Pleistocene, Oakland, KY, and Apple Island, NY.

Sparkling time tube travel and ensuing complications.

The two women walked hunched over along the low-ceilinged tunnel, talking quietly about rescuing Hugh first, then going into the green tunnel to find Brian. The rock walls sparkled around them, illuminated by their headlamps. After about fifteen minutes, the passageway became brighter than the sparkles. Once around a final bend, they saw daylight ahead. They emerged from the tunnel at the base of a rocky slope, into the cold open air on that overcast, sullen, ancient afternoon.

Janet looked around at the flat horizon stretching off in all directions. She asked, "Is it acceptable if I don't like it here?" Lena managed an unconvincing laugh. They climbed the slope and saw the rock-pile cairn Dave had mentioned. At its base sat a plastic-wrapped package labeled "MRE Assortment – Case Pack 12 meals with heaters." In the distance, a human figure could be discerned trudging in their direction.

"Think that's a caveman, or modern man?" asked Lena.

"Based on Dave's sterling example, there isn't much difference," replied her mother, and this time Lena laughed out loud. The trudging figure stopped, lifting its head at the sound of laughter. It broke into a shambling jog, shouting. The words soon became clear.

"Help, help, stop, stop," came the cries, as they waited. "Don't go away! Please! Wait for me!" A filthy dirty skinny shaggy Hugh Hynes came running up. He was crying.

He said, "Oh my God, is this the day, is this finally the day?" and held out his hands to them. Janet took one, Lena the other.

"It's all right, Hugh. We're here to take you home," they said, as he heaved and wept.

He finally seemed to recognize them and shouted, "You two left me here!" Hugh sobbed with rage and relief. They could not hug him – he smelled so bad. The day was fading – dusk was approaching. They heard in the distance a humming mechanical sound.

"That racket started about a month ago," said Hugh. "Every day, right after I get up here, about when I see the pile of food next to the rocks." He looked at them, at the food, and stared into space. "I'm real sorry, but I gotta go, it's in the daily script. Pardon me." He walked back the way he had come down the slight slope, and they turned away to give the poor fellow some privacy.

Janet spoke to Lena, who was examining the homing device, looking for power buttons and controls. "I don't think we want to be stuck here overnight – we might have to start all over again tomorrow." Lena nodded, pushed a button, turned a dial, and a pink glow shone from the device, matching the pink pulsing light emanating from the base of the hill they had climbed.

"All set, I think," she said, as Hugh came back toward them.

"Can we go now?" he asked, dignified but shaky.

"We're hoping that part will be easy," said Janet, as a helicopter roared overhead. The two women ducked. Hugh grabbed the MRE 12 pack and stuffed it into his backpack.

"These are pretty good, let's take them," he said, adding, "That helicopter has done that every day at this time for the past three weeks. I suggest we hurry. It spots me every day and comes back around for another look. That's when I hightail it back down into that cave with the sabertooth family." He gave them a wild, unhinged look that mingled horror with glee.

They ran for the pulsing pink spot and scrambled into the sparkling hole low on the slope. Moving quickly back along the tube passage, Hugh led the way, swearing to himself quietly and continuously. He was not waiting for instructions! Soon they emerged from the pink tube into the big cave chamber, partway up the pile of glowing time tubes.

Hugh looked around and said, "OK, you got me. Where to?" Lena led them out of the room and up the winding passageway to the ladder.

As they walked, Hugh said, "Where the heck are we? This isn't in the Park, is it? The rocks are different. Are we under the sinkhole plain? Is this those cavers? Gabby said they had a secret project. Is this it?" He might have been filthy and injured, but he was the same relentless guy.

Lena said, "Yes to all that. Some crazy stuff has happened," as she watched Janet climb the ladder and try the lid. It was locked. After all, they were not expected back yet. This had been a quick rescue effort. Janet began to pound on the lid.

"Why aren't you dead? Everyone thinks you're dead," Lena asked Hugh, who was looking around for something to break the lock with.

"Rocks rejected me, that's all I know," said Hugh. "I was pushed back through the tunnel under the river and fell down to the floor of that big room. Bruised, and maybe a cracked rib. And that's where I've lived, each day the same, sneaking past the sleeping tigers for my daily walk outside." He crouched to dig into his pack.

Neither woman mentioned that he could have returned any time through the reopened passage, once he got past the tigers. He looked so grubby and pitiable as it was, why drag him any lower?

Hugh looked up at Lena and asked, "What happened, anyway?"

Lena said, "It's a long story, but it starts with Tom King pressing the reset button in the Park's control room while we three were in the passage under the river."

"OK. That's all I need to know," he said, pulling a rock hammer from the bottom of his pack. "I'm gonna get him. Forget modern man, I'm a caveman now." He swung the hammer aggressively through the air and walked over to the ladder.

Lena said, "Hugh, we aren't coming back up with you. Don't go right back to the Park – that would be dangerous for you. Stay at this house – we're in Oakland – and let the cavers fill you in."

He stared at them and nodded that he got it. "Tell me this, is there coffee and a hot shower up there?" he asked, taking over from Janet in pounding position, raising his hammer. Just then the lid creaked up, and the pleasant face of the homeowner peered down at them, smiling.

"I heard you," he said, "come on up. The cavers are gone for now. I bet you want coffee and a hot bath, after what you've been through."

Hugh scrambled up the ladder and into the room, engulfed by warmth and electric lighting and modern odors. The homeowner was always delighted to meet yet another caver. He and his wife found these people fascinating and funny.

"Come right this way," he said to Hugh. "Do I have the honor of speaking to the long-lost head scientist at the Park?" They walked into the house, toward coffee.

"You sure got that right," said Hugh, becoming aware of his smelly self. But first, the coffee.

"Where are the two others?" asked the homeowner, heading back to look down through the cave access doorway. No one else came up. No one was at the base of the ladder. Hugh came to look, already draining a large mug of excellent coffee.

He shrugged. "They'll be back. I think they had other business to attend to. Where's that bath? And more coffee." He grabbed spare clothes from the pile in the equipment room and headed into the house. The homeowner, accustomed to the strange behavior of cavers, shrugged and followed him, closing and latching the lid, turning off the lights and closing the door behind him.

As soon as Hugh was out of sight, the two women had spun around and run back down the slope, into the big room. They moved quickly up the sparkling rockpile and into the green-labeled passageway. The trip through this time tube was different than the Pleistocene passage. In places the walls were crumbling. They had to climb over and around piles of newly fallen sparkling rocks as they headed steeply downhill. Big rocks fell out of the ceiling behind them, rumbling and tumbling. In places they slipped and slid in thick mud.

After twenty minutes of strenuous effort, they came to a place where the ceiling was only three feet over their heads. The air was still, stuffy. First Janet, then Lena waded through a wide shallow stream that crossed the passageway from a side passage, flowing who knew where or when. The water glowed, a neon green-yellow, casting rippling reflections on the walls and ceiling. A chilly breeze blew along the water surface from the dank side passage.

"I don't like this," said Lena. "This is scary." She looked behind her, wondering if they should turn back.

"Just keep moving," said Janet. "If Brian came through and went back, we can do it." They heard a rumble behind them, and in the light of their headlamps saw the ceiling of the passageway falling in a rippling sheet of rock, moving fast toward them. Fear a spur, they ran and scrambled forward. Soon the noises and destruction had been left behind. The passageway tilted upward and dried out. They paused to rest and drink from their water bottles.

"I think we're past the point where Gollum lives," said Lena.

"No Gollum jokes, please," said Janet. "This passageway is not healthy. Let's just keep going." Lena was feeling relieved and hopeful, and wanted to hiss and ask a riddle, but understood her mother's anxiety and subsided. Soon they smelled fresh air – and a distinctive scent.

"That's like a flower's perfume," said Janet. "What could it be?" Rounding a bend, they saw the glow of daylight. Pink and white flower petals lay scattered thickly on the cave floor. They quickened their pace and saw a small hole through which bright daylight gleamed.

First Lena, then Janet squeezed out, pushing their packs ahead. They found themselves beneath a blossoming apple tree, having emerged between its roots. Overhead, a canopy of pink and white blossoming trees stretched off in all directions. The air was warm, the hum of bees pervasive. "Where are we?" Lena asked in wonderment, gazing around.

"Brian mentioned an apple orchard when I saw him last fall," Janet said happily. "Let's go looking for him. But first – after that scary experience – let's eat lunch."

They dug into their packs for food that Dave had provided, which turned out to be sandwiches and chips from a Kentucky highway gas station market and two cold cans of Mountain Dew. Tasted like fine dining in this quiet bower. They ate slowly and stared around at the vast soft ceiling of flowers, held aloft by branches and gnarled tree trunks.

Up above them and through the woods to the Hollymount Inn, Maeve was dozing lightly before the fire. The Innkeeper was worried that she was not yet back to full summertime strength, so he cosseted her with fresh herb teas and fireside naps.

At a table nearby sat a small group of her animal friends, squirrels visiting from distant woods with their local family, along with the crow and that potbellied piglet, now grown, still wearing its bonnet. They were chatting quietly, to not wake Maeve.

However, with the arrival of Janet and Lena, her sleep was disrupted. Maeve sat up straight and cried out, “Someone is here!”

The animals stared and the Innkeeper, who had been lounging nearby reading a magazine of air fryer recipes from a human grocery store, put it down. “Who would that be, dear?” he asked.

“Friends!” said Maeve. “Helpers.” She gazed through the thick walls of the Inn down the lane, along the path, and into the orchard on old Apple Island. “Oh, how curious,” Maeve said. “Brian’s family.” She smiled at the Innkeeper. “We will have enough helpers, if Mary Anne returns.”

The little house in Horseheads, the NYS DEC Environmental Conservation office in Syracuse, and eventually Apple Island.

Yet more pizza, donuts, and information, and a happy reunion.

Rita sat on the front porch swing of the little house she shared with Harris, and now Brian. The porch ceiling was painted robin’s egg blue and decorated with glow-in-the-dark stars and planets. Climbing roses on the wooden trellis were starting to bloom. She was waiting for a carpool ride to the SUNY campus in Binghamton, while listening to the others try to resolve Brian’s confusion over what time it was.

It all started because Brian was up bright and early for his and Harris’s drive to Syracuse. They had made an appointment to examine the Highway Bypass Project files at the Department of Environmental Conservation office, and he did not want to be late. No one else was up, so he got into a nervous tizzy and rousted Harris out of deep sleep. An indignant Harris said he had another hour, and burrowed back under the blankets. But Brian persisted.

Rita, awakened by this sleepy uproar, agreed with Harris that the time on her watch and phone matched his – they were both 63 minutes earlier than Brian’s watch and phone. A disgruntled Brian came out onto the porch, sat on the old couch and set his watch

63 minutes earlier. “I could have stayed in bed,” he grumbled. More loudly, “I’m tired of being an hour early. It’s not just you two – it’s everywhere I go – everything is an hour behind me. Plus three minutes! I can’t get it right.” His watch time stayed where he set it, but his phone remained steadfastly 63 minutes earlier.

“Don’t blame me,” said Harris sleepily. He emerged from the house and slumped into a decrepit rocking chair.

“Is it always exactly one hour and three minutes?” asked Rita, standing up as her car ride arrived at the curb.

Brian nodded. “I started keeping track yesterday.”

Rita turned to speak as she walked down the porch steps. “Maybe it started when you came back through that time hole,” she called as she climbed into the car, waving goodbye as it moved down the street.

“Harris, I apologize. I’m sorry for being rude. I had to sit and wait for things to get going. Made me jumpy,” said Brian. Harris had not had breakfast, and his shoes and socks were in his lap, because he had grabbed them while scrambling to catch up.

“We have all morning to do good work, man, it’s all right,” he said. “Let’s go. Good excuse to get donuts!”

Brian and Harris drove two hours to the Department of Environmental Conservation office in Syracuse, to view documents in the highway bypass project that threatened Apple Island and Hollymount. They were looking for information that could stop it from being built. A box with the remaining donuts stayed in the car for later.

The older, paper documents were rolled out for them on a big cart in a quiet workroom. Digital documents were available online. They took photos with their phone cameras of the good stuff. But by early afternoon, after sorting through files and boxes of documents and reports, they had found only a mystery.

Harris came back into the room after talking to a staff person familiar with the project. “I asked her if there was anything missing, maybe out on someone’s desk for review, and she said no, this was all of it.”

“It looks like the highway company was following the rules

like they were supposed to, at the start," said Brian, who had been going back through the documents while Harris was away. "They submitted highway maps and reports on different route options, and got started on the environmental review process. I found the proposed timeline, and tentative dates for public hearings."

Harris nodded, "Yeah, that's what the staff just told me. They were all set to start notifying and involving us, the great unwashed public, and then the highway company stopped communicating. But – they're building the project anyway."

"So we're not imagining things?" Brian asked.

"Right. The whole public input and application review process is missing from the files – because none of it has happened. The highway company is just going ahead and building it. They won't respond to the office's queries. They kick state enforcement staff off the property!" The staff person Harris had been talking to entered the room.

"It's beautiful outside today," she said. "Let's go eat lunch at the picnic table out back." The weather was still cool around the edges, so they sat at the table soaking up the hot sunshine and exuberant birdsong from the surrounding trees, watching cars and pickup trucks come and go in the agency's parking lot. The grass needed mowing, as it always does in springtime. Harris shared out the rest of the breakfast donuts.

The staffer rubbed her face and held out her arms to the sun, trying to shake off that airless, cold dead office feeling.

"I'm going to say some things that I shouldn't," she told them, between donut bites. "But you two are the first and only people to ask questions about the situation. And there's something wrong here."

Harris had submitted their request to review the documents under the SoTier group name, and the staff person was relieved that someone was asking questions about this secretive project. She looked around to ensure they were not within hearing distance of anyone, and spoke quietly.

"Like I said to you before, the highway company won't talk to us. And they're now working with a bigger company, and maybe several other companies, to get the work done quicker. We've even seen some pickup trucks with federal agency license plates, but you didn't hear that from me."

She started talking faster as a co-worker approached, carrying two fast-food bags, a lit cigarette dangling from his mouth.

"What you need to know – this is a lot more than a tiny bypass project. You did not hear a word from anyone here that we think it is a Department of Defense project. They are gonna tear down that little village and inn up there, and build a research lab. Put a roof over that island. It's top secret." She had their full attention.

"These donuts are stale but delicious," she went on, licking sugar off her fingers as her co-worker arrived, threw his cigarette butt in the grass, and tossed the food bags on the table.

"Eating dessert first, huh?" he asked, sliding onto the seat and smiling at Brian and Harris, who hung around for a few chatty minutes before heading to their car.

As Brian drove south from Syracuse, Harris stared out the passenger window at the beautiful wide valley below the highway and at the steep forested hills beyond. Signs announced this gorgeous place as Onondaga Nation Indian Territory.

But Harris did not notice. He was feeling disillusioned about the Department of Environmental Conservation office they had just left. "Can you believe those guardians of the state's environment eat fast food and smoke cigarettes?" he said in disgust. Overwhelmed by what they had learned, he focused on irrelevant details.

Brian turned his head away from the road ahead to glare at Harris and responded energetically. "They're just trying to survive, Harris, be compassionate! I sure couldn't work in that building. Like a mausoleum! Anyway, she gave us the information we needed. And it's sooo bad. Now we know what that creepy Tom King is up to. He's going to turn the whole area into a time research lab!"

Harris said, "I guess the highway company doesn't have to follow the law when they're working for the Department of Defense."

Brian asked, "How are we gonna stop them?"

Harris poked around in the compartment between their seats and found a roll of mints. They chewed, racking their brains.

"Let's take a leaf from the recovery community," Harris suggested after a few minutes. "Ask ourselves, 'What is the first right step to take?'"

"Talk to someone," said Brian. "How about Ravi Sen-Ellis. He's cool. How about him?"

"Ravi. Exactly right! Yeah – I have his number. He said to use it if I needed help – oh yeah." Suddenly Harris felt better, with an excuse to contact Ravi! He pulled out his phone.

By evening the next day, Ravi and the three occupants of the little house were sharing pizza, chicken wings, and a little bit of salad at their kitchen table, comparing notes on the situation surrounding Apple Island and the Inn.

"That's enormous news you got from that state employee," said Ravi. "Tom King wants to move the residents out, tear down the houses and Inn, and build a time travel research lab. And put some kind of protective roof over Apple Island." There was no need to tell them that he had already heard this via Steve Roberts. Good to have it confirmed! Ravi fit in this information with King's activities at the Park in Kentucky and realized that the Time Tsar was thinking big.

"The highway spur project will link the lab to the interstate highway, for speed and convenience," said Harris. "That's why the highway is being built. Maybe they don't have to get public permission or permits, because it's top secret or in the national interest or something."

Brian was mulling over the intrusive groups of visitors that Acton and Greenwood had described. "Remember that strange guy Ard Sprinkle, who works for someone in D.C. who will pay them cash for showing them the time holes? What's that all about?"

"I think Ard wants to steal the whole thing from King," said Ravi, "weird as that might seem." He shook his head. "Maybe Ard is working for the President. But who is the President working for?"

"President of what? You mean of the USA?" asked Rita. "That dude is a criminal. I hate to think what he has in mind for time travel." She slid the last piece of anchovy pizza toward Ravi, who had an unseemly craving for the local pizza from Mushroomy Fields Forever.

"Can we call Maeve and talk to her? Or should we just go see her tomorrow?" Ravi was all business, eating that final slice. Rita had taken control of the salad.

"Better go in person," said Brian. "She can't stay focused very long over the phone. We also need to talk to the two guys on Apple Island, and they don't have phones. And – 'Who is the President working for'? What do you mean by that?"

"Not my President," muttered Harris.

"Let's just say Russians," Ravi replied.

"Russians? You mean this is an espionage situation?" asked Rita. "I really need to get my dissertation done so I can join you. This is just too wild. The world's problems coming right to our doorstep here in New York State's southern tier!"

"People think they can find safe haven from the world's problems, but the world's problems follow them," said Ravi.

Brian wondered, "The two guardians on Apple Island said they voted for the President. But would they support Russians?"

"Wait," said Ravi. "Last thing I knew, your theory was they were some kind of supernatural forest protectors. Now they're right-leaning U.S. citizens with voting privileges?"

Harris replied, "Yeah, Brian's romantic magic hero dreams have been demolished. Turns out that Greenwood and Acton are right-wingers from an isolated community at the far end of a time tunnel. Racist, too."

"Well, you have to admit," said Ravi, "those two guys are pretty strange, magic or not!" He was feeling uneasy, worried that Harris and Brian and Rita, apparently rational people, were caught up in a cult or something. These stories were spinning out of control.

"We're just taking it as it comes, nowadays," said Brian. "Acton and Greenwood also told us that they are really, really old. Something about the time tunnel, and the place they live. But they won't tell us much."

"How old do they say they are?" asked Ravi, and an ancient

feeling shivered along his spine.

"One of them is a hundred seventy-five years old, the other is one hundred and eighty," said Harris. A shudder rolled through the little group as they contemplated these strangely ancient human beings. Harder to accept than magic.

"And is Maeve some kind of ancient human, too?" asked Ravi, feeling a little disappointed while hoping for a normal reply.

"No, no," replied Brian. "She's a real fairy queen, who came here through a time tunnel maybe 400 years ago, to get away from a debauched fairy scene in Ireland."

"And you know that how?" demanded Ravi. How could he explain *this* to Senator Maximus?

"I saw her. She flew! In a shower of sparkles!" said Brian. This sounded childlike, even though he had been there. He tried again. "She flew down and landed on Apple Island and begged the two guys to let her through the time hole back to Ireland. She asks every spring, they said. They wouldn't let her, because she brings back bad fairies and such." Ravi stared at them. The sounds of children playing, and the scent of roses, came through the window. The streetlights winked on.

Harris saw Ravi's doubt and said, "It's like Brian said, Ravi. We're just taking it as it comes. If you have a better explanation, we'll take it."

"May I change the subject for one minute?" Rita asked. "It's not often I have a brain trust gathered like this." Her two roommates gazed at her inquiringly, while Ravi brooded that his time was being wasted on a cult or shared hallucination.

Rita plunged ahead. "One of my profs is a botanist, and he asked me to ask you if there are plants native to Ireland around the highway project site. And if there are New York State plants, native or introduced, in Maeve's world." She gazed at her friends expectantly, but they only stared and shook their heads.

"All right, I'll tell him that no one knows," she said. "Is it OK if he comes to have a look?" Brian shrugged and Harris started to speak, but Ravi's sudden outburst ended the discussion.

"How can you talk about any of this as real?" he demanded.

"Everything I'm hearing here is ridiculous. What has got into you people?" He felt the exhaustion of a long day. Draining his iced tea, he stood up.

Harris spoke, protective of his friends. "Ravi, please understand we are knowingly practicing active suspension of disbelief. Just step back a bit, cut some slack, and juggle all the points of view. It's not rocket science," he ended, grinning at the idea of rocket science mixed with fairies.

"I'll sleep on it," Ravi said. He contemplated the comforts of his upper-end motel. "Back here right after breakfast – is 8 a.m. all right?"

"No, make it 6," said Harris. "We have to traverse that roundabout to get to Maeve's hidden community. Before the highway crews arrive to start work for the day."

"If you insist," said Ravi, rolling his eyes.

"Well, yes we do, we do insist," said Harris, quietly admiring the grace of this capable man.

By seven the next morning the three men were creeping, crouched, through open fields beyond the roundabout, toward the hilly edge of Maeve's upland realm. They had walked counterclockwise around the roundabout, so they were in Maeve's world as they crossed the magic-made parking lot, paid for with New York State tax dollars. The little lady on the hill above watched from the doorway of her cottage.

Up the slope on the flower-lined path, they moved quickly through the arched stone tunnel, untouched by the fire of the previous Halloween night. Around the tunnel the fields and trees were scorched, but regreening rapidly in this young season.

Brian waved at the creekside cottage as they passed by, following the path through open fields and up the slope into the woods. The entire route was outlined with wooden markers and neon pink plastic tape.

"How did they get the highway project into Maeve's world?" asked Ravi.

"Same way we got here," replied Brian, "They went counter-clockwise around that roundabout. It was part of a grant that

I helped Maeve apply for. She wanted to lure in people to pay her annual tithe to that devil she brought from Ireland."

"I bet she didn't expect all this to happen," said Harris. The three men turned left at the crosspaths and headed downhill toward Apple Island.

"It's not smart to mess with human beings," Harris continued. "The most dangerous animals on the planet."

"From what I've read and experienced, fairies are a lot meaner, and faster," said Brian. "They're badass predators, like velociraptors. I doubt our technology measures up to their magic." Around a bend in the trail, they saw the stream and footbridge at the bottom of the slope, and heard people talking, at first a low murmur, then words and laughter.

Brian's face brightened. He turned to smile at the others and ran, skidding down the slope and across the log bridge. Ravi and Harris watched as two of the four people seated around the campfire rose and ran to meet Brian.

"It's the ecoterrorists!" said Harris with delight, scampering forward to witness the joyous reunion. Mother and children were hugging and laughing. Acton and Greenwood watched, smiling.

Ravi slowed to a halt just across the bridge, painfully aware of his position as top aide to a prominent U.S. Senator. He had met Janet and Brian the previous year on a time travel research trip at Ten Thousand Secrets National Park, as an official observer for Senator Maximus. He had helped rescue Brian from being trapped in the past.

When the Park casino was blown up soon after and the three family members were implicated, he had barely avoided being caught in the spotlight. Since then, Senator Max had repeatedly and emphatically warned Ravi to stay away from anyone involved in this situation.

Janet untwined from Brian's hug and walked toward Ravi.

"Hi!" she said. He bowed his head in greeting. "We're trouble for you, I guess," she went on.

"I'll figure something out," said Ravi, quietly. He stood apart from the group, drinking the tea that Acton handed him, gazing at the sunny spring day. He walked past the hemlock grove, up the slope and out into the blossoming orchard.

The green path took him between the rows of fragrant flowering trees, past daffodils and tulips, to the edge of the water. The valley was quiet, with just a hint of springtime chill, and the sky overhead was deep blue. He could see stars beyond the daylight.

Ravi understood nothing about this place and the strange phenomena of time portals, an apparently eternal spring day, and daylight stars, but he knew this area had to be protected and treasured, not exploited.

Across the small lake, the everyday world was turning green. The old grey apple trees stood out vividly. The cliffs rising above the water were crowned by evergreens and budding trees. Ravi knew that the Hollymount Inn was right over there, atop the cliffs and through the woods.

He envisioned Apple Island under military control. A dome would arch overhead, to hide and protect the portals. The lanes and paths would be replaced with paved roads. The Inn would be modernized as a guest house, at the far end of a big parking lot surrounded by nondescript lab buildings, replacing the neighborhood of small homes. Industrial lights on tall poles would illuminate the entire area. Most of the trees would be cut down, including the apple orchards, to provide better access to the portals, and for security.

Ravi had never thought much about nature. For him, the outdoors was how he got from one indoor meeting to the next. But he was learning from Harris and his friends, and appreciated their passion for nature. Certainly this area, probably globally unique, must be protected from bulldozers. It was easy to make a choice, after all. Ravi hoped that Senator Max and her New York State colleagues would agree. He walked back to join his friends.

Part II
"So get to the point, dumbass"

Chapter 6

A farewell to Washington, D.C., and a visit to the new Time Fort & Barracks in the Pleistocene.

An eventful weekend for Mary Anne, Tom King, and cat Pixie.

That Friday was Mary Anne Washington's final day of work for the federal government. She had gradually emptied her office of personal items. She was leaving everything else in place – work supplies, electronic devices, files, all her project records, a guide to passwords. Simply walking away. She did not want to provide an electronic trail when they came after her.

Tom King was out until Monday, so now or never had arrived. Mary Anne had procrastinated long enough. She returned from placing her potted plants on a colleague's desk, closed the office suite door behind her, and headed to the elevators. On this warm summer Friday the office had emptied out early, so there was no one to note her departure except the security cameras, and they saw nothing amiss. She was soon outdoors in the humid afternoon. The hum of traffic-clogged roads and highways was loud as office workers headed toward cookouts and cold beer.

Later that evening, Mary Anne submitted her letter of resignation via email. Her apartment was cleared out, the rent paid, the car sold. She had many weeks of vacation time built up, so there were no regrets about quitting without the official two-week notice. Especially because her professional career was about to come to a screeching halt.

Sometime after midnight, Mary Anne shut the apartment door and was on her way with a backpack and a walking stick, her small striped cat Pixie in a carrier riding atop the backpack. No phone, no laptop, a few hundred dollars in cash, a bundle of folded paper maps, and a small device that masked her departure. She was headed into deep hiding, on her way to the Hollymount Inn.

By the following Monday afternoon, the hunt was up, the dogs loosed. With her security clearances, Mary Anne had to return – to be reasoned with, constrained, or disposed of. She was not allowed to quit and vanish. To Tom King, she was a tool, a valuable tool with top secret clearance. Also he had trusted her, and felt injured by her betrayal. They tracked her via train and bus west into Virginia on I-66, but after that she could not be found.

The President, meanwhile, was enraged at the supposed insults made to his "cute little Russian envoy" during the security conference at the Park. He publicly accused King of attacking, confining, and forcibly removing Martina Putina (ignoring the fact that she was not authorized to be there).

These accusations were escalating into a national scandal, so King had to quit worrying about Mary Anne. The President's radio and television hosts howled for King's blood, and a second Congressional investigation was being considered.

King sat in his darkened office watching as a FIX News anchor ranted onscreen. "First, this King guy tries to take away our God-given time travel rights! Next thing you know, his thugs arrest and imprison a top foreign diplomat who last week had dinner with the President at the Florida White House! Next thing, King will come for our guns." Images flowed across the screen of the President patting Martina Putina's bottom while winking at the camera.

King successfully made a cup of coffee without Mary Anne's assistance and watched as a trio of blond people sitting on a couch speculated about his future.

"That so-called 'Doctor' King is such a snob. I mean, tea and crumpcts in Merry Olde England? Lobsters in Maine? Yuck, those are just giant bugs! Go all the way to Italy just to eat pizza? We make better pizza than they ever did. Where does he get off with this hoity-toity stuff?"

"When the President's family takes over the time travel program, where do you want to go first?"

"Oh, definitely ancient Rome. I want to lie on a couch and have a slave feed me peeled grapes. How about you?"

"Gambling in old Havana. The President says that's tops on the list. He is gonna offer luxury trips, led by him personally, to all the hottest gambling dens in history."

"Don't tell anyone, but my fantasy time trip is to shoot Indians from horseback, riding with the cavalry to rescue a wagon train." There was a brief pause as the two others on the couch wondered if this comment went too far, even for FIX News. The screen switched to an advertisement with a mustachioed man shouting about pillows, and King turned off the drivel.

He picked up his jacket and bag and headed out to the waiting driver and car. King was flying to Kentucky for a tour of the new Time Fort & Barracks, across the Green, Green River in the Pleistocene. It had just been installed.

This was the first USA time base, from which scientists would test small improvements in future events, moving the base forward as they edged toward the present moment. The dazzling scenarios emerging from Vatson's computers mapped a timeline of small successes and adjustments resulting in an improved present day, with the USA untouchably in charge of the entire planet.

King and his teams knew that this research had to remain deeply secret. If the President took control of the program, this carefully calculated series of time improvements would crumble and vanish. Billions of dollars would be wasted. Although everyone claimed to love him, they also agreed that "the President is not good at this kind of thing."

As his personal jet blasted into the sky, King settled into his seat with a glass of beer and spoke to Hrudlu Vatson, seated next to him. "The President is well intentioned, and I'm glad I voted for him, but he is not a scientist."

"You are certain he doesn't know about this project?" asked Hrudlu, trying to ascertain how much King knew or suspected. For the first time in his life, Vatson's research was fully funded with so much government money he could not ever possibly spend it all. He was being treated well by these innocent and trusting Americans. He *almost* felt guilty about being a spy for the President and his – their – Russian masters.

King said, "We need to keep this away from the President, Hrudlu, you know that. It's not like we're the only ones withholding sensitive information from him. The CIA and some of the other agencies are not telling him everything. He doesn't have the government and policy background. With all due respect."

Hrudlu agreed, maybe too heartily, "The President is enthusiastic, can't keep stuff to himself. He wants to share with everyone. When he says he wants to make America better, 'great' again, I feel love." He took a sip of his diet soda.

"It's not him I'm worried about," replied King carefully. He knew about the problems with Vatson's background check, and other concerns. Maybe he could trick him into revealing something.

He went on, "It's the Russians I worry about – know what I mean?" He lifted his beer, watching Hrudlu through the glass.

Hrudlu looked down at the backs of his hands, flipped them over and examined the palms, while considering his reply. "I am excited to do research, Dr. King. Grateful for generous support. I don't want anyone to interrupt or interfere. Not Russians, not President." He glanced out the window.

King nodded. That was a good reply, but not to the question he had asked. "We don't want anyone to steal this project from the USA," he added, lifting the end of the sentence into a question.

Hrudlu looked up at these words, meeting King's gaze. "How could that happen?" he asked. King laughed, took a long sip, and explained the obvious. "If Russian military interests get involved in time research, our entire program will be jeopardized and undermined. We can't have more than one political force moving forward through time, attempting to correct and improve its past trajectory. If we add in a second force with an opposing or conflicting agenda, we will fail."

"With respect, sir," said Hrudlu, in an intense, low voice, "I have run scenarios. Out of simple scientific curiosity. Outcomes for two opposing forces are not all bad, or negative, for U.S. interests. Or Russian."

"Hrudlu, man, that's crazy talk," snapped King, sitting up straight in his seat. The flight steward peered out at them from behind the front curtain, but King shook his head. "Don't need anything, thanks," he said. The steward nodded and ducked back behind the curtain.

"I will run scenarios for you at time base, Dr. King," Hrudlu said quietly. "There are synergistic interactive effects to benefit both powers."

"You can do that, if we have the time, but you will then have to terminate and destroy that work, Dr. Vatson." The two men became more formal as the tension rose.

King went on, "I cannot have you doing ambiguous or conflicting research that benefits our global nemesis!" He wondered how Vatson dared tell him about this – this – treasonous research? King stared angrily at the man next to him as the aircraft began its descent.

Vatson was undeterred by his employer's anger. "I have been wanting to tell you, Tom," he said, in a conciliating tone. "Maybe I have more than one interest," he went on, in a vague way admitting his multiple loyalties. "But math and future outcomes are good. I set the problem to my team, stayed out. Was shocked like you, but one force cannot adjust history alone. At least one other is needed for optimal outcomes."

"That's treasonous bullshit," snapped King. He watched as Vatson pulled out a pen and began to sketch on King's beer napkin.

"Let me speak, Tom," he said. "Core team is afraid to speak.

I promised them to try. Here are basics." He drew an x and y axis, with "time" along the bottom and "improvement in global status" along the vertical axis, and began to construct two lines, one labeled USA and one labeled Russia.

"Actually modeled in four dimensions, not two," Hrudlu said. Fascinated, King was drawn in. As Vatson added dots for adjusted time events and showed the rise over time in mutual improvement, they talked, absorbed, until the plane landed in Bowling Green.

Two hours later, they stepped off the Ten Thousand Secrets National Park boat onto the cold rocky soils of that gloomy Pleistocene afternoon. King gazed behind him at the glowing doorway on the north side of the Green, Green River – expanded in height and width to accommodate trucks, troops, and matériel.

Their military vehicle took ten minutes bumping across the stony plain to the Time Fort & Barracks. Once they had parked, a crisply uniformed Time Service scientist approached and introduced themself as Turing. The group walked toward the low brown building that blended with the icy setting and leaden sky. Mud season would not arrive here for several thousand years, and their boots crunched on the ancient surface.

"We enter here," said Turing. The trio popped through a membrane into a small lobby, waited until interior air pressure and temperatures adjusted to their presence, then popped through a second membrane into a reception area.

The climate-controlled modular building had been brought through the river portal on a single day and assembled in a few hours. If done this way, a thing or activity usually persisted from one day into the same next day. The scientists did not know why, and it did not always work. No one had yet dared to stay overnight.

As they led King and Vatson toward an inner door, Turing spoke about King's visit. "We've been discussing the pros and cons of switching from a repeating single day to a repeating week schedule or longer, and we're hoping you can help us decide," they said. The inner door opened onto a well-lit space that took up most of the building. A group of people clustered around screens. Turing made introductions and then stepped over to the screens. As the project's leading mathematician, they had everyone's full attention.

The Science offices, Ten Thousand Secrets National Park.

Dissembling, shyness, tea.

Late springtime was in full flower at the Park, and Steve listened to abundant birdsong on his walk from the parking lot to the Science offices.

He was spending a full week here, working with the team of builders who were installing three docks along the Green, Green River to accommodate the flow of visitors who, come November, would be embarking for daily time trips to Oxford, England; Venice, Italy; and Eden/Bar Harbor, Maine. The site for the Tennessee River Ghostlands Cruise was surveyed but not yet constructed. These were all waterway destinations, so tourists would board historically appropriate watercraft along the river shoreline, for the quick time transfer.

Steve was coordinating the construction work with engineers from the Time Mechanics Division, Mid-Ohio Office, Federal Parks Service. Their gnarly task was to create four neighboring portals for the time destinations.

One major adjustment was underway – the docks were too close together for the force field surrounding each portal. Three had to be moved farther apart, so right now the Green, Green River shoreline was a mess. Nothing like this had been done before, and it had to be safe and stable for everyday use, and secure from power overloads and terrorist attacks. It also was top secret, though not very.

Also, a new coal-fired power plant would soon be built to raise the energy capacity in the central-western Kentucky power grid. Senator Harlan Styce promised that the permits and building process would be streamlined, with no environmental review. His office was touting the new mining jobs from the long-shuttered coal mines. The potential military uses for this tourism-focused activity were enormous.

As a result, Steve was feeling the heat and the excitement from all directions. This week, the legal team from the Federal Parks Service's Time Mechanics program was onsite to finalize day-use contracts and insurance policies at the three time destinations. The Italian government had not yet been able to come up with a coherent plan, despite the best efforts of the University of Milan's tech community. The State of Maine's Office of Tourism was enthusiastic, had inserted the tour into its state marketing plan, and was demanding a high fee for the Park's access to Maine's past, citing "longterm infrastructure wear-and-tear costs" and "multidimensional labor costs."

Today, Steve's office was anticipating the arrival of a time trips consultant from Oxford, England. An enthusiastic intern had sent an email query to the Oxford City Council, asking who should be contacted about a daily use fee for a date with good weather in May 1910. The intern expected to wait a while, assuming that Oxford was just a sleepy old college town, and that a time travel query might confuse them. However, a reply had appeared in her in-box five minutes before she sent it.

"Thank you for your time travel query," read the reply.

"Apologies for this automated message, but we receive too many time travel queries to respond individually. Please contact Chronos, Ltd. at this address (provided). Their fee-for-service staff are standing ready to help with every arrangement, including high teas, punting availability and guides, weddings, pub crawls, side tours to Stratford-upon-Avon, Blenheim Palace, etc.

Please understand that these options are dependent on availability of venues on preferred dates. Sorry, no Blitz, no wartime visits, no Plague. A full list of exceptions will be provided, and more may emerge during consultation. Permits and fees all-inclusive. Insurance is provided via a standard Lloyd's of London policy, 1965."

This message was signed by a member of the Planning Team, Oxford City Council. Below the signature was an additional statement, in italics.

"Preliminary NOTE: May 1910 is COUNTERINDICATED for visitation owing to a change in national government. Sensitive dates preclude permission."

While waiting near the front door of the Science building for the arrival of the representative of Chronos, Ltd., Steve met a Time Mechanics team member walking toward her office. He handed her a printout of the Oxford City Council message.

As she read it, he asked, "So we're not the only country with time travel?" She gave a dismissive shrug. "Those Chronos guys are flaky," she said. "We tried to work with them, but they can't keep it together. They promise stuff and then vanish for months at a time. Bunch of grad students, history and languages, no engineers. No supervisors, no management."

Emma Brown was a busy woman on a short deadline, and walked away.

"I don't get it," said Steve, to her back.

"Oxford, England is the global leader in time travel," she replied. "You know that, right?" Her body language signaled impatience.

"Actually, this is the first I've heard of it," Steve said, a note of irritation entering his voice. 'The rudeness of New Yorkers,' he thought, not for the first time.

Emma realized she should not cut this short, restrained herself from looking at her watch, and turned to face Steve. "Oxford's so-called science community started fiddling around in their crummy little college labs about a century ago, and began making time jumps. Sometimes with grisly results – hands missing, half-bodies, dead sheep. They didn't start with subatomic particles!" She grinned gleefully. Steve's eyebrows shot up as Emma went on.

"Back when Cornell Tech was developing a process to open the Pleistocene gate, we worked with Chronos for about a year – shared a couple jumps, had them send computers and monitors back in time to figure out how it worked. But halfway through, the data stopped flowing."

"Do you know what happened?"

"They said the machinery was broken. And they lost our equipment. After that, we didn't hear from them again. But we had learned enough to move forward. Why are you talking to them?"

"The U.S. Department of State requires us to have contracts and insurance and a mini-treaty, for international destinations. And Chronos, Ltd. is our official contact."

"With direct ties to Brit security services and the Foreign Office," said Emma, turning away. "Better you than me, for that work." At that moment, a young man materialized outside the Science building, and began walking up the steps.

"Oh my God, here comes one now," said Emma. "I know that guy. I'm out of here!" She sprinted down the hallway to get on the other side of her office door. The tall willowy man entered the building. His brown hair was cut long in front so that it flopped over one eye. He was wearing a button-down shirt, baggy tweed jacket, and corduroy trousers. On his feet were suede desert boots.

"Sorry to trouble you," he said, approaching Steve. "I'm looking for Mr. Steve Roberts. Could you direct me to his office?" He was looking around for the person in charge, and assumed it was not this Black man, whose uniform suggested a building custodian, perhaps.

Steve had not experienced this type of dismissal in many years. He stuck out his hand and pulled the young man into a hearty, all-American handshake. "I'm Steve Roberts," he said. "And you must be Peter Saint-John?"

"Yes, yes I am," said Peter, a startled – no, amazed – look on his face. He stared searchingly at Steve, and his eyes filled with tears.

Steve stepped back and said, "Are you OK? Want to sit down?" Peter shook his head and collected himself, pulling out a big handkerchief to wipe his eyes.

"Forgive me," he said. "This is my farthest forward jump, from 1965. Seeing you in this position of authority gives me great hope. Wait until I tell the others. This is incredibly good news."

"But you're not allowed to tell them, Peter," said Emma, reappearing at Steve's side. To Steve she said, "Turns out I have to attend this meeting," rolling her eyes in irritation.

Emma turned back to Peter. "If your Chronos security overlords find out that you're sharing information about the future, they will wipe your mind. Nasty!" Peter had fully recovered and spoke to Emma.

"Oh, is this the project from Cornell Tech? I remember you, Emma. But you're different."

"Yeah, I was a lot younger then," she snarled. "And you're only one year older. Amazing how that works." The three of them climbed the stairs and entered the conference room, where they settled around the big table. Turing was already seated, looking through their phone. They whipped it out of sight, but not before Peter had seen it.

The room had been cleared of present-day technology – no screens or laptops, and the projection equipment in the ceiling was covered. The rules for this meeting included strictures against contemporary technology, no discussion of events between 1965 and the present day, etc.

The goal was to avoid influencing the past by giving Chronos staff any details about the future. However, the Chronos workers were curious – and devious. They plied clients with trick questions, and pooled their information at the 1965 office.

For this meeting, someone was going to have to take handwritten notes on actual paper using a vintage ballpoint pen, and each of the three present-day staff was determined that this would not be their demeaning task. Fortunately, coffee and hot water for tea were available on the side table, so there would be no class or gender skirmishing about who would make coffee.

Last to come in the door was Christina Lopez, who had arrived the previous night from D.C., where she wrote contracts for the deeply buried Office of Net Assessment. Peter was visibly struggling to determine where the social order dictated that he should sit, so she pulled out the chair next to hers and steered him into it.

To his stammered thanks she said briskly, "No problem." Chris had arranged a kayak trip on the Green, Green River for that afternoon and did not want to waste a moment indoors. "I'll take notes," she went on, placing a yellow legal pad of paper and period-correct pen on the table. This offer erased the social fears of Emma, Steve, and Turing, and everyone relaxed.

A few minutes were spent in getting coffee and helping Peter with tea, with the inevitable small talk about tea bags versus loose tea.

"I know that we're not supposed to tell you anything," said Turing, "But I think it's OK to say that everyone here loves that television show *Doctor Who*. The Tardis, the Daleks."

"Really!" said Peter, looking pleased. "I was at school with a member of the cast. But in my time, the show has only been around for a year – how strange that you would recall it over fifty years later." Steve glared daggers at Turing, who looked pleased with themself.

"Let's get started," Steve began, but Peter excitedly went on talking. "Emma, someone on your team mentioned the Tardis when we met, which for me was last year, and for you was 1999. How is it possible that this small English television show has remained on your minds for so many years? Over half a century! Did someone write about it in a book?" There was a studied silence.

Peter turned to Turing. "Does it have anything to do with that small machine you were holding when I came in?" Turing looked away.

"Remember the rules, everyone, please," said Chris Lopez. "Could we focus on the task at hand? I have the happy job of writing the contract to allow the feds a two-hour time access slot in a specified area of Oxford, England on a sunny day, approximate date pre-World War I, specific date to be stipulated by you or others at Chronos ell tee dee." She waved her coffee spoon for syllabic emphasis and went on.

"Others in my office will negotiate all fees, to be paid by Homeland Security. There's a lot of details to sort out, so let's get going."

"Thank you," said Peter, "for pulling me back to this task. However, before I become officious and overbearing, I just want to say that if this team is an indication of future United States society and its workplace, I am thrilled to bits about what's coming."

The others gazed at him, wordless. How to begin to explain? That was not allowed, and so many apparently unsurmountable problems remained. Peter appeared ready to start crying again. Turing patted his hand.

Peter sniffled, "Your name, especially – have you ever heard of an eminent English mathematician, Alan Turing? He was top secret and very obscure, so I doubt it." Turing opened their mouth to reply, but Steve spoke quickly to Peter.

"I appreciated the warning in the cover note from the Oxford City planners stating that May 1910 is not available because of a change in government."

"Right," said Peter, tucking away his handkerchief. "We are concerned about the destabilizing effects of time travel during sensitive periods. Did you have any trouble finding out what happened that month, so long ago?"

"Not at all," Steve replied, "took me about twenty seconds." He sensed that the others were holding their breaths, and Peter was staring at him. "Umm, I mean, twenty minutes. The *Encyclopedia Britannica*, you know?"

Chris pushed the situation past this awkward moment. "Yes, we read that you lost a king and gained a new one that month, with a royal funeral. Good thing to avoid. Do you have a preferable date to suggest?"

"May I smoke?" asked Peter, pulling out a silver cigarette case and attempting to hand it around. The others leaned back in their chairs with shocked expressions.

"Goodness no, you can't do that," said Turing.

"Oh, you American Puritans," laughed Peter, putting away his case. "All right. We came up with a list of four potential dates, but first I want to make sure that we understand your purpose. A daily two-hour visit, on a small watercraft resembling those we have on Oxford's River Isis at the selected date – is that correct?"

Steve nodded. "Yes, with a maximum of fifteen travelers. We've made two short reconnaissance visits, and we think that the boat cruise should be from Port Meadow through the heart of the city. We request that your office help us designate a start and end point for a 45-minute trip. Passengers, all wearing appropriate clothing, will disembark after the cruise and walk back to the beginning via a carefully selected, unvarying route that will maximize atmosphere and charm. It will avoid human interactions and complicated situations. Then we climb back on the boat and head upstream to a spot overhung with willows, where we rejoin our own time on the river here."

"That sounds quite reasonable, really," said Peter. "Once you select from our proposed dates – and I invite your team to test-travel each one before deciding – we can suggest romantic details and history-drenched walks. But – " and he looked at them. "I don't want to be rude, because really this is all very wonderful and exciting – "

"Oh c'mon," said Chris, "we're Americans, we invented rudeness. Go for it."

"But that's exactly it," Peter went on. "You are being far too conservative in your planning. Oxford is a world city, even at that date. Oddly dressed people were accepted. Americans were widely accepted, if perhaps looked down upon for their loud voices and forward behavior. And don't you want to offer a pub lunch, a high tea, and shopping?"

"We have to keep them safe, bring them back alive and unhurt, and not affect the past or future," said Steve.

"Once we've done this exact tour for a year or two, we'll understand the situational parameters and be able to add a refreshment stop," added Turing.

"All very well," Peter replied. "But what's done is done. Whatever happened then is part of your present day. We encourage our clients to roam freely, with a pocketful of coins, make fools of themselves, explore, and have fun. Nannying them along the route is undignified."

"Legally, we cannot do that," said Chris. "Our laws oblige us to get them back safely and on time. Speaking of which, we need to discuss the insurance coverage."

"Oh, yes," said Peter. "That's the easiest part. A Lloyd's of London 1965 standard policy will cover you, your visitors, and all circumstances. That's why we're stationed in 1965, where Lloyd's is a byword for simplicity and security in the insurance world. I'm a 1957 man myself, but am being trained in 1965, tested well in 1999, and will soon be promoted to 2000. I requested 2002, but they said I wasn't ready for that. Something must have happened in 2001?" He looked around hopefully, but no one replied.

Chris stood up to refill her coffee, and the others followed suit. Emma took advantage of the pause to speak quietly with Peter.

"We should make a date to meet up, Peter. You'd like me in 2000." They smiled at each other, caught up in the emotions of ships passing in the abyss of time. Emma went on, "I'm in the phone book, Peter – Somerville, Massachusetts. OK?"

He nodded, suddenly shy. "Actually, Emma, I must admit. I looked up your timeline of addresses, after we first met." She went bright pink and stared at the table, shocked and pleased, as the meeting resumed around them.

"Aren't you concerned about the adverse impacts our tourists could have on future time, Peter?" asked Turing, who was thinking about the Time Travel Best Management Practices. These restrictions on behavior and activity when visiting the past had dominated time research until Dr. King had taken over the program. Under the earlier management of Ed Zanetti, almost no time travel had been allowed because of the potential to harm the future. How far could these rules be relaxed?

"Time is a beautifully flexible thing," said Peter. "I know that Emma understands the elegance of its flow. So a brief daily trip by a few law-abiding people will not affect much down the line. Cause and effect are not that precise. It is all looping back upon itself, you know. Time is more of a pool to play in, not a timeline from past into future. We have learned things from theory developed after our time. It's necessary for the success of Chronos, Ltd."

Emma was nodding thoughtfully. They would enjoy one another's company in 2000. Already had. He was her longtime husband, after all, though he did not know that in 1965. Turing was nodding thoughtfully, too. This made sense to them and would be helpful to the time defense research going on at the Deep Space labs and at the Time Fort & Barracks.

Peter stood up. "I have to get back," he said. "Not allowed to stay more than 45 minutes, you see. Afraid I might go native, I suppose." This 1965-appropriate comment caused a dead silence in 2017, and he spent two of his remaining minutes apologizing for his "insensitivity. We Englishmen are such brutes."

Peter turned to Steve and said, "I assure you there will be no adverse impacts from your proposed daily visit. We checked all that before offering you a Lloyd's contract. So if you let your visitors go off on their own for thirty minutes, and give them some pocket money, they will all show up back at the river. If not that day, then the next day. We already know this."

"We can't do that right away, Peter," said Steve. "But eventually, I hope. This has been a surprising meeting. Thank you."

"Your country still has that delightful puritanical streak," said Peter. "Learn to relax a bit. Bye-bye." He and Emma walked together to the front door. He kissed her on the cheek, walked out into the Kentucky heat, turned to wave, and vanished.

A new life in Horseheads and Hollymount, NY.

Accompanied by the spirits of Pennsylvania's Endless Mountains.

Outdoors, the evening sky was filled with a pearly light, and a soft breeze ruffled the trees. The small house in Horseheads, NY was packed with young people sharing a potluck meal and discussing next steps in their campaign to save the Hollymount Inn and surrounding area from Tom King. In her upstairs office, Rita quit trying to write the Results chapter for her dissertation and came downstairs to get a plate of food.

She sat next to Ravi and Harris on the saggy sofa and dug in to the amalgam of vegetarian and vegan gluten-free goodies on her plate. The two men were deep into the details of what to name their campaign and how best to explain the situation to the public.

Ravi remained incredulous. “You’re saying that we tell the public this is a magic world in a different dimension, and needs to be protected from the U.S. military and our President?”

“Why not?” asked Harris, undisturbed by mockery from a guy who was, after all, five years older and therefore out of touch. (With whom, he realized, he was falling in love.) Harris knew his message would do really well with people his age, and probably with a ton of others.

“Let’s just tell them the truth as we know it,” Harris said. “Anything else will backfire. If we talked about protecting water quality or endangered species or something boring like that, people will tune it out. Then they hear from somebody else that it’s actually a magic immigrant community from old Ireland, and where would we be? Our reputation for truth and accuracy would be in the toilet!”

He had stopped after two beers, still felt them, was speaking more boldly than usual. He somewhat regretted the word “boring.” Ravi was laughing, and Harris joined in. Rita smiled as she ate.

Out of his laughter Ravi cried, “How can I possibly take this tall tale back to Washington and my boss, Senator Max? I can’t expect her to support this insane story. Two competing groups, one led by the President of the USA and one by the head of a federal agency, are fighting for the right to militarize a fairy community in upstate New York, to gain access to its natural time portals?”

He stifled his mirth and went on. “Senator Max can’t get New York’s own Senators to pay attention to this stuff. They aren’t calling back." Ravi was feeling both appalled and delighted. He could not deny that something strange was going on. But the D.C. world of policy and precedent would dismiss the situation as crazy. What a wonderful mess.

He grinned at the increasingly cute Harris and his old college pal Rita, and looked across the room to where Lena and brother Brian were working on a communications plan with Mary Anne. She was using a pad and pencil to make notes, because an electronic device would signal her typing style to the surveillance bots. Anyway, pencil and paper felt better to her.

Mary Anne had hiked to the Hollymount Inn across northeastern Pennsylvania's Endless Mountains, she and her cat Pixie, immersed in the deep beauty of June. Even the noise and traffic of Pennsylvania's gas drilling in the small towns and on hilltops could not interrupt Mary Anne's meditative state. Nature has found ways to persevere, and rural northern Pennsylvania is no exception. She and Pixie opened themselves to the spirits who inhabit the thickets, the woods and valleys, brooks and lakes of that beautiful countryside. The immigrant Irish fairy Maeve is not the only unhuman in these woods.

As Mary Anne trekked north, sleeping in old barns and sharing provisions with Pixie, she was rebuilding her interior self for a new life, and making friends with the spirit allies she encountered. Many of them are patiently waiting for the return of the area's indigenous peoples. These nature spirits have no love for Maeve, who had driven away their people as viciously as had the European settlers, land speculators, George Washington, and his generals.

In this manner, while the miles piled up behind her, Mary Anne gathered power and strength, becoming an ambassador to the Hollymount community on behalf of the nature spirit people she and Pixie encountered.

One day, a brilliant sunny day, the pastures were alive with birds and all the early summer flowers at their peak, when human and cat followed the Crystal Hills trail down to the Hollymount Inn through the Stone Door, a natural portal between two rocky outcrops. There was no need to walk backwards around a church or to incantate archaic, amoral words. Mary Anne did it herself, thanks to her new spiritual allies.

Maeve walked up the woodland path above the Inn to greet her and saw that Mary Anne had deepened since they had last met. She now contained the knowledge of King's wicked hungry world from her old life, and the wisdom and reach from her ongoing transformation. (The Innkeeper, while still attractive, was less important to Mary Anne now.)

"I have known for years that I could do this," were her first words to Maeve, as they walked together down the grassy path to the Inn. "Thank you for making it possible." Pixie rode in her arms, gazing around at their new home.

"Oh, my dear," Maeve replied, "I am so grateful you have arrived. We have a young excitable group of humans here, and I hope you can explain them to me. They have heroic plans to protect Hollymount. You must help."

"If I can have a shower or bath, I will tackle any life form!" said Mary Anne, still human in her needs. They entered the Inn to find her a bath, followed by deep sleep in a featherbed with Pixie purring by her side.

Now here she was laughing and working with others to protect her new world. If anyone was fit to move back and forth between different truths and realities, it was Mary Anne. She sought Ravi and Harris's attention.

"We need your advice for our list of proposed actions," she said. Flipping back through her notes, she read, "'Mobilize the population to help. Local communities, young people, etc.' What do you think of that – it's our biggest planned action so far – and how might we carry it out? Keep in mind I'm the new kid."

Harris nodded vigorously and Ravi leaned back to listen, uncomfortable at the idea of widespread publicity. He preferred doing good things behind closed doors. Across the table, Brian was grinning in anticipation of Harris's words.

"OK! So you already have two big groups to support this," Harris began. "There's our SoTier activism group, protesting the highway project, and seventy thousand followers on Facebook who've been following the Brian Owen Safety Watch page ever since he was unjustly imprisoned. They will be behind this in a heartbeat. That's a ton of reach, right there!"

Rita added drily, "Never mind that both of those campaigns are mostly just you and your laptop."

"Hey! Ouchies!" Harris said, laughing at himself a little bit. "But that's what works nowadays. And," he continued to Mary Anne, "I assume you're good with the narrative that this tiny rural community, established by Irish fairies 400 years ago, is under siege by our own government, which wants to take it over for military purposes?" Mary Anne was feverishly writing, capturing his words.

"Yes, of course," said Lena. "What other narrative is there?" Ravi began laughing again, and Harris ventured a pat on his arm, to comfort and reassure. "Gotta stick with the truth, man," Harris said. "This region and the whole country are ready for it. Where have you been?"

"In air-conditioned offices and marble hallways," Ravi replied, sitting up straight. "I just have to warn you that the Senator and her team in Congress, and your own New York Congressional delegation, may not get fully behind this approach." The others gazed at him thoughtfully.

Harris said, "Excuse my cliché, but with all due respect … what they feel and think in Congress is not very relevant to what's actually happening here."

Nods of agreement around the table.

Brief sulfurous interlude, Washington, D.C.

Time is money.

"The plot is sickening," said Senator Elizabeth Maximus to Ravi Sen-Ellis, who had hustled from Hollymount back to D.C. to report in person. The Senator's office was dark – nightfall had crept in around them while they talked. They were sunk low in their chairs, dispirited and uncertain how to proceed.

Max stretched her arms over her head. "I am going to ignore the weird details, and focus on the facts," she said. "Two bad actors, Time Tsar King and the President of the USA, are competing to seize control of time travel portals in Kentucky and in New York State near the Pennsylvania border, for military and pecuniary reasons." She listened to her words as she spoke and knew it would make no sense to her fellow Senators, particularly her esteemed but stodgy New York colleagues. And yet it was true, and the outcomes could be catastrophic for the country's future.

"How can I pitch this to the Senate, Ravi? Those young friends of yours can go right ahead with their 'magic Irish community' appeal, but we can't."

Ravi's eyes were closing with exhaustion. He rallied to suggest, "Could you call Senator Styce and feel him out? See what he'll share with you? And maybe find out what he's hiding?"

Senator Max smiled and picked up her phone, instantly energized. In a neighboring vast building, Harlan Styce's cell phone rang, causing him to jump. He, too, was sitting in his darkened office, thinking over the potentially traitorous conversation he had just concluded. He could feel the warmth of Hell's flames just below his feet.

Who could be calling now? He saw that the caller was E. Max, and flushed with shame. Of all people – a stickler for honesty and honor. Occasionally his rural, devout boyhood caught up with him. It had all started about an hour earlier when he'd taken a surprise phone call from the President.

"Yes, sir," Styce said enthusiastically, "happy to talk time travel. My assistant Ard Sprinkle is among the country's best informed about this rapidly expanding military resource. He's here right now!" Across Styce's desk, Ard sat up straight, attempting to look guileless and helpful, having arranged the call in advance with the President's staff.

Senator Styce turned on the phone speaker, and that mellow

synthetic warmth flowed into the room. "Styce-Styce baby, we're buddies, right? We work pretty good together, am I right?"

"Can't say we agree on every detail, Mr. President, but I am getting a kick out of watching you torment the liberals."

"Sure, those losers. Pathetic. So I guess it's time you and I did some business. Keep the good times coming, right?"

Styce smiled and said, "I don't really have a lot of control over the time travel programs, sir – Dr. Tom King is who you need to – "

"Don't want to hear that name, OK? Guy is a dead man walking. I just need one more reason to fire his ass. My son is taking over, to get time travel cooking for me and my investors. They are *drooling*. Say – before we get to that special favor you said you would do for me – "

Ard watched the Senator's jovial expression turn to puzzlement as the President went on. "I know you want to get in on the ground floor with my personal time investment opportunity. We have three levels of influence, and you can move from one to the next whenever you're ready. Just released today, for our closest friends and colleagues. Want in?"

"Mr. President – " said Styce, trying to slow the man down. New Yorkers!

"That's what I thought, I can hear your enthusiasm all the way over here on Pennsylvania Avenue. OK, you are in at the entry level, but we'll move you up as soon as there's room. My guys will do the necessary with your guys and your preferred bank account."

A loud bleep from Styce's laptop announced the arrival of a long and complex email message bristling with attachments, titled, "Time is Money."

"And the money starts flowing as soon as you do this little favor for me that you promised."

"Mr. President!" said Styce sternly, indignation taking over from his Southern politeness.

The President kept talking. "I heard, a little birdie told me, that there's a place in my home state where you can get into the past without letting the government know. Am I right? Does this guy Ard

Sprinkle, what a name by the way, know anything about it?"

Ard rose to his cue, leaning forward eagerly to serve his true master. "Thanks for the nice words, sir! So excited to speak to you in person."

"So get to the point, dumbass," said the President.

"OK, sir, sorry! Yes, I have been researching naturally occurring portals to the past, and found this cluster down on the New York-Pennsylvania border."

"Ard," said Styce, "That is a top secret project we are doing for Homeland Security, with Tom King. You can't – "

"But the President of the United States wants to know about it," said Ard, flushing with embarrassment, his voice sharpening.

"Yeah, buddy," said that President, "I can't believe you would hide this from me, Senator. If it's top secret, it belongs to me now."

"I beg to differ," snapped Styce. "This project belongs to the people of the United States, for their benefit, and for the enhancement of our national security."

"You just really stepped in it, Styce," snarled the Commander-in-Chief. "Trying to hide this place from me! Now you owe me big time. No more little favors, like the one you promised me." Styce opened his mouth to reply, but no words emerged. How had they gotten here? The President's voice switched back to warm honey.

"It's so easy to get along with me, you know? I am the most reasonable guy. And it's simple – my investors want that little valley. To make money for them, and for you, too – you're part of it now. They'll be excited to hear you've joined up. I'll call you back later after you calm down. It's a simple real estate deal! Just see things my way – OK? Bye."

The call ended, and Styce found himself staring at Ard Sprinkle, who ventured a shrug and smile. "Isn't the man wonderful?" he said, sighing like a lovelorn teenager. Rage boiled up from Senator Harlan Styce's gut. Nobody treated him this way. He rose to his feet and screamed at Ard.

"Get out! You treacherous piece of sh*t! Scram! You little f*cker!" Ard gathered up his stuff and ran out the office door into the marble halls.

An hour later, sitting in the dark, after much bleak reflection, Styce answered his cell phone. "Hi, Senator Max, it's been a long time," he said.

"Big changes, Senator Styce, since we last talked. Such as our new President. Just for starters, you are being way too nice to him."

"Oh c'mon, Liz, he's great for business, and the good folks in the Commonwealth of Kentucky love the guy."

"But he's *evil*, Harlan!"

Ravi listened in, fascinated. He worked for one big shot Senator and knew many others. He could never get over how this alien life form interacted among themselves. In public they appeared to hate one another, but privately they were often warmly informal and chummy. Sometimes this contradictory relationship led to compromise and teamwork – as it did now.

"Funny you should say that, Liz. I have just been thinking about evil, and I'm kind of worried." There was a pause, and Senator Max and Ravi held their breaths, intrigued by Harlan's tone, hoping he would say more.

"Well, you can trust me, Harlan, we go back a long way," Elizabeth Maximus said softly, which reminded him of the time when everyone was younger and they were both new to their illustrious positions, helping each other learn the ropes and tropes.

"All right," Styce replied, taking a breath. "Suppose – just suppose – that a very senior member of the White House administration contacted me about that little valley near the New York-Pennsylvania border – you know the place, I reckon?"

Ravi's eyes widened.

Senator Max said, "I know a little bit, sure, Harlan."

"Well, that senior person wants to use it for his own personal financial benefit. We're talking about a place of great strategic value to our country. My staff has been checking it out and reporting to me and Dr. Tom King, for the past six months. It's a national military priority, top secret. Not even our esteemed New York Senators know about it."

Senator Max gave a thumbs-up to Ravi, and continued speaking in her gentlest, warmest, most trustworthy tone. "I don't need to know all the details. But I am wondering, why does this very senior person want this little place? How did he hear about it? And most of all, Harlan, are you in trouble somehow? Can I help?"

"It's a business opportunity for this person and his group of investors. Turns out my so-called trusted assistant Ard has been feeding him our top secret information. This senior guy didn't tell me what he plans to do with the portals – uh, military resources in the valley there – but – "

And here was the sin of it, for Harlan, the personal grip on his flesh by evil. His voice dropped to a whisper. "I gotta tell someone. He conned me – *me!* – into joining the investor group."

"Ahhh …" said Liz Max, whispering in return. "He thinks he's got you, Harlan, right?"

"No one has tried anything like this on me for decades – no one would *dare* – how DARE this damn Yankee charlatan from New York City do this to me – to *ME?*" Harlan's badly shaken ego was recovering fast, and he went directly from a whisper to a shout. "And that lousy disloyal Ard Sprinkle! Carrying all this top secret stuff straight to the White House, maybe for *months!* I – I'm madder than a boiled owl."

"Harlan, I understand! This is an awful situation, and I'm grateful you trust me enough to tell me about it," cooed Senator Maximus. "Want to meet for lunch tomorrow? We could go to our favorite place from the old days – they have a new menu, all the latest trends, and I've been wanting to check it out. We can get a private table and work out how to handle this. And Harlan, honey, that's a cute expression, about the boiled owl."

"Oh, that's what they say back home. I am *that* mad! Liz, I have never been treated with such disrespect. I'll break a date with a committee member and see you there tomorrow."

Senator Max ended the call. She shook her head in wonderment. “As far as he’s concerned, this is all about him!”

“That was spectacular, ma’am!” Ravi replied. “Can we talk again after your lunch with him? I’m taking another quick trip to that little valley – two days tops – I’ll be right back.”

Chapter 7

Hugh Hynes returns to Kentucky's Ten Thousand Secrets National Park.

Lunch for everyone!

It was a warm day at Kentucky's Ten Thousand Secrets National Park. The cicadas were buzzing loudly in the trees, and the visitor parking lots were packed with cars and SUVs. In deep shade, dogs on leashes panted.

In the Science building, Steve Roberts was reviewing a video with the two time travel communications staffers. They were completing the first round of advertisements for the new travel program. In one week, the Park would start taking reservations for Venice 1959, Eden/Bar Harbor 1900, and Oxford 1908 (the perfect day had been found).

A weary team of time explorers walked past Roberts's open office door, ready for their debriefing session. They were loosening garters and girdles, shedding itchy underskirts, urgently stripping off thick wool stockings; untying bonnets, unbuttoning collars, removing wigs, false moustaches, and sideburns. Steve heard loud voices downstairs in the lobby.

"There's a guy down there who wants to talk to you," said one of the explorers as he passed the door.

A guard came running up the stairs and burst in on the video session. "Steve, sir, can you help? There's a crazy guy who says he's the boss, and wants to come up to his office here. I called Security, and Officer Turner is on his way over."

Behind him in the doorway loomed the Park's chief scientist, Hugh Hynes, assumed dead in the Pleistocene. Steve jumped to his feet in shocked delight and rushed to embrace Hugh.

Pushing the security guard aside, Hugh demanded, "Steve – can you unlock my office?"

Steve said, "Hugh, I was hoping they'd find you. I went – "

"Yes, I know all that. Don't talk about it here. And thank you!" snapped Hugh. He gripped Steve by the shoulders and looked into his eyes, speaking with quiet intensity. "I am aware of what is going on here. But I am not sure you are."

"Well, I need to warn you about some changes. You were presumed dead, so Dr. King emptied and remodeled your office – " Steve started explaining the new situation, but Hugh shook his head impatiently, looked around and began to shout. At Steve, at the others in his office, and at the likelihood of security guards approaching to shut him down.

Hugh was making noise. "Let me into my office right this minute! Steve! Wake up! Do you understand what is happening?" Hugh ran down the hall to his corner office and began kicking the locked door. *Boom boom.*

"How dare they lock me out," Hugh roared, continuing to kick. Heads popped from offices along the hallway, and the science and support staff from Hugh's era ran to hug him. The new people hired by Tom King were on their phones, calling and texting.

Their theme: "Warn Dr. King that Hynes is back. Somebody needs to remove him ASAP."

The Park's head of Security, Officer Lee Turner, sprinted up the stairs. "Oh, good," cried King's staff. "Go get him, Officer Turner! Arrest that trespasser." Shouting and fisticuffs broke out between Hynes and King loyalists.

Officer Turner ran up to Hugh Hynes, hugged him fiercely, and unlocked Hynes's office door. Inside, new grey carpeting covered the floor and a light gloss green coated the walls. A steel, teak, and chrome desk dominated the room, and beyond it a red leather armchair beckoned. Red and black upholstered chairs and a plush leather couch framed a low glass table. A fully stocked bar with refrigerator covered the nearest wall between the two big windows, which sported fancy accordion blind treatments.

On the desk were two brand-new nameplates, one for the hallway wall and one for the desk. They read "Dr. Thomas King, Time Tsar." The room was unused – the new boss had not yet moved in.

Hynes was momentarily struck dumb by all this splendor, and began to laugh. He grabbed the nameplates and tossed them into the hall, where he could hear voices raised on his behalf as Turner strove to restore workplace civility.

A lowly staffer of Hugh's era came in, carrying his old desk nameplate. "Dr. Hynes, I saved this. It was all I had to remember you by." The man was crying.

They hugged and Hugh said loudly, "I'm back. Science is back." He leaned into the hallway and called, "Can somebody get Steve Roberts in here? At 1 p.m. we'll have a general staff meeting to get caught up, meet the new folks, tell them how things work around here, and update the work plan."

Hugh said to his staffer, "Can you order lunch for everyone? On me. I've been living on field rations and glacial meltwater, and I've got a lot of back pay coming."

The uproar reaches Washington, D.C.

And New York's Southern Tier.

King took the call from the Park at his D.C. office desk. "What do you mean, 'Officer Turner will return my call – later'?" (rapid chatter). "Look, you already know this – Hugh Hynes does not work for the Park – he is officially deceased, declared dead! And that's *my* office! Kick him out on the street! What do you mean, 'He's declared himself undead'? How *dare* you speak to me that way."

Fulminating with rage, King found himself glaring at his silent cell phone – the Park staffer had ended the call. He emerged from his office – no Ard, no Mary Anne to help – and grabbed the nearest Time Travel intern.

"Car! Get my car! And driver! Plane! Get my plane!" he roared. The tender 19-year-old, a wealthy youth from suburban Louisville, stammered in awe, his eyes rolling toward more competent friends across the room.

He cried, "Yes, yes – sir! Right this, this minute – sir!" as two youngsters came running to assist.

From his car, on the way to his plane, King was soon shouting into his phone at Senator Styce, who was shouting right back. They were *both* mad as boiled owls. Fresh from his private lunch with Senator Liz Maximus, Senator Harlan Styce was taking no instructions from anybody, least of all that hopped-up sex fiend Tom "Cat" King.

Where he got "sex fiend" from he had no idea, but it sounded great, screaming at King over the phone. And surely this damn mad scientist was also in cahoots with Ard and the President! Sweet Miss Lizbeth, his dearest and only true friend in this nest of vipers, had warned him to not trust anyone but her. Maybe the two stiff bourbons he'd had with lunch were contributing to his mood.

"I am not a f*cking sex fiend!" King bellowed at Styce over the phone, raising the eyebrows of his driver. King went on, "Harlan! Listen to me! Calm down! We could lose control of our program. I'm headed to the Park, got a new problem there – " (loud ranting).

"What do you mean, I'm in cahoots with Sprinkle? Wait, what? He works for the President? Stop swearing, Harlan." King thought about Hollymount. Had Ard told the President about the natural portals there? He ended the call, leaving Styce shouting, "The President of the United States is a lying rattlesnake!" – raising the eyebrows of *his* driver.

Not wanting to talk directly with the formidable Senator Max, King called Ravi Sen-Ellis, her top staffer. According to security reports, that tough young man was involved in every aspect of this situation. 'Maybe he could come work for me,' King thought.

Ravi answered immediately, not giving himself time to think. Newly arrived from the Elmira airport, he was just sitting down to supper with Harris, Mary Anne, and Rita. "Hello, Dr. King, how may I help you?" he asked smoothly, breathless, leaping up and away from the dinner table and out to the front porch. Harris crept after him, leaning out the door to listen.

"Yes, I and Senator Max can verify that the President wants the time travel programs for himself and his cronies," Ravi said, listened, and went on. "Yes, both the engineered time entrance at Ten Thousand Secrets National Park and the natural portals in New York State. He wants them all." Ravi turned around to Harris and gave him a wink.

"I don't know who Mr. Sprinkle is working for, but he has been here – uh that is – at the Hollymount site – several times since last fall. I thought he was working for you! Me? Where am I right this minute? I'm in D.C., same as you, sir," said Ravi, attempting a smooth save. "Oh, you're headed to the Kentucky park? Pardon me – did you say that Hugh Hynes is back from the dead?" Ravi stared wide-eyed at Harris and the others clustered in the doorway.

"No, sir, thank you for thinking of me, but I like working for Senator Max," Ravi said, as the call ended, "Yes sir, I will keep it in mind. Talk to you soon? OK, sir."

Ravi sat down suddenly on the porch couch, cradling his phone, and stared across the well-tended lawn into the distance. He said to Mary Anne, "Any minute now, King will figure out that you're here." Mary Anne Washington shrugged.

"No need to worry about me," she said. "I'm no longer frightened of him. Come in and finish your supper." Ravi returned to the table. Harris fiddled with the extra wall switch near the front door, and they went back to their meal, listening for sounds of approaching law enforcement.

Twenty minutes later, an unmarked black SUV with opaque

windows pulled up quietly in front of the house, and the neighbor kids stopped playing to watch.

"Nobody lives there, mister," shouted the biggest girl as a black-clad helmeted man, hand on his gun, walked through waist-high weeds and mounted the broken-down steps to knock on the door. The security team fanned out into the backyard. The front and back doors were not locked so they swarmed inside and found an empty house, with collapsing old furniture, a sagging staircase, broken windows, and dried-up mattresses on cobwebbed bedframes. In the kitchen, a long-dead refrigerator sat near a broken-legged table, four chairs upright around it.

Ravi and the others sat still in the chairs, breathing lightly, as the enforcers slammed their way through the apparently lifeless house. This was the first full test of the masking system, and it held true.

They listened as the security team headed back to their vehicle, reporting via radio. "She's not here. Nobody's here. The house at this address is derelict. Neighbors say nobody's lived here for ten years and it looks it."

The SUV zoomed away. Harris did not rush for the off switch. The four crept up the stairs and looked out of windows on all sides of the house. The black security SUV was parked on the next block, and the spooky security team was going door-to-door in search of Mary Anne.

"Those guys came for me last fall," Brian whispered. "There's a place out near the airport with some warehouses. That's where I spent three months. My next check-in is in two days, and I was going to skip it." His phone began buzzing in his pocket, and he pulled it out. "Wow, they want me there now – it's a random check-in, because I am 'not at my official domicile or place of work.'"

"They're checking up – I think you better go," said Ravi.

"I'll drop you off near your apartment, so you can take your car," said Harris. "I'll trail you from there."

"Assuming they let me out," said Brian, "I can meet you at the McDonald's down the street."

"Assuming that works out, let's meet at the Inn," said Ravi.

"How long should I keep the house mask turned on?" asked Rita. "I promised the neighbors to turn it off after an hour."

We will leave them for now, devising code words, agreeing on rendezvous details, and sketching out a Plan B.

The Time Fort & Barracks.

In the Pleistocene epoch on the Green, Green River.

Tom King arrived at Ten Thousand Secrets National Park from the airport with two urgent tasks: check on the new Time Fort & Barracks in the Pleistocene, and throw Hugh Hynes out of the Park.

After entering the Pleistocene via the Green, Green River portal, he was driven by Turing to the Time Fort & Barracks. The first full week of time residence in the Pleistocene had started, and this was the second day. So far, it looked remarkably like the first day, which the time staff had been experiencing repeatedly for several months. However, on this new day there were bound to be weather changes, and differences in movements of Pleistocene wildlife, so technicians had fanned out to do monitoring. This day seemed greyer than the previous one, and King wondered if a storm was coming.

"We all survived the first night, sir," said Turing, who was filling King in during the ten-minute ride to the Time Fort.

"Good, so the situation is stable," said King. "Do you think it's all right for me to stay here tonight?"

"No, better not. Let us take the risks this first week, and maybe next time around you can bunk here with us," said Turing. Quietly relieved, King nodded.

Back in his grad school days, King had been casual about the technology for his pioneering exploit into the past. His bravado then had long since been replaced by caution. Now he was haunted by what he did then – killing his grandfather to test a theoretical point for his Ph.D. at Cornell Tech.

It had seemed like an excellent career move. The action was minimal, surgical, and harmed no one in the present day, as he thought then. He had proved that if carried out at exactly the right time, the past could be changed without affecting the future.

King and his family were unaffected – or so he thought at first. He had assumed they would be so proud of him, and of their family's role in furthering the frontiers of science.

His findings had led to a revolution in time research. The math and physics now pointed to manipulating micro-moments of the past to adjust the future in tiny but significant ways. And that's what the Time Fort research was all about, with funding from the Department of Defense.

But science, folklore, and morality point to an unbalancing when someone is killed. King had come to expect that karma, the working out of a physics formula, or some other form of rebalancing was coming for him sooner or later.

Most of life's comforts and pleasures passed King by as he waited for the shoe to drop, the pendulum to swing, the weight to shift. He was always vigilant, on guard against that moment. He had no time for a wife, a partner, friends, a social life.

"The news is not all good, sir," Turing went on, heedless of King's brooding silence. Startled out of his reverie, King looked sharply at Turing.

"The energy cost of a full week of operations is – um – well, devastating is one word to describe it. We're spending our entire annual energy budget just for one week of continuous time access. That's the estimate based on the first twenty-four hours."

"That can't be right," said King.

"Sorry, sir," said Turing as they parked next to the Time Fort and climbed out. "We didn't anticipate this massive surge. We had budgeted for a week – you know, seven times the energy use for keeping the portal open for one day." Turing popped through the air hatches into the Fort's reception area and waited for King to follow, while continuing his careful explanation.

"So we are wondering if the Fort itself is an energy sink somehow. We have our best people working on this here and back at the Park's Deep Space labs. Also, we're watching the server farm down by Oakland to make sure it doesn't overload." They headed into the main conference room. The prefabricated Time Fort & Barracks was built according to international space station dimensions, compact and easily crowded.

The staff was waiting, worried looks on their faces. Energy overload was not the news they wanted to deliver to their boss at a moment that should have been triumphant. Taking a chair at the table, King mustered a confident smile and was rewarded with smiles from Emma Brown, Chris Lopez, and Security chief Lee Turner.

"Congratulations on transitioning to the week-long schedule," said King. "I bet you smart people already have some good ideas about solving this energy glitch." Everyone relaxed a smidgen.

Chris said, "Yes, sir. Turing instructed us to brainstorm while they were getting you, and this is what we have so far." A several-point list appeared on the wall screen.

1. End the research until we understand what's going on.
2. Go back to one-day visits.
3. Shut down the Fort and live in tents until we find the surges and leaks.
4. Shut down the exit portal during each week-long deployment.
5. Carry out a detailed energy audit at all locations until we find the surges and leaks.
6. Aggressively search for natural time portals.
7. Shift to natural time portals, if these become available.

"We're starting at number five, sir, because we assume you don't want us abandoning the work or retreating," said Chris.

"But we included numbers one through four because deep caution is the basic hallmark of safety in time travel," added Emma. She had worked with Ed Zanetti to develop the original federal time travel safety guidelines and was loath to abandon them.

"I don't see 'rapid development of new energy sources' on this list," said King. "What's your reasoning?"

Turing replied, "Senator Styce is already in trouble over fast-tracking the new dual coal and fracked gas power plant out in Paradise for this project." King cocked his head at the strange place name.

Emma said softly, "Paradise is the old name for the little Kentucky community where this plant would be built."

Turing went on, "The Pleistocene project is already overloading the central Kentucky energy grid. The federal parks office is questioning our need for all this power, and the local communities are worried about power outages. That means it would not be politically wise to ask for more energy. We also have the three new Time Tours starting soon and have to provide for their energy needs, too."

"You know I have the jurisdiction, the power," said King, "to seize the flatlands around Ten Thousand Secrets Park for a massive solar installation. Think about it – all those dumpy little towns along the I-65 corridor could be replaced with a sea of solar. And lay new tracks to bring in gas and coal trains. This project is that important to our nation's security, you know."

Lee Turner spoke: "Most everyone who works at the Park lives in those towns," and he did not say sir.

"Look, I like this list," said King. "But I will do that if I have to. The possibility of that action will inspire us to work hard on the other options, so it doesn't become necessary."

Officer Turner's face remained impassive, and Emma looked down at the table. There was a pause to contemplate the power this one man held.

Turing said, "Let's get back to work after we eat lunch. We

need to finish business in time for Dr. King to get back to the portal this afternoon."

By 3 p.m. King was recrossing the Green, Green River, warming up in the hot Kentucky sunshine from the Pleistocene's deep chill. He stripped off his winter coat, ignoring the jolt of nausea when the motorboat went through the time transition point as it approached the dock, originally built to ferry Park visitors back and forth for visits to the Pleistocene. That tourist attraction was shut down, the portal now exclusively for use by the military under King's direction.

As they docked, King gazed down the river shoreline toward the three new landing areas nearing completion for the Time Tours to Oxford, Eden/Bar Harbor and Venice. Safely distant from one another to prevent energy overloads, each was built and landscaped according to the charm of three fictionalized olden times, and staff would be costumed appropriately.

King cared nothing for these human entertainments, a public façade behind which military funding could flow freely. His mind was buzzing with the possibility of carrying out a military seizure of the Hollymount community and the natural time portals on Apple Island. He might be able to get away with actions like that in Kentucky, but probably not in New York. In any case, he needed to take control of Hollymount before the President did.

King ignored Officer Turner's helping hand, climbed out of the boat, and headed up the path to his car, intent on dealing with Hugh Hynes at the Park's Science offices. But Hugh Hynes was not in his office, the locks had been changed, and no one had a key for the enraged Dr. Tom "Cat" King. Also shut down was Deep Space, the subterranean military research center, undergoing software upgrades.

Soon, King's car was speeding through parkland woods downslope to Wilcher Boulevard, seeking a night's shelter in the sumptuous home of the other, junior Kentucky Senator, near Bowling Green. The driver took a shortcut to I-65 through charming little Oakland, about five hundred feet from where Hugh Hynes was engaged in a sharp argument: five hundred feet horizontally, and one hundred and fifty vertical feet down.

A subterranean interlude in the vicinity of Oakland, Kentucky.

Wherein Dave Caver has a bad hangover.

Across a shady lane in peaceful Oakland lies a tangle of downed trees, vines, and wildflowers. These cover a steep drop into a rocky sinkhole, with a small natural drain at the bottom. That day, rain fell all afternoon, laying the dust, breathing new life into the warm summertime greenery, calling out the birds to sing and the insects to hum. By evening, water was trickling down through the limestone rocks of the sinkhole.

Far below, the drip-drip of rainwater into a small cave pool punctuated Hugh Hynes's agitated conversation with Gabby – Dr. Gabriella Greene to the rest of us, coordinator of the regional university's cave science programs. They stood in the big cave room near the sparkling pile of time tubes.

Dave Caver had just gotten back from the tube that probably connected to New Orleans, date uncertain, maybe 1806. At the far end of that tunnel he had found a lantern-lit community at dusk, where a riverboat crew was drinking around a fire. They were celebrating their arrival from Kentucky, following a rugged month-long journey down the Ohio and Mississippi rivers. He had joined their celebration; now back with Gabby and Hugh in the big room he was feeling a bit delicate, resting quietly against the cave wall.

His return trip had been harsh. Dave grasped foggily that Hugh Hynes had dropped down through the house entry, looking for someone to talk to. Or shout at. Dr. Greene was up for the challenge, and Dave let her go for it. He chugged water from his canteen and wondered if he could creep away unseen, go upstairs and take a nap.

"But how could you keep all this a secret from me?" Hugh asked.

They had already been over this, and Gabby would not budge. "These caves are not in the Park. You're the Park's scientist. It was our own project to develop," she said firmly – again. "And it had to be top secret, to keep out the military and the spies. So we left you out of the loop."

"Who all knows about these – these creepy sparkly time tubes?" Hugh asked.

"That's a secret too, Hugh. And if you tell anyone about it, you will have to die." This startled him, but shouldn't have. Cavers are ferocious.

"You mean that, right?" he asked, just above a whisper. They were both calming down and could talk conversationally again.

Gabby nodded. "Can you imagine what we went through to decide to rescue you? We're a very small group. The landowners upstairs, our gracious hosts, think these are just caves we're exploring. Steve Roberts pretends he doesn't know about it. We recruited the two ecoterrorist gals to get you. Dave gave them a hint that a person they were looking for was down another tunnel, and now they're gone, looking for him, and that tunnel has partially collapsed behind them. I don't know if they were caught in it or not."

"You rigged it to collapse?"

"Not saying," Gabby snapped. She crouched down to slow her heart rate, scared at what she might have done to protect this crazy phenomenon, these shimmering tubes. She saw Dave tottering away toward the cave passage, one hand on the wall for support, and called to him. "Dave! I might need you here!"

He paused to look back, and spoke weakly. "Gotta go sleep it off, Gabby. Have pity. That was bad whiskey. You're doing great, and Dr. Hynes is trustworthy, you know that." He wavered out of sight.

"OK, so, I'm in the loop now," said Hugh. "And I'm telling you, I want to use this place right here against Tom King. And that wacko in the White House. And the spies and spooks who have turned the Park into a military base." He was starting to shout again.

"You know my first loyalty is to the resource. I will do whatever is needed to get our Park back," cried Hugh, exalted and exhausted.

With Hugh gone, presumed dead, Tom King had transformed Ten Thousand Secrets National Park into a military time travel research center. The three upcoming Time Travel Tours provided a screen of normality for the public. Park visitors were also looking forward to the in-cave casinos and hotels, scheduled to reopen the following spring.

These changes obliterated Hugh Hynes's science programs and water quality monitoring. The excavation and construction of Deep Space blasted holes in the subterranean rivers.

The unsighted cave shrimp and other vulnerable species, monitored for decades, were blown to smithereens. Chemicals poured into the damaged rivers and, via springs, into the Green, Green River.

But Hugh was back, "undead," said the office jokers, supportively. The Park Superintendent reinstated him as Park Scientist. Attorneys were filing a lawsuit on his behalf against Tom King for pressing the button to reset the Pleistocene into the present. That action had almost killed Hugh, Janet, and Lena.

Hugh felt both grief and rage. Gabby Greene understood his losses. She and he, with her students, had worked together for many years on cave research and exploration. That work had ended for the foreseeable future. They had to drive this military menace out of the Park before restoration could begin.

"If King finds out about these tubes," Gabby said, slowly and clearly, "he will seize and militarize them. Like he's gonna do with that place in New York State."

"I missed the memo," said Hugh, "out there on the Pleistocene prairie. What are you talking about?" She explained that a cluster of natural time portals had been found in southern New York State. Furthermore, Steve Roberts had told her that the President of the USA and Tom King might go to war – with one another – to seize control. Gabby called the place Apple Island.

"Is anything being done to protect it?" Hugh asked. "I doubt that New York State would let it go without a fight." A native New Yorker, he knew his people, arrogant and pugnacious.

"I'm waiting to hear more from Steve," Gabby said. They walked around the big shimmering hill, peering into tubes. The ones that had been explored had signs outside with location and approximate time at the other end. About half were unlabeled.

Gabby explained, "We can't use GPS trackers because there are often no satellites in the sky at the other end, so we have to approximately locate it on the globe. Establishing the time – the date and year – is even trickier. You have to get that from people, or clocks, newspapers, books."

She scrambled around fallen rocks and continued, "Some of these places don't have any of that. Where Dave was, the people were so drunk and backwoods that they didn't know the date. So we take photos of the night sky, when it's clear, to establish dates from star maps. It's slow work, and we have to do it undetectably."

Gabby pointed to a sparkling tunnel entrance with a pink sign outside it. "That's where you came out. That's the Pleistocene portal. And up there," she pointed upslope to an entrance partially obscured by a pile of rocks, with a green sign next to it. "That's where we sent the ecoterrorists, chasing a family member back to New York."

"It goes directly to that Apple Island site?" Hugh asked.

"That's a weird one – comes out in the apple orchard, and the time difference is tricky – it's exactly 63 minutes later there than here. Two very strange men sit guard over the area. They told Dave that an Irish fairy queen keeps trying to get into one of the other portals on the island."

Hugh's gaze was skeptical.

She shrugged. “That’s all we know. Dave has only been there once. But recently we saw a guy come out at our end, and watched until he went back in. We identified him from the media as Janet’s son, Lena’s brother. We told them about it and they – uh, took the bait, after they rescued you.”

“I liked those ecoterrorists,” said Hugh. “Janet’s my kind of gal. I know I should hate her for harming the cave with those explosives, but damn, she did good work.”

“You have got to be kidding me,” said Gabby. They were strolling back up the cave passage now, following Dave, all three seeking comfort in the house overhead.

“I sure hope they’re all right,” said Hugh, as they arrived at the ladder. “I’ll keep your secret here, Gabby, but this is not your caver playground any longer. This is now a base to take back our Park.”

Later that day, Hugh saw from his Park office window that Officer Lee Turner was heading toward his vehicle to drive home. Hugh ran downstairs, and they stood talking next to Turner’s pickup truck. “About those two women terrorists,” said Hugh.

“Folks have been protecting them, sir, but I finally found out where they holed up last fall,” Officer Turner said helpfully.

Hugh shook his head. “In fact, I’m going to ask you to handle this differently. I don’t think you’re going to like it.” Turner’s face remained impassive as Hugh continued.

“Janet Harper and Lena Owen rescued me from the Pleistocene, using a route I am not at liberty to share.” Turner knew about the pile of time tubes underneath Oakland; he also knew how to keep a secret. So he gazed blankly, stupidly, at Hugh, forcing him to do all the work.

“So, I am grateful to them.” Hugh said. Turner nodded. Hugh saw this as a positive reaction, and went on with more confidence.

“Please do me the favor of just letting them go, OK?”

“You’re right, I don’t like it, sir.”

“And I owe you big time, Officer Turner.”

'That devil is quiet today,' the little lady thought, 'but a bad thing is coming.'

Trouble arrives in the magic parking lot, headed toward the Hollymount Inn.

Rita drove Ravi and Mary Anne to the enchanted parking lot beyond the roundabout. "I need to learn the entry procedure," Rita said, "because I'm bringing a colleague over later this morning to do a plant survey." She looked at Ravi. "It's the botany professor I mentioned. He's curious to see the vegetation in Maeve's world and ours."

Ravi said incredulously, "He believes all this stuff?"

"Yes," she said, sharply. "You better catch up, Ravi, or you'll be left behind. He's a historical botanist, and he suspects there are some interesting things going on with the plant introductions from Ireland 400 years ago. He asked for a field trip. When Brian and Harris get here, they'll show him around."

"Makes sense to me," said Mary Anne. "He thinks there's Irish plant species mixed in with the local ones?"

"Yes, that's part of it," said Rita, as they turned into the Highway Spur Project site. The work had started up again and there were trucks on the move. Rita drove along the graded dirt and gravel roadway toward the roundabout. She was silent, upset by Ravi's skepticism.

In turn Ravi, stung by her criticism, endeavored to display polite interest. "Can you explain more, for the benefit of my bureaucratic self?" They were old college buddies, after all, and Rita relented.

"This botanist, Professor Hill, says that Maeve and the others must've brought Irish plants with them four hundred years ago, both deliberately and as seeds carried in their clothes, you know, what we learned in fourth grade. He wants to survey the plants around the Inn. He's wondering if there are plant species native to New York *and* plant species from Ireland long ago."

Rita looked at Ravi in the rear-view mirror to make sure he was keeping up and went on. "He also wants to check what species might have been carried back and forth through the time portal at the roundabout. Maybe birds and other animals have learned the widdershins route around the little church, and pass back and forth between Maeve's world and ours. Also he thinks the highway project is accelerating changes."

"Explain to me, the non-scientist, what that means," said Ravi.

"If a stable, unique assemblage of Irish and local plants and animals has grown up here over the past 400 years, the trucks and bulldozing may destroy it," said Rita.

"An argument for stopping the project while impacts are assessed!" cried Mary Anne, still a creature of Washington, D.C. Rita nodded, slowing the car as they approached the roundabout, church spire at its wooded center.

"I go around this thing counterclockwise, right? Oh – but that's the normal direction!"

Mary Anne replied, "Yeah, you unlock access by driving counterclockwise, *widdershins*, around that little church there. That's how we enter this outpost of fairyland." The car crept carefully around the roundabout, circling the old church, almost hidden in the overgrowth of many years. Ravi sat mute, resisting this apparent nonsense. As they emerged from the roundabout, the Special Heritage Area Parking sign appeared and directed the car down a narrow lane to the parking lot.

Ravi and Mary Anne climbed out, shouldering their backpacks. They both felt a golden intensity and caught a hint of distant music, just beyond hearing. Rita (who was too intent on her Ph.D. work to notice anything else much) joined them and pointed to the tiny white flowers growing between the porous paving stones.

"For example, those probably aren't from here," she said. "That may be Irish moss, or pearlwort. I described it to my friend, and he wants to have a look."

"That's cool, Rita, very cool indeed," said Ravi. "It's the kind of thing that works really well with my Senator – scientific data. Tell me more about Professor Hill."

"His name is Royal Hill. His family is originally from the area, so he's curious to see it. I'll tell you what he finds when you get back – tomorrow, right?"

"Yes, I'll be right back," said Ravi. He and Mary Anne headed toward the trail leading to the crosspaths and the Hollymount Inn. Ravi needed to gather more information for Senator Max; Mary Anne wanted to get back to Pixie.

Rita drove back toward the roundabout, mentally rehearsing how she would traverse it to return to the so-called normal world ('Clockwise – then turn left. Clockwise – then turn left.')

Atop the hill near the parking lot, the little lady in her long dress and Hello Kitty apron stood outside her cottage, one eye on her playing children. She watched Ravi and Mary Anne trek up the trail and through the stone tunnel. 'That devil is quiet today,' she thought, 'but a bad thing is coming.' She gathered up her darlings and took them indoors for safety, and the hikers emerged from the tunnel and disappeared around the edge of the hill.

An hour later, the little lady observed Rita's car returning, her passenger Dr. Royal Hill. They had been chatting easily, but as they approached the roundabout he grew quiet. Royal was tall, a big man, his black hair worn in a single braid down his back. He said, "Sorry if I'm not talking, but this was our land a long time ago, and I need to focus."

They pulled into the parking area, and he saw the carpet of white flowers between the pavers. "That is so *weird*," he said, climbing out of the car and hunching down to examine them. He stood up and looked around at the surrounding meadow, the moss-edged trail up the slope, and waved to the little lady atop her hill. She waved back.

"Who's that?" asked Rita, who had never before noticed the woman or her tiny cabin.

"She's the guardian here. She watches both sides," Royal replied.

"How do you know that?" Rita asked.

"It's an old story," Royal said. "Let's talk about these plants. There are several that jump out as Northern European, not native here. And I see a couple of seaside species, very far from home." Royal pointed to a distant pale patch of flowers. "I wonder if I'm seeing eyebright?" He added, "*Euphrasia*, you know?" – thinking that would help Rita, who shrugged gracefully. To each their own expertise.

He gazed around in wild wonder. "This is unusual, all right." Royal walked up the slope into the meadow, hearing the humming musical song of the landscape. The air was golden with meaning. He bent to look at the plants, touching and sorting, making notes in a small notebook.

"Do you feel and hear it?" he asked Rita.

"I can't hear the highway, if that's what you mean. It's nice and quiet here." Rita was unobservant outdoors.

"What's all that?" he asked, waving his hand at the hillside.

"That's the trail, and it goes through the creepy stone tunnel and along the base of the hill, and eventually to the big old Inn where Maeve lives. I haven't done that part by myself, so we're waiting for my friends to get here and show you around." She glanced back toward the roundabout, but Harris's car was not in sight.

"Let's go up the trail a bit," Royal said. "I won't do any detail work today, but I want to understand this meadow and slope area. We'll be able to see your friends arrive." They made slow progress on the trail, Royal stopping to check flowers, muttering Latin plant names as he went. He came to a stop at the tunnel's entrance archway of massive carved limestone blocks. Overhead, a neon sign glowed red at the top of the arch, announcing ENTRANCE.

Royal did not like the sign or the tunnel and turned to look at Rita.

"Can we wait here?" Rita asked. "I don't like to go through this. It's got a bad vibe. Brian had some trouble here last fall." She glanced below at the parking lot and roadway – still empty.

"This is not a good place," Royal replied. "That little lady up there keeps her eye on it." He waved again to the woman, now tiny and distant. She did not respond, but stood with her arms folded.

Royal laughed. "She doesn't want me to go in, I get that. So let's go around." He walked to the outer edge of the tunnel and confronted a wall of thorny briars.

After examining the stems closely, he turned to Rita. "This is some type of bramble – *Rubus idaeus*, or whatever. I didn't see this before, did you?" Royal watched as clumps sprang up around the tunnel. Thorny brambles soon covered the hillside, stopping the two from walking anywhere but forward through the tunnel or back down to the parking lot.

"Or maybe *Rubus fruticosus*," Royal said, "bramble or blackberry. Found across the British Isles, closely related to its North American cousins. It's just finished blooming, and the fruit is forming. But we can't walk through it. How did I not see it before?" Tall thorny thickets now stretched across the meadow all the way to the parking lot.

"Can we please go back down the hill, away from this doorway?" Rita asked uneasily. She had never seen this happen on her several visits.

"There's something bad in there," Royal said, peering into the dark tunnel. "But my people were here first, so f*ck it," he said, stepping forward.

"Oh, thank goodness, here come Harris and Brian," said Rita, watching their car emerge from the roundabout and travel the short distance into the flower-speckled parking lot. She ran, or fled, down the path toward them. Royal waited at the tunnel entrance, watching as Rita spoke to the arrivals, jumped in her car and drove away, around the roundabout and back to town. Harris and Brian waved up to him, locked their car and soon joined him at the tunnel entrance.

"Hey," said Royal, extending a hand to each of the younger men. They shook hands while he continued, "Rita was kind enough to take time out of her work schedule to bring me here. Can you show me around?"

Brian said, "We'd like to show you the crosspaths and Apple Island and the Inn."

Harris was looking at the looming briar thickets. "Brian," he said, "something's up. I think we should go back to the car." But now the path below them was nearly overgrown.

"Forward, through the tunnel?" asked Royal.

"I guess we have to," said Brian. "You can see the daylight at the far end. We'll just run fast and stay away from that red glow." The two men peered in, moving back and forth to see the tiny dot of daylight at the far end. Royal waited for them to collect their nerves to go in. They all saw the red glow shimmering along the floor at the tunnel's midpoint.

Harris said, "This is summer. It's months until the end of October" – he did not dare name the holiday out loud – "What could be bothering…um, it…?" The brambles had spread along the pathway and loomed overhead, blocking their view of the parking area. Over the rough green and purple growth, Royal could glimpse the little lady on her hilltop, now standing straight, arms at her sides.

"Might be me causing it," said Royal. He raised a fist to the little lady, who returned the gesture. He stepped inside the tunnel and turned to look at the other two.

"I didn't expect this, but I'm not surprised. My people are from here. We had a village, and traded with the Cayuga and Seneca to the north, around the lakes. Our old stories say we were driven out by a magic woman who had a devil to help her. And then the settlers and soldiers came." He gestured for them to follow him in and walked forward into the dark, his voice floating back to them.

"This thing you're nervous about is not my devil. It was brought here by the magic woman when she first arrived. It has no power over me. So come on."

The three men walked steadily forward. At the center of the tunnel, the red glow pulsed in the floor, as Brian and Harris recalled from an earlier visit. Royal Hill walked straight across the pulsing area. The other two edged along the walls. Beyond that point they felt fresh air on their faces, the daylight grew, and they soon emerged at the far opening.

A neon red EXIT sign hung atop the tunnel arch, its light blinking on and off. The pathway was clear ahead.

On her green hilltop, the little lady had turned at the sound of loud engines, as three big black vehicles pulled out of the roundabout and roared into the parking lot. Black-clad helmcted figures leaped out, covering all approaches with their weapons. An explosion bloomed on the hillside, carving a smoldering hole into the wall of brambles. The little lady ducked back into her house and set about making it less visible. Trouble had arrived.

Outside the uphill end of the stone tunnel, Royal watched as the grenade opened up the dark green brambles to his right. "That's bad, right?" he asked. The three men jogged up the trail and around the bend toward the creekside cottage. Brian led the way, because he knew the people who lived there.

Hurrying feet could be heard running toward them through the tunnel. But only a few of the pursuing soldiers made it past the pulsing center, where a pit opened to engulf them. Emerging from the uphill end of the tunnel, the remaining handful of soldiers huddled defensively, guns bristling, below the neon sign that now read NO EXIT. The gate at the downhill end of the tunnel slammed shut and the neon sign now read NO ENTRANCE.

Royal Hill, Brian, and Harris were out of sight, in the cottage. Now two black helicopters circled overhead, flying fast and low toward the wooded ridge above Apple Island and the Hollymount Inn. The remaining black-clad soldiers swarmed forward along the trail.

The old creekside cottage is home to the small gentleman with his black cat tail and the lady with her soft white-tipped fox tail. They had opened their door to our friends. Brian asked Mr. Cat and Ms. Fox if they could warn their community about the invasion.

"Maeve already knows," said Ms. Fox.

Up the trail from the cottage, into the woods and straight on past the place where the paths cross, the land opens into Hollymount Valley, with its cottage homes and the old Inn, white against the deep green of the majestic holly trees around it. Maeve walked out onto the Inn's top step, listening for news and new arrivals. She had already informed Ravi Sen-Ellis that his friends were approaching, and had made irritated remarks about Royal, whom she called a "trespasser out of the past."

But now she stood silent. Mary Anne Washington came walking down the lane to the Inn, having bartered for garden vegetables with the lady in the pink tracksuit. She stopped, seeing Maeve silent and watchful.

"I'm afraid we have visitors," Maeve said as two black helicopters rose over the trees. The noise of the machinery was appalling. One helicopter hovered over the Inn as an amplified voice shouted unintelligibly. The other 'copter landed in the nearby pastures, driving the small ponies to the fences.

Helmeted and armed black-clad figures poured out of the machine, dementedly running to corners and edges, securing the valley for their master in Washington, D.C., and the ultimate master in Moscow. Spiderlike figures dropped on ropes from the helicopter hovering over the Inn. They circled the building, shouting orders to stand still, submit, hands up, surrender, drop your weapons, resistance is futile, and so on.

These words meant nothing to Maeve. She could not care less. But she saw that her followers in their cottages and her human allies were frightened. Ravi stood behind her in the doorway, the Innkeeper beside him. Maeve turned to Ravi as the first troops approached the steps.

"These fools are from the warlord in the D.C. palace," she said.

"Not from Tom King?" Ravi gasped.

"This is not his style," said Mary Anne. "They must be from the President." Maeve raised her hand at the soldiers who, climbing the Inn's steps, were pointing their foul weapons at her head. Two soldiers burst into flames and blew away in puffs of smoke.

From behind a black mask, a woman's voice, in a foreign language, directed the others to stay where they were and lower their weapons. She shouldered her gun and walked toward the Inn to speak to Maeve. These conventional military gestures, so familiar to our hunted and haunted humanity, meant nothing to Maeve.

"Hello, ma'am!" shouted the leader over the helicopter racket, snapping open the faceplate on her helmet.

"Are you speaking to me?" Maeve asked.

"Yes ma'am, you're Ms. Maeve, correct? We're here to help you pack your essentials and depart. I hope you will cooperate. It will go better that way." The leader stood still, gloved hands open to signal peaceful intent. Maeve turned to look at the armed troops positioned around her. Ravi was stunned into silence, wondering why this person wore no identifying insignia. And why her accent was distinctly foreign.

Mary Anne shook her head. "Careful, Maeve," she said.

"You must evacuate, ma'am," said the leader impatiently. "This area is under new ownership, as of now. Once you and your friends are safely relocated, you will be paid for your land and buildings." She turned to two men in black standing at her back.

"Go help them pack, as we discussed." She added a phrase that sounded like military code, until Ravi realized she had said "no prisoners" in Russian (one of the languages he had acquired in pursuit of a diplomatic career, before he was beguiled by a summer internship on Capitol Hill).

The two soldiers walked past the group on the steps and into the Inn. (It is noted here, ahead of the coming mayhem, that they were never seen again.) The leader called to the helicopter crewmembers standing near the cottages.

"Get these citizens packed and out of here. They can't take the animals. Assure them that their animals will be taken care of." Meaning, "We will shoot the animals while these people are being dumped on the streets of a distant city."

"This is not reasonable," said Maeve in a mild voice. She was smiling quietly.

In a tone combining exasperation with infinite patience, the leader replied. "Ms. Maeve, I have a special presentation, made just for you. Then you must go." The leader removed a breadbox-sized grey device from her backpack and pointed it at the Inn steps.

In the projected beam, a human figure flickered and grew. It loomed over everyone else, a twelve-foot hologram projection of the USA President, in his obese suit-clad glory. His gilded hair shone under the lights of the distant projection room.

The glossy figure spoke, small mouth wrapped around the words. “Hi, Maeve! I can’t see you, but I know you’re there. Thanks for doing this for me – and my investors – and for our beautiful country. I know you’re as thrilled as I am that this high-value spot will soon be a major center for peace-loving All-American investment and financial growth!” The flickering figure moved its arms and small hands in expansive, positive gestures.

“It’s gonna be great, I know you agree! And lemme tell you, you’re safe with these people, that soldier lady, and her troops. They will make sure you get what you need. Do exactly what they tell you, so that nobody gets hurt.” The giant figure flickered and faded away.

“That was a huge honor, ma’am, and I hope you appreciate it,” said the leader. She turned to check her troops, and watched in vain for the team that should have been coming along the trail through the woods.

Part III
The return of the natives

Chapter 8

Three methods are used to dispose of unwanted visitors to Apple Island.

The first one is to ask politely that they leave.

The second and third are rougher and more effective.

But first we need to catch up with Janet and Lena.

Since arriving in the Hollymount community, Janet had preferred the company of Acton and Greenwood. They reminded her of the older westerners she had known at the national park in Nevada. But that does not mean she liked them. It's just that they were preferable to Maeve and what Janet saw as her little cult at the Inn. Women can be like this.

The Hollymount area felt crowded, not a comfortable situation for a solitary person like Janet. Also, she was watching Maeve closely for any sign that she was still trying to seduce Brian.

Mothers are often like this! Lena enjoyed the more youthful company at the Inn and craved to get out, in a car, to the regular world. Children are always thus.

The two ecoterrorists had set up camp in the woods near the crossroads. Today they were on Apple Island, enjoying the eternal soft spring weather and cajoling the two old guys – Lena's words – into showing them the Island's portals. The women did not mention the pile of sparkling time tubes back in Kentucky.

"So that's the route to Ireland," said Lena, gazing at the sparkling shine at the base of the big hemlock tree. "And the time is hundreds of years ago at the other end, right?"

Greenwood nodded, but did not add any information. They were sipping endless cups of tea around the campfire, and Lena thought she would burst from the tedium of sitting with these horrible old men. But she had promised her mom she would help this morning. And then she could go up to the Inn where things were happening.

"Yes, and we came through that tunnel down there in the orchard, from Kentucky," said Janet, attempting to create momentum for further revelations about the other portals. But it was hard slogging.

Acton smiled at her. "And over there – " he waved his arm vaguely, "is where Brian fell into Venice, Italy, at the same time that you and others were there for some reason." Silence fell. The two men stared into the fire, poking it with sticks to yield a bit more heat.

"And your home is at the end of another tunnel, right?" said Lena brightly. They nodded, not looking at her. Lena turned to her mom and carried on. "So that makes four, but I don't know where theirs is." They did not offer to tell her where, so she said, "And there's more, right?" She looked at the silent men.

Acton finally stirred. "Why do you want to know?" he asked. "You aren't from around here. You two women are not well behaved to my mind. Why should we tell you anything? Your idle curiosity is dangerous."

Janet stood up. "Some powerful people are coming to take this place away from you. If we know what's here, we can help you protect it from them." She was losing patience.

"We can take care of ourselves," said Greenwood. "You two are as bad as Maeve. You better go join her at the Inn with all the colored folk. It is a crying shame she is letting them stay."

The two women sat silent, stunned by these ugly words. Greenwood collected their teacups and stood up, waiting for them to depart. If the beautiful spring day could have turned stormy, this was that moment, but cheerful May sunshine continued to pour down out of a robin's egg blue sky.

"Some other time, ladies," said Acton, bowing in the direction of the log bridge over the little stream. The middle of a quarrel is a bad moment to encounter a mutual enemy, so they were thrown off guard as three black-clad helmeted soldiers ran down the path and across the bridge.

Janet recovered first, pulled out Gene's purloined handgun, and shot the bandit coming at her. The other two raised guns to their shoulders, covering her and the two men.

"Lena – the Inn!" Janet shouted. Lena ran behind them, across the bridge, and up the forest path to get help. Acton and Greenwood turned and ran along the stream shoreline, but not very fast. They were leading the remaining two attackers to a portal for disposal. They disliked the strange place it led to, so they used it to dispose of unwanted visitors to Apple Island.

As Janet watched, the soldiers followed the two guardians into a thicket of white pines. Startled birds flew out, disturbed from their nests. After a few minutes, Greenwood and Acton re-emerged. She waited as they returned to the campfire.

Greenwood said, "All right, now you know another one. There's a hole in the ground – we step aside, they fall in."

"Where's it come out?"

"In a city somewhere. It's foreign. Cars all the damn time driving around a big circle, on the wrong side of the road. Crazy World, we call it. It's a good place to dump unwanted visitors."

They were listening for more intruders when the helicopters flew overhead on their way to the Inn. The clatter of the rotors was horrific, echoing off the cliff walls above Apple Island. Much as she disliked Maeve, Janet figured she would be more useful up there than with these unpleasant men. Without a word, or a glance for the fallen figure she had shot, she trekked uphill after Lena. The two Apple Island guardians were glad to see her go.

Acton and Greenwood moved back into the shade of the hemlock grove by their fire, waiting to trap any further invaders. Ever since that highway company had caused trouble last year, there had been problems, most of it because of women as far as they were concerned, and it was all Maeve's fault. They agreed to allow no one else onto the Island. The dead soldier lying at the entrance of this strange and sacred place would be a warning.

An evening with Tom King and Harlan Styce at home in a stately D.C. suburb.

Headed to Hollymount.

"Harlan, I'm back in D.C.," said King, calling the Senator as soon as his plane touched down at Dulles. "Can we meet and talk?"

"Tom! Good to hear from you, my boy. Sure, we need to get caught up. But first things first, I owe you an apology. I was not quite myself the other day and said some things to you that I shouldn't of."

"Oh, it's all right, Harlan, you and me, we go way back. I was kind of upset myself. But look, I need to see you. Your Senatorial colleague in Bowling Green hinted that I might be in some political trouble – "

"Yes, yes indeed you are," said Harlan. "And I'm sticking my neck out to meet with you. But this phone talk is no good. Say you come over to my place, and we'll get the staff to rustle up some country grub."

His long gusty sigh blew through the phone. "I tell you, I am ready to go back home to Kentucky and stay there. The atmosphere here is pure poison, under the new President. And I voted for him. Yep, Tom, just you come on over. Bad news, and worse coming."

Supper at the Styce home included some of the same ceremonial Kentucky dishes King had been served the previous night in Bowling Green, but he was not complaining. Tonight's main course was a hot brown. New to King, it was the ultimate comfort food for Senator Harlan Styce after a hard day on Capitol Hill.

"Puts me in mind of a good old New York special, the beef Manhattan sandwich," said King, as he used knife and fork to cut bites from the hot brown's layers of bacon, cheese, sauce, tomatoes, turkey, and toast.

"Stop right there!" said Styce, shaking his knife at King. "You damn Yankee! How dare you compare this heavenly Kentucky dish to anything from New York City!"

King smiled and they ate in contented silence. Styce's wife Marian was at a business meeting, so they found two comfortable armchairs in the living room following their meal. The staff set out coffee and brandy, and left them to talk.

"No drinks for me tonight, Tom," said Harlan. "I am doing penance for my bad behavior last week." He waited as they both poured coffee and then continued, almost shyly. "I am feeling the hot breath of sin nowadays. Like the Devil is gaining on me. Does that ever trouble you?"

Tom King was startled at this quiet statement. "Every day, Harlan, every waking hour," he replied. Their eyes met for a moment, Harlan's old brown eyes and Tom's sharp blue gaze, and then they both glanced away.

King shrugged. "But I'm not a godly man, Harlan, you know that. So it's the laws of science and the physical universe that are gaining on me. I did something reckless when I was younger, and I know it is gonna catch up to me."

"Sounds like the Devil, pure and simple, to me," said Harlan softly.

"We all have our different ways of understanding," said Tom. "Back then I made a choice in pursuit of academic glory. And last year I made a similar choice, in pursuit of career advancement. Something has been out of balance ever since, worldwide. I wonder if my actions caused the imbalance, the things that are going wrong." He sipped his coffee and closed his eyes, trying to quell the panic that was never far away.

Harlan was a wise old monster and did not want one-sided confessions added to the balance sheet between them. "Well, as for me, it's this new President," Harlan said. "He is making me think and do things that ain't right. And my anger at him is not seemly. I feel tempted into wickedness every time his name comes up." He set down his cup and cleared his throat. "Which leads directly to the trouble you are in, Tom King."

King nodded, sat up straighter, and poured himself another cup of coffee as Styce continued. "It starts with my once-trusted assistant Ard Sprinkle. Who we thought was working for us, to find natural time portals."

"A lot easier than building and opening new portals," said Tom. "I learned out in Kentucky they are big energy hogs."

"And less red tape to use them," said Harlan.

"Regulations haven't strangled them yet," agreed Tom. All this was familiar ground, and he awaited the new bad news.

"Cut to the chase," said the Senator, "Ard now works for the President's time travel investment group." He raised his head to look at Tom King. "I sure as hell hope you have heard about them?"

"I have been busy with the military and tourism time programs, so you better give me the details," said King, getting a glimmer of the trouble he was in.

"The White House Office for Time Travel Development," Harlan replied, "has hired Ard as their top consultant. Have you seen their website?" King's eyes widened and he shook his head.

"You go look at it later, but not at your leisure. It's required viewing, soon," said Harlan. "It reads like you are already gone. To your knowledge, you still have your job – correct?"

King checked his phone for messages and thought about the mail in his office that Mary Anne was no longer there to sort through. He had to hire someone – he was letting things slide – got to get back on the ball!

"To my knowledge, yes," he said quietly. "I am still the USA

Time Tsar, Departments of Homeland Security and Interior, with close ties to the Department of Defense. But not for long, you're saying?"

"Well, from what I have been able to find out, no one can fire you," said Harlan. "So I think you have a little bit of time. But they want to put the President's son in charge of the time programs, and they want to plunder the past for an investor group."

"'To plunder the past,'" King repeated. "What do you mean?"

"Seems that the Grosch Brothers and big-money boys like them are hungry to get at the wealth of ages past. From the history books, any kid can tell you where and when the gold was still in the ground, where the diamonds were embedded in the untouched South Africa kimberlite, where the big oil finds were waiting to be discovered. And the coal in Kentucky and elsewhere. They want to go in and bring it all to the present day. And that's just a taste of their plans."

King leaned back, closing his eyes, and stretching to relieve his rising tension. He said, "The President talked about these insane ideas back when I first met him, and he sent me a follow-up memo last month."

"And you – ?" prompted Styce.

"I laughed it off," said King. "Thought it was unbelievably stupid. No one would do something that dumb." There was a silence, and Styce shook his head.

"All right," King went on, as the late-night caffeine kicked in. "As far as I know, he can't get at our stuff in Kentucky. That's pretty well protected, and the military is on our side." He looked at Styce in sudden alarm. "Right?"

"For the moment, maybe," said Styce, "that's still our turf. But that place in New York State – that little valley and community that Ard was investigatin' – I heard that the President is going after it, right now, with a private army."

King stood up, his fear and weakness falling away. "He can't have it. Damn, man, what are you telling me!"

Styce was pleased with this reaction. He gazed wide-eyed at

King, gleefully fanning the flames. "His soldiers are not Americans, they're Russian," he said flatly.

King jerked, galvanized by the shock of this information.

Anticipating his question, Styce said, "We don't know how they got over here. Maybe in the private jet that accompanied Air Force One back from the President's trip to Moscow last week."

"I'm not set up to handle this," said King, sitting back down, pulling out his phone, running a hand through his hair. "The potential threats we modeled – that Hrudlu Vatson modeled – were all at the Kentucky site. The New York site was safe."

King stared at Styce as he realized what his own words meant.

"Well, well, so the Russia-born scientist on your team, appointed by the President, fiddled with the research results, you say?" said Styce, spreading his hands expansively. He sat back to watch King manage this crisis.

Maeve's voice flared inside King's head, letting him know that her valley was under attack.

King rose to his feet, shook Styce's warm dry hand, and moved toward the door, apologizing as he picked up speed. In the silence after his hasty departure, Harlan took off his glasses, put his feet up on the ottoman, and had a little nap.

"Yes, I need to talk to the Governor, please," King said, but to little avail, based on the chatter coming through the car phone. "Tell him there's a Russian invasion – " the call ended. King then called his office, and a late-working Time Travel intern answered. King's young political wizards quickly contacted the New York State National Guard and Congressperson Speed, whose district included the Hollymount community.

Speed's staff called the nearest State Police substation, and they dispatched two cars to check things out, it being a quiet evening. Twenty minutes later, they reported finding a tiny traffic circle on a private road in the middle of a field, and beyond it a parking lot with three big black SUVs, apparently abandoned, doors open, no license plates. Military hardware was scattered across the parking lot, and they had found the remains of three grenades.

The astonished police further described a fire smoldering uphill in a blackberry patch, and a closed door on a stone building with a flashing NO ENTRANCE neon sign. They had no idea this place was here and thought maybe it was an artist colony. They were interviewing a small woman who lived nearby.

"How about a drone overflight?" suggested the Time Travel interns, who deserve naming, in lieu of wages – Aggie, Stuart, and Ade. While coordinating King's travel to the site, they wished aloud to him that they could go along.

"Maybe later, when this is stabilized," said King, mindful that they were the children of influential people, and he did not want to put them in harm's way.

Early the next morning, King's plane landed at Elmira Corning Regional Airport. As the new business day dawned, he called the security office at Ten Thousand Secrets National Park and directed Lee Turner to cut off Hrudlu Vatson's access to his lab and offices. King also put in a request for an investigation into Hrudlu by the Department of Homeland Security. The person he talked with took the inquiry as a personal insult.

"Hrudlu's a good guy, an all-American patriot," said this middle-level Presidential appointee. "I reviewed his dossier myself. You got better things to do, Dr. King, than getting in his face with this false accusation."

Down along the Green, Green River.

In which science prevails momentarily, and an evil deed is named.

The day dawned overcast and hot at Ten Thousand Secrets National Park, already muggy at 7 a.m. In the hickory trees above the old ranger cabins, birds called to one another in low and dismal tones. Even the cicadas' buzz-saw whine was lackluster.

Steve Roberts sat outside his cabin on the old couch drinking from a mug of strong coffee, in a desperate attempt to wake fully. His in-person work with the Time Teams and dock engineers was nearly complete. After a final walk-through today, he would soon head back to his family in Ohio and get a good rest.

But right now he needed a clear head for the bigger situation. Yesterday evening, Hugh Hynes had taken him out for a chat along the Green, Green River by the old ferry crossing, where the far bank was deep in greenery. Upstream of the fenced-off Pleistocene and portals area, this old-fashioned spot was untroubled by shimmering lights and power grids.

"Remember when it was all like this?" Hugh said. They watched the cable-drawn ferry put off for the other shore, two cars onboard. The trip took about a minute. Upstream to their left, the steep-sided river valley rose into the darkness, filled with the summertime noise of buzzing insects and frogs wailing their love songs. Downstream to their right, the glow of the portal area shimmered through the trees.

"Can't go back to then," said Steve guardedly.

"Hell we can't," said Hugh. "It wouldn't take much to pull the plugs on all this high tech trash. Literally pull the plugs out of the walls, then pull the walls down. Drag it all to a landfill."

He tossed a pebble toward the quiet green river water, and it went in with a small plunk. "Exactly what do you think you're doing, Steve?" Hugh asked, leaning in to capture Steve's gaze.

"My job," snapped Steve. "And I'm damn good at this work."

"It's not what you were hired for."

Steve shrugged, wondering if he could just walk away, knew he could not.

Hugh pulled him down to sit next to him on a green bench. "And you're not working in the spirit that you used to bring to your work."

'Uh-oh,' thought Steve, 'he's got me there.'

"Where's my subversive buddy Steve? The man who brought the highest standards and ethics to coordinating the research of two massive federal agencies, seeking the truth at the heart of our work, and ensuring that we did it right?"

Steve let this sit a bit, then replied. "Hugh, the situation since last fall is so delicate. I could have been fired, maybe imprisoned, for associating with the ecoterrorists. Tom King told me that, and then he gave me a new start, as head of thc time travel program for the public. I don't want my career to die. My family needs me to have this job."

"So he's blackmailing you."

"OK, yes. But so what."

"So I'm back now. Doesn't that count for something?"

Steve nodded.

"And we've got Ed Zanetti back into the D.C. office. Remember him, the guy who directed our time travel research for twenty years? Your direct supervisor?"

Steve Roberts turned to look straight at Hugh Hynes, close beside him on the green bench. "I hear you loud and clear," he said. "But – " Steve gestured widely, to include the Park and his enormously complex task, which he was doing so very well. It was extraordinary creative work, and he felt good about it.

"Look, Steve," said Hugh. "Your work is astonishing. But we need you back as our science coordinator, to help us rebuild a safe and honorable time program. You know what these greedy monsters have in mind – Tom King, and the President, and Senator Styce, and their military allies. They will do irreparable damage to our planet, to nature, to humanity, to history, to the future."

Steve smiled at the energy and passion of his friend and fellow scientist. "What do you want from me, old friend?" he asked.

Hugh nodded and spoke rapidly. "Some big changes are coming in the next couple days, and I need you to be ready to support them. Officer Lee Turner and the security staff are onboard, as is most everyone I used to work with before King tried to kill me. Even some of the new folks here prefer science over military might. And the old program in D.C. is coming back to life. King's takeover is on very shaky ground."

"'Big changes,' like what, exactly?"

"Steve, we're heading across the river tonight. I need you to be ready to help Dr. Greene and her associate Dave Caver when you hear from them, OK? That's all I'm asking of you right now."

Anyone watching would assume that the two green-uniformed men were discussing some detail of Park policy. And they were. Steve looked at the river, then back at Hugh.

"All right, Hugh, that's good, I can do that much. But I am not going to sacrifice myself for a lost cause." Hugh nodded, adding a few details that Steve reluctantly agreed to. Then they stood up and headed back along the trail.

Remembering this conversation the next morning shocked Steve fully awake. He stood up from the bench, shook out his mug, and climbed into the Park vehicle for the short drive to the Science offices. His mood was positive because he no longer felt alone. And Hugh had named the cloud he was under: blackmail. Steve was glad that his family was a safe distance away from whatever was coming.

So many stars in the Pleistocene night sky.

Unpleasantness at the Time Fort & Barracks.

That night at the Green, Green River, the half-built dock for the Oxford Time Trip gleamed in the moonlight and shifted slightly under the weight of three stealthy intruders. A small motorboat engine quietly put-putted to life and headed toward the Pleistocene portal on the far bank. Insects and bats played overhead in the security lights along the river.

The boat pulled up just downstream of the portal, which was humming with energy that discharged in a sparkling shimmering curtain along the riverbank. The portal doorway was a dark opening through which the three figures moved quickly.

The deep chill of the Pleistocene night hit them hard, and Dr. Hugh Hynes shuddered in disbelief that he was already back at the scene of his torment. A Jeep was parked next to the portal on the frozen ground, and a pile of discarded beer cans gleamed in the starlight of that ancient night sky.

The blaze of stars overwhelmed the trio – Hynes, Dave Caver, and Dr. Gabriella Greene – who sank deep into her puffy coat as she gazed upward, stunned by the vast dark sky, white with stars, thickly spread out in a sparkling blanket overhead across the entire night sky, from edge to edge of the endless plain where they stood in a cold and rising wind. The creak of the Jeep door opening called Gabby back, and she climbed in with the others.

Hugh turned the vehicle around, its headlights illuminating the eyes of a passing group of low-slouching beasts. He edged forward toward a light at the Time Fort, gleaming in the distance. The beasts stood where they were, not moving, not hostile, just curious. After a few nudging tries, he drove around them.

No one spoke. They bumped over the frozen hummocky soil, gazing at the illuminated dashboard map that displayed the few known landmarks of the surrounding area. Hugh nodded with interest to see the new mapping and monitoring appear on the screen, including notes about animal and big bird sightings.

Soon the outer edge of the map included the area along the ancient line of the Green, Green River, including the location where Hugh had been stranded. Notes appeared regarding the habits of the tigers inhabiting the old cave entrances along the river. Hugh shuddered and concentrated on creeping quietly toward the Time Fort.

He halted the Jeep and turned off the lights so they could look at the one-story, dirty brown prefabricated building, about a quarter mile ahead of them. Several other vehicles sat around it; there were piles of fuel containers and machinery. A shed at a distance held a small helicopter. The scene was neither sinister nor impressive.

"It all looks so normal, if you don't think about it," Dave said quietly.

"And yet, this basic bivouac is the first major step by the military-industrial complex to change the future," said Hugh. He turned to look at Gabby and Dave, all three sitting quietly in the darkened vehicle.

"King and his engineers are using that kook Hrudlu Vatson's plan to jump forward in time from here."

"I burrowed into some classified documents, thanks to the hacking skills of my very best student," said Gabby. "They have a lab in that nondescript building, and big computers to calculate jumps forward in time. So they can establish more forts between the Pleistocene and the present day across the river."

"And for why?" Dave asked plaintively.

Gabby replied, "They want to correct things in history, to make the USA dominant. They want the USA ruling the world, in the past, present, and into the future."

"That ain't right, somehow," said Dave. He glanced out the open window as Hugh started the engine and drove to the fort. "They better not do that. I gotta admire my man the President's attitude – it's the beauty of simplicity. He likes these time travel projects because there's big money to be made."

Hugh backed the vehicle up to the building for a quick getaway and shut off the engine.

Dave was not quite done. "But that ain't right, either. My man should leave the past alone. So should these guys," he finished, climbing out of the Jeep.

They walked to the fort's small door. One by one they climbed through the seals into the quiet reception area, where a low light gleamed. At a table in the conference room beyond they saw a human hunched over their laptop, deep into work, typing like blazes.

This was Turing, who felt the change of air flow and looked up. They rose and leaned over to turn on more lights at a wall switch.

"We have visitors!" they called to unseen sleepers. "Hello Dr. Hynes, it's an honor to meet you. I'm Turing," they said, one hand resting lightly on the laptop keys, ready to resume work.

"Pleasure," Hynes said, walking past Turing to the mass of humming hard drives and blinking screens assembled on tables along the far wall. Thick cables ran in every direction. Dave and Gabby stayed in the reception area as two sleepy people emerged from the bunkroom.

Gabby said “Hi” in a friendly way, because she had seen them at the Park.

“So what’s this?” asked Hugh, gesturing to include the tangled array. “More of King’s so-called science, to promote USA world domination?”

“I love this work,” Turing said mildly. “It’s very interesting. That there, please don’t touch, is our set of information boards for moving to the next Time Fort location. Calculating the ways and means. I was monitoring and tuning it, and you interrupted me.” Turing sat down and resumed their quiet keyboard work, uninterested in the discussion.

“You should be ashamed of yourself,” said Hugh to Turing, who had tuned him out. Hugh turned to the others, Chris and Emma. “How can you sleep when this is going on around you?”

“This is not your research, Hynes,” said Chris Lopez sharply. “You are out of date and out of line. You should not be here. How did you get here?”

“I’m in charge of science for Ten Thousand Secrets National Park, you bitch,” Hugh replied. “Tom King tried to murder me and steal my job, but he failed. And this is not science. This is an apocalypse-level attack on our planet and our human and natural history. For the glorification of one damn country. For shame!”

He glowered at Emma Brown, who huddled into her robe and looked down at the floor, in silent agreement with what he was saying. Suddenly the exciting adventure was over, and her conscience came roaring back to life.

“As of right now,” said Hugh, “I am in charge of this research and this facility.” Turing, at a difficult moment in their work, glanced up and nodded at the new boss, then returned to the screen.

“You’re not going to get very far,” Lopez said. “This is a joint Homeland-Defense project, top secret, and has nothing to do with your little Park, which is just a convenient place for us to do this. You need to give up now before you get hurt.”

Even pleasure-seeking slackers like Dave Caver have their limits. He got right into Chris's face, shouting, "Then you and your military asshole buddies can get the hell out of our Park. No one asked you to butt in here. This Park is for public enjoyment and the protection of nature. Go somewheres else with this destruction and pollution. You people have ruined the rivers in our cave. Killed the cave critters. This time travel crap is a total waste of government money."

Dave was sputtering bravely toward incoherence when Hugh recalled him to their mission. "Dr. Greene, can you take our gallant hero Dave out of here?"

Gabby grabbed Dave by the elbow and propelled him outside. They took their bags and cave equipment out of the Jeep and set off on foot. They were heading to the present day via the back route, with some judicious spying and monkey-wrenching along the way.

Hugh gave them twenty minutes as a head start, distracting the Time Fort staff, before returning in the Jeep to the river portal. Back at the Science office in the present day, he would sit tight until Gabby and Dave reappeared. After that, the real fun would begin. The team was ready to roll, and even Steve Roberts had agreed to help. Hugh was impatient to dismantle this mess and begin to restore the Park.

A brief Oxford, England interlude, around September 2012.

That midnight, rain fell steadily on rooftops, gardens, and streets. Water gleamed on the pavement, under streetlights illuminating narrow ancient alleys and broad new thoroughfares. Church and college spires were shrouded in low cloud, their tolling bells muffled. This was a cold rain, presaging autumn.

Snug in college rooms and homes, people noted the blue lights and screaming sirens of passing police vehicles. Some shuddered at the thought of having to deal with trouble on such a nasty night.

Two police cars and an ambulance converged on the small sweets shop situated just north of the Kennington Roundabout, not far from the international campground. A man was slumped in the phone box, telephone dangling next to him. He looked up when help arrived and asked, "Did you see them? They headed down Old Abingdon."

The ambulance attendants shushed him, lifting him into the vehicle while tending to his wound, a gunshot to the arm. Sirens on, the ambulance sped away. The sound of shots and screams pulled the police on foot and in vehicles toward the campground, where a few hardy souls were camped in the rain.

"Oh please, no children," whispered a police officer over and over as he and his partner ran through the poorly lit campground entrance toward the few remaining tents. His flashlight illuminated a Travelers caravan wedged into the trees and shrubs at the rear of the open area, its occupants out on the grass trying to calm their frantic ponies.

These men and women turned to the policemen, shouting and pointing to the west, away from the town center, toward the low hills that lay beyond the rail line and ring road.

"It was spacemen!" one man shouted.

"Nazis!" screamed another.

The slashing headlights of arriving police vehicles revealed a wider scene of knocked-down tents and underclad young people staring transfixed into the lights, most of them shouting. No one was hurt. They had been singing in a quiet circle by the Travelers caravan, huddled under ponchos and blankets, when three "giant men" appeared out of the night.

"Nightmare robots from a film, screaming and shooting," cried a young woman.

"They stole my car!" a tall Scandinavian man said. "Forced me to give my keys! Shooting their terrible weapons into the trees!"

"Their heads were covered in black plastic globes!"

"Black suits of armor!"

"Enormous black spaceguns! Russians – they spoke Russian!" This last came from a woman holding her small shaking dog. A police vehicle took up the chase westward, powering through the roundabout and uphill toward Boars Hill. Spotlights shone into homes and gardens and across the river meadows, seeking the missing car.

"It's that damn hole, it's come unstuck again," muttered the foot patrolman to his partner. He pointed to a dim glow at the center of the roundabout, distantly visible through the rain.

The two men slipped off toward the roundabout on foot, as other officers took names and statements from the campers and cajoled the night manager into opening the small administration building for overnight shelter. The two officers ran through the concrete underpass below the circling roadway into the roundabout's center, planted with shrubs and grasses.

At the lowest point, a pulsing, shimmering glow poured out of a circular hole in the ground, casting an eerie light on the roundabout overhead, where noisy vehicles circled endlessly in the night.

"We'll need someone on guard here until they can fix it," said the officer to his partner, making a call on his cell phone. At Chronos, Ltd., he was invited to leave a message. "Right, lads," he said. "Your last fix did not work. We have an emergency, with three spaceman-style armed terrorists on the loose up Boars Hill. That doorway is open. This is your problem. Come close it so it stays closed."

The Chronos staff had trouble controlling this portal. Someone from their 1965 office needed to manually step into the streaming future to check for problems, and they did not do this regularly. Nor could they keep it closed.

This phone message went unheeded for a week. Meanwhile, the trio of terrorists was killed off by specialists, who pursued them on Boars Hill across Matthew Arnold Field, and cornered them atop Jarn Mound. Their futuristic Russian gear vanished into the Ashmolean Museum. Eventually Chronos resealed the portal and promised better results "in future."

The portal had first blazed forth during construction of the Kennington Roundabout in the 1960s, when a big yellow bulldozer dug it open. Chronos, Ltd. receives a princely fee to keep it shut – in cooperation with unnamed national security services. A long-term study is underway to develop a visioning statement to create a task force to design a plan to send in an exploration team from the Oxford end, with no progress to date.

So far, the portal traffic was one-way, and rare – small North American wildlife such as racoons and opossums have crept out into the English rain; and two young hikers from the USA emerged who never, ever have figured out what happened. Returned home via airplane, they were years younger than they had been, or everyone else was years older.

Chapter 9

The Battle for Hollymount Valley, Part 1.

Choices are made.

By 9:30 a.m. King had arrived via a police-escorted SUV at the magic parking lot beyond the roundabout.

"I guess he's just a hands-on kinda guy," said the New York State policeman in wonderment, watching Tom King climb aboard a black National Guard helicopter that would carry him from the parking lot over the devilish brambles toward the Hollymount Inn.

The 'copter flew above the NO ENTRANCE stone tunnel, swerved over the path beyond, and touched down in the meadow by the small creekside cottage. King climbed out, hoping that someone here could tell him what the situation was on Apple Island and at the Inn. He walked through the long meadow grass toward the cottage, hands out to show he was unarmed. The black helicopter behind him belied this gesture.

As a rule of thumb, a well-dressed tall broad-shouldered white man with expensively styled white hair posing as harmless should never fool anyone. A drone buzzed overhead, transmitting every move back to the New York State Police troops in the parking lot.

The cottage door opened, and Ravi Sen-Ellis stepped out to meet Tom King. Behind Ravi was Harris. Watching through the window curtains were Royal Hill and Mr. and Ms. Cat and Fox. Brian was fast asleep under a nearby tree, following a busy night.

The previous day, Maeve (and the little lady, on her hilltop) had watched magically as Royal directed his friends and animal allies to trap and tie up four of the seven black-clad foot soldiers – the few who had gotten through the tunnel. Three evaded them and ran off toward the crossroads, where they had made the mistake of turning left down to Apple Island.

Royal, an Iraq War veteran, asked Maeve's special friends – the enchanted cat and fox and smaller wildlife neighbors – to help. He directed his human companions to act as lures, bringing the invaders close, so they could be trapped and disarmed.

Later that night, the captives lay near the cottage, each wound thickly with brambles, bound at hands and feet with tough grass ropes. Chipmunks and voles, the smallest animal helpers, had been ingenious and enthusiastic with the winding and the binding. Royal was shocked at the little beasts' willingness to help and wondered if Maeve had harmed their animal selves in her need for friends and supporters.

In the warm evening darkness, he, Brian, and Harris huddled around a small campfire, talking in low and urgent tones. Mr. and Ms. Cat and Fox had retired for the night into their cottage, which was small and a bit too animal den in its styling and scent to be comfortable for the three men.

"I have a class to teach tomorrow," said Royal. "And this situation is not what I agreed to help Rita with. I got very little information about the native plant species today, and I tell you honestly I don't want to return here."

"So you don't feel like this is a homecoming, huh," said Harris.

"The distant past of my family and tribe is interesting, and important, but I want to do other things. I'm a global guy, not a local guy. Don't want to get stuck here, that's certain."

The three had attempted to eat the cache of grasses and seeds generously donated by their tiny allies, but gave up, stomachs rumbling.

"Let's get some sleep – " said Harris, but Brian interrupted.

"I'm going to the Inn," he said, standing up. "I need to know what's happening there."

"And can you give that message from the Park guy to Janet?" said Harris. Hugh Hynes, trying to reach Janet, had contacted Harris via Facebook. "You think you'll be OK?" Harris asked, rising to his feet.

Brian said only, "See you," and was gone, moving away silently along the path to the crest of land between the cottage and the community around the Inn. At the crosspaths he turned left downhill to the bridge at Apple Island. There he was warned off by the sight of a dead black-clad soldier lying next to a lopsided pole flying a yellow "Don't Tread on Me" flag, with its coiled rattlesnake.

There was no sign of Acton and Greenwood, because they had returned through the tunnel to their home for instructions in this emergency.

Alarmed, Brian walked quickly back uphill, turning left on the path through the dark nighttime woods toward Hollymount Valley and the Inn. He realized that the trees above and around him were filled with birds, disturbed and agitated, all speaking at once. Two foxes sat in the path looking out toward the Inn. They were silhouetted by bright white light and ran back into the woods as he approached.

Brian crested the rise to find the small valley and Inn pinned down under spotlights. Generators grumbled noisily, powering the harsh lighting, which pried into every nook and cranny around the homes and Inn. Animals and people were cowering indoors, seeking quiet darkness and not finding it. The path ahead of Brian led straight to the Inn, and every foot of the way was visible to observers.

How could he get there? Brian walked along the edge of the woods, looking for an unobtrusive route. He would have to go a long way around to stay outside the lights. He considered climbing down into the Apple Creek valley, to his left. But there were big vehicles over there, and he saw the outline of a helicopter, with people and machinery moving. Bats were flying above the lights catching bugs – the only sign of normal woodland night life.

Maeve's voice spoke inside his head: *"Move forward. You are cloaked."*

Brian looked around, and across the valley he spied a tiny figure standing outside the Inn. So he stepped forward into the light. He showed no shape and cast no shadow, and a thousand cameras and trembling electronic trip wires did not see him jog along the path. Brian crept past a second helicopter, averting his eyes from the blinding lights that demanded his surrender.

They were waiting for him inside the Inn's big doors, which the Innkeeper swung open just enough for him to slip inside. Maeve let the cloak drop as Brian entered, and he appeared suddenly to her, Ravi, and the others.

"Hey – hi!" Brian said to them all, adding, "Thank you," to Maeve, who bowed her head quietly. She stepped past them out the big door, into the night, to continue her watch.

"I was with that plant scientist and Harris at the Fox-Cats' cabin," Brian said. "Figured I'd better check in here and find out what's going on." To Lena he added, "I have a message for you and Mom, from the Park."

"From the Kentucky Park – Ten Thousand Secrets?" she asked in astonishment, wondering how anyone there knew where they were. Her emotions rose toward panic, but Brian's steady voice was calming.

"Yeah, from the Park," he said. "Did you hear that the dead scientist came back?" Lena turned to their mom, who had appeared from upstairs to hug Brian. "Yes, we found Hugh," Janet said briefly, not wanting to overshare about anything in this dicey situation.

"Well," Brian went on, "he called us and said to tell you that he needs your help back at the Park." Janet leaned her head against Brian's strong shoulder, then stepped away from the group to think.

"BOTH of us?" Lena cried out in dismay. Her mother turned to look at her, sadness in her eyes. "Mom, I don't want to go back," said Lena, her voice rising, "I feel safe here for the first time in a long time." Janet pulled her away gently, and they went to sit near the fireplace, crackling with aromatic flames, to talk quietly.

Brian watched them, then turned back to Ravi and Mary Anne. The Innkeeper had set a big table for the entire group, so they settled there to talk and eat.

The Innkeeper leaned over to pour fresh tea for Brian, who eagerly sipped the hot liquid. He picked up a cookie and popped it into his mouth, eyes on the covered dishes that the Innkeeper was carrying to the table. Once upon a time, Brian feared being trapped by the fairies if he ate their food. After six months confined by the thuggier parts of the U.S. government, he was a lot less particular. He was hungry, so he would eat.

"The very thoughtful mice and voles and the Fox-Cats pooled their best tasty tidbits for us, but the pickings were kind of lean," Brian explained, peeking under the lids to see a stew, a savory pie, and vegetables. A mighty platter of cheeses was added. The Innkeeper, smiling, topped up Brian's tea.

Unaware of the apparent dangers inherent in eating fairy food, mortal man Ravi lifted a wedge of the pie onto his plate and passed the dish to Brian, who served himself and handed the dish along to Mary Anne, who served herself and put a slice on the Innkeeper's plate next to her. The remaining pie came to a rest next to Lena's place, to be served when she and her mom came back from the fireplace. It was a big dish, mushrooms and carrots in gravy spilling out of the steaming crust, with enough for Maeve, were she to alight long enough to eat.

"What's going on out there?" Ravi asked Brian, who was seated next to him. "I have to urgently report to Senator Max. She needs to know that Russian-speaking soldiers directed by our nation's President have invaded U.S. soil. There's a bunch of laws being broken here, and I hardly know where to start. How can I get out?"

Brian replied, "Wow, man, please slow down. Give me ten minutes to eat. I am famished." Ravi nodded, and they all ate the good food gladly, in silence.

Maeve glided in to sit near Mary Anne, and started the conversation going again. "Who are these black-clad soldiers? Where are they from? They are mortal, like you, but their speech is different. From the East." She gazed around the table.

Ravi spoke up. "They're from Russia. The new warlord in D.C., the man we call the President, is allied with Russia's top warlord. But these soldiers are breaking our country's laws by being here. By taking over American land. And the President is a traitor for using them."

This was a good style for talking with Maeve.

She said, "America, the USA. That's what the people who worked on that grant, and who are building the big road, told me is the name of this land." She looked around the table for agreement, receiving warily unbelieving glances from the others.

Maeve smiled winningly. "I have been tucked away here so cozily for a long time – a long time according to you brief firefly human beings. You flicker with light and life, and then you are gone."

Brian felt her young, ancient blue eyes on him, and did not look up. The Innkeeper leaned over to refill Maeve's tea. She picked up her cup to sip and went on.

"This was not a named place, except by Royal's people, when I arrived, for me such a short time ago. I will have to ask him what their name was, because I have forgotten – it was not important to me."

Janet was replete with the good food, but felt ensorcelled by Maeve's style, and chafed to break out of it. She compromised by turning her chair to face the fire, sipping at her tea and watching the flames. She steered a new log into place with her feet and tried to relax.

Lena felt her mother's impatience and faintly understood her dislike of Maeve. Janet disdained glamor and mistrusted women who weaponized femininity.

Also, Lena knew that Janet was now eager to be gone – to go back to the Park and help Hugh Hynes. But Lena wanted a quiet place to live her young life in safety. She liked it here, and being with her brother and the others in that small house in town.

The Innkeeper and Mary Anne (who had no intention of ever again leaving what she had found in Hollymount Valley) cleared the table and brought out a dark aromatic cake. Even Maeve had a slice.

Ravi tried again. He was eager to leave, and needed to report to Senator Max. "Brian, can I hike back with you to the cottage? What was going on there when you left?" Brian finally lifted his eyes from his plate and began to talk.

"That plant scientist professor Royal Hill is a military veteran, so he got us and the animals to trap four of the soldiers. They're tied up near the cottage, and I have to get back to help with that. We're near the entrance tunnel, Ravi, but right now that's closed."

He pushed back the cake plate with a contented sigh and nodded his thanks to the Innkeeper, who bowed in reply. From the fireside Janet was watching him, face soft with memories about her boy. The three family members smiled at each other, aware that partings were coming soon.

Brian said, "If Maeve can get us past the lights and vehicles out there, Ravi, you can come with me. I know that Royal also wants to leave, because he has a class to teach." Brian smiled at this mundane detail.

Maeve spoke up. "I have summoned Tom King from D.C., the warlord's fortress town. To stop this warlord. But Tom King wants this place for himself. He wants to drive us all out of Hollymount Valley."

"And he wants to put a weapons-proof dome over Apple Island," added Ravi.

"You know this?" asked Maeve, startled, turning to him.

"That is Tom King's plan, yes," said Ravi. "How did *you* know?"

"Oh, I listen in," Maeve replied airily, reassessing Ravi as more influential than she had thought.

Ravi repeated his request to Brian. "I really need to reach the Senator. Can we go soon?" Brian nodded, getting up from his seat. The Innkeeper gave him a basket of food to take along. Brian thanked him and turned to his sister and his mother.

Janet leaned close and murmured in his ear, "I'm heading back to the Park. You stay safe and take care of your sister, and let's meet again soon in a more comfortable place. I love you." Brian hugged her fiercely, his strange mom.

He whispered, "See you soon," to his sister, with a hug, and looked at Maeve. She nodded, and he and Ravi vanished. They cracked the door open and jogged steadily on the path under harsh lights toward the distant trees, while Maeve kept watch on the steps of the Inn.

The two men were soon back at the Fox-Cat cottage, carrying the food basket from the Innkeeper. In the darkness Royal Hill stepped away from the deeper shadow of the tree he was leaning on, and came forward to greet them. A sleepy Harris sat up. Nearby lay the four tied up soldiers.

"Is that food?" Harris whispered. Brian handed him the basket, from which a scent of mushrooms was rising. Harris laughed, and handed around small pies as appetizers. While they took the edge off their hunger, the four men exchanged news about the Inn and the situation at the cottage.

"My top priority is to get back to D.C. and tell the Senator what's happening here," said Ravi. It was four a.m., and they could hear nothing from the distant parking lot. They listened, captivated by the quiet sounds of owls and insects, and birds calling sleepily.

"The tunnel and slope are still blocked," said Royal, "but Harris has an idea, if he can stop eating long enough to tell us."

Harris held up his hand, asking them to wait. He carried the much-lighter basket of food to the cabin door, set it down, and returned to the group. Eventually the Innkeeper's feast was shared with their hosts, the prisoners, and the smallest vole and chipmunk.

Harris said, "Yes, I think we should try to get an Internet signal here. Maybe it isn't magic but the hills here that interfere with cell tower reception. There's a tower close to the highway project parking lot. If we connect, we can send messages for Ravi, and I can alert Rita to the situation here."

"It'll be getting light soon," said Royal. "Harris wants to climb up on top of the tunnel to see if that helps with phone reception. Let's wait for dawn and try it. I think things will start happening today." While he spoke, they heard distantly the sound of cars approaching the parking lot, soon joined by the chatter of helicopters.

As dawn crept across the land, the little woman watched the parking lot from her cottage on the hill, and Maeve observed the latest moves by the black-clad occupiers of her valley.

During the night, the soldiers had unloaded two small bulldozers from the big helicopter parked across the valley from the Inn. At first light, one dozer was noisily tearing down the fences around the valley's small homes. The other was scraping and widening the path from woods edge to the Inn. Two men with chainsaws were felling the tall, ancient trees where the woods began. This destructive approach had worked for the President when he was a real-estate developer, because it forced people to leave a place he wanted. As President, he figured it would work here, too.

Maeve knew the time was approaching when she would take her valley back. But not quite yet. Her human helpers had been busy during the hours of darkness, and she wanted to see the outcome of their actions. But not for much longer. Her curiosity about the outside world had come to an end.

The biggest challenge to her peace of mind was not these black-clad soldiers, but Royal Hill. In him, an older power had returned to her valley. He had a natural affinity for the land here, and the animals recognized him. She had even heard the trees whisper, in their sibilant leafy tones, that the first people were coming back.

This would not do. Long ago, she had taken this upland valley as hers, creating a trusting family with her animal friends, and she would not let it go. Beneath her nostalgic longing for Ireland, she knew she would never return to that overpopulated frantic fairy land. This, here, was home. Maeve did not know what a veteran was, but she did not want him here. Royal would tear apart her peaceable kingdom.

Yesterday, Janet had told them that three Russian soldiers had run down toward Apple Island – but had gotten no farther. She had said no more, but Maeve knew how they were disposed of. This too worried Maeve – the tough female power wielded by Janet. Neither Janet nor Royal were beholden to the devil Maeve had brought with her from Ireland. They could easily overwhelm Maeve and drive her out.

The fairy was puzzled by human beings. Reckless, generous, foolhardy. And when they got deeply into an endeavor, they lost interest in the sensual side of our shared worlds. Their brief lives were filled with conflict and confusion, and had ceased to interest her. The fun here was gone, Maeve thought. Time to bar the door.

King stepped down from the helicopter. Crouching beneath the rotors he walked toward the small reception committee waiting outside the Cat-Fox cabin. "Mr. Sen-Ellis!" he exclaimed. "Not in the office after all, I see." He did not approach the cottage, which the helicopter crew was surveilling for signs of danger.

Ravi shrugged off his comments as impertinence. "We have these terrorists for you, sir," he replied, gesturing at the four soldiers, who had had an uncomfortable night. Their weapons lay in a pile near Tom's feet.

King poked the pile gingerly with his foot and asked, "Who sent them here, do you know?"

"I was over at the Inn yesterday," said Ravi, "And heard them speaking Russian. There's about twenty of these guys over there, commanded by a Russian-speaking officer. With two helicopters. If they're not your troops, can you help get the situation under control?"

King replied, "The New York State Police don't like the Hollymount Inn setup – it's an armed compound, with foreign terrorists and kidnapped American citizens. They want to clean it out." He smiled tightly and walked closer to Ravi and Harris as he spoke.

"So sure, I can offer Maeve and her little band of hippies a safe exit from the area, if that's what you mean."

"Appreciate the offer," Ravi replied, "but Maeve has directed me to tell you that everyone has to leave. She said, 'I will take it back.'" He and Harris did not move.

"I'm in control here," said Tom King, Time Tsar.

Ravi smiled, polite but dismissive. Emerging slowly from the cottage, empty hands visible, Royal Hill saluted the 'copter crew and stood next to Harris, listening to Ravi and King's conversation. Shocked awake by the helicopter, Brian joined them.

King said, "We'll head over there now and deal with these invaders. After that, we have plans for a nice new cottage village for Maeve's group, a few miles away. I want to clean out the weirdos living in that old inn with her." King wrinkled his nose in disgust.

Royal Hill stepped up to Tom King. "You ignorant piece of shit," he said. King backed away, stepped forward, and realized he could not dominate this hard man.

"Sir! Control yourself!" he barked.

Hill turned away, walked over to the prone prisoners, lifted one by his ropes and tossed him into the open helicopter door. He had tossed in the second one before the 'copter crew stopped staring and took over the task.

Ignoring King, Royal walked over to Harris. "Let's get you set up," he said. "I'll help here a while longer to make sure this damn fool doesn't add to the damage."

He turned to Brian. "Come on. Don't waste another minute of your precious and irreplaceable time on this rat bastard." Royal winked at Ravi, standing next to the stunned King. "I'll send that message for you, if we get through," he said.

Hill, Harris and Brian headed along the path to the tunnel, where Royal climbed the rock wall to the curved roof. There he was clear of the surrounding slopes, and the sun peeked around the hill as it rose. With a boost from Brian, Royal hauled Harris up beside him. They stood atop the stone structure looking down the briar-choked slope to the parking lot, busy with vehicles, helicopters, and pcoplc in uniforms.

Royal sat down at the edge of the tunnel, legs swinging over the "NO EXIT" neon sign. Harris did not like edges, and sat a few feet away, hoping to find stray Wi-Fi or satellite signals for his phone.

"I've seen some weird things in my day," Royal said to Brian, who was standing on the path below. "But this – this situation – is truly unusual."

Brian paced around the end of the tunnel and trail, watching for approaching dangers. Monitoring the four cardinal directions, and above and below. The dark purple brambles pressed close.

"How can you be so relaxed?" he called up to Royal.

"Probably because I'm ignorant of the danger," said Royal with a smile. "Have you been involved with this place for very long?"

Harris, on the verge of Internet success, whispered to Royal, "Brian is the guy who went to jail for supposedly colluding with those Kentucky ecoterrorists – " followed by "Yes!" as his phone linked into our teeming world.

Royal called delightedly down to Brian, "You're the son of the woman who blew up that damn casino?"

"That's part of it, yeah," said Brian.

"Those developers destroyed the last known population of a rare goldenrod species when they built that resort," said Royal. "Got in there before we could stop them and poured poison all over it. We couldn't prevent them from building that monstrosity. In a national park! I was so GLAD when she, and wow, your SISTER, man – blew it up. Cool family."

All three raised their heads to watch the black helicopter rise from the cottage, carrying Tom King and Ravi over the woods toward Hollymount Valley.

"They're off to see the fairy queen," said Royal, "and Russian soldiers led by our nation's President!" He tipped his head back to laugh, then turned to Harris. "You get in?"

"Believe it or not, yes!" said Harris, bent over his glowing device. "I sent a message to Rita and she'll put out the call. We got it all lined up."

Royal called the good news down to Brian, then said to Harris, "'Lined up'? Like what exactly?"

"We have almost one hundred thousand followers on the Save Brian Owen and the SoTier media pages. A lot of them are nearby and ready to come here. Rita just posted about the "'Local fairy community under siege,'" and the numbers – oh my goodness, it's – up to one hundred fifty thousand – two … " Harris looked at his phone, as dozens of calls and texts flowed in from friends, strangers, and media.

Royal began working with his phone, sending messages to his office about being late, missing his class, telling his mother and family that things were weird and they should check the Brian Owen news online, and asking his grad students to find out about certain Northern European plants and shrubs. And, at Ravi's request, he sent a brief message to Senator Elizabeth Maximus, to update her.

This intense ten minutes of connection was broken abruptly when a second New York State Police helicopter lifted out of the parking lot and roared low overhead, following Tom King to Hollymount Valley and the Inn. The three men fell flat, climbed down from the tunnel roof, and walked back toward the cottage. They waved to Mr. Cat and Ms. Fox, and continued up the path toward the Inn.

Meanwhile, heeding the social media call to gather, hundreds of cars, trucks, vans, and motorcycles began flowing onto roads and byways toward the Highway Spur Construction Site and the enchanted roundabout beyond.

To Apple Island and the sparkling portal to Kentucky.

Mother and daughter make choices.

During the night, Maeve had stood on the front steps of the Inn, watching the destruction of her community. By mid-morning the next day the Russian commander was directing her troops to lay waste to the Hollymount homes. The bulldozers scraped clean a circular perimeter and were knocking down fences and small outbuildings. The residents of the valley clustered in and around the one remaining small house.

The commander's plan was simple. Soon these discouraged people, separated from their animals, would climb on a bus and be carried to a distant town, to be dumped on the streets, a method that had always worked for shopping centers, casinos, and golf course resorts. Just business, for this President and his family.

The Russians had separate, secret instructions to build an independent command post nearby, so drones were buzzing around the heights above the Inn, seeking a defensible location.

Janet was ready to go back through the time tube to the sparkling pile under Oakland, Kentucky, and help Hugh Hynes at the Park. The destruction in this valley was not her concern. She did not have a minute more to spare for Maeve worship, or for what she regarded as the turbulent "East Coast politics" of Ravi, that psycho Tom King, the ego-driven U.S. Senators, and the peculiar New York City man in the White House. They would resolve their problems as Eastern elites always do. She preferred the action-oriented Kentucky team at the Park, and she trusted Hugh. There she could be useful.

Maeve was glad to see Janet depart. She gave the two women advice and supplies, and whispered to Lena that she was welcome to return. Cloaked by Maeve's invisibility device, they were soon past the worst of the noise and destruction. Lena followed her mom through the woods to the gorge overlook, a good place for their secret descent to Apple Island (they wanted to avoid Acton and Greenwood). She had yet to make up her mind whether to accompany her mom or to stay with her brother. Lena wanted to stay – but she was fearful that Janet would have trouble in the unstable collapsing time tube.

So when the helicopter carrying Tom King flew over the Apple Island gorge, Lena was dangling on a rope halfway down the gorge cliff. She closed her eyes at the shock of the noise. Crows flew away in a cawing crowd. Janet watched anxiously from below, belaying the rope for her daughter's descent.

Once the engine echoes had subsided, Lena continued down the rope, landing next to her mother on the rocks at the creek's edge. Leaving the rope hanging, the duo shouldered their packs and splashed through the creek to the shimmering shore of Apple Island, where sunshine and apple blossom scent awaited them. They moved past the portal to Venice and into the heart of the orchard.

Janet turned off the path to walk under the blooming trees to the one with a glowing opening at its base – the time tube back to Ten Thousand Secrets National Park. They slid inside and scrambled along the passage downslope from the entrance, then paused to breathe.

Even now, Lena could not say goodbye. She wanted to make sure her mom made it back safely through this unstable time tube. It had partly collapsed behind them when they came through to Apple Island. Was it passable?

As they walked forward into the glowing tunnel, Lena eased into the topic of goodbye. "You know how in New York our family always is ready before anyone else, up earlier in the morning, at the Inn and in town?"

Janet was absorbed in climbing over the piles of loose rock that had fallen since their last trip and watching for unstable ceiling rocks. She nodded, trying to pay attention to Lena's conversation.

Lena went on, "Brian and I think that's the time difference between the Park in Kentucky and Apple Island in New York, if you travel through the time tube. It took us a while to notice the difference." They had reached a clear stretch of tunnel in its descent toward the low point.

As they walked side by side, Janet said, "I wasn't paying very close attention, honey. Sorry. But I don't mind being out of step with others."

"Exactly, Mom! At the New York end we are sixty-three minutes earlier than the rest of the world. I think that means we're safe with our New York friends. Or safer, anyway."

"I don't get it," said Janet. The cave ceiling got lower, and they hunch-walked toward the dark and oily cross-stream ahead. "I didn't feel any difference."

"We're just a little bit out of sync," said Lena. But now the passage changed, and they grew quiet. They splashed through the nasty dark cross-stream and began to walk uphill toward the far opening below Oakland, Kentucky. Here the floor was covered with new rockfall from the ceiling, but moving cautiously they found a clear path and could walk upright.

After another five minutes of climbing alongside her mom, Lena saw ahead the sparkling light of the tube's end in Kentucky. She stopped. Janet realized Lena was no longer with her and, fear clutching at her heart, turned to look at her daughter. Their headlamps gleamed, illuminating droplets of moisture in the air.

"So, Mom," said Lena. "You and I have to do this next part separately. You know I love you forever." Janet could not speak, and simply nodded, her helmet light moving up and down. Lena saw this and said, "When you get to Hugh, can he send us a message that you arrived safely?"

Janet found her voice, deeper than usual. "All right, that's good, I understand. And you're safer there. I can warn you ahead of time. You take care of yourself and your brother, and we'll get through this. And then we can find a place and time to all be together for a while. I love you both so much."

"OK, Mom, I love you and already miss you," said Lena. She wanted to go with her, but she did not move. Her mother turned and walked away, the glimmer of her headlamp vanishing as she climbed toward the big room in the Kentucky cave.

Lena headed carefully back the way she had come, across the stream and up the sloping passage beyond, the apple blossom scent growing stronger as she neared New York daylight. They were both crying, but they kept going.

On Capitol Hill, Washington, D.C.

Senator Elizabeth Maximus speaks out, with consequences.

Morning looked a lot like the night before in Senator Maximus's Capitol Hill office. The cleaning crew had done what they could by removing dust and emptying the trash baskets, but the fact that the Senator's workload was overwhelmed by events was evident in the piles of policy documents on her staff's two desks and in semi-orderly heaps on the floor.

In contrast to this disarray, the top edge of her desk was lined neatly with orderly stacks of important papers: pending bills. The only sign of morning life was the coffee machine, aromatically chugging its way through the brew cycle, and a stray beam of sunlight that had found its way past the thick curtains.

It illuminated the Senator's hands where they lay folded before her on the desktop. She stared at her hands in the sunshine and smelled the coffee. Max felt as if she might burst with tension, and held her hands still as an act of self-control. She suspected that Tom King and her old buddy Senator Harlan Styce were up to something, but all she had to go on was "a bad feeling." She craved the facts, which could only come from Ravi. But he had not returned as promised.

"Yes, thank you sir," said her aide Ayesha, ending a call with Steve Roberts at his Ten Thousand Secrets National Park office (in the final throes of the Oxford trip planning). Ayesha shook her head at Senator Max: Ravi wasn't there, either.

"Try his phone again," said the Senator, who was too worried to do this herself. But it only rang. Two days of silence – he always reported in every evening, and he had said he would be back by now. It was nearly 11 a.m. Senator Max sighed and got to her feet, putting her phone in her bag. "I have to go. I'm voting Yea on this one, right?"

Ayesha nodded, patting the top left pile on the Senator's desk. When she was nearly at the door, Max said, "Keep looking for him. Can you find the number for that place he visits in that little New York town, Horseheads – I think the people there are named Harris and Rita. Not much to go on, but – " and she headed out for a vote in the Senate Chamber.

Ayesha had heard about these people from Ravi, so she tried social media first. Twenty seconds later she was reading:

Magic Community Under Siege by Armed Gunmen

> Two days ago, the Utopian/Faerie community of Hollymount was attacked by unidentified gunmen in black uniforms. We don't know much yet, but you need to come now, join us, and help free these gentle, wise people.
>
> This beautiful 400-year-old community in the hills south of Corning, NY is under siege from Russian-speaking troops, who have shot up the countryside and destroyed woods and homes.
>
> Community organizer Harris reports from the scene that he is barricaded in a secret location and is calling for us all to come help. Bring food, tents, bicycles, and all your media. (Directions follow.)

Photos of a black helicopter flying above treetops and vague views of countryside accompanied this message. It had been posted three minutes earlier. Ayesha sent it to Senator Max, who emerged from the elevators, head down, reading the news release. As she crossed the hall to the Senate Chamber, she received a phone text:

> Madam: Ravi (last name?) asks me to inform you he is safe but unable to depart from rural site. Constrained by force incl T King. R says pls investig. use of Russian troops by POTUS hope you understnd. Bad here mst go. – R. Hill

Liz Max was electrified and enraged by this message. She entered the Senate Chamber and walked directly to Senator Harlan Styce's desk on the Republican side of the floor, causing consternation among those hoping or fearing she was switching loyalties on this important vote.

"What – what – can I do for you, my dear?" Harlan asked, drawing back at her fierce expression. As his fellows gathered eagerly around to listen, she came to her senses.

"Afterwards – outside!" Max snarled. She turned away and headed for the Democrat side of the chamber. Following the roll call and vote, and subsequent declarations of virtue and insinuations of vice, the U.S. Senate in its grandeur adjourned for lunch.

Senator Styce found Senator Max waiting for him just outside the Chamber doors. He chose a pleasantly bland approach.

"Liz, I have a hankering for the bean soup today. Shall we keep it simple, or go whole hog to the dining room?" He began walking.

"Stop right there, Harlan," said Liz. "Talk right here."

"But – " he protested, looking around at colleagues and staffers passing by, curious, straining to listen.

"Fine with me," she replied, loudly. "This scandal will be national news very soon. Already is, on social media."

"Ah, yes," he replied soothingly, "my grandson has been trying to teach me about the Internet. He says it will help me understand our country today. I hope he's wrong, I really do," he went on, in the fretful whine of the upper-crust Southern male. 'What does she know?' he wondered, catching the eye of his top staffer, who cut through the crowd like a shark and stood, silent and attentive, at Harlan's side.

Liz shrugged. "Beefy protection is not going to help," she said. "Tell me what Tom King is doing in New York State, Harlan."

"Oh that, ha hmmm," he said. "You mean that little place up there that you and I discussed at our recent cozy lunch? He might be there checking something out."

Styce shrugged to suggest that he knew nothing more, ending lamely, "I think he's due back later this afternoon, so just get the details from him." He turned to walk away, his aide flanking him protectively.

As the gap between him and Liz widened, she called loudly, "I think you know that my staff and members of the public are under attack there – from Russian troops. In New York State! What is Tom King doing there?"

The crowd around them had thinned, just in time for a passing cable TV news crew to hear her words. Turning on their microphones and readying their cameras, they headed in her direction.

Ten minutes later, the President ended a call with the news crew. They were interested in his reaction to Senator Max's announcement of Russian troops in New York State.

The President spoke to the aide hovering at his elbow. "Max needs to have her free-speech rights rescinded." He looked around at his ever-present admirers, and continued, "Let's do that. Target individual loudmouths on Capitol Hill. Especially the women. Get that done. Dial her down so she can't speak." The aide nodded and ran off.

The President said, "Am I smart or what? Nobody else thinks of these things. I am the right guy to bring this country back to greatness." He glanced at the gaping faces around him. "Right?" They all nodded, made supportive noises, and some clapped.

Back in her office, Senator Maximus stuffed a briefcase with laptops, chargers, and papers related to the next two bills. It was time to get off the Hill and stay with friends in an undisclosed location. Ayesha had put together a work kit for herself and rushed out the door with her cheerful warning – 'don't answer the phone and keep your head down' – hanging in the air behind her.

Senator Max immediately answered her phone, to be asked by a friendly reporter what she thought about the President threatening to take away her guaranteed Senatorial full free-speech rights. She replied, "I am just leaving," and within ten minutes was outside the perimeter of the free-speech control zone, via the back doors and secret golf cart routes and subterfugeous corridors known only to her ilk.

In the multiblock belt of giant federal agency buildings surrounding Capitol Hill, there was turmoil within and between the departments of Interior and Homeland Security. No one could reach Dr. Tom King, the federal Time Tsar, whose office intersected these agencies.

Also, the young talent was on the road: King's trio of interns had read the social media call to protect Hollymount and were in a car speeding north through Pennsylvania. "Bigger than Woodstock," many people shared as they drove.

Armed observers from one of New York's numerous Southern Tier private contractor defense companies were on their way to the roundabout, concerned but skeptical about reports of Russian troops. The Russian Ambassador to the USA spoke on talk show radio and television, denying the presence of Russian troops on American soil. He and his family then boarded a private jet to Moscow. A retired four-star general explained to the public radio audience about the international ramifications if Russian troops were found in the USA. Fighter jets stood ready as the National Terrorism Advisory System declared a heightened threat alert.

A team of investigative science reporters from the premier New York newspaper had been nosing around the rumors of "time portals" for several weeks and suspected that this small besieged "artist colony" was part of the story (they could not abide "Utopian" or "Faerie"). Their main informant, Ard Sprinkle, was nowhere to be found – he had been severed from the outside world at the President's most obscure golf course community.

The reporters' other source, Ed Zanetti, was known as the brainy genius who had built the time travel program back when it was managed by the Federal Park Service. When interviewed, Zanetti had steered clear of politics by feeding the reporters details about Best Management Practices and other science-based tools that keep the past safe from impacts by visitors from our time. But now he, too, had quit answering his phone and email and social media queries.

A sharp intern hacked into a top secret bibliography listing a report by Tom King, *The "Grandfather Paradox": Results of a Field Study With Defense Applications,* and they were trying to get permission to read it (provided in the Appendices to this novel, page 298).

The President sent out a media message:

Had a great visit with Russia's President in Moscow – shared important information. He's helping me with a private deal in upstate NY. It's just business. Private business.

Kentucky, both Pleistocene and present.

Sneaking past the sabertooth tigers – all the way to the Deep Space complex.

After leaving the Time Fort, Dr. Gabriella Greene and Dave Caver walked under the blazing star-packed sky about two miles to where Lena and Janet had rescued Hugh. There, they headed downslope to the rock shelter where he had slept while trapped in the Pleistocene.

Next to that small stony cavity was a hole leading to a larger cave, home to a sabertooth tiger family. Beyond their smelly lair was a big cave room. On its far wall, Gabby and Dave planned to climb up to a small cave passage that leads under the Green, Green River and into the present day.

More climbs would take them to the cave passages beneath the Park's science and administration buildings. They knew this route from Hugh, who had come that way with Lena and Janet the previous autumn. On the day he was trapped in the past by Tom King.

Their planned route then lay through the ruined casino and hotels, damaged by Janet Harper's bomb and the ensuing fracked gas well explosion last November. Finally, they would reach Deep Space, the subterranean suite of meeting rooms and science labs installed for Tom King and his military allies. Once in the Deep Space complex, Gabby and Dave had several goals:

Explore the facilities and exit the cave safely.
Map as you go (*expert caver technique*).
Find the other entrances to Deep Space – where do they connect to the surface?
Take control of all access in and out.
Take control of power, lights, air, security, water, etc.
Don't get hurt.
Report back to the team.

As they walked through the giant night, Dave felt oppressed by his surroundings. "How cold is it here?" he whispered, appalled at the eternal stillness around them. The starlight was bright enough to illuminate the flat horizon ahead, and the rising moon cast their shadows on the frozen rocky ground.

Gabby did not reply: She grabbed his arm and shook her head. He remembered with a shock that they were prey to ancient predators and began to pay close attention. They were being stalked.

On the single repeating night Hugh had been there, the tigers had slept in a big warm pile of parents and children. But tonight was a different night, and a tiger was out. Their flesh crawling, Gabby and Dave crept down the slope toward the rock shelter and walked out onto its stony roof.

During Hugh's several-month stay – the same twenty-four hours endlessly repeating – he had checked out a hole in the cavern roof beyond the tigers' den. Gabby and Dave hoped to bypass the tigers there.

The tiger following them was the youngster who had terrified the waitstaff at a Ten Thousand Secrets National Park casino restaurant the previous year. They had found him rooting around in the dumpster, snarfing up discarded burgers and chicken. This was the same young tiger that Janet and another park ranger had chased into the cave passages below the Casino. That night, he had run back through the cave to his family in the Pleistocene, reeking of ketchup and BBQ sauce. Tonight he smelled these foods on Dave and wanted a bite.

His parents had kept him close after his return. He was too young to be following delicious odors into strange places. But now he was a big, big boy. He roamed in search of his own territory and hunted to satisfy his growing hunger. He moved closer, easing up and over the bouldery surface to come alongside the tasty-smelling human.

Anticipating this as the most dangerous part of their trip, Hugh had waived two Best Management Practices for Time Travel. Specifically, the duo could ignore:

"BMP #3.1.a-d.: Do No Harm. Breathe Shallowly (mask where possible). Touch Nothing. Do Not Speak.

BMP #3.2.: If anything is bent, broken, twisted, etc., by participant (see Footnote 3.2 for full list), ABORT TRIP."

Gabby and Dave each carried a handful of flash-bangs, small nonlethal explosives intended to frighten. Not on the list of approved Time Travel BMPs! Dave was holding a spray can of bear repellent. Gabby was doused in mixed herbal oils, which both the tiger and Dave found disgusting.

Dave could smell the tiger now. He positioned his spray-holding hand as they moved toward the hole into the cavern. Gabby readied a flash-bang. They were going to have to jump into that hole, and the landing was going to hurt. Walk – don't run – walk very fast – but *don't run.*

The tiger felt a surge of warm affection for his prey and moved in to embrace Dave. His hug would be savage and fatal, so Dave began to squirt spray as they jogged toward the hole in the rock, black under the starlight. Most of the spray went into the tiger's fur, making him itch; enough went into his eyes to slow his crushing embrace.

"Go! Go!" shouted Gabby, and Dave leaped into the hole, rolled into a ball, helmeted head tucked. The tiger turned on Gabby, who threw the flash-bang directly toward his muzzle, where it ignited with noise and light. The big boy recoiled.

Gabby followed Dave down the hole, controlling her descent, and landed on a ledge five feet below the surface, sliding toward the edge and the big space below. She held on, and called quietly down into the darkness.

"Dave!"

"OK! Kind of!" he called back hoarsely.

Gabby scrambled toward the cavern floor below, where she could see his headlamp shining.

Aboveground, the tiger was not burning bright, but the ground around him was – the frail wisps of vegetation crackling with a low flame. He was unhurt, except for his dignity, and ran off in the direction of conventional food on the hoof, determined to restore his self-respect with a great big bloody treat for his family.

We cannot pause right now to consider the butterfly effects of those burning grasses, but rest assured, empires rose and fell as a result, ages hence.

Dave was on his feet when Gabby reached him, feeling his shoulders and arms. "I didn't break anything," he whispered – the tiger den was nearby, across the big cave room they had dropped into – "but my shoulder hurts pretty bad. Let's go!"

They edged around a heap of mud and rocky debris toward the rear wall of the room. Water trickled from a hole twenty feet up the rocky surface. That was their route.

How did we get here?

This is the place where Hugh Hynes was ejected from the cave passage by a wall of mud and rock when Tom King pushed the CONFIRM REVERT TO THE PRESENT DAY prompt on the Time Re-Set panel in the control room far above in Ten Thousand Secrets National Park headquarters. Far below, the muddy deluge propelled Hugh fifty feet across the cave room, where he lay unmoving for several hours.

Unaware that the passage had subsequently reopened, Hugh emerged from his concussion sufficiently to creep away from the mess of rock and mud. He lay in a hole in the rock near the outdoors. The tigers were terrified by the explosion and stayed away.

Because of the Park's time control setting to keep the Pleistocene in a single repeating day, this series of events repeated for many agonizing days, leading to trauma for Hugh, and also to determination, tenacity, and murderous intent toward whoever had done this to him. He eventually remembered enough of the movie Groundhog Day *to adjust his daily repeating narrative.*

He had explored, looked down the hole in the cavern roof, walked uphill to look for humans, and had a daily bowel movement in the wilds of the Pleistocene.

After several months, a new element materialized: a package of ready-to-eat meals appeared near the path, with a note: "Help is on the way." When he awoke each repeating day with a splitting headache on the floor of the cavern, the idea of those meals helped him get moving.

One day, while approaching the food, he heard a helicopter and felt a strong urge to hide. That was not how his friends would come looking for him. When would help arrive? Many repeating days later, he saw Lena and Janet standing by the food, and began to run and shout.

Hugh had drilled this experience and information into Dave and Gabby. They carried old-fashioned compasses to add directional detail (taking into account the movements of magnetic north over the intervening millennia). The compasses were not very accurate, but provided directional suggestions in the flat, overcast, sometimes foggy Pleistocene landscape.

Gabby and Dave climbed up the wall in the cave room and entered a small passage, about the size of a narrow tall hallway. Water splashed underfoot in a shallow stream. They scrambled over rocks, debris from the flood when the passage reopened. Soon the ceiling overhead began to drip, plunking on their helmets.

"We're under the river!" Gabby said, her voice muffled in the tight cave passage. They both felt the moment of nausea indicating they had moved into the present day, out of the Pleistocene. After a few hundred feet, the tight passage opened into a beautiful bowl-shaped cave room. A tattered rope and badly lacerated inflatable raft lay in a pile of rocks and mud at the base of the narrow stony canyon that led upward to the next cave level.

Dave spared a glance back from where they had come, at the small wet passage that led under the river to the big cave room and the Pleistocene. This was where Lena and Janet had realized that Hugh was no longer behind them – when the passage was suddenly choked with mud and rocks. Today it was gently blowing air.

Far above, in the Park's time settings control room, Hugh Hynes had set Officer Lee Turner on guard to ensure that no one was meddling with the time controls while Dave and Gabby were in these cave passages.

The climb up the stony canyon was no big deal for these tough cavers, especially as there was no water flooding up toward them from beneath, as had happened with Janet and Lena. The space narrowed near the top, where they squeezed around several boulders that had gotten stuck when the passage reopened. They had to take off their packs and shove them up around the obstructions.

The duo popped out, like workers out of a manhole, onto the dry floor of the cave lake. They could see the roof of the cave overhead. Another thirty-foot climb and they would be on a tourist trail that connected to the old cave exploration areas, the ruined casino-restaurant zone along the Styx River, and Deep Space beyond that.

The two easily finessed the final muddy side passage upward and were soon resting on the wooden dock, staring down at the bed of the empty lake below. Here, Lena and Janet had been rescued by Steve Roberts and interns, leaving Hugh behind, assumed dead.

"That was easy," said Dave, rubbing his shoulder, legs dangling over the edge of the pit.

"Where do you think they should install the tiger gate?" asked Gabby mischievously. The route was open all the way back to the tiger den, and their scent would linger for a long time. Dave jumped to his feet and began walking up the tourist trail away from the lake room, Gabby following.

They were soon in cave passages that led to the surface, and could feel and smell fresh air. The small streambed alongside the trail was dry, its flow diverted elsewhere by the big blast the previous autumn. They walked in the streambed to get around the broken cave walls where the fracking gas well had blown out, littering the old tourist trail with limestone boulders.

Ahead, daylight streamed in from far above through holes punched in the domed roof of the casino complex by Janet Harper's bomb and the ensuing gas well explosion. Shafts of light illuminated the battered and broken casino and hotel district along the Styx River. In its bed, the water flow was at its summertime low, a trickle they could step across. The two cavers heard trucks and people on the terraces above. Cleanup was complete, and new construction had begun.

On the far side of the river in the cave wall, they found the small ventilation shaft that Hugh had located on a diagram of the Deep Space conference center and military command post. They removed (and replaced behind them) the gridded vent cover and crawled for twenty feet, emerging into a large dark space that smelled of engines and chemicals and damp concrete.

According to the diagrams Hugh had found online in the Time Tsar's office, they were in the security services bay, part of the interlocking set of workshops and labs surrounding the Deep Space center. They crept along the floor, staying low to avoid laser beam intruder-detectors. Pinpoints of light shot back and forth across the room as they crawled. Gabby eased herself up the wall next to a set of illuminated red buttons and began to shut it all down.

A door slid open in the wall, and they walked through a medical suite and weapons and munitions storage areas. Dave took some items, and Gabby pretended not to notice. They made note of two big ramps with doors for the wheeled vehicles in the security area, and locked the mechanical wall devices marked "outside access."

Lights were on in a room across the next hallway, and they heard voices. This was marked on the diagrams as a Time Research Lab. Dave waved a newly acquired handgun hopefully at Gabby, but she rolled her eyes. They passed by silently, out into the big conference room.

In every space, Gabby was turning off security and control devices, and adjusting settings to "low" or "off." Officer Turner had provided a tangle of key fobs and metal devices that further disabled and disarmed the security coverage. As Gabby walked through the meeting rooms, turning stuff off and noting locations, she found a master control panel in a small room next to the EXIT panic capsule. She turned off every glowing light, but an unmarked red button under a metal grill she left alone, only taking photos.

Gabby eventually found Dave in the food service area near the rear wall, filling his pockets with packaged treats. He had already slid a couple bottles of Kentucky's best bourbon into his pack.

"We ready to go?" he asked pleasantly. "Just getting back some of the taxes the government steals from me," he added, shoving a twelve-pack of mixed salty snax into his bulging pack.

"Give me a break, you don't pay any taxes," Gabby said.

Dave grinned at her. "We need a private way in and out of here," he said. "Come see what I found." Beyond the dining area was a small kitchen, at its rear a storage closet full of cleaning supplies, mops, and boxes of disposable food containers and plates.

Dave shined his headlamp into a dark corner, revealing an old wooden door with a lockable metal knob. There were no control panels – this was old-school. He bowed to Gabby, and she stepped forward to open the door. "You already looked?" she asked.

"Just a peek," Dave replied. "It's real dark, wherever it is. Smells like a cave." She reviewed the Deep Space diagram on her phone, said, "Wow!" and opened the old door. A healthy scent of mud and water breezed in as Gabby peered into the darkness. Her headlamp illuminated stalactites overhead, and the metal of an old tourist trail railing. Dripping water was the only sound.

"It's the Frozen Waterfalls trail!" she whispered in delight to Dave, who already knew. This trail was not far from the secret cave exit in the wall of the old staff laundry room. They stepped through the door, and Dave closed and locked it from the cave side. The two tired cavers began to relax, having safely completed their mission. Now they had to report to Hugh.

"I'll come back and change out this lock for something sturdier," he said. Fifteen years earlier, this cave trail had been a popular tourist route at Ten Thousand Secrets National Park, so they knew it well from their younger days as park rangers. With the arrival of the Casino, hotels, and Pleasure Domes, the cave tours had ended, leaving these trails in the dark.

Today they trod their well-loved labyrinth in the cool comfortable cave darkness. In a side passage, they came to a short metal ladder with a manhole cover in the cave roof overhead. Dave climbed the ladder and poked at the metal disk with his flashlight.

"It's unlocked," he said, carefully pushing it open. Light filtered down to Gabby as Dave climbed into the closed cupboard on the wall of the room above, peeking out to make sure that no one was doing their laundry.

Moving fast, they climbed out of the stone-lined cupboard into the laundry room, closed the manhole cover, replaced the jugs of detergent, shut and latched the cupboard door, and stepped outside past the old couch onto a familiar woodland trail of the Park. After dropping off their packs at Gabby's car and changing clothes (in the parking lot: cavers are like this), they combed their hair with their fingers and headed to the Science offices.

Officer Lee Turner looked up from the front security desk and winked at them. "How'd it go?" he asked coolly.

"Missions accomplished," said Gabby, heading off to the glories of a modern bathroom. Dave tossed a snack pack to Lee, embossed with the Deep Space Conference Center logo (not very top secret). Lee grinned, and phoned upstairs to tell Steve Roberts and Hugh Hynes that their late afternoon visitors were here. Gabby emerged from the bathroom, the hand dryer howling behind her.

"Is Hugh in?" she asked.

The smile vanished from Lee Turner's face. "He's got that ecoterrorist b-i-t-c-h in there with him," he said.

"Damn, I thought we'd gotten rid of her," said Dave, as they climbed the stairs.

Lee called after them. "Hey, you two, I think he's sweet on her. Let me know what you think, OK?"

Chapter 10

The Battle for Hollymount Valley, Part 2.

The situation is explosive – Ravi, run!

As they approached the place where the paths cross in the woods, Royal insisted on seeing Apple Island.

“It’s bad, man, something ugly happened,” Brian warned the others as he, Royal, and Harris jogged down the Apple Island Trace.

“My grandmother told me the old stories about this place,” said Royal. “I want to see it.” At the foot of the slope, they looked across the stream at the dead Russian soldier, draped with the collapsed yellow “Don’t Tread on Me” Gadsden flag and its coiled rattlesnake.

This tableau was too much for Royal, who roared, “What the F*CK is WRONG with people?” He stomped across the log bridge, lifted the flag, and opened the black helmet faceplate to reveal the pallid face of a young man.

“We need to put sacred things in the right places,” he said gently, rolling up the flag and wedging it into his backpack. He carried the dead man back across the stream and laid him at the foot of a big pine tree on the wooded slope. Brian and Harris helped pile branches and leaves over the slender youth. A moment was given for silent farewells.

Back on the island, Royal looked around to contemplate the sighing evergreens, the fire ring, and the path to the eternal apple orchard, shining in spring sunlight. A young woman walked down the orchard path toward them, and Brian ran to meet his sister.

"Mom went back to the Park," Lena said, drying her tears. They hugged one another with sadness, relief, and a dawning sense of liberation.

"Where are the two wacko racist vigilantes you told me about?" asked Royal.

Harris said, "Hey, that's not nice. They're just protecting their culture. Um – I take that back. You're right." He walked toward the log bridge and called back, "Thanks for speaking the truth, Professor. We sure don't want to meet them here, and we need to get to the Inn." The others followed him up the path.

"That was our farmland, that island, in the old stories," said Royal as they turned left at the crosspaths toward the Inn. "The apple trees are a nice touch, but they're settler crops."

"Where do you learn these things, sir?" Harris asked respectfully.

Royal eyed him skeptically but replied gently, "At home, and in college. You should try it."

They crept forward toward the open land of Hollymount Valley, hearing loud noises and shouting. Big trees that had shaded the path lay fallen around them. Ahead was an ugly scene. The path to the Inn was torn up. A circle had been bulldozed around the edge of the community, and one of the small houses had been reduced to a pile of debris. Wooden fences separating the cottages had been torn down and set on fire atop the demolished home.

The heat and flames had driven away the little ponies and other yard and farm animals, who huddled behind the cottage of the woman in the pink tracksuit. She and the animal-human inhabitants were clustered on her porch to watch the confrontation at the Inn. Animals and birds looked on from the shelter of the surrounding woods.

No one was looking in their direction, so the four humans walked slowly forward on the rutted path. Ahead, Maeve was facing the two bulldozers, which were roaring and huffing to get to work on the Inn behind her. The Russian troops were massed around the machines, awaiting orders from their leader, who stood in front of them. All were focused on Maeve.

Weirdly, the giant President hologram had been redeployed and loomed, wavering and flickering, again reciting its greeting and warning. The volume had been turned down, so they could hear its menacing tone, but not the words.

The approaching group saw Ravi, standing near Maeve. He had edged toward her and away from Tom King, who stood with troops and crew near the State Police and National Guard helicopters. Mary Anne and the Innkeeper were behind Maeve, up on the Inn's broad steps. Royal stopped and turned to the others.

"Any of you know about engines?" he asked quietly. Harris shook his head.

Brian said, "We do," gesturing toward his sister.

"OK, then – Lena, right? You come with me," Royal said.

As they moved away he called to Brian and Harris. "Leave the King guy one 'copter for evacuation, but hurry. The fairy is about to take back this valley." (Royal Hill's awareness ran deep; Maeve was wise to be uneasy about him.) Lena and Royal ran past the crackling fire toward the two Russian helicopters parked near the wooded edge of the valley.

Brian said, "I know what he wants – c'mon." He and Harris moved quickly in a wide loop around the edge of the action, toward the State Police and Guard helicopters.

"I am warning you, come no further," Maeve said to the intruders. "You have harmed me and mine. You are about to pay." She gestured around the valley and beyond. "Everything will be as it once was."

Maeve stood alone on the grass, surrounded by flowers. She was fairy-like indeed, lit from within, shimmering in the sunlight, seeming to float.

"Maeve, Tom King wants me to tell you that he can help," called Ravi, "but you know better than that."

"Hey, damn it, young man," said King, walking toward Ravi

with intent to silence him. He spoke to the nearest National Guardsman. “If he says that again, arrest him.”

“Can’t help you with that, sir,” replied the Guardsman. “Our orders are to maintain order and avoid bloodshed, and to control the foreign troops.” His eyes and weapon were trained on the bulldozer drivers. The other Guardsmen and State Police focused on the Russian leader and soldiers. One Guardsman shifted his position to better cover the Russian troops standing between the two bulldozers. All Russian eyes were on their leader and Maeve.

“Backup is on the way, sir,” the police trooper said to King, who finally had the sense to step back, out of the several lines of fire.

“Ravi,” he called, “come back here.” Ravi stayed where he was.

“Maeve,” said Mary Anne. “Give them a deadline.”

“A dead line,” Maeve echoed, not taking her eyes off the Russian leader.

The ghastly President flickered on and off overhead. The projection was stuck on, so the thing was spieling, stuttering, whispering. “Th-thanks f-for doing this for me – me – me…”

Mary Anne spoke to Maeve over the sound of the droning specter. “Tell them how much time they have left. And not all of your friends will be staying. Give them a chance to get away. Let them know.” Mary Anne watched Hill and the others move toward the helicopters and saw what they were doing.

“There is no time left,” replied Maeve, and raised her hands, while sending a warning to her human supporters. Behind the Russian soldiers was a mighty roar; they felt the heat on their backs as one helicopter blew up, and then the second helicopter ignited and exploded. Their leader shouted an order, and the troops moved toward the steps of the Inn.

Around the remaining cottage, humans and animals fell flat as debris and flames flew toward them.

“Run for it,” hissed Royal to Lena. “She’s taking it back.” After sabotaging the ’copters, Royal and Lena had run to the wooded edge of the valley and flung themselves down among the thistles and goldenrod. Flaming chunks of debris now sizzled around them. They jumped down the wooded slope into the creek valley and ran splashing across to the far shore, where they ran upstream toward Apple Island.

"Ravi, run," called Harris, and Ravi ran toward his two friends, who were pelting back along the path. The New York State helicopter they had messed with burst into flames, ejecting hot metal and glass.

Maeve threw Ravi forward to the treeline, watched the three men get away into the woods, and knew that Royal and Lena, such a good girl, were down in the creek valley, already crossing the water to the uphill trail from Apple Island. They would all meet at the crosspaths and escape back to the parking lot.

But they had to hurry. Maeve was taking back her valley, just as she had promised. Not even Royal Hill understood the immensity of what she was about to do. King and the Guard troops crowded into the larger helicopter and shot aloft as the smaller 'copter burned.

Maeve drew a deep breath. Humans were a disappointment, a waste of her endless time. She gently brought her arms down. The Russian troops vanished; every human thing brought into the valley during that fateful attack was erased. The damage remained for a while, but was soon made whole once more.

Somehow spared, the bloated President hologram grew massively in size, shadowing out the sunlight as it rose, spewing threats into the sky, drifting dismally past the fleeing helicopter.

"We stand waiting at the edges of your fields."

Can this be love?

Sticky summer heat had settled over Washington, D.C. From the fifth-story office of the federal Time Travel Agency, Dr. Hrudlu Vatson surveyed the horizon. The Washington Monument was almost invisible through the heat haze. He shuddered, thinking about less-salubrious places where he had worked in the service of Mother Russia, long ago. The shudder became a shiver as he realized how cold the building was. Air-conditioning in the USA was superb, one of his favorite things about this wonderful, generous, naïve country.

Sitting next to him at the large conference table was the beautiful Russian spy Marina Putina. Many people in the USA enjoyed her attractive presence on all the talk shows. Protected by the President, she went everywhere and talked to everyone.

Marina was wearing a cute little short-sleeved outfit to show off her beautiful shoulders. She loved the deep cold of industrial-strength air-conditioning, for her a marker of great wealth.

Marina leaned forward for emphasis as she spoke to Ed Zanetti, who sat facing her and Hrudlu Vatson. Yanked out of suburban exile, Ed had been appointed Chief Scientist for the Time Travel Agency in a quick Congressional committee vote. He was now second in command under Dr. Tom King – who had not been consulted on this decision. And right now, Ed felt that he was in way over his head.

"But Ed," Marina said, "you underestimate yourself! While Dr. Tom King is away, you are decision-maker. Dr. Vatson here is under threat from Tom King's jealousy and paranoia. Please help him." Marina sat back and looked at Vatson for his approval. Receiving in return a cool stare, she went on the attack again, leaning toward the hapless Zanetti.

"This important scientist has been locked out of his offices. King removed him from top secret military time research. He is under investigation as possible security threat to USA! So ridiculous. This man is great American. You must reinstate!"

Vatson shifted uneasily, wishing that Putina (whom he had known since their early days in Moscow) would tone it down. He enjoyed working with Tom King. While he was shocked that King had locked him out of his offices, surely a friendly conversation was all they needed. "Marina," he said, "I think it was all big misunderstanding. When King gets back, we can have nice chat and work it out between us. Please, there is no need – " Under the table, the sharp point on her stiletto shoe connected with his ankle.

He yelped and subsided.

Somewhat at random, Zanetti found forceful words. "Ms. Putina," he said, "I am not making any big decisions without input from Dr. Tom King. I appreciate your strong feelings about Dr. Vatson, but it is not up to me to reinstate him."

"My 'strong feelings'!" she hissed, rising to her feet. "Are you accusing me of having affair with this man?" She gestured dismissively at Vatson, stalked around the table, and leaned in toward Ed, who slid his chair backward to get away. "I have been warned about left-wing environmental radicals!" she shouted. "Your beloved President told me. False accusations against him! Sex-trap scandals! He is victim of your country's lies. Now you attack me!"

Marina spat at Ed and turned toward the door.

"I take this to the media! Come, Hrudlu!"

She paused in the doorway of Ed's office, chin up, radiantly enraged, glaring at Vatson. He shrugged apologetically at Ed and followed her to the elevators.

Outdoors, Marina headed toward the cable television crew hovering on the hot sidewalk, hungry for the big story she had promised them. In the office, time travel staffers came running at the sound of Marina's shrieks. They joined Ed Zanetti at the windows, where he was watching Marina gesturing and speaking, weeping for the camera.

A banner began flowing along the bottom of USA screens: "*BREAKING NEWS: TIME TRAVEL OFFICIAL FALSELY ACCUSES INTERNATIONAL SCHOLAR OF SEXUAL MISCONDUCT.*" Certain media sources were quick to spread this story.

Ed's desk phone began to ring, and he stepped away from the windows to answer it. The office receptionist took the call and said, "Dr. Zanetti! The White House is on the line. You are out to lunch, correct?"

"How the heck can anyone get work done around here?" Ed cried. He foolishly took the call. "No sir, I did not do any such – " he shouted, as sharp phrases poured out of the phone. The staff and receptionist listened in horror.

"A Russian spy is gonna lie," Ed said in between the angry words coming at him. "Why would you believe her?" The President ended the call, having gotten what he wanted, and his flood of online messages commenced.

> Time Travel IDIOTS make fake sex accusations!
> TT King & Zanetti scum Incompetents!
> TT is a top Program - Needs new Leaders!
> TT King in Hiding? Deputy Zanetti Insane?
> TT Zanetti defames International Gun Scholar Putina!

And so on.

Around this same time, the helicopter carrying Dr. Tom King emerged from the hills south of Corning, NY where Hollymount and Apple Island lay hidden, and made an emergency landing on Interstate 86. Or what was left of it.

The highway's four lanes were covered with trees, hundreds and thousands of trees that were bursting through the pavement, growing to thirty feet high or more in under a minute. Several miles away, both east- and west-bound, police were redirecting highway traffic onto side roads to bypass this phenomenon. But that was hard to do, because the new forest was pouring like lava across all roads and buildings in its way.

Several miles south of I-86, Route 416 and the Highway Spur Construction Site were engulfed in tall trees and flowering meadows. The trailers, trucks, supplies, the little church, and the bulldozed lanes curving south toward the hills – all replaced by forest.

The river of trees had first flowed downslope from Hollymount Valley above, and kissed the Canisteo River with returning timelessness. The golden green sylvan abundance then surged unchecked swiftly north over and between the hills, gilding the banks and cleansing the waters of the Cohocton River, and spilled out across the interstate highway.

The cars and bikes, parked along the roads by all the people responding to Rita's social media call, were gone. Now there were meadows filled with nothing but flowers, the tall native flowers and shrubs of midsummer.

South into Pennsylvania, beautiful huge trees — oaks, hickories, hundreds of years old – surged out of the ground. Their deep green hues and vast canopies filled the sky as people in cars and on foot stopped to stare. Woodpeckers and blue jays, crows and ravens, passenger pigeons, salamanders and bees, foxes and rabbits, and larger animals, long gone in the modern world, were living ancient lives of untouched abundance.

Vanished were the toxins, the pollutants, the microplastics, all the plentiful human debris that cripples and extirpates wildlife. Big fish swam in the renewed streams and creeks, joining their meager modern brethren, having emerged from seemingly nowhere. The land was restoring itself to a past time – to what Maeve had found here when she first arrived.

"Why didn't you land at the highway project parking lot? Where's my car?" King demanded as he and the helicopter pilot and troops stood by the side of I-86, on the edge of the river of flowing, emerging, flourishing woodlands.

"Sir! It's gone! Just – trees. No roundabout, nothing. Just woods. And flowers. It's all covered with flowers. I had to land here." The pilot turned away and walked over to the police and National Guard personnel. They too were wondering where the highway spur parking lot and road construction vehicles had gone. Where were the factories and businesses?

The state police gave Tom King a ride to Elmira Corning Regional Airport, where he watched the overhead TV screens while his plane was fueled. He soon learned via FIX News that his job was in jeopardy, under threat by the President and his weird Russian pals.

King knew that he needed to focus on this power crisis and ignore his surging thoughts. But as his jet carried him south into the dome of dirty haze over the nation's capital, he stared unseeing at the landscape below, his mind in turmoil: 'Why has Maeve shut me out?' He had known for a while that he was drawn to her. 'We are a lot alike. Surely she recognizes this and appreciates it.'

He wanted to help her find a new place to live and to enjoy life a little bit more. 'Get her away from those filthy hippies, get some pretty dresses, go to some restaurants. Do the things women enjoy.'

Dr. Thomas King, Time Tsar and rational man, regarded love as a biological urge – to be ignored and denied. Romance and tender emotions, all these sweet things, are caused by body and brain chemicals, designed to lure human beings into having babies – to perpetuate the species. He refused to be fooled. On the other occasions when he had been trapped, as he saw it, by feelings of love, he had managed to outlast the flow of chemicals until they faded away. He now struggled to overcome that initial harsh biochemical and mental surge.

As soon as the plane had landed and was taxiing to the terminal at Dulles, King called Senator Harlan Styce, who answered right away. Senator Elizabeth Maximus was not reachable, her phone unresponsive.

"Tom! What a bad time to sneak away for a wild weekend!" said Harlan. "You are thiiiiis close to losing your job, if the talk show hosts are right." King easily imagined the tiny space between thumb and forefinger in Harlan's gesture.

"I think we've lost contact with the New York site," said King, cautious of being electronically overheard.

"Yessir, we've been watching helicopter news reports from that area," said Harlan. "Giant trees! They grew right across the interstate highway – watched it live – a forest pushed up through the pavement like it wasn't there. Never in all my born days."

Hearing these words from Harlan, King was thrilled by Maeve's power. Punched deep in his gut. Dazzled. He drew a shaky breath and could say only, "I saw some of that before I got a ride out of the area. Harlan, I need to go, and get to my car."

"Come straight to our home, my boy. Senator Max – well, I won't say any more. You get caught up on the news, and I'll see you soon."

King stopped by his office first. He moved through the damp

summer air between car and building, took the elevator and emerged at the Time Travel Agency office floor to find the lights on and people working in their offices. What a relief – he had imagined that it was all gone, replaced by a forest. Maeve –

As he approached the glass doors of his office suite, his eyes were caught by an addition to the lobby letterboard, just below his own name and title: Dr. Edward Zanetti, Chief Scientist. Suffused with a healthy, restorative rage, Tom King entered the suite, stalked past the unattended reception desk, and slammed his office door loudly behind him. He then lost steam and stared out the window at the parking lot. Almost immediately he heard a soft tap-tapping at the door.

"Come in!" King shouted. His Time Outcomes modeler came in, appearing timid but speaking firmly.

"Dr. King, great to have you back. So glad you escaped from whatever's happening at the natural portals site in New York."

King glowered at the man, John somebody, who edged forward with his news, hoping to survive this encounter. "Sir, you may have noticed that the desk out there is empty. Our top intern and her two friends aren't answering their phones, and their parents are very upset."

King felt a deadly chill and sat down, hard.

"Where were they last heard from?"

"They got caught up in the media excitement and drove to the New York site, and called to tell their parents they had walked to a magic parking lot past the roundabout. With a lot of other young people. Since then, nothing."

Tom King's final defenses went down, and he was overcome by anguish, thinking only, could he join them, and be with her again? He could not speak or move, paralyzed by this piercing thought, gazing out the window, silent and blind. His staffer had been expecting an explosion of rage and action, not this sudden silence. He turned to see Ed Zanetti entering the office.

With impeccably bad timing, Zanetti was there to get over the awkwardness of his presence on King's staff. Then he would get to work. He had charts, graphs, lists, plans. Improvements would be made, and his Best Management Practices for Time Travel needed updating for reapplication to all the new initiatives. Some of which he would toss out.

Zanetti smiled at his longtime colleague John and moved around him toward Tom King, missing a warning gesture to stay back. "Hi there, Tom!" Ed said, going for hearty informality. "A massive time restoration effect is happening in New York! Incredible, unprecedented. New to science! You were there! Can you tell us what you know? We'll get right on it!"

John grabbed Ed's arm and pulled him back toward the door as Tom King seemingly, and actually, in a trance – that is, entranced – turned to stare at them. He rose from his chair, a big handsome man of middle age, well dressed though disheveled, his ruddy face pale and in need of a shave. He moved toward them, looking past them.

John, scared of King's famous temper, broke for the door. Ed stood transfixed as King loomed over him. But King backed away and collapsed into his office chair.

"Hi?" Ed said again, shaky in tone, but resolute.

"Yeah. Ed Zanetti, right? Been a while. Excuse me," said King. "I am going through something." Head in hands, massaging his face, trying to break out of it.

"You need to drink some water," said Ed, getting up and calling out the door, "Hey, John or somebody, can you bring in water for the boss?" In a moment, John was in the doorway with bottled water and glasses. He poured water for King and dared to place a hand gently on King's shoulder.

"Are you going to be all right, sir?" John stepped away as King leaned back to drink the water, gazing at the two men as he set down the empty glass. He said, "I'm all right, for now anyway. Thank you."

"Shocking experience, today," John offered. "Do you need medical evaluation? Are you possibly concussed?" This solicitude threatened King's brittle self-control. He put up a hand to ward off the kindness being offered. "Please," he said. "Stop." There was a silence while Ed and John eyed him. He shook himself mentally.

"OK," he said. "Can you get me some black coffee?" John darted away. Dr. Tom King, Time Tsar, looked around his office and willed himself into a semblance of normality. That meant asserting control.

King gestured for Ed to seat himself in one of the chairs facing his big desk, and said, "Ed, what are you doing in my agency? I did not express any interest to anyone at any time that I wanted you around. What gives?" Ed had to think about that for a moment.

King went on, "You are a nitpicking perfectionist. Nothing ever got done with you running the time program. Just rules, rules, rules. All those wasted years. It was so satisfying to throw you out. I am about to do that again."

John reappeared with coffee and cups and said, "I ordered sandwiches." King filled and quickly drank a cup, refilled it from the carafe, and gestured for John to join him. Both men, armed with black coffee, stared at Ed Zanetti, awaiting his reaction to King's harsh assertions.

"I was kind of enjoying my back-to-the-land experience in the suburbs," said Ed, "but they called me." King raised his eyebrows and waited. Ed found confidence as he went on.

"Basically, Tom, people felt that your programs are weak on science. They brought me in to back you up."

"'People'?" King asked.

"Long-time science and policy staff in Homeland and Interior are really worried about the new President's antiscience diatribes. They talked to their House and Senate subcommittees. Putting me in here was their solution."

"Not seeing it," said King. But his self-assurance had veered into a nosedive. He looked at John, pushing away the intrusive thoughts. "You got any insights?"

"It kinda makes sense, Dr. King. You were isolated on top of this big new tech and science initiative. And it's so important. You need some solid science guys right below you. Especially with this unstable President."

John got up to accept a plate of sandwiches from someone in the hall and set them down in front of King, who picked one up and began to eat, suddenly hungry.

"The President is deeply ignorant, Tom," said Ed, "and greedy. He wants his son in your job to convert the Time Travel program into a moneymaker for the family business and his investor buddies." He started in on a sandwich.

"But they can't do that," said King. "It's government. We have rules and procedures." He ate another half sandwich, definitely feeling better.

"It's a new day with this President. He just does what he wants," said John.

"So who in Congress decided to stuff you down my throat, Ed?" King asked, smiling. Ed had, to his knowledge, never before seen him smile. He smiled back.

"People I know and trust. Senator Liz – "

King made a scornful sound.

John said, "You hear about her, sir? When the news broke this morning – " he paused at King's startled, guarded glance.

'What am I about to hear?' King wondered, bracing himself.

John continued. "This morning, we the public learned that you and Senator Max's aide, and the local landowner, and others were under threat by apparent Russian troops, on American soil, in a remote and isolated location. And it was Senator Max who broke the story."

John looked at Ed to continue. King let out his breath. He could handle this.

Ed said, "So, the President attacked Senator Max. Went on TV, said the soldiers were there as a private favor, helping him with a real estate deal, and that Max was responsible for any deaths and injuries if the situation went wrong." Tom King stared, amazed, and Ed went on.

"He tried to remove Max's free-will waiver, said he'd put her in prison. But she fled, she's in hiding. A U.S. Senator, hiding from the U.S. President. For truth-telling."

"You owe her big time, Dr. King," said John.

Tom King's phone rang, and he glanced at his watch. "I'm on my way, Harlan," he said into his phone, pulling on the jacket he had thrown down in his wretchedness. "I'll be back in tomorrow, and I agree to listen, Ed," he said, heading out the door, "but nothing more."

King's driver took him to Senator Styce's gracious home. Harlan Styce opened the front door for Tom King, peering around the front steps for intruders and media. Seeing none, he turned and padded in his slippers back toward his study.

"This way, Tom. We're in here," he called back.

King felt the lock catch as he closed the door and followed Styce down the hallway. His internal wrestling match had continued on the ride over, and right now he felt fine. He felt great – exalted, in fact. The world was his to command; he was floating on air. The Styces' home was beautiful, with fine old rugs and early American furniture. Everywhere he looked, he saw beauty and felt deep emotion. It was a wonderful world, and nothing could stand in his way.

Senator Styce stood waiting as King entered the wood-paneled, gleaming study, and gestured to the room's other occupants, seated in comfortable chairs. King nodded with pleased recognition of Harlan's wife, Marian, and grinned at the sight of Senator Liz Maximus. She was startled into smiling back.

"She's safe with us," said Harlan. "No one would look for Liz here." He gestured to a chair for Tom, who sat, still smiling.

"What a lovely home. I need to settle down into something like this," he said. The cheerful pleasantry was so out of character for this no-nonsense, driven man that Harlan wondered if he were delirious or hallucinating; and both women knew instantly what was up.

"Tell us what has happened, Tom," said Marian, handing him a cup of coffee.

"Happily," said Tom, "But first, Senator Max – "

"Liz, please," she murmured, wondering why she had never before realized how attractive he could be. She wondered, who was the unlucky lady, to call down this toxic lightning?

King adjusted his attack. "Liz! I am mad as hell about the appointment of that idiot Ed Zanetti as my chief scientist, but let's discuss that later."

"I retract the charitable thoughts I was just having about you, Tom," she snapped back. King's coffee cup stood empty. By now he had had more than enough coffee and politely refused Marian's offer of a refill.

She rose to accept a tray of brunch foods from the smiling young household staff, today wearing a rainbow tie atop his summer uniform. The delicious midday dishes were shared around the table. But Tom King was again losing steam. The room and the pleasant people around him were dimming, seen through a thickening mist.

He pushed on. "Harlan and Liz, and perhaps you too, ma'am," he said to Marian, "know that we have an important top secret time travel site in southern New York State. I went there to investigate Harlan's report of a disturbance. We have a landowner there," he drew a deep breath, "who needs our protection."

"You can talk freely, Tom," said Liz Max. "The story has been outed on social media and cable TV, and the President has confirmed that the Russian troops were there at his request."

"'In return for helpful information' he provided to the Russian President on his recent Moscow visit," said Marian. "Unbelievably dumb, to admit all that!" She looked at her husband. "Surely you can get him impeached and removed from office for treason." Marian passed the fried potatoes to Harlan as she spoke, and he took a generous second helping.

"I hope so, my dear," said Harlan, "but let's hear Tom's story."

King was shivering, and a bite of omelet caught in his throat. He drank from his glass of water and hurried on.

"Your assistant, Ravi, is very good," he said to Senator Max. "Capable young man. But he prevented me from providing emergency assistance to the local landowner. We were going to evacuate her" (Marian perked up at the female pronoun, glancing at Liz, who smiled briefly), "but Ravi told her that she shouldn't trust me. And she said we all had to go. And now she's shut us all out."

He ran out of energy to continue, and stared down at his hands. The void loomed, and he fought down panic.

"Well, well," Senator Styce muttered at a level only his wife could hear. This was unexpected, but not unprecedented. 'We all have our weak moments,' he thought, but did not say aloud. They continued their meal quietly.

Tom shook himself mentally and looked around. "I seem to be going through something," he said. "You will have to pardon my lapses until I am myself again." This verbal formality sounded strange, coming from the unruly Dr. Tom "Cat" King.

"These things happen to all of us," said Harlan. He was put in mind of his young grandsons and said gently, "Now eat your bacon and drink your juice. You need food and sleep." He turned to Liz Maximus. "Maybe you can tell Tom what Ravi reported before we lost contact with him."

Senator Max did not like Tom King. He was a menace to science and policy, arrogant, and a bully. Also a killer, according to the top secret reports she had finally gotten access to. And now, lovelorn and vulnerable? Bah! Liz smiled in a chilly way and commenced her attack.

"Ravi has been to the Inn, and neighboring Apple Island, several times. And he found out that Tom here, with the help of Harlan's slimy aide, was scouting the place for secret government seizure, with plans to kick out the residents and landowner, and to build a top secret time lab." King glowered at her, Harlan smiled; Marian sat back to listen.

"It all seemed far-fetched to me," Max went on, "because Ravi described the local landowner as a fairy immigrant from Ireland. He said she had bewitched local animals and people. I figured she'd cast a womanly spell over him. And now you, Tom, appear to be a victim of her attention."

Max was trying to stir up a reaction, and King replied, angrily but in control. "I don't trust Ravi. He assisted that ecoterrorist in Kentucky. He has continued to consort with her son, who was interrogated for months by our security agencies until the liberals got him released. Today I saw Ravi with the rabble hanging around Maeve." Tom leaned toward the Senator, who sipped her coffee and did not meet his eyes. He continued, "You should have fired Ravi, and he should be in prison. I don't need to listen to this nonsense from you."

"Children, children," said their host, "Not at the table. Manners!" To Liz, Harlan said, "Be nice! Play nice!"

"But he isn't nice," said Max. "Tom King is – "

"Hush, Liz, please. Eat your dessert," said Marian. "Tom, would you care for some fruit salad?" Harlan and Marian played at being genial hosts, while the antagonists simmered down.

Cooling, Tom threw a peace offering to Liz. "Admittedly, Senator Max, I would forgive that young man all his missteps if he'd come to work for me. He's that smart and capable. Any chance you'd let him go?"

Liz snapped, "He told me you asked. Please don't steal my staff." To Harlan, she sniped, "On the other hand, old friend, you are well rid of that bum Ard Sprinkle."

Styce went bright red. "He carried all the top secret information about the Hollymount site straight to the President – who took it straight to his friends in Moscow!"

Marian reminded them, "The President today said that the Russian troops were there to help him with a business deal, in return for favors he gave to Moscow." She waved her hand, napkin flapping. "He sees nothing wrong with this – says it's 'just business'! How is this treasonous man our President?"

"Well, the Russian role for now is mere hearsay," said Harlan.

"Until such time as we can get back into the Hollymount Valley area," agreed Liz Max. She turned to Tom King. "I'm not big on magic and fairies, Tom, and I doubt you are either. What do you think accounts for the sudden closure of that area? And for all the trees?"

King's eyes widened at her words. He said, "Actually, Senator – I can find nothing in science that accounts for the strange phenomena there, with its weird requirement for entrance, and the numerous naturally occurring portals to other places and times. And now this instant forest!" He shifted in his chair, his mood spiraling down as he continued.

"Our country has spent billions of dollars to engineer a time portal to the Pleistocene, and we spend millions in energy costs every *month* to keep it open. Sprinkle's discovery of naturally occurring time portals on little Apple Island is – was – an incredible breakthrough for the Department of Time Travel, and for our country's military interests."

It was indiscreet to let Senator Max know these things, but King could not help himself. He stared at the backs of his hands, the palms of his hands, and around the room, seeing nothing. "For the time being, I'm calling it magic, and she – the landowner, Maeve, no known last name – is a fairy from Ireland." He leaned back and closed his eyes. The house staff quietly cleared the table.

Marian said, "Tom, I don't think you had any sleep last night. You need to get some rest. We have a spare room, of course, and then you should go home, take a break with your family."

"Oh, ma'am, I don't have a family."

Harlan huffed, "Nonsense, bullpucky, boy, get control over yourself. I talked to your dad at the club last week." Harlan was thinking that professionals and agency heads should never indulge in self-pity.

King shook his head. "You all know about my Ph.D. research, right?" Harlan leaned back to explain to Marian, while Liz leaned forward.

"Yes," she said, "I just found out. My staff finally got clearance for me to read that report, 'The Grandfather Paradox.' I'm not sure I can bear to talk about what you did. So deeply shocking. Your own grandfather!" Liz Max shuddered. Marian's reaction to her husband's whispered explanation was audibly horrified.

King replied, "At the time I thought it was necessary, for science, and for time travel research progress, you know? I wanted to demonstrate that we CAN go back in time and change the future – if we choose the correct inflection point. In fact – " He was listening to himself speak, again heedless of his audience. "My study is the basis of the work we're doing at the Deep Space Time Lab in

Kentucky. So we can improve our country's military history and our global – "

"Tom, snap out of it," said Harlan, who did not want these military secrets revealed to his nearest and dearest. Too late, of course, because Senator Max was filing away everything King said for Ravi, should she ever see him again, to dig into.

"Yes, sorry," King said, uncaring. "But I was mistaken, after all. My actions soon had impacts on me."

"You have not vanished, Tom. You are solid, and real, here with us." Marian spoke softly.

"I'm on borrowed time – running on empty, call it whatever you want to," said Tom King. "When my parents saw that the family history had changed, and that my grandfather died a decade earlier than they remembered, they came to me for an explanation. I was the brilliant grad student in time travel, a brand-new field, right? They figured I might have the answer."

"What did you tell them?" Marian asked. Tom King rose from his chair and walked toward the fireplace, then turned. Rays of warm afternoon sunlight and shimmering tree-leaf shadows touched his pacing figure.

"I was proud of my work. I told them exactly what I had done. I thought they would be all for it, supporting me like they always had."

"But no?" Softly, from Marian.

"But no. At first they didn't believe me. They tried to get me to check myself into a mental health recovery program. They thought I was overworked and imagining things." He gazed at his audience, who were focused on his words. "Look, I've never talked to anyone about this before, and you three of all people are not who I had in mind to share this with."

Marian Styce, retired family therapist, replied. "This is a good place and time to talk, Tom." She glanced at Senator Maximus, who stared back at her wide-eyed, and at her husband, who was gazing at Tom King.

"Maybe you're right, Marian," King said. He pulled his chair away from the table and sat down facing them. "I have a lot of empty quiet time to think things through, since my family disowned me. No holidays, no family meals, no interactions with my sister and her kids. And most of all, no birthdays. My parents' attorneys wrote to tell me that I'd been removed from all family records, all the photo albums – my entire life has been erased. That I no longer exist."

Liz was shocked – and pleased. Family vengeance cuts deep! She kept a tight rein on her reaction, ever the public servant. "But your birth certificate, they can't touch that."

"Wanna bet?" said King, meeting her eyes for a moment and seeing the deep dislike there. "The family attorneys are working on that, and on getting my birth expunged from the Census records."

"But you're here, Tom," said Marian, "and real."

"You can feel my dislike, Tom," said Liz. "From one living, breathing human being to another."

Tom said, "I'm here, and alive. But for how long? If I killed my grandfather, can my dad erase me? Or is there some kind of mathematical time balance requirement that's coming to take me out? There's always a first for anything – I'm already proof of that."

Tom smiled and looked again at his hands, both sides. "Still here, right this minute," he said, and then looked up at Marian. "Can I take you up on that spare room offer? I need a nap. Hope I can sleep. And then wake up, and get going."

In the quiet bedroom at the top of the house, Tom King lay awake for a long time, hands clasped behind his head. His thoughts were calm and cool.

He had been distracted by the idea of natural time portals. They did not require costly engineering or energy use. But they required relationships, which were treacherous and unstable. She had kicked him out and locked the door.

So now he would focus on the Pleistocene Time Fort and research facilities at the Kentucky park. He had glanced at a coded report in the office that morning, which stated that the Time Fort engineers were closing in on the calculations needed to create a time jump to the next inflection point. He could get back there tonight.

'Also,' he thought drowsily, 'the President does not have a foothold in the Kentucky research – oh wait, yes he does – Hrudlu Vatson.' Tom King fell asleep.

The Science building, Ten Thousand Secrets National Park, Kentucky

A plan unfolds – water flowing underground.

As they approached Hugh Hynes's office, Dave Caver and Gabby Greene could hear the heated argument. Both Janet Harper and Hugh glanced their way as they entered, but continued their debate. Janet was soaking up sunshine, sitting on the window ledge. Through the open window, fresh tree-scented warm air wafted into the room, diluting the chilly air-conditioned office space.

"Vengeance does not work, Hugh," she said. "This isn't the Wild West, where you shoot down the bad guys in the street."

"But that's how I feel. King tried to murder me, pushing that reset button. I almost died in that tiger hole." Hugh gestured toward Dave and Gabby. "These guys and you and your daughter found me and rescued me. Now King has to pay."

Janet turned to look at the new arrivals and said, "Hi there, you failed to get rid of me." They slid onto chairs near Hugh's desk.

"We need to report to you, Hugh," said Gabby, ignoring Janet.

The fancy office, renovated for Tom King as Time Tsar, was an eyeful for humble Park staff. Hugh said, "Glad you two made it out alive! Grab a drink and a snack – we're living like gods here." He gestured toward the bar and mini-kitchen. Then he turned back to Janet. "Fair is fair! You blew up the casino and gas well. Now it's my turn."

Dave was not shy. "Crock a shit!" he said, opening soft drinks for himself and Gabby.

Gabby said, "You're just being playful, right, Hugh?"

Dave added, "Priorities, man! Why is this woman not under

arrest?" He gestured toward Janet while pressing microwave buttons on two frozen burritos.

Gabby tried again. "Be *quiet*, Dave. Hugh, we both need showers and sleep, and Dave needs his shoulder looked at. Can we give you a brief report on our findings and actions? Then you two can get back to your pointless discussion."

Janet said, "'Pointless' is right. Men have dreamed of final retribution since before the ancient Greeks, but it just doesn't work that way." Dave's scornful guffaw at the pompous words cut her short.

Hugh asked, "Dave's shoulder?"

"He had to dodge that tiger by cannonballing down into the cave."

"Needs looking at, is all," said Dave, wolfing down his burrito and eyeing Gabby's, which she did not touch.

"OK," said Hugh. "Sorry, I was distracted, arguing with our guest over points of principle." Gabby rolled her eyes.

Hugh pulled himself together, saying, "So give us a brief report, then go take care of yourselves. We can have a planning meeting after you rest up."

"With her here?" Dave asked, taking a big bite out of the second burrito, gesturing with his head at Janet.

"Yes," said Hugh. "She made it back, taking a dangerous route. She is now part of our team to rescue science, rebuild the Park's programs, clean out this scum."

"But there's "Wanted" posters for her in every Post Office!" objected Dave.

"All the more reason to not discuss it," said Hugh pointedly. "Officer Turner has agreed to stay quiet for the time being. Let's move along." He and Dave glared at each other.

Gabby worked on her phone screen. After a moment she looked up, having sent her notes from their mission to Hugh. She did not feel like sharing this information with Janet. "Where's your daughter?" she asked, pointedly preferring the young woman to her mother.

"She's not here," said Janet briefly. None of their business.

Steve Roberts knocked at the door and came in.

"I'm taking a break from the final run-throughs on the Maine time trip," he said, "and just wanted to say hi to our returning explorers." He smiled at Gabby and Dave. "Have you heard the news out of New York?" he asked. "Just now."

Catching Janet's eye to prepare her, he turned on the room's big screen. They watched the helicopter's-eye-view of a forest that grew and spread before their eyes. Trees thrust up through guardrails, ditches, across the Interstate 86 highway lanes and medians: stately white pines, elms, hemlocks, maples, oaks, smooth-skinned beech, and an occasional big chestnut tree. The natives were returning. Carpets of flowers surrounded the woodlands as the trees burst forth and grew, their soaring green canopies emerging like blooming fireworks.

The televised view shifted upward to include the southern horizon, where the new forest had spilled down the slopes from the area known to humans as the old Pinnacle State Park, then north across the sparkling Canisteo River. Massive sycamore trees with golden and white trunks now lined its banks.

Beyond the river, woodlands and meadows had surged, engulfing roads and farms and homes and businesses. Onward the new ancient trees had spread, up over Beeman Hill and across the Cohocton River, to cover the I-86 corridor.

The helicopter swerved to show the view north of I-86. The forest edge was spread out in a massive fan, across Frog Hollow and the surrounding creek valleys and uplands. Outside the woodlands lay vast grassy meadows and wetlands filled with flowers, bees, birds, frogs, salamanders, turtles and their kin. Birds fed their babies, and bats slept under the shaggy bark of hickory trees. Larger animals lay low, waiting until darkness to explore.

Human figures, alone and in groups, were emerging from the forest. No vehicles, though. Not a single automobile or truck of any kind. Many people were walking through the flowery meadows in the direction of I-86.

Janet climbed off the window ledge to get close to the screen.

She asked, "What has Maeve done?" while trying to see the

tiny humans. She sat down, or fell, into a chair.

"What was happening when you left?" Hugh asked.

Janet concentrated her mind to reply. "My son was heading back toward the entrance, the parking lot, with Ravi," she said. "And my daughter refused to come here with me. She went back to the Inn, to Maeve and the others. Soldiers were swarming all over the valley – Ravi said they weren't American." She paused to take deep breaths, trying to calm herself.

"They said there was a giant blow-up doll, or something like that, of the President," she continued. "He told Maeve that everybody had to leave right away. Lena and I got out of there and entered the time tube to come here, but then she went back."

Janet turned to look at the busy screen. "I don't like Maeve – I think she's a cult leader. But this forest is a wonderful transformation. Much better than me blowing things up. But what has she done? Where are my children?" Her usually measured voice was rising unsteadily.

Hugh was speaking quietly on his phone. "No one has come through here," he said to the others, referring to the secret tangle of natural portals below the house in nearby Oakland.

"I need to go check – " said Janet, standing up. Hugh walked over and put a hand on her shoulder, daring to comfort and console. There was no hugging a stern person like Janet.

"For now," he said, "you stay here. These two need to rest while we carry out the next steps of our plan. You, me, Steve, and Officer Turner." He spoke quietly. "If anyone shows up here, we'll know soon enough. OK?"

"But those are my kids!" she cried out.

Hugh nodded, and they all turned to watch as Tom King filled the screen… *FEDERAL TIME TSAR…*

"Yes, there were armed troops, apparently Russian, threatening our national interest at a hush-hush facility I was inspecting. No, I don't know what has happened since we departed. We'll tell you when we learn more." King turned and climbed into a police car.

The reporter said, “The Time Tsar is heading to Washington. Back to you,” as the television studio reappeared.

“What was that nasty crack about a blow-up doll?” Dave asked Janet.

“It was big, and floated, and threatening words came out of his tiny mouth,” said Janet. “The others told me about it.” She was distracted, weighing her options, deciding to stay for the time being.

“Best to not speak against my man the President,” said Dave, as he and Gabby left the room in search of showers and sleep. They brushed past Officer Lee Turner, who entered the room and sat down at the conference table. Hugh and Steve joined him. Janet sat away from the others, positioned so she could continue to watch the news screen, sound off, captions on.

Gabby’s notes from their trip, alongside a diagram of the underground Deep Space, came up on the room’s projection screen. She had color-coded her findings and actions. The group of three reviewed possible points of entry (the ventilation screen, the vehicle doors, the old doorway, and two other doors she had marked and disarmed, but had not checked where they led); storerooms with arms, vehicles, supplies; laboratories; that interesting control panel; and a scattering of glowing green dots indicating the doorways, lights, security system, and controls she had disarmed or turned off.

They looked and learned, mostly in silence, with only the occasional “There!” or “Look at that,” or “Can you scroll up to that again please.” These innocent comments were spoken aloud, in case someone was listening in.

Janet jumped to her feet and strode to the news screen where she leaned in close to listen, while the others focused on Phase I of the plan for the disarmament and takeover of Deep Space. Restoration of the Park lay far in the future. This was just the first step.

Janet resumed her seat – *smiling.*

Hugh said, “Let’s take a break. Janet, why the happy face?” he asked, startled by the gleam of sunshine on her normally impassive face.

"That was Ravi Sen-Ellis, they just interviewed him," she said. Her smile broadened. Hugh realized he was seeing relief in her stoic demeanor. "Ravi said – 'Our entire party is accounted for.'" She was grinning, and hopped up again to look out the windows at the bright summer woods around them.

"This calls for more coffee and snacks!" said Hugh, heading to the kitchen area with the others. A new, interesting face was on the screen, and Steve walked over to turn up the sound.

... *PROFESSOR ROYAL HILL, BOTANIST*... "The young people who came here to protect this area are walking out with us now," he said, appearing to float through a field of flowers toward the highway. "These are all native species, some not seen for decades," Hill went on, gesturing around him. "These new woodlands are typical of what we popularly term 'primeval,' the untouched woodlands of the pre-European era." Hill turned to look at the forest he had just left, and seemed about to go back in.

A voice offscreen – *Lena!* – Janet knew, said "C'mon, we need to rest, then you can return." Royal Hill nodded, turned, and spoke again to the camera. "One last point. This ancient forest needs immediate and full protection. Besides its grandeur and pristine condition, it has unique qualities that may be new to science."

The camera moved away from the professor to show a large group of young people sitting and lying among the flowers, and then went to a commercial break. Steve turned the sound down and sat back in his chair, a cup of black coffee and a highly unhealthy, delicious snack unwrapped before him.

As the others settled into their chairs, Hugh spoke to Lee Turner. "Can we do this thing, Lee?" He was referring to their Phase 1 plan: disarm and take over Deep Space.

"Damn straight, with a little luck and gumption. We need to get started today, now." Lee Turner was not usually so talkative! He drained his coffee, dusted crumbs from his hands, and walked out the door. "We gotta stay ahead of them," he said. "Ready when you are."

Some details about their plan to take Ten Thousand Secrets National Park back from the Time Tsar and his military allies:

The Plan, Phases 1-4, had been developed during long woodland walks, away from cameras and listeners. Guided by Hugh, Gabby and Dave had paced out the perimeter of what lay below as they strolled. They mapped the locations of vents and air circulation systems.

In the surrounding woods they found truck ruts and blasted rock and dirt piles, left behind by contractors who had worked quickly and sloppily to build this underground research fortress at top speed.

The more our little team of saboteurs looked, the more they realized that this vast facility was run by only a skeleton crew of hired security staff. The place was reliant on cameras and surveillance devices when the Time Tsar wasn't around. Officer Turner kept track of the boat traffic to and from the Time Fort on the Pleistocene side of the Green, Green River.

Right now, only the scientists were making regular use of the vast outpouring of money to develop this site. This was the time to strike, now that Gabby and Dave's reconnaissance trip had prepared the way.

At the close of their meeting, Janet returned to her hidey-hole in an empty staff apartment, focused on watching media reports for glimpses of her children. She had seen Brian in the crowd, but maybe he was avoiding cameras. Steve went back to his work team, tweaking the details of the Eden/Bar Harbor Time Cruise.

Hugh Hynes walked out into the early evening summer warmth. A breeze scattered leaves off the trees with just a hint of autumn, as sometimes happens in July. Dave and Gabby had showered and cleaned up, and sat waiting on a bench to talk with him privately. They sauntered along a paved park trail that featured inclusive interpretive signs and wheelchair access.

Hugh said, "That red button in the cage worries me. I think it calls up the troops, so to speak."

Gabby nodded, "I didn't know how to disable it without triggering it." They peered at its image on her phone.

Dave smiled and removed two AA batteries from his pocket.

"Is this what you're looking for?" he said. "I looked at that button after you did, and pulled these out of the little compartment below it. The red light went out."

Hugh stared at him, and smiled a giant smile. "Incredible, a major emergency response system powered by a couple of batteries."

"People don't think too clearly nowadays," said Dave.

Gabby's eyes slid sideways toward him as he continued, "That's why we need to make America great again. The President, he's my man – "

"And that's a big red button you really need to stay away from, Dave," she said. "Don't you understand what would happen to our environmental protections if he takes control?"

"He is a total ignoramus about nature, I know that perfectly well," said Dave. "But that's what experts are for. We can guide him to do the right things. I am such a fan of that man. I just trust him, you know? It's the sincerity and love in his voice. For all of us. He embodies a deeply Christian forgiveness." The other two let these words float by without reacting.

The saboteurs were now walking along the edge of the area underlain by Deep Space, the massive military and conference facility. The ground surface here had become noticeably drier since construction of the rooms below, and the trees were parched, leaves drooping. Shrubs were withered, and the usual summer wildflowers had not bloomed. The mycelium – the threads and roots and networks that bind us all together – had been ripped apart here.

The dry conditions brought water to their minds – the water needed for the success of their sabotage. Hugh said, "Steve has the water almost ready." Gabby nodded, and Dave looked wise. Hugh was referring to the underground river diversion needed to wreck Deep Space.

He went on, "Steve is nervous about helping us. But he's doing it. The two interns for the Park are doing the grunt work."

"Do they know what it's for?" Gabby asked.

"Don't ask – don't tell," said Hugh, grinning wolfishly. "Trustworthy youngsters."

The pathway took them to a viewing platform, where an underground river emerged from the caves beyond to join the Green, Green River.

Hugh talked through rising anger. "While I was 'presumed dead,' Tom King and dear old Kentucky Senator Harlan Styce bypassed our environmental laws to build their research citadel here. Every day since I got back, I see more of the damage they've done to our park."

"Where's the cave river water?" Dave asked, leaning over the tourist railing to look into the low cave entrance. The riverbed was bone dry as far into the darkness as they could see.

"Once we shut down this illegal military operation," said Hugh to Gabby, watching as Dave climbed over the railing and walked up the streambed into the cave entrance, "we'll put you in charge of a major restoration project." She nodded as they watched Dave's flashlight play around the walls and floor of the cave. He came trudging back into daylight, shaking his head.

"This cave's water flow has gone somewhere," said Gabby. "They blasted out those rooms without any planning. I suspect the water is now pouring into a lower cave passage. We'll figure it out, but we'll never get it back the way it was."

"I hate to tell you this," said Dave, climbing over the railing to rejoin them as a tourist family watched, scandalized at his rule-breaking. "But there's no salamanders, and no waterflow for the cave fish. Plenty of cave crickets – those guys will eat anything. They must have gotten fat on all the fish and crayfish carcasses."

"King broke a lot of laws here," said Hugh. "And – he attempted murder. Of me. I still haven't gotten over it. I get these surges of rage."

"Maybe you need to talk to someone about it, a therapist," Dave suggested as they continued on the trail, looping back toward their offices.

"I know what you mean, and I appreciate the thought," Hugh replied, "but vengeance is my therapy."

"Wow, man," Dave replied. "Like Janet said, that never works for nobody nowadays. World is way too crowded for that shit. Some tyrants try to get away with it, and we got our eyes on them."

"Vengeance didn't work for Janet," said Gabby, a pleased note in her voice.

"Yeah," Hugh agreed, "she told me to forget about revenge. She said there's no satisfaction to be had in blowing stuff up. Only regret and doubt."

"But you're going for it anyway," said Dave. Hugh nodded, and Dave laughed, admiring this old-school aggression. As they approached the Science building, Hugh spoke once more.

"Let's start tonight, all right? King could come here anytime, now that the place in New York is shut off to him. In other words, we better hurry."

"Ten p.m.," said Gabby. "We'll notify the others."

At 7 p.m. that evening.

Just after 10 p.m. that night.

Just after midnight.

And at 3 a.m. the following morning, when water began rising in an obscure river cave passage.

At 7 p.m., Dr. Tom King's flight arrived at the Bowling Green airport (the closer one was closed for runway repairs), where he was met by the son of Kentucky's junior senator. Together they drove to the Senator's golf course residence outside town for a relaxing afternoon – that is, to a private fundraiser for the Senator's 150 closest donors.

The family took King with them in a flock of golf carts to the catered barbecue at the clubhouse. All the local politicos were there, and King was the main event. "Getting a little tired of the President as the featured guest," a friendly inebriate shouted.

"You sure make a pleasant change," his wife said, leaning in close. "Tell us about the magic Irish witch!"

She and her friends cackled at her wit. King smiled, looking for an escape route through the relaxed, boozy crowd. The hot sun sank to the horizon, and a warm dry breeze spilled across the patio like an oven door opening. People drew apart, drank their drinks, got refills, and set aside their half-eaten plates of potato salad and pork barbecue.

"Hot one tomorrow," a bank president remarked to his lawyer brother.

"The power grid is straining at the seams," was the reply.

"You reckon there might be a brownout?" asked their mutual friend the accountant. They were all thinking about the county's industrial park, which was only partially leased, and subject to sinkhole collapses beneath new buildings. It did not need any more bad news.

"What I hear," said the lawyer, "is that the time travel facility up at the Park" – they all turned to look over at Tom King, who was still fending off admirers – "is taking more than its share of power during this unseasonably hot summer."

They drained their drinks and went for dessert, returning to huddle while they nibbled at platefuls of small chocolate this-and-thats. They had pulled the county's Judge Executive into their circle.

"Yep. I can confirm it, to you gentlemen only, of course" – they nodded. "Tomorrow morning, we'll give the Park twenty-four hours to voluntarily shut down the Oakland server farm. Or else we'll do it for them. They can start up their top secret shit again in the fall after the weather cools down." The words ""top secret"" tend to drift, and several heads turned their way.

"Good thing that King guy showed up," the Judge Executive went on, a tad too loudly. "Maybe he needs to hear that we got jobs to do down here, not just his airy fairy – " The Senator appeared, and put his hand on the judge's arm.

"Please, hush now. The gentleman is our powerful guest. Break it up." The group dissolved, each man heading off to stand next to his spouse. The Senator circled though the crowd toward his guest of honor and realized he needed rescuing.

'Tom is not his usual outgoing self,' he thought. 'And there's bad news for him tomorrow morning. I sure hope he doesn't have any big research plans until late autumn.'

The waitstaff had kept Tom's drink topped up. He had not budged from when he had first sat down, engulfed by the merriment of local honchos cracking hobbit jokes and straining to sing old Irish ballads in honor of his fairy queen. A fiery discussion about redheads got tangled up with a drunken debate over Kentucky's role in the Civil War.

The two Black couples, professors at the nearby university, had departed long ago. They knew this crowd. Someone tried to sing "My Old Kentucky Home," but couldn't remember the words. People hummed the tune, swaying.

The Senator expertly extracted Tom King to a waiting golf cart with a flurry of apologies and "early day tomorrow" remarks, and soon had him reclining on the couch in the big, deeply air-conditioned home.

"Hot out there," said Tom faintly. The Senator placed a glass of iced tea into Tom's hands. King's eyes popped open and he said, "Thirsty! Thank you," and drank deeply. He sat up and gazed around the pretty sunroom as he finished the cool drink.

"Kentucky is good for a person," said the Senator. "You planning on an extended stay?" They turned to see a black SUV pulling up outside the front door.

"Here's my ride to the Park," said King, smiling as he stood up. "I have an urgent appointment with the distant past. Now that the New York research site is shut down, I need to focus on work here for a while. Going across the river tomorrow, to the Pleistocene."

He and the Senator said their goodbyes, and King asked that his grateful thanks for hospitality be shared with family members still at the golf clubhouse. His hired car drove away into the warm evening, under the bright security lights of the gated community.

The Senator immediately called the Judge Executive, who answered from the party. "He's heading to the Park now. He plans to go into the Pleistocene tomorrow. So when are you letting him know he has to shut it all down?"

"Tomorrow morning, I got a 10 a.m. appointment with that Groundhog Day scientist. Got a guy from the economic development team and a field specialist coming with me. We've been warning them about the energy overload for months, and now they gotta turn it all off for a while."

The Senator was uneasy. "Would it be OK if I call Tom King later tonight and give him advance warning?"

"Hell, no. He'd call upstairs to someone in D.C. and stop us. That's the last person you should be notifying. We're doing this purely bureaucrat to bureaucrat. That Groundhog Day scientist – "

"You mean Dr. Hugh Hynes, the Park's scientist?"

"Yeah. The guy who came back from the dead. He has to give the OK to shut the power down. He'll understand the situation." And there the Senator had to leave it.

Just after 10 p.m. that night, Dave and the trustworthy Park interns from Steve's office sneaked into the Deep Space center via the back door he and Gabby had found off the Frozen Waterfalls trail. This time, they were there to carry out active sabotage – ripping up control panels, blocking doors open, removing protective covers to expose delicate circuitry to water.

Gabby had pointed out where chemicals were stored that would react in violent and flammable ways when exposed to water. Storage bags and boxes were ripped open and contents scattered. The trio placed heavy objects in front of the ventilation panels and other floor-level openings so that water would be blocked, held inside. It would rise to, they hoped, ceiling height.

Moving through the rooms, they scavenged goodies, supplies, foodstuffs, and weaponry for their large backpacks. (Dave had a hidey-hole in the dry upper cave that Gabby did not know about.) They left laptops and other traceable electronic devices alone. These and all the vehicles would perish in the flood. No one was in the lab rooms that night, so they padlocked the offices and laboratory doors to minimize the possibility that people would get trapped.

All outside doors were secured. They found a locked cabinet that had been overlooked. Inside was an array of circuit breakers and the holy grail of their search, emergency generators. Once these were disabled, the place finally sounded – dead. Empty. No distant electronic hums, no airflow. Deep quiet within Deep Space.

The trio departed the way they had come, having locked all other entryways from the inside. That unobtrusive door at the back of the supplies closet had a new lock and key.

Just after midnight, news spread rapidly among Park staff that Dr. Tom King, the nation's Time Tsar, had returned and was checking in to a guest cabin. Officer Lee Turner notified the others.

"Where's he headed?" asked Hugh, horrified. The ongoing sabotage process needed another twelve hours for complete destruction of the underground facility. He had not expected King to arrive quite so soon.

"You'll be interested to know," said Turner, "that today at 10 a.m. he is heading straight from his cabin to the Pleistocene river crossing. One of our security guys will go with him, to the Time Fort." Hugh began to breathe again.

Out prowling in the warm darkness, Janet saw a shiny black vehicle pull up to a tourist cabin. The porch light revealed Tom King, whom she recognized from the news. He went inside, and a light came on. After the vehicle departed, she heard the crunch of footsteps approaching in the dark. Janet caught a glimpse, in the moonlight filtering through the trees, and walked over to scare the heck out of Hugh Hynes.

"I saw that man, Tom King," she whispered when Hugh's pulse had slowed.

"Yeah, you saw him?"

"He's in that cabin," she said, pointing.

"I just learned that he's heading into the Pleistocene at 10 a.m.," Hugh replied.

"Not going to Deep Space tonight?" she asked.

Hugh nodded. "Right. So our project should be complete by the time he returns."

They walked back along the path to his car, and he offered her a lift to staff housing. "No, thanks," she said, vanishing into the night. "I need to walk."

"OK," he said forlornly, and drove home to his small house in Brownsville. It felt especially empty on this warm summer night, but his little striped cat was waiting beneath the light by the front door, and they went in together.

At 3 a.m. water began rising in an obscure river cave passage that now intersected with the subterranean conference center's plumbing system. Water was soon pouring out of the toilets. Water pressure gradually built up in the wall, finding its way in through the backs of mirrors and the heating elements of hand dryers. Electric outlets spouted little fountains.

By noon, the restroom walls had collapsed, and water was soon ankle deep, spreading across floors and through the open doorways. No alarms were triggered. No signals were transmitted that anything was amiss.

Nothing protective kicked in. Water was moving faster now, and some rooms began to fill up while others provided pathways for water to spread out. In the darkness, chemical fires ignited and fumes filled the rooms. Water found its way into the conference center, the main elevator shaft, and the emergency escape elevator, and began to rise.

Meanwhile, Steve Roberts and family departed for a long-deferred family vacation, and the two Park interns headed home to get ready for the upcoming college year.

Chapter 11

The Emergent Hollymount Woodland.

Governmental response to a radical reforestation event.

Ravi Sen-Ellis was back in Washington, D.C., to the great relief of Senator Max and of his family. Today he was underslept and caffeine-fueled, moving from one emergency meeting to the next on Capitol Hill as the U.S. Congress struggled to come to grips with the uncanny developments in New York State. Few in elected office would admit to believing in magic, so physicists and plant scientists were called back from their vacations to explain what had happened.

Russian officials in Washington easily denied reports that Russian troops had invaded New York State because the evidence was gone: Hollymount Valley and Apple Island were no longer to be found. Helicopter and drone overflights revealed only thick woods where there had once been an Inn and small houses. No apple orchard was visible. No roundabout.

The President released a simple message: "No people, no problem." His whisperers circulated rumors that left-wing Senator Elizabeth Maximus had made up the entire episode.

Ravi was repeatedly shocked by finding seedlings from the emerging woodlands growing in his jacket pockets and clothes. In a state of near hysteria, he had showered long and hard, washed his hair several times, and put his clothes in a plastic garbage bag. He had collected around a dozen of these tiny plants, all with healthy rootlets and sprouting green and gold leaves. In rising desperation, Ravi called Royal Hill for advice.

"Man, me too!" Royal shouted. "Isn't it wonderful? I found them growing in my backpack! My socks!"

"Actually," said Ravi, "I find it creepy. Have they invaded my body, do you think?" He had a bad case of the creepy-crawlies.

"I don't think so!" laughed Royal. "But put them in a safe place. You have any potted plants? Good, so just tuck them into the soil, sprinkle a little bit of water on them, and keep an eye on them. I'll put out a Facebook call for all our returning supporters to do this. I'll tell our group. Leave it to me! Seedlings of change, man!"

In this, his third meeting of the day, Ravi was resisting examining his hair and eyes, and under his fingernails, for tiny growing trees. Senator Maximus had assigned him to work with Ed Zanetti and Steve Roberts, who was on a video link with them from a vacation spot in the Smoky Mountains outside Asheville, NC.

The three men were preparing the agenda for what Ravi hoped would be the final meeting of the day, to be convened that afternoon by Senator Max. They had invited top-level staff of the Federal Park Service, the Environmental Protection Agency, the National Guard of the United States, the Federal Emergency Management Agency, and other government entities concerned with environmental protection and emergency response.

In preparation for the upcoming meeting, the trio was compiling an experts resources list. "How about the Secretary of Transportation?" Ravi asked. "I-86 is their interstate highway, and all those local roads are affected."

"That office has been captured by the President, but I think the Secretary is still facts-based," muttered Steve. He was the note-taker.

"Someone from the Hawaii federal parks – lava flow experts, people who work with lava-impacted communities," said Ed Zanetti. "Those trees poured down the slope and spread out."

This upcoming meeting was heavenly for him. He was dreaming up all the government experts and areas of jurisdiction that might possibly relate to the situation in southern New York State – *and* he had the power to pull them in for an emergency meeting! Heady stuff.

Ed's cell phone lit up: "White House, Office of the President." He shook his head and did not touch the phone while it rang. The noise stopped, then started ringing again right away, so he carried his phone into the next room and closed the door on it.

Jittery and fatigued, Ravi with the others reviewed the agenda for the Emergent Hollymount Woodland meeting, set to begin in 45 minutes.

Emergency Federal Task Force
The Emergent Hollymount Woodland
Steuben County, NY

Protection & Mitigation

Introductions
Goals
Summary of the present situation – Ravi Sen-Ellis
Field report and assessment – Dr. Royal Hill
Background overview – Harris Jay Smith
What we know
What we do not know
People to include/Experts list
Next steps

Ravi reached into his jacket pocket for a pen and brought out a tiny, beautifully formed tree seedling along with the pen. He screamed silently, pulled his hand away, and the seedling landed on the table.

"*What* is that!" said Ed Zanetti sharply.

"Enchanted tree," said Ravi, pawing through his pockets and

digging into the linings, finding three more. “Oh gawd,” he shuddered, dropping them onto the table, where they shone and gleamed.

Ed poked at them with his pen. “Animal, plant, what?”

Ravi stood up and shook out his jacket, patted his shirt, ran a finger around the collar. He sat down, took off his shoes, and totally lost his cool while checking his socks. Didn’t find any more.

“Those came out of the woods with you, right?” asked Steve after Ed described them and held them close to the video screen.

“Yes. But I didn’t wear these clothes in the woods!”

“And do you think everyone else came out with them, too?”

“That botany professor, Royal Hill, he was overjoyed to find them. Me not so much.”

“He’s in today’s big meeting,” said Ed. “Steve, let’s add state and federal invasive species experts to that resources list.”

“Rare and endangered, too,” muttered Steve, typing busily.

Ed dug into the possibilities. “Do we have a record of the four hundred young people who emerged from the woods and went home? They’re going to be spreading these beautiful little trees everywhere.”

“All those people are in close touch with Professor Hill and the local activists via social media,” said Ravi. “We’ll get a brief report from Harris in this meeting.”

“Better include the Centers for Disease Control. You don’t know what these plants are, or what they’re carrying,” said Ravi. “Or even if they’re plants,” he added, shuddering.

“They may be new to science,” said Ed, picking up each little tree and examining it closely.

Steve said, “Or very ancient. Add someone from the Smithsonian? And how about an extremophiles expert. I know a couple of caver extremophiles people.”

“These tiny trees have a strange texture,” said Ed, touching one with his fingertips.

“Read my field report,” said Ravi. “We walked and ran between the trees as they shot up around us. Touching them was strange. They were solid, but we couldn’t get a grip on them.”

Ed picked up two of the jewel-like trees (the trees had begun to grow, with daylight), felt them with his fingers, and nodded. "It's like they're not completely here. Or partly somewhere else," he said, puzzled.

"Both in our world, and another one?" asked Steve.

"Come off it," said Ed. "Hocus-pocus talk. We'll open up a couple of these and get them under a microscope."

"No!" said Steve and Ravi together, fiercely. Overcoming his aversion, Ravi picked them all up and put them in his empty lunch bag, observing, "I'll take very good care of them."

Their meeting preparations complete, they ended the call. Ravi tenderly tucked the bag of tiny beings into his backpack and glared at Ed, who obliviously checked his watch. The two men rose and headed to the conference room.

Several giant buildings distant, the three interns had returned in triumph to the Time Travel Agency offices. Office celebrities, they repeated their story many times. After parking along the highway with hundreds of other people, mostly their age, they had walked through fields and around the roundabout as instructed by their Facebook group. They suddenly felt they were "in a different space."

"There was all this singing in the air," said Ade. "It was eerie, but not sad."

"Nature was singing," said Stuart, blushing at the intense scrutiny from the office staff. The third intern, Aggie, looked at the adult faces around her, expecting to see scorn or disbelief. But this was the Time Travel Agency, and the staff were all strange and geeky experts, which she was beginning to appreciate. Like maybe she fit right in.

The three youngsters were listened to intently and with great respect. "Wish I'd gone," said a grey-haired man.

"But we lost our car!" said Ade. "We were just getting started on the path to the Inn, walking in a big group. With all the other people."

"I bet that was wonderful," the older man whispered.

"And suddenly – coming down the hill in front of us, and all around us, giant trees began to rise up out of the ground!" The three interns spoke rapidly, together. "It got crowded in a hurry! The trees were pushing us out of the way. Everyone was trying to stay calm but shouting, too, and I for one was kind of scared."

Aggie took up the tale. "Then around the corner of the path down the hill a big man came, walking fast, with people around him. They were telling us to head back to the parking lot. The man kept shouting, 'Big magic! Big magic! Everybody get back to safety!' So we all turned and started moving back to our cars."

Stuart said, "But they were gone! The parking lot wasn't there – just a big grove of tall trees and little white flowers in the ground. Birds were singing. The big man – he's a botany professor – said 'Follow me, everybody,' so we walked out together."

The three spoke in turn. "Trees were popping up from the ground around us. Then we came out of the woods into flowery meadows. Most of us slowed down and sat down, and we all talked for a long time, and we made friends with each other in person, and on social media."

"Took a lot of photos. The professor didn't want us going back into the woods and told us to call our families because they'd be worried. There were some police, and a whole lot of media. We tried to dodge the cameras, but some of the kids did interviews."

They told their story many times, wrote about it, and became experts; their future careers gleamed more brightly. But they did not mention the little trees, growing safely in their apartments. Professor Royal Hill had sent plant care instructions to the interns and to four hundred others.

Back at the Capitol Hill conference room, two hours into the Emergent Hollymount Woodland meeting, a plan was being hammered into shape. It was rough and ready, to both contain and protect this emerging presence in the landscape. The plan was cautiously positive, not fearful.

Senator Maximus smiled across the table at Ravi. He was sitting between the Federal Emergency Management Agency staffer and the top environmental aide from the New York State Governor's office. (New York's two eminent Senators had pled prior commitments and were not present. They did not want to be associated with something this weird, and were delighted to let California's senator take the heat.)

"I need to get out there and see this," Max said to the assembled group. "When can we arrange a quick tour?" Ravi nodded and bent to his laptop, making arrangements for transport. The group relaxed toward the meeting's end, convivial and hopeful. Senator Max's team had just reported out a proposed boundary-buffer-zone map after hearing from other groups about a relocation plan for displaced landowners, residents, and businesses; and had assigned a summary of partially implemented short- and long-term traffic flow remedies to a New York State staffer.

They still had to discuss public access versus protection of the woodlands and meadows, and how to manage the massive flow of curious people to the area. All campgrounds, rentals, and motels were filled, and people were trying to sneak into the enchanted woods at several points, even paddling in on small boats along the Canisteo and Cohocton rivers.

The most challenging area was the hilltop where the flow of trees seemed to have started. It was sparsely populated, with trails and small roads climbing out of the village of Addison to the old hilltop state park. Hikers and drones found an impenetrable holly tree forest where Hollymount Valley was speculatively located. After agreeing to a helicopter and bus tour over the weekend, the group broke up for the day.

Harris sat, hot and tired, against the rear wall of the crowded conference room. He looked at the backs of the people in front of him, sitting around the big table, all of them big shots. His presentation to them had not been too bad. He had arrived late from the airport to address the attentive group, and described the public campaign he and Rita had devised to protect the area from the road project, how they had expanded its focus when Brian was incarcerated, and how they had dealt with the attack by Russians and the President.

"I'm trying to decide if you're a patriot or a scoundrel," commented a hard-bitten old often-elected cynic during the question and answer session.

"This is how things get done nowadays, sir," Harris replied. The end result was more work: He'd agreed to cooperate on a big social media plan with a cross-agency team from the State of New York. He was chafing at the thought of all this grim laptop labor with the new forest calling him. What a tiring day. In this noisy city. And he was stuck here for two days more.

People smiled at Harris as they edged out of the room. He felt the doors downstairs opening and heard the sounds of birds and traffic, and could smell new-mown grass. Harris watched Ravi, and dared to dream. They had not spoken since his arrival, and now Ravi was easing his way through the attendees, smiling from his height, talking, taking notes, reacting to comments, walking toward the door with Senator Maximus, nodding goodbye as she left the room.

'Walk my way, Gorgeous,' Harris thought.

Ravi turned and moved toward Harris, smiling. "Welcome to my town! What do you think of it?" he said, sitting in the chair next to Harris, who sighed, leaning his head back.

"That meeting was hard work. I'm pretty tired. How do you keep up this pace every day?"

"Ever since your great presentation, I've been thinking that I need to take a day off. It's been a long time since I did something for myself," Ravi said, gazing at Harris.

'He's not so shy after all,' Harris thought, startled, his heart rate rising rapidly.

"So what do you say?" Ravi asked, pulling Harris to his feet, helping him with his backpack and laptop.

"I say yes," Harris replied.

"Let's go get a beer," said Ravi, as they walked out together.

The small house in Horseheads.

A celebration and a safe haven, for the time being.

There was a big party tonight at the little house. Cars were parked along the streets for blocks in every direction, and bikes were piling up in the front yard. In the tree-shaded backyard, every chair in the house had been set out on the grass. These were filled with talking people and surrounded by blankets, on which children danced and babies gurgled. Two charcoal grills were fired up, one for meat and one for grilling vegetables and yet more pizza.

Shaky old folding tables held a groaningly large grad student potluck feast, for Rita Morales had successfully defended her Ph.D. dissertation, and everyone was here to celebrate. Her work was titled, in part, "Ways and Means: An Interpretation," and we will leave it at that.

Rita sat at the old picnic table in the deep shade of a maple tree, enjoying a celebratory nonalcoholic drink with her major professor. He had dropped in for a few minutes to share the happy moment, but would not stay long, because the graduate students could not relax with him there. Ancient custom.

Over at the grills, Brian wielded spatula and tongs among the corn and peppers, and peeked under foil at the almost-perfectly-grilled mushroom pizza. He stood back-to-back with Lena, who turned hotdogs and hamburgers, plopping them onto buns for children and adults. Ever since that cold winter in the cabin, she craved hamburgers, so she was in the right place.

They were surrounded by people who were fascinated with the Hollymount Woodland situation, from the TV news. Children and grownups asked:

"How could you tell she was a fairy?"

"How does a forest grow out of nowhere?"

"Is your mom really the ecoterrorist who blew up the cave?"

"Will they impeach the President for allowing Russian troops on American soil?"

Ten Thousand Secrets National Park, into the Pleistocene...

... and quickly back out.

At noon that day, the Warren County Judge Executive and his team clattered down the stairs of the Science building at Ten Thousand Secrets National Park, their message of doom delivered: Either the Park turned off the electric energy flow to the Pleistocene, or they would do it for them.

Hugh sat transfixed at his desk, having been handed Tom King's fate on a platter. He was scrying the outcomes of possible actions. Dave Caver dragged Gabby Greene out into the corridor for an urgent conversation.

"You see what's happening here?" he whispered, hoarse with strong emotion.

"I see that Hugh wants to trap King and the Time Fort crew in the Pleistocene for a few months while the power's shut off. And we can't let that happen," said Gabby. She pulled out her phone to call Janet Harper, who seemed to have influence over Hugh's decision-making.

"No, no, not that, I mean the other thing," Dave hissed. Gabby had a bad feeling about what she was going to hear, but she made an encouraging noise and Dave went on.

"So the New York State time tubes are out of commission, and the Park's Pleistocene access is about to go down for several months. That means the place we cannot speak of" – he rolled his eyes at the window in the direction of Oakland – "is the only access point to the past."

"Yeah, so what?" Gabby was waiting to call Janet until Dave finished speaking. She wanted to ask Janet to stop Hugh from acting on his revenge fantasy.

"So, our President needs to know about it. Our secret."

"No, he does not," said Gabby.

"But it's unfair! I've seen how eager he is to get involved with time travel. He was trying to get into Hollymount, and he snuck his people into that secret meeting at the Park last spring. And they were kicked out! The government experts always snub him because they think he's stupid! It's just not fair." Dave's voice was rising. "It's a national security issue, and he's my President," he said, "and I'm gonna tell him."

"But then we have to kill you, Dave. That's what we cavers agreed when we found it. Secret means secret!" Gabby hissed.

Dave turned away from her to walk down the stairs to the front door, but Gabby got in front of him and grabbed his arms hard.

"Did you hear me, Dave?"

"You couldn't do that," he said, upset at her words. "You and me are good buddies."

"I couldn't, but Janet would do it in a heartbeat," she replied. Dave Caver's mouth opened into a round O of shock, because he was frightened of Janet Harper. At that moment, Officer Lee Turner came up the stairs three at a time on his way to Hugh's office, answering an urgent call to report in.

"Howdy, folks," he said, moving past.

"And *he* would happily silence your sorry caver ass," Gabby snarled. She turned away from Dave and called Janet.

In his office down the hall from this standoff, Hugh was on the phone with Steve Roberts at his family vacation hideaway.

"We're about to send in a time team today for a final run-through of the Oxford trip," Steve said. "What do you mean, you're 'shutting it down'?"

Hugh shrugged and said, "I'm real sorry, Steve, the energy grid is overloaded in the hot weather, and could go down at any minute. The Judge Executive said that a hundred thousand customers are in jeopardy. We have until 5 p.m. to shut it down from here, or they shut it down for us."

Steve said, "I've got to call the time team and stop them!" and ended their call.

Hugh turned to Officer Turner, standing in front of his desk. "It has come to my attention," Hugh said, "that Dr. Tom King, a member of your security team, and the three-person Time Fort research team are all presently in the Pleistocene."

"Sir! If we're shutting it down, we better send in someone to retrieve them immediatcly." Turner spoke with forceful sincerity.

"That's an idea," said Hugh, "but first we should consider if they have the supplies they need to survive for several months, um, in situ. In case we can't rescue them in time." He hoped he sounded blandly official.

Officer Turner saw the gleam in Hugh's eye and said, "Sir! You need to let the Superintendent know about this situation. Immediately!"

"Another excellent idea," said Hugh, leaning back in his chair, in no hurry to do anything. He smiled at the thought of Tom King trapped, as he himself had been, with no expectation of ever escaping. 'Yet another excellent idea,' he thought.

But at that moment of deep satisfaction, he heard rapid light footsteps coming along the hallway. Janet stood in the doorway. Turner stepped back from Hugh's desk to give her space.

"Oh no you don't, you wicked man," she said, walking toward Hugh's desk. Behind her, Turner bent his head to hide his smile and relaxed a little bit.

"I just had a call from Dr. Green, who says you want to trap King in the Pleistocene," Janet growled.

"But Janet, this is a beautiful opportunity," Hugh said. "I can just let it happen. Not going to send anyone over there to get them," he said, his voice louder.

"Then I'll go get them," said Janet.

'Attagirl,' Turner thought. 'You tell him.'

"Are you crazy, if the Park authorities find you here, they'll throw you in jail!"

'Present company excepted?' thought Officer Turner. Janet turned and ran back down the hallway, Turner following, with the greatly diminished amoral mastermind Hugh Hynes a distant third. Gabby and Dave chased after them. They all headed to the Pleistocene dock on Kentucky's Green, Green River.

Earlier that morning, Tom King had crossed the river into the Pleistocene to bury himself with work at the Time Fort & Barracks. He knew that the research team was just a few million data-crunching and programming steps away from (a) determining how far forward in time to go for optimal results; and (b) where exactly in time-space the next fort would be placed.

This work was what he needed while he recovered from his losses in New York State. A couple weeks of living cold and scrappy doing big computing under uncomfortable conditions, eating ramen noodles with ketchup sauce from the little packets, solving hard problems — all that would clear his mind. The perfect getaway!

At 10 a.m. sharp, King and a Park security team member loaded their bags into a small motorboat, started it up, and disappeared through the tall gateway in the shimmering wall of light and flowing energy that lined the bank of the Green, Green River. Inside the gate, a Jeep was their ride to the Fort.

The shock of entry into the Pleistocene cold from the 85°F (29°C) heat of a droughty Kentucky summer morning was exhilarating. And the Pleistocene's steady 32°F (0°C) was not that bad. Even so, as King and security guard Robert Mullins jolted across the permafrost toward the glowing light on the dashboard map screen showing the Time Fort, King felt the ancient cold seep into his bones.

He needed a deep rest, something positive to focus on. He would be the camp cook for the young team and immerse himself in their sustained difficult brainwork. He would have brilliant ideas and insert the final puzzle piece, help to test the links and get a signal from their future target point. That's what he needed.

They arrived to find a white pickup truck parked next to the Fort, its doors open. A young woman King did not recognize was in the bed of the truck, wedging a plastic tub filled with hard drives and laptops in between several padded hard drive containers. He saw pillows and sleeping bags farther back, and overloaded backpacks on the ground next to the truck.

Emma had heard the Jeep approaching and assumed it was someone coming to help them evacuate, following Chris Lopez's arrival earlier with news that the portal might blow at any moment. Emma was in a deepening panic, terrified they might get stuck in the past.

She was muttering the fear litany that she had learned from reading *Dune*: "I must not fear. Fear is the mind-killer…" but to no relief. Wishing she had a "Don't panic" towel from Doug Adams's books to chew on, Emma turned toward the new arrival – to see the big boss, the head honcho, the Time Tsar himself, staring at her with evident anger.

She screamed, short and hard.

"Where do you think you are going with that equipment, young lady?" he thundered, climbing out of the Jeep to loom over her.

"Emergency evacuation – sir!" she replied, close to tears.

"You stay here and keep an eye on her," said Tom King to Mullins, who nodded, assumed a wide stance, and loosened his holstered gun. While his hand hovered in readiness he stared gimlet-eyed at Emma, whom he knew from seeing her around the Deep Space command center laboratory.

Emma began to sob, crying incoherently, "Can't we just go – can't we just leave this stuff – surely people are more important…"

King pushed his way through the two-layer entry into the Fort's center. Here was Chris Lopez, whom he remembered vaguely from that big gathering at Deep Space. Today Chris had on several layers of jackets, coats, and hats, and was about to depart, arms full of tote bags jammed with electronic devices and chargers and cords.

"Hello, sir," said Chris, adapting smoothly to the shocking sight of the top boss. "Very good of you to come help us evacuate. Can I get by you?" Edging past the nonplussed Time Tsar, Chris walked out to the truck and slid the armload of stuff into a nearly full plastic tub on the back seat.

"We're just waiting on Turing," Chris said to the weeping Emma. "Nice of the boss to come check on us – " and then saw the pistol that her Park pal Robert Mullins was shakily pointing.

"Sorry, Chris," he said, "but please put up your hands."

With an eye roll, Chris complied, as did Emma, her weeping subsiding to sniffling. She had burned out her panic and felt better. All three turned their heads as the Fort door popped open. King emerged, followed by Turing, who was speaking quietly in their compelling monotone.

"Can't argue with Dr. Hrudlu Vatson. His data are always impeccable. When he says evacuate, we go. Chris came to tell us. Too much electricity in use across Kentucky – the portal could blow at any time. Sir, please come back with us to the river crossing in your vehicle now – because we can't be responsible if you stay."

Handing a bunch of important small objects to King, Turing closed and locked the Fort door with digital beeps and boops, and for good measure snapped a padlock in place. Ignoring the transfixed law enforcement tableau, Turing took the small valuables back from King, walked to the driver side of the pickup truck, and climbed in.

The engine started. Mullins put away his gun, Chris and Emma lowered their hands and climbed in, and Turing drove off. The battered Jeep with Mullins and King followed close behind, back across that dusty cold plain. Very large birds wheeled overhead, forever hopeful. Tom King's working vacation had lasted just over two hours.

Jogging through the woods, Janet cut across the curving Park roads and arrived ahead of the others. She gained access at the gate by telling the guard that she needed to retrieve a tool and was soon on the dock alongside the Green, Green River. Janet climbed into a small motorboat, hoping she could start it. The river's edge was stifling hot in the rising heat, and her legs were scorched by the boat's hot metal surfaces. Across the river, the containment fencing for the Pleistocene rippled with white and colored lights, dim in the hot sunlight.

The buzz-saw whine of insects in the trees was the only sound until a puffing Hugh Hynes ran up, his shadow looming over Janet.

"Don't try to stop me," Janet growled. She found the starter, and took the wheel.

"You have to get the motor into the water," Hugh said, and climbed in to assist. As he adjusted the outboard motor, Janet stared across the water at their destination, the Pleistocene time gate, twenty feet high. It was a quarter-mile downstream. The opening was outlined by shimmering, pulsating purple sparks.

"Look, Janet," Hugh said, "I admit, you're right, right about everything. I can't be playing with other people's lives. I can't do a bad thing just because you did. Because Tom King did. Two wrongs, no right, right? Let's get these folks out safely and then please come have dinner with me tonight? Over at the Porky Pig Diner?"

Janet snorted at the name and spared him a quick glance, not totally unfriendly, and said, "Maybe I can think about that later. Right now I gotta go rescue Tom King and the team at the Fort, and it looks like you're along for the ride."

Then two things happened.

A motorboat emerged from the sparkling Pleistocene time gate. It held Tom King, Robert Mullins, and the three researchers from the Time Fort. The three were standing, hunched over, holding boxes and plastic tubs, backpacks on their backs. King was sitting on a heap of equipment, holding a piled-high plastic tub. At the rear, Mullins steered the heavily laden boat, its gunnels only a few inches above the water, upstream toward the dock where Hugh and Janet were now scrambling out of the motorboat.

As the boat neared the dock, the second thing happened. On the far shore the sparkling containment fence began to buzz loudly, drowning out the summer insects. The full length of the fence buzzed and hummed, and a moaning *waa-waa* sound commenced, rising and falling like an old-time air raid siren. Loud bangs – explosions – shook the hot air, up and down the fence line. An alarm sounded, whooping its warning.

The boat reached the dock, and hands quickly secured it; people began handing off their loads to those onshore. Dave, Gabby, and Turner arrived to help. As Tom King stepped onto the dock, he watched the Pleistocene gate flare up in blue flames. Everyone stepped back as the crackling flames outlined the opening. The heat could be felt on the opposite bank.

The alarm continued to wail, and wind picked up along the river. Everyone sighed as a cool breeze blew through, announcing the approach of a thunderstorm. Distant rumbles and dark clouds could be seen coming quickly from the west.

As he stepped off the crowded dock onto the paved walkway, King looked up to see Hugh Hynes staring at him. Janet had moved out of sight. The burning portal and moaning alarm framed the scene, and the siren of an approaching fire engine added to the cacophony.

The only thing King could think of to say was, "Hello, Dr. Hynes."

"Looks like the hot weather has blown out the power grid," Hugh shouted over the noise and rising wind. "How fortunate that you evacuated when you did." He did not appear overjoyed at their narrow escape.

"Thanks to the Time Fort team," King said, gesturing toward the others as they quickly reloaded the data drives and equipment into two Park trucks. Needed to get it all under cover ahead of the rain, which was already landing in big smacking drops.

"The power will be back up in the morning," said King, smiling stiffly at the man he had tried to kill. And Hynes stared searchingly at King, trying to make eye contact with the man he had, but no longer, desired to kill. The two were locked in this brittle exchange as the others worked around them, fastening tarps and tops over the truck beds. The fire company was calling for emergency support from the surrounding towns.

"No, it won't be back up in the morning," replied Hugh. "Maybe in October or November. This project overloaded the power grid for the entire western half of the state. That's the news I got from Warren County and the state people this morning. They don't want this place back online until the summer is over – and even then, long-term changes will be needed."

Emma came up and handed King his bag, and walked off under her backpack load toward one of the trucks. King remembered his deep dislike of Hugh Hynes, who today seemed strangely intense. King started to move toward Mullins, waiting by their vehicle, but Hugh blocked his way and put a hand on King's chest.

King said, "Hey," swatted down the hand, said, "Out of my way. See you tomorrow in the lab," he called to the departing Time Fort team, and heard shouts of agreement as the trucks moved off.

Hugh lowered his hand and stood there, staring. A woman King did not know walked out from under the trees and took Hugh by the arm, bending in close to speak to him. King heard her say something about "your victory."

Hugh was distracted, so King eased past. His ride was soon spitting gravel as they headed back to his cabin.

Hugh turned to Janet and said, "Thank you. I still want to fight him."

"Tonight or tomorrow, he'll know what's happened, Hugh. Relax," Janet said. She turned away and began walking back into the woods, the trees blowing wild in the arriving storm.

"Still on for an early dinner at the Pig Diner?" Hugh called after her.

"Sure. See you at my cabin at five," she replied, and was gone. Hugh got into his truck just as the rain came on strong.

King's choices are eliminated.

"I hope you can handle the President," said King. "Goodbye!"

Tom King got back to his cabin at dusk, following an awkward meal at the Porky Pig Diner. He had sat alone, two tables away from Hugh Hynes and his companion of the afternoon. They ignored him. On his other side, the Time Fort team was a happy group, giddy with excitement at being back from the Pleistocene, especially after such a close call. The place was packed with other diners.

The power was still out, so everyone ate in the dark, the room barely lit by candles and flashlights and lanterns. King and the other customers packed away sweet iced tea, pork barbecue, catfish and hush puppies, salmon patties, gravy, cornbread, okra, tomatoes, grilled chicken, pork chops, greens and beans, and vanilla pudding with cookies crumbled in. The ice cream machine was not available.

On their way out, Turing came over to tell King that the Time Fort team was heading over right away to the Deep Space lab to get their equipment in place, so they could restart their work tomorrow morning. They would do the time research here, though not as quickly as at the Time Fort. The field testing would have to wait.

King replied that he would be there to help in the morning. He promised Turing that he would call the Senator and see what could be done to get the Pleistocene back online sooner than October.

After leaving a tip, Tom King walked past Hugh Hynes's table. Hugh and his friend were having fun with the Ohio cavers at the next table, arguing and quoting poetry, on the topic of revenge. He heard applause behind him as he stepped out into the gentle summer evening, soft and fresh after the big thunderstorm.

A phone call from Turing came about an hour later, just as King was pulling clothes from his backpack, wishing the power was on so he could have a hot shower. Part of his brain was wondering why the Senator and others in Bowling Green had not told him about the pending power shutdown while he was at the golf club party. But he pushed that away, trying to keep negative thoughts at bay so he could get some sleep before the intrusive thoughts about Maeve came back in full force.

"Dr. King, can you come right away? To the elevator entrance of the Deep Space conference center and labs." Turing sounded agitated, almost shouting.

"Surely," King demurred, "you don't need me there tonight? We agreed on 9 a.m. tomorrow."

"It appears that a catastrophe has taken place. We need your advice immediately. I called the Park security team, and they're bringing lights so we can see better."

"The stuff we brought out of the Fort today is OK?" King's small measure of serenity was evaporating.

"Yes, sir, we have it all here, ready to carry it down the elevator and into our labs. But we can't – " the call ended.

In ten minutes, King had jogged to the parking lot behind the darkened casino. The original back door, kept propped open with a rock, had been replaced with a glass and chrome pair of doors, and the tiny elevator replaced with a larger model. This was the official entrance to the Deep Space complex, belowground. He had last been here in the spring for that big announcement about the public time trips and the military research conference.

What a fog he had been in. Maeve had just begun to trouble his mind with her voice and messages. Her murmuring interfered with his ability to get work done. At that time, he just wanted her to leave him alone. But now she was gone. And that was no longer what he wanted.

He turned his head in the direction of distant Hollymount Valley, where she summoned him, sleeping and awake. King stood in the darkness for a long minute, staring unseeing, while he wrestled with focusing either on the present situation or on the only place he wanted to be.

He stood spellbound among the pickup trucks and security vehicles parked close to the Deep Space doorway, all shining their headlights into the opening. Bright emergency lights were being switched on, and generators began chuffing loudly. Turing found King there and urged him forward, shouting over the noisy generators.

Emma and Chris turned as he came up to the doorway, shaking their heads, horrified expressions on their faces.

"We opened the door, sir, and got into the elevator to take us down to the conference center and labs floor," Emma said. King saw that the elevator car was down about a foot below the hallway floor. Its floor was four inches deep in water.

"I don't get it," he said. "What am I seeing?"

"The elevator descended a few inches and then stopped," Emma shouted in his ear. "And then water started to come in, covering our feet. Turing pressed the emergency button and the door slid open. We stepped up to the hallway and ran out here."

They watched as Officer Lee Turner leaned into the elevator and pushed a button. The elevator car rose back to its starting position. He pushed another button, the doors closed, and the elevator car rose out of sight toward the closed-for-repairs Casino floor above. Turner shined his light down into the elevator shaft and mouthed two words beginning with "Holy." Others rushed in to look. King stepped forward to see that the shaft was filled with water. It smelled of chemicals. Pieces of wallboard floated on the oily surface.

A Park police van swung in and parked, and security guard Mullins climbed out. "I checked the vehicle entrance," he said. "The ramp is underwater almost up to the road. Can't get the doors to open."

Turner spoke to Mullins. "Can you check the escape capsule? Maybe we can get in that way." He nodded toward the Casino, where the tiny elevator from the Deep Space conference center emerged in a back corner of the first floor.

Mullins and another officer headed off around the big building to check, entering via the front door. They soon called in to report that when they pressed the button to summon the capsule it had come up promptly from the conference center below. But it was filled with water, which they found out the hard way when they opened the door. They could hear the elevator shaft below sloshing with water. No way in.

"Who's going to say it?" whispered Emma to Chris Lopez, who shrugged and said it.

"So it looks like the entire facility is flooded?" said Chris.

Everyone turned to look at Tom King for leadership in this crisis. Weirdly, he was looking away, into the darkness. After a long moment, he turned back to the group. "Sure looks like it," he said. "Any idea as to the cause, the source, of so much water?"

"A leak from one of the underground rivers?" Turing said. "I'll have a look at the – hmmm, the maps and blueprints. Those are all online, right?"

"I saw all those plans," said King, "before they started blasting rock out of the space. The water sources were safely re-routed. And we're in a drought. I don't understand." He dropped his head in thought, wondering if it was sabotage, or a design flaw. If it was sabotage, was the President the culprit? He didn't think it was a design flaw – how could he and the engineers have missed an underground water source big enough to do this much damage? He never considered the possibility that the – to him, inept and incompetent – Park personnel could have done it.

Beyond the lights, a safety perimeter was being set up, closing off the parking lot and other approach points to the building.

King's head came up. He shrugged off a large burden in the darkness. "But I don't really care," they heard him say. He continued in a brisk tone. "However, I am responsible for my staff and this work. We'll reassign you to our offices in Washington. You can get some of the Time Fort work done there – eventually. Right?" He gazed at the demoralized Time Team scientists.

Turing shuddered at the thought of working in a city.

"Yes, sir," they said glumly, as the others nodded.

"I'm very sorry about all this," said Officer Lee Turner to Tom King, who was staring straight through him, unseeing. "Tomorrow we'll send in people to find the leak and get started pumping."

"Thank you," King replied. He focused his eyes to look at Turner and added, "My choices have been eliminated." Turner understood at least part of that and nodded as King walked away into the dark.

Next morning, the entire staff of Ten Thousand Secrets National Park was summoned to a meeting with the Park Superintendent to discuss what had happened and how to move forward. People who had heard rumors arrived excited and curious.

Those who paid the Park's bills were upset about the loss of bountiful top secret government revenue. Still others – the perpetrators, our protagonists – were either mentally prepared or physically absent.

Sitting near the back of the room, Hugh Hynes listened as Officer Turner described the previous night's unfolding events. Steve Roberts listened on a phone connection from the family vacation; Gabby Greene did not attend, claiming teaching duties as the school year approached. Dave Caver was, let's face it, in hiding until things cooled down.

For the time being, said the Superintendent, Ten Thousand Secrets National Park would return to basics, offering the public their beautiful walking and biking trails, cottage rentals, and maybe a few of the old-time cave tours. Staff work schedules would be adjusted, and everyone needed to be patient. The Park was closed to the public for two weeks while these changes were implemented.

Hugh listened to these announcements, but he was not feeling victorious. Instead he was awash in sadness. He thought of the loss of the Park's science programs, of the total destruction of nature and entire species in pursuit of political and military gain. Shutting down Deep Space in the face of these losses felt hollow. He was grieving. Victory can be like that.

But he held tight to a small piece of personal good news. When he'd dropped Janet off at staff housing the night before, she'd said she was moving – downhill, to Oakland, to help with the secret project there. Janet Harper and Dr. Gabrielle Greene had decided they could work together. Not as friends, but as team members. This meant that Janet would be nearby, and for this Hugh was grateful.

Dr. Tom King, America's Time Tsar, was long gone. The previous night, back at his cabin, he had packed up and gotten on the road, borrowing a Park vehicle. He drove it all the way to Washington, D.C., along back roads through the beauty of rural Appalachia and its perennially hopeful, bedraggled, and historic small towns.

The radio informed him that the President had easily evaded the accusations that Russians under his control had attacked a New York State community.

"What Russians? What community? All I see is woods!" he said. No Russians – no problem. The next day, he called for big bombs to be dropped "on those creepy woods, to see what's in there. Those are not American woods!" No bombs were dropped.

King checked in by phone with his D.C. office and had a conversation with Ed Zanetti. While they talked, Tom's feet rested on the vehicle dashboard, and he drank a chocolate milkshake. He was parked under shady cottonwood trees in West Virginia. King would soon emerge onto the monster highways that merge into the D.C. maw, and he was savoring his final hours of solitude.

He listened to a long, learned discourse from Ed about time travel priorities and practices. King took advantage of a pause to speak. "It's all yours now, Ed. When I get back I'm submitting a formal letter of request for an extended leave of absence, and you as Time Tsar. That should last you a while."

Ed's exuberance was quenched; he could not reply.

"I hope you can handle the President," said King. "Goodbye!" He ended the call, dropped his empty cup and paper straw in the nearby trash bin, and set a course for the D.C. suburbs. There he dropped off the car at a federal lot and arranged for his plane to be flown from Bowling Green to its D.C. home base.

Free to go?

Whatever the cause, King feels the loop closing.

After that, calls to Tom King's phone went unanswered. At his apartment the next day, he submitted his leave request and recommendation for Ed Zanetti to succeed him, and paid all his bills ahead for six months. He shipped his work equipment and phone back to the office, and mailed power of attorney paperwork and a simple will to his estranged family, without comment. Let them figure it out.

There was no food in his refrigerator except one frozen pizza, which he heated and ate. He turned off all the appliances. He pulled the window drapes shut.

After placing his backpack in the car, King went back in, removed his suits and ties and fancy nice shoes and shirts from the closet and placed them in the hallway outside his door, with a "Free" sign on them. He piled up other stuff alongside, and then walked out of his life, just as Mary Anne Washington had done. He, too, was heading to Hollymount Valley, but he had forgotten about Mary Anne.

King was now free – to follow his compulsion. Was he pulled by the spell Maeve had cast? Or, perhaps, was the imbalance he had triggered in the physics of time and space finally being resolved? Other words for this situation include love, a guilty conscience, or that concept of cause and effect known as karma. Perhaps one or more of these explain the internal force that both pushed and dragged him toward Maeve.

In any case, King felt an unresolved loop closing as he drove north toward the newly named Emergent Hollymount Woodland. At long last, he felt calm and serene about what he was doing. Once he escaped the East Coast cities, Tom King's drive north was beautiful, especially the sinuous route into New York State from Williamsport, Pennsylvania on Route 15.

Summer was at its height, and people were kayaking and fishing in the creeks. The road was packed with water trucks and white pickups for the fracking operations on the surrounding high ground. King, however, no longer noticed the things that had once delighted his pro-development, anti-regulation brain.

He soon became aware of the occasional tall golden tree that stood out above the lush late-summer greenery gracing the slopes and valley bottoms along his route. He knew they were guideposts to Hollymount.

'But are they for me? Will she take me in? Why won't she speak?' he wondered. A few miles after entering New York State, King turned off Route 15 and went west onto the smaller Route 417, toward the town of Addison. He was looking for a place to leave his car. Several miles ahead, the road was blocked by the newly ancient forest, so he would go forward on foot. The once-convenient Highway Spur Project parking lot no longer existed; in its stead were towering trees.

Tom King, ex-USA Time Tsar, left his car in a factory parking lot off 417. A note inside provided the phone number of his family. Again, let them figure it out – this was the outcome they thought they wanted.

King took his backpack out of the car trunk, beeped it locked, and left the key fob on the top of the rear right tire. He shouldered his pack and headed south along a wooded fence line toward the Canisteo River. At the river's edge, he stood looking at the gentle murmuring late summer flow, delicious with its muddy freshwater scent.

He turned west, walking in the narrow fringe of woods along the river. To his right were farm fields, and beyond he heard the hum of Route 417. To his left across the Canisteo, a hill's steep bulk rose sheer above the waterway. The green-wooded slopes soaked up the westering sunshine. Birds were gathering, flying, meeting to plan their southern trip as autumn neared.

Here and there King could see patches of the newly ancient forest rising head and shoulders above today's green tree cover; golden and tall, it had flowed like lava from Hollymount Valley far above. He walked until dark, ate from his provisions, and slept untroubled on a soft bed of pine needles in a grove of white pine trees, the river murmuring low.

A few hours later, King woke and walked forward again under the full moon, which was riding high, illuminating a shallow place to wade across the Canisteo River. He splashed through the cool moonlit ripples, unknowingly observed by three black bears out for a predawn swim and fish feast.

Here the south bank widened into a floodplain, with fields and a few small houses. He headed toward the hillslope, through pine and beech groves, and along a small stream flowing to the Canisteo River. A pair of owls hooted overhead. For a while they flew in front of him, seeming to announce his progress with their calls.

The moon set beyond wooded hills to the west as he felt the warmth of the rising sun on his back and shoulders. It rose to illuminate, ahead of him, the Emergent Woodland spilling down the slopes from Hollymount Valley. The woodland was hundreds of feet across. Massive golden trees, mingled with ancient hickories and oaks, swayed in the dawn breeze. The shade beneath them was dark and called him forward.

Tom King breathed in the intoxicating green aroma of their trunks and leaves, heard the chatter of birds, and came to the flowery meadows he had to cross to enter the big woods and climb toward Hollymount.

Stepping into the open, he looked around. To his right, across a pond and fields toward the river, he could see fences and warning signs to keep people and cattle out of the Emergent Woodland and the buffer of flowering meadowland enclosing it. To his left were trees, in the wild crease between meadow and slope.

King walked forward into the meadows, toward the woodland on the slope that would lead him up to Hollymount Valley. He pressed through fields of goldenrod, the huge honey-scented heads of blossom humming with bees. The rising sun warmed the flowers' color and aroma. Red-winged blackbirds stood and sang on the swaying flowers, enjoying one last day, or maybe two, before heading south.

The sea of goldenrod was punctuated by the purple blooms of ironweed and the sultry scent of dusty pink milkweed flowers. Monarchs and great spangled fritillary butterflies drifted overhead in the warming air. Nearer to the ground, the white cabbage butterflies in their flirtatious pairs scattered as he approached.

Tom King soon reached the edge of the Emergent Woodland and walked between two giant golden-trunked sycamore trees into the arboreal hush of big oak-hickory woods. It was cool and dark in the cavernous spaces beneath the tree canopy far above, and he went forward as surely as if he trod a path. The human presence was gone, but the shape of the land remained the same beneath the forest cover.

He knew when he had crossed the place that had once contained – or perhaps, in the future, would contain – the roundabout, and then the parking lot with the small white flowers. Some of these flowers grew in a ring at the feet of young, healthy chestnut trees. Tom King felt under his feet the land beginning to rise. He walked among tumbled rocks, unaware of any sleeping demon below.

Green branches arched far overhead, pierced with sunlight and opening up as he approached the stony bluffs. He waded across the small creek and followed its course upstream around the rocky corner and toward the slope that once had been, or perhaps someday would be, the site of a path leading to a crossing in the woods.

Did he but know it, the little lady on the hilltop watched him go past. The couple in the cottage, buried under the layers of enchantment or freedom that Maeve had unleashed, quietly watched him go by as he splashed in the shallow stream.

Tom King climbed the slope where his feet remembered a path, and walked into an open space at the once or future crosspaths. This clearing was floored with tall green ferns, and on the far edge a shapely old tree held mosses deep around its base. It was now the middle of the day, warming up.

He was very tired. He would nap here before he walked onward to where he knew the Hollymount Inn and Maeve should be. He had gotten this far; he did not know what would be required. He did not know what would happen; this was all he knew to do. Tom King could think only of Maeve.

King took off his pack and sat down with his back to the big tree, relaxing into the deep green mosses and ferns. He drank deeply from his water bottle. The tree trunk did not support him in a firmly treelike way. It felt insubstantial, and yet he did not fall backwards. In fact, it seemed to take hold of him.

Tom King soon fell into a refreshing slumber. His breathing was light and easy. The woodland afternoon moved forward around him, and carried him along with it. As the sun sank into the west, King's breathing slowed and became imperceptible.

You could call it a coma, or a deepening spell, and maybe understand that he was slowing down to match the pace of the woods around him, that he was being absorbed, and accepted.

The night drew on, and he lay there in quiet repose, unsought and undisturbed. The two owls watched in silence. When dawn broke, he was no longer there.

Appendices

TOP SECRET – CONFIDENTIAL
NOT FOR PUBLICATION
EMBARGOED UNTIL FURTHER NOTICE

The "Grandfather Paradox":
Results of a Field Study with Defense Applications

Thomas King[1]

Abstract

In the emerging field of temporal transfer, basic principles must be established for researchers to proceed expeditiously toward real-world applications, emphatically the enhancement of past military outcomes for present-day national interests. Of lingering concern is resolution of the "Grandfather Paradox": Can the past be altered without unforeseen outcomes in the present day? Results indicate that it is all in the timing. The principal investigator (p.i.) entered Wichita, KS in February 1902. At that time, p.i.'s grandfather was 35, father to two sons, including the p.i.'s future father. Using approved techniques, p.i's grandfather was harvested. To minimize biomass loss and other essential impacts, the carcass was (hygienically) disposed of in 1902. No unanticipated outcomes of this action have been measured by the p.i. and lab into the present day. Although repugnant to the p.i., this personal sacrifice demonstrates conclusively that, when timing is taken into consideration, targeted past events can be altered without present-day unanticipated outcomes. Implications for defense applications are significant.

---

[1] Professor King holds the Endowed Chair of Business Biology, GOBI (Global Online Business Institute), Dartmouth College. He is the principal investigator (p.i.) of the project detailed in this report.

Key words: defense applications, harvest, temporal transfer, unanticipated outcomes

Introduction

When temporal transfer was first established 20 years ago as a replicable phenomenon in the laboratory setting (Cadwallader, 2008), the implications for the defense applicability of targeted temporal adjustments were profound and exciting (Tuttle and King, 2008).

However, what then seemed admirable scientific caution, in terms of carrying out necessary basic research in advance of real-world applications, has since degenerated into what can only be called alarmist foot-dragging. The early promise of this revolution in scientific understanding has faltered due to what the present author suggests are roadblocks deliberately set in place by extremists (Zanetti, 2010; Mackey and Terwillegar, 2012; UN Review Committee, 2012).

In a nutshell, the original 20-year partnership between the Department of Homeland Security and the Department of Interior for the study of temporal transfer is in shambles, and is due for a shake-up, preferably a complete overhaul.

While this is not the first time that calls have been made for necessary changes (King and Styce, 2010; Styce and Granger, 2011), the present study provides real-world research support that was previously lacking. As a result of the findings detailed below, it is suggested that we can fast-track forward with improved experimental design and proceed – finally – to reap the real-world benefits of the temporal transfer revolution, for the improved defense of our nation in an uncertain world. … (report continues)

Conclusions

The success of this apparently "high-risk" study, while it required actions personally repugnant to the present author, calls into question the continued funding of the present "more research needed" approach favored by the Homeland-Interior Liaison Office. A shift in research focus is called for, toward real-world temporal transfer actions in support of our national defense, and away from the presently dominant "impact study" approach.

The present focus of temporal transfer research on support of tourism in our national parks (best exemplified at the Ten Thousand Secrets Casino Park) is a shockingly unconscionable misuse of our private and public funds. Our nation's business interests deserve better.

TOP SECRET – CONFIDENTIAL
NOT FOR PUBLICATION
EMBARGOED UNTIL FURTHER NOTICE

Recommended further reading

"A Sound of Thunder"

Ray Bradbury published his short story "A Sound of Thunder" in 1952. I first read it in the 1960s, and more recently found it again in his short story collection *Golden Apples of the Sun* (first published in 1953, Rupert Hart-Davis Ltd., Great Britain), in a 1970s (Grafton Books, London) paperback. The story involves time travel safaris, a dead butterfly, and the impact of its accidental death on our present day. I had written most of the first two books in the Apple Island series when I found this story again and realized how deeply embedded it is in my brain, and in our culture.

A song about the return of the trees

"Trees" is a song by Laurie Lewis. It can be found on *TREES*, her 2024 album. The song's first line is quoted on page 237:

> "We stand waiting at the edges of your fields."

Learn more at laurielewis.com.

www.ingramcontent.com/pod-product-compliance
Lightning Source LLC
LaVergne TN
LVHW010605100826
845148LV00014B/2849

9798218906931